In 1940, when E.V. Thompson was a small boy, his home in the East End of London was destroyed in a night raid by German bombers. In the dead of night he was taken to Oxfordshire possessing only the clothes he wore. He woke to begin a new life in the village of Swinbrook, on the fringe of the once-great Wychwood forest.

E.V. Thompson was born in London. He spent nine years in the Navy before joining the Bristol Police Force. Later he became an investigator with BOAC, worked with the Hong Kong Police Narcotics Bureau and was Chief Security Officer of Rhodesia's Department of Civil Aviation.

He returned to England committed to becoming a full-time writer and moved to Bodmin Moor, the powerful background for *Chase The Wind*, the book which won him the Best Historical Novelist Award.

E.V. Thompson continues to live in Cornwall, where he shares a house overlooking the sea near Mevagissey with his wife, two sons and a wide variety of family pets.

Also by E.V. Thompson

Blue Dress Girl
Chase The Wind
Harvest of the Sun
The Music Makers
Ben Retallick
The Dream Traders
Singing Spears
The Restless Sea
Cry Once Alone
Polrudden
The Stricken Land
Becky
God's Highlander
Lottie Trago
Cassie

Wychwood

E. V. Thompson

HEADLINE

First published in 1992
by Macmillan London Limited

First published in paperback in 1992
by HEADLINE BOOK PUBLISHING PLC

10 9 8 7 6 5 4 3 2 1

ISBN 0 7472 3918 5

Typeset by
Letterpart Limited, Reigate, Surrey

Printed and bound in Great Britain by
HarperCollins Manufacturing, Glasgow

HEADLINE BOOK PUBLISHING PLC
Headline House
79 Great Titchfield Street
London W1P 7FN

Wychwood

CHAPTER ONE

Colonel Sir Nelson Fettiplace, fortified by a good lunch and a couple of extra brandies, crossed the wide pavement from Brooks's Club to the waiting carriage.

The light hackney sagged to one side as Sir Nelson placed his considerable weight on the first step of the vehicle, but before he could climb inside the driver called, 'Where to, guv'nor?'

'Essex Street, if you please. I understand it's off Hoxton Street.'

The driver and the Brooks's Club doorman, who was holding open the carriage door, exchanged glances. Hoxton, in London's East End, was not an area visited by officers and 'gentlemen'.

'You sure you've got the right Essex Street, guv? There's another one not very far from here . . .'

'Dammit, I've just told you where I want to go. Take me there, and be quick about it.'

The irascible baronet settled himself on the padded leather seat and the carriage jerked into movement.

Sir Nelson Fettiplace was not usually so irritable. Neither was he used to visiting places on the poorer side of London. Today he had a duty to perform. A promise to keep. The sooner he got it over and done with the better.

The carriage bowled along fashionable Pall Mall, with its tall and impressive buildings, and passed

Trafalgar Square, where Admiral Lord Nelson stared out over London from the top of his tall fluted column. In the busy Strand the vehicle was forced to a halt more than once by the sheer volume of traffic on the wide thoroughfare.

Threadneedle Street and the City were almost as busy, but from here the character of London changed markedly as the wealth and glitter were left behind. The streets became narrower and litter-cluttered, the houses small and dingy, the lack of colour reflected in the drab clothes worn by those who lived here.

The traffic had undergone a change too. A carriage was an oddity among the handcarts and the trundling wagons. Soon they entered a street where there was a market, the cries of the vendors vying with each other, offering everything from hot meat pies and live eels to buttons and dress materials.

The driver leaned down to speak to his passenger. 'This is Hoxton, guv'nor. I'll need to ask somebody where Essex Street is.'

Sir Nelson Fettiplace nodded. 'Be quick about it. I want to be back at my club before nightfall.'

'Don't you worry, you will be. You won't find me hanging around this area after dark.'

The hackney-carriage driver cleared the market before pulling the horse to a halt and calling out to a ragged urchin at the side of the road.

'Whereabouts is Essex Street, boy?'

'I'll tell you for a penny.'

The driver grinned and flipped a coin to the boy. 'Here's a halfpenny for your cheek. Where is it?'

'It's better known as "Kill-copper Alley" around 'ere. It's the second on your right. If that's where your taking 'is nibs, you'd best tell 'im to 'ide 'is watch and any money before 'e steps out of yer 'ackney. They'll 'ave 'em orf 'im afore 'is foot touches the ground.'

Inside the carriage, as he transferred everything of value to an inside pocket, Sir Nelson Fettiplace frowned at the graphic name given to his destination – and the picture conjured up by the urchin of what he might expect there.

It seemed the hackney-carriage driver was having his doubts too. 'You quite sure that's where you want me to take you, guv? I don't know what it is you're looking for, but I could probably find it elsewhere. Somewhere a bit more salubrious . . .'

'I'm going there to visit the widow of one of my soldiers who died in Africa. I made him a promise. I intend to keep it.'

'Ah! Well, a promise to a dying man now, that's something different. You've got to keep that, you have. All right, giddup there.'

The driver flicked the long reins on the horse's back and the carriage rattled and bounced over a decidedly indifferent road.

Essex Street was all the young informant had promised. The doors of the houses had paint peeling from them. They opened directly on to the street and many doorsteps were occupied by women, children and pipe-smoking men. Few were clean, most were ragged and untidy and one or two looked positively diseased.

The arrival of the hackney carriage caused such a stir that Sir Nelson Fettiplace doubted whether a wheeled vehicle had ever been along the street. Certainly, the road was heavily cluttered with a great deal of evil-smelling rubbish. It was gloomy here too, as though even the sunlight shunned 'Kill-copper Alley'.

'Do you know what number, guv'nor?'

'No . . . it's twenty-something, I think. The widow's name is Quilter. Dolly Quilter.'

Dolly Quilter was seated by the small open window in the room overlooking the backyard, trying to stitch a tear in the threadbare elbow of a coat that belonged to her son, Seb. It was not easy. The cloth was so worn it was difficult to make the stitches hold, but it had to be done. She could not afford another, not even a second-hand one from the pawnbroker.

She was thinking of Seb when she heard her name being called. At first she ignored it, thinking someone wanted to borrow something. In Essex Street there was always someone wanting to borrow something – unless they could steal it first.

The calling became more insistent and there was an unusual urgency in the sound that sent a chill of alarm through her. Seb was out somewhere. Perhaps he had suffered another of his attacks . . .

Dolly dropped the jacket to the floor and was down the stairs and along the dark passageway to the street, her feet scarcely pausing to touch the ground.

At the entrance to the house, the woman who occupied the front, ground-floor room lolled in the doorway. 'What's the hurry, Doll? There's a gent to see you, but slow down. It's my experience that gents from "Up West" like their women to tart themselves up a bit, not run to meet 'em.'

'Someone to see me? Who?'

The woman jerked her thumb. 'Him out in the street. I hope he's not bringing you anything of value.

He'll not have a thing left by the time them urchins have finished with him.'

When Dolly emerged from the house into the street she saw Colonel Sir Nelson Fettiplace surrounded by a crowd of children aged from three to fourteen. All had a hand outstretched to beg from him, but a few were using their hidden hand to search inside his pockets.

'Clear off! Get away. Go on, off you go, if you don't want a good wallop from me.'

Dolly waded into the crowd of thieving youngsters, boxing an ear here and there until the children scattered.

'Are you Mrs Quilter? Mrs Dolly Quilter?'

'That's right.' Dolly was puzzled. This was obviously a gentleman. Why had he come here looking for her?

'I'm Colonel Fettiplace. I was your husband's commanding officer in Natal, in South Africa.'

'*Sir* Nelson Fettiplace?'

'That's right. Your husband was my batman. I was with him when he died . . .' The baronet glanced at the crowd of all ages, gathered around them, listening unashamedly to their conversation. 'Is there somewhere we can talk?'

'Yes . . .' Dolly hesitated, her room was no place to take a gentleman. But there was nowhere else. 'Come into the house.'

'Cabbie! Wait here for me. I won't be long.'

'You'd better not be, guv'nor, or these thieving little urchins will pinch everything except my horse.'

As Sir Nelson Fettiplace passed the woman in the doorway, she hardly moved to let him by, forcing him to brush against her. When he glanced at her she winked brazenly and said, 'Hello, luv. Where do you hang out in the West End? I go up there some nights. I could come and visit you, if you liked.'

Sir Nelson made a strange sound in his throat and followed Dolly Quilter. It was dark in the house and the stench violated his nostrils.

Inside her room, Dolly picked up Seb's coat, hastily punched some life into the tired-looking cushions resting on the room's two chairs and invited Sir Nelson to have a seat. Closing the window, Dolly said, 'I like the window open, but the privy is just down below and sometimes the smell's a bit strong.'

Sir Nelson Fettiplace sat down gingerly. It was cleaner in here than he had expected, but it was not of the standard to which he was accustomed, even when campaigning with his regiment.

'Would you like a cup of tea? I've got some here.' Dolly put the question proudly. She had kept the tea for a month now, not expecting to be able to offer it to a titled gentleman.

'No, thank you. I can't stop for longer than a few minutes.' Sir Nelson had only just arrived, but he was already eager to leave this sordid area. 'Before he died, I promised your husband I'd call on you when I returned to this country. He nursed me when I was ill and close to death. In truth, I regret to say that he probably caught his illness from me.'

Dolly closed her eyes and fought back tears. It had been a year since she had been informed that her husband had died while on active service in South Africa. It had been the unhappiest day in the lives of both Dolly and her son, and things had gone from bad to worse since then.

When she had control of herself, Dolly nodded. 'It's

kind of you to come here. I wish Seb, my son, was home. He'd have been proud to know that his father's last thoughts were here, with us.'

'They were indeed, Mrs Quilter. The British army lost a good soldier when your husband died. One of the best. I hope it will be some consolation when I tell you he was buried as befits a soldier. His grave was dug by his companions and I myself read a passage of the Bible over it.'

'Thank you, Sir Nelson. It . . . it *is* a comfort.'

'And you, madam. How are you coping with things now your husband is dead?'

'It hasn't been easy. It was all right while I was working as parlour-maid to Lady Spalding. But since she and her husband left for India, times have been hard.'

'Oh dear . . .'

From somewhere, not too far away, two women began screaming abuse at each other, with interjections by a male voice. Sir Nelson rose to his feet and reached inside his waistcoat. Taking out a soft leather pouch he counted out ten gold sovereigns and handed them to Dolly. 'Here. Take these. I was afraid those rascals out there were going to steal them. I fear they have taken everything else. My handkerchief . . .'

The sounds of the altercation were reaching a crescendo now.

'Thank you, Sir Nelson. You're very generous, but I would be happier if you could tell me where I might find work. I need to support myself and Seb. He's not strong . . .'

'Hm! My home is the manor at Swinbrook, in Oxfordshire. I'm rarely there, but my sister runs the house and I keep a full staff on. If ever you find yourself in that part of the country there'll be something for you, I'm quite sure.'

'With accommodation?'

'Pardon? . . . Oh, yes.'

Sir Nelson Fettiplace was not giving Dolly his undivided attention. The screaming was now accompanied by sounds of a fight. It was time he left.

'Thank you, Sir Nelson.' Dolly dropped him a curtsy. 'Thank you very much.'

'A pleasure. Your husband was a good soldier. Damned good.'

It sounded as though half the street had become involved in the fight. A dog too. It was barking furiously as Sir Nelson hurried from the room.

In the street two men lounged by the hackney carriage and their appearance gave Sir Nelson pause. He hesitated and one of the men drew a length of heavy lead piping from beneath his jacket and began walking slowly towards the baronet.

Sir Nelson Fettiplace carried a light walking stick. He took it in both hands and twisted the handle. A narrow, sharp-edged sword blade emerged from its wooden case and now it was the senior army officer's turn to advance.

Neither the man carrying the pipe nor his companion waited to test the effectiveness of a lead club against a skilfully wielded sword-stick. They fled, and Sir Nelson hurried to the carriage without a backward glance at Dolly who had taken a broom from inside the passage of the house to go to the baronet's assistance.

'Drive off, cabbie. Back to Brooks's, I feel like a drink. Let's get out of this part of London as quickly as possible. The people here are as foul as the air they breathe.'

CHAPTER TWO

For four long and extremely uncomfortable days Sebastian Quilter endured the bone-rattling jolting of the unsprung horse-drawn cart. Throughout the whole of the journey the regular and monotonous squealing of the front nearside wheel had recorded their progress along eighty miles of rough English country lanes.

When he rode on the cart, Seb shared what space there was amidst the Quilters' worldly possessions with his mother. In front of them the surly carter perched precariously upon a wagon shaft, speaking only to hurl curses at the sway-backed, ribby horse plodding along, head down and dejected, beside him.

At times, unable to endure any more of the nerve-jangling noise from the ungreased axle, Sebastian would climb from the wagon and explore the unfamiliar world of fields, hedgerows and trees.

He had no fear of becoming lost. The raucous altercation between axle and wheel could be heard half a mile away. The sound drove crows and pigeons from nearby cornfields far more effectively than the small children who were being paid a penny a day to perform this tedious task.

Sometimes Dolly would join her son in his explorations. Her delight at discovering flowers, strange insects and colourful butterflies banished some of the resentment and rebelliousness that smouldered deep inside him, but only for a while.

A few miles to the west of Oxford they entered the Wychwood Forest and the cart jolted along a narrow, rutted track carved through a carpet of bracken and ferns that covered the forest floor. High above, the branches of great oak trees fought endless duels, encouraged by the wind.

Dolly thought the forest was gloomy and forbidding and she remained on the cart, finding comfort in being surrounded by the familiar items of furniture which she had gathered over a penurious lifetime.

'Seb! Mind you don't get lost – and don't tire yourself out. I can't have you laid up when we reach our new home. I've a job to attend to, remember.'

'I don't know why we had to come all this way, miles from *anywhere*.' It was a complaint Seb had made many times before. 'Look at it . . . nothing but *trees*! What are we going to find to do? We should have stayed in London. In Hoxton. At least we had *people* to speak to there.'

He spat out the words with such venom that it brought on a coughing fit. Within moments he was hunched over in distress, his shoulders heaving in time with the coughing and gasping that racked his thin body.

'Stop the cart, Seb's having one of his turns.' Dolly snapped the words at the carter.

Making no attempt to do her bidding, the surly carter growled, 'If I'd stopped every time he had a coughing fit we'd still be looking at the streets of London now.'

'You're getting paid for your time. Do as you're told or I'll knock a shilling off your money when we reach Swinbrook.'

The undernourished horse was hauled to a stop and Dolly hurried back to her son although she could only watch helplessly, biting back her anxiety, until his shoulders ceased heaving and he was in control of himself once more.

Dolly knew better than to try to touch him when he was having one of his coughing bouts. Seb was sixteen years of age. Not yet a man, he was no longer young enough to be publicly cuddled and comforted.

'You all right now, Seb?'

He nodded, still too breathless to attempt a reply.

'Come back to the wagon and ride awhile. It won't be long before we reach Swinbrook.'

'In . . . a minute.' It came out as a strangled whisper.

'If he doesn't soon move himself we'll be spending the night in this forest. You might be 'appy in the company of cut-throats and fierce wild animals, I'm not.' The complaining voice of the carter carried to them.

'I'm all right now, Ma. You go back to the cart. I'll walk for a while longer.'

The impatient carter slapped the reins down upon the sagging back of his horse. As the cart lurched into motion Dolly hurried to catch up with it.

Ensconced among the few pieces of ageing furniture, Dolly took a look back to satisfy herself that her son was following the cart. She wondered, as she had on many occasions recently, whether she had made the right decision in bringing Seb so far from the city that had been their home for all of his young life.

Dolly had struggled desperately hard to keep Seb and herself free from the clutches of the workhouse master. When Sir Nelson Fettiplace had found his way to the dingy house in Hoxton, it had seemed like the answer to all her most fervent prayers. He had offered nothing for Seb in Oxfordshire, but Dolly was convinced there would be something for him there.

She could not know that with Hoxton left behind, Sir Nelson had breathed a sigh of relief. His relief was mingled with a feeling of self-satisfaction. His rash promise to a dying soldier had been fulfilled. He was convinced Private Quilter's widow would squander the money he had given her and he did not expect ever to see or hear of her again.

Knowing nothing of Sir Nelson's private belief, Dolly gave his offer long and troubled consideration. She had ventured outside London only once before. That had been when her husband first joined the army and was sent to barracks in Chatham, in nearby Kent. She had returned to London soon afterwards, when she knew she was expecting Seb.

Had it not been for Seb she would not have considered leaving London now. In spite of the abject poverty in which they were living, London was her home. But Seb was a bright and perceptive boy. He knew he was very sick – dying, perhaps – and people were often telling them both his only hope of recovery lay in getting away from the fogs, smells and river vapours of London.

At first Dolly had taken little notice of such advice. However, more recently Seb's condition had worsened and she had become desperate enough to try *anything* that had the remotest possibility of giving Seb a few extra years of life.

She made up her mind to accept the baronet's offer, disregarding Seb's protest that there were probably just as many sick people in the country as in London. Settling her affairs, Dolly hired a carter with his horse and cart to take them to the Oxfordshire village of Swinbrook.

Little of Sir Nelson's money remained now, but Dolly said farewell to lifelong friends with pride. Usually, when a widow-woman moved house in Hoxton she ensured there were few people around to witness the event. Such a move invariably took place in the dead of night, household chattels being loaded quietly on a handcart and sleepy, bewildered children cowed to silence.

Dolly was leaving her home in daylight with head held high and not a penny owed to any man.

'I'm feeling better now.' Seb caught up with the cart and grinned cheerfully at his mother, aware of her concern for him.

Dolly looked anxiously at the pale face and dark-circled eyes behind the grin.

'You'll be better with good country air in your lungs. Everyone says so.'

'I've been breathing "good country air" for four days now – and I'm coughing worse than ever—'

The horse threw up its head in sudden alarm, causing the cart to jerk suddenly, shifting the few pieces of furniture and unbalancing Dolly.

'Whoa! Whoa there, I tell you . . . What the 'ell do you think *you're* doing?'

The question was hurled at a young girl of about the same age as Seb, dressed in ragged clothing and carrying a large basket. She had emerged unexpectedly from behind a tree at the side of the track farthest away from Seb. Her appearance was so unexpected it had galvanised the carter's horse into more life than it had shown at any time during the long journey from London.

'Buy some pegs? A bell for your horse?' The girl shook a small metal bell that made a soft musical sound, alarming the horse even more.

'You frighten me 'orse and nearly tip me bleedin' cart over, then want to sell me some pegs? I wouldn't take a gift from you – or from any other gipsy. Clear off, 'fore I take this whip to you.'

'A lucky hare's foot – tipped with real silver? A sprig of scented heather for your lady . . .?'

The girl offered more goods for sale as though she had not heard the carter's threat, but the cart was on the move once more and suddenly the carter said, 'Gawd 'elp us – 'ere's another lunatic! It's busier than Whitechapel market around 'ere.'

The carter's observation referred not to another gipsy, but to a horseman who was coming along the track towards them at a breakneck gallop.

'If he keeps that speed up he'll kill himself for sure – and do *us* no good.'

The carter slid hurriedly from the shafts to the ground. Taking the bridle of his horse, he drew animal and cart to the side of the track, combining brute force and loud-voiced haranguing.

Seb looked back to where the gipsy girl still stood in the centre of the lane. Her view of the oncoming rider was blocked by the cart and the sound of drumming hoofs drowned by the shouting of the carter and the squeaking wheel of the cart.

'Get out of the way! *Quick!*' Seb shouted a warning to her.

The cart was still moving, but it had two wheels off the track now and the girl should have been able to see the approaching horse and rider. The pair had almost reached them, yet showed no sign of slackening their reckless pace.

Standing where she was, holding her basket, it would be impossible for the horse and rider to pass by the girl without knocking her over.

Seb sprinted to where she still stood as though rooted to the spot. As he reached her he could hear the pounding of hoofs close behind him. For the first time it seemed the girl realised her danger – yet she hesitated, as though uncertain which way she should go.

Seb bowled the gipsy girl over, knocking her into the undergrowth at the side of the track and falling with her. As the galloping horse swept by, mud thrown up by the animal's shod hoofs spattered Seb's back.

Scrambling to his feet, Seb's relief changed to sudden anger. Rounding on the girl, he said, 'What the hell did you think you were doing? You might have got us both killed. You should have seen that madman long before he reached you . . .'

'Anna has seen nothing since she was eight years old.' The explanation came from a dark-skinned young man. A gipsy like Anna, he too had appeared unnoticed from the forest. His expression of anger matched Seb's own as he added, 'My sister is blind.'

For a few moments, as Seb stared at the girl, pity and anger fought for possession of his face. Then his recent exertions caught up with him and he began to cough once more. This time it was a severe bout that brought him to his knees.

Dolly climbed from the furniture cart and hurried to

the side of her son, even though there was nothing he would allow her to do. As she stood helplessly looking down at him, the gipsy man took Anna's arm and began to lead her away.

She went without protest for perhaps ten or twelve paces before suddenly pulling free from her brother. Turning back, swiftly and cleverly feeling the ground ahead of her with bare feet, she hurried to where Seb kneeled coughing, his head bowed low to the ground.

Crouching beside him, Anna put an arm about his shoulders and raised him until he leaned against her. For a moment the spasms ceased. During this brief time the girl's fingers passed methodically over his face, touching eyes, nose and mouth and tracing the shape of his features with sensitive fingertips.

When Seb pulled away from her and began coughing once more, Anna released her hold and stood up.

'You . . . the woman with him. What's his name? Where does he live?' The gipsy's voice was surprisingly soft and gentle, in sharp contrast to her wild and unkempt appearance.

Dolly hesitated for a moment, unsure whether she should tell this girl, who had held Seb in a way she had not been able to for years. Then she said, 'My son's name is Seb. Seb Quilter. We're on our way from London to Swinbrook Manor. I'm to work there.'

It was far more than Dolly had intended saying, but it brought a quick reply from the brother of the gipsy girl.

'Then you'll be seeing more of the madman on the horse who almost killed my sister. He's Meredith Putt, Sir Nelson Fettiplace's nephew. You can give him a warning from me. Tell him it's time he learned a little caution and some manners. If he doesn't he'll find the forest's a dangerous place for the likes of him.'

The gipsy took Anna's arm once more and led her away. A few minutes later they were lost to view amidst the dense, green undergrowth of the Wychwood Forest.

CHAPTER THREE

Swinbrook Manor was an attractive, grey-stone house occupying a site close to the ancient church in the heart of the small village. Not as large or impressive as some of the great mansions Seb and Dolly Quilter had seen during their journey from London, the manor nevertheless possessed an air of quiet durability, which for three hundred years had given reassurance to the villagers in times of trouble.

The air of warmth generated by the house was in sharp contrast to the attitude of the maid who opened the kitchen door to Dolly's knock. Sharp-featured and middle-aged, she looked the London woman up and down from head to toe, making it quite clear she was not impressed by what she saw.

'If you're selling anything we're not buying – and don't waste time begging, there's little enough to spare for those of us who work here.'

'I'm neither begging, nor selling.' Dolly's air of haughtiness was calculated to outdo that of the maid. 'Sir Nelson Fettiplace asked me to come from London and work for him here. A post with accommodation, he said.'

'*Did* he now. Well, no one's said anything about it to *us*.'

Having failed to cow Dolly, the maid said grudgingly, 'You'd best come in the kitchen while I find Mrs

Putt, Sir Nelson's sister. She's his housekeeper.'

Jabbing a finger in the direction of Seb, she snapped, 'He can wait outside. I've spent an hour on my knees scrubbing the floor his morning. I'll not have him treading mud everywhere.'

For a moment Dolly was tempted to argue the point, but Seb said, 'It's all right, Ma. I'll wait out here and keep an eye on the furniture.'

From the doorway the maid could see the cart with its pathetically small load. 'You don't need to guard belongings in *these* parts.' Sniffing disdainfully, she added, 'And from what I can see there's nothing there anyone might want to steal.'

'Never mind what you can or can't see. Are you going to tell this Mrs Putt I'm here? Or do I have to come in and do it myself?'

Dolly entered the house and the door was firmly shut behind her. Outside, Seb thought despondently that his mother had not got off to a very good start with the Swinbrook maid. He hoped they would not have to see too much of her and comforted himself with the thought that she was only a kitchen-maid while his mother had come to Swinbrook to take up the post of parlour-maid.

Inside the house the sour-faced maid left Dolly waiting in the corridor between the kitchen and the back door of the house while she went off in search of the housekeeper.

When the maid returned she was accompanied by a tall, unsmiling woman dressed like a widow in a severely cut, faded black dress.

Without any introduction, the housekeeper snapped, 'What's all this nonsense about Sir Nelson telling you to come here for work? My brother is not in the habit of employing the household staff. That is *my* responsibility, as well he knows.'

'Begging your pardon, ma'am, but it isn't nonsense. Sir Nelson came to see me in London. You see, my husband was with him in the army out there in Africa. He died after nursing Sir Nelson back to health. Saved his life, I believe. Sir Nelson asked me what I was doing in London. I wasn't in work at the time, but when he heard I'd been a parlour-maid for Lady Spalding he said I'd be better off here, working for him. Said there'd be accommodation too, for me and Seb. He's waiting outside. You'll find him a good boy. He won't be any trouble and though there's not much of him he's not afraid of hard work . . .'

'The boy's got no more flesh on him than a blade of grass,' said the maid, maliciously. 'And if that was him I heard coughing a while back it's a doctor he needs, not work . . . Begging your pardon, ma'am.'

'You've brought a sick son here with you? I'll not have *him* in the house, whatever my brother promised. It was bad enough having to listen to my husband's consumptive cough before he died. I'll not put anyone in this house at risk of the same thing. Besides, we have no work here for a parlour-maid. A *scullery*-maid's work is the best I can offer. You can take it or leave it. As for accommodation, there are two rooms over the old stables. They'll need to be cleaned out thoroughly, but there's nothing else.'

Amelia Putt knew better than to defy her brother's wishes, but she had no intention of making things easy for Dolly. Swinbrook was a small, insular community. Bringing someone in from outside – from *London* –

was likely to prove disruptive.

Dolly's initial reaction to the offer of a post as a scullery-maid was to refuse, but she realised that was exactly what the housekeeper hoped she would do.

A scullery-maid was the lowest grade of servant in any large household. Dolly was proud of having risen to the position of *parlour*-maid during her years in service.

For a few moments she fought with her pride over Amelia Putt's take-it-or-leave-it offer. Eventually common sense prevailed. Pride would not provide a future for Seb. Besides, most of the money given to her by Sir Nelson had been spent in paying off debtors and in bringing her belongings to Swinbrook. She had effectively cut all her ties with London.

'I'll take the position, thank you, ma'am.'

Dolly thought she would carry out whatever tasks were given to her and appeal to Sir Nelson when he returned to his home.

'Very well. Cook will instruct you in your daily duties, but I shall expect every pot and pan to be cleaned and put away before you finish work at night. In the mornings you will light the kitchen fire, scrub the downstairs floors and have everything ready for Cook when she comes down to make breakfast. You will work for six days a week and have Sunday off – but you and your son will attend the church services, morning and evening. Your salary will be seven shillings a week plus food – but I will not have your son fed from my kitchen. He will need to find work for himself – and please ensure he *does*. The devil finds work for idle hands, and my experience of young London boys is that they are more idle than most. Florence will send someone to show you to the stables. When you begin work tomorrow morning Cook will acquaint you with anything I might have forgotten. That's all.'

When Amelia Putt had gone, Dolly followed the servant named Florence from the house. 'Did you need to mention my Seb's cough to Mrs Putt? Where I come from servants try to *help* each other, not do 'em down.'

'It's the other servants I was thinking of. We've got troubles enough here, without running the risk of catching lung fever. If you don't like our ways you can always go back to where you belong.'

'*This* is where we belong now, so you'd better get used to it. You and anyone else who feels the same way.'

'We'll see. Servants from outside the village have never lasted long in this house. I doubt you'll prove any different.'

The rooms above the old stables were piled high with rubbish and Dolly felt like sitting down and crying at the first sight of this, the future 'home' for herself and Seb. Mildewed leather tack, broken tools and mouldering hay were heaped around the rooms and the accumulated rubbish of years was strewn everywhere. There was also an impressive selection of cobwebs adorning the walls and unceilinged roof. The sounds of horses could be heard through the worn board floor and in one place, where the boards had parted company, it was possible to look down into the stables.

It was the only view from the rooms. The glass of the single, small window in each room was stained and thick with grime, providing an effective barrier against even the most determined sunshine.

Looking around her in dismay, Dolly's determination to remain in Swinbrook wavered. 'This is *horrible*. We can't possibly stay here.'

Unexpectedly, Seb said, 'It's not all that bad, really. It'll be fine once we've got rid of all this rubbish. It don't look as though the roof leaks . . . and there's more room than we had in London.'

'But . . . it reeks of *horses*!'

'There's nothing wrong with that. It's a sight better smell than some we've had to put up with.'

Now Dolly understood why her son was pointing out the advantages she was unable to find in their new surroundings. Seb had inherited a love of horses from his soldier father. In London, whenever he was missing from home and Dolly needed to find him, she always began her search at the nearest stables – and rarely needed to go farther afield.

For the first time that evening, Dolly saw a glimmer of hope in the situation in which she had placed herself and Seb. Things improved even more when Sir Nelson Fettiplace's head groom, Tom Hanks, climbed the outside stairs to introduce himself to them and offer help to clear the rubbish from the two rooms.

The task was completed much sooner than Dolly had believed possible. It would take days, perhaps weeks, to bring her new 'home' to a state of acceptable cleanliness, but in the meantime they would be snug enough.

Tom helped greatly to allay Dolly's fears. He assured her the stable roof was as stout as that of the manor itself and the fire drew exceptionally well. What was more, the family would enjoy almost exclusive use of the privy attached to the stable – a degree of privacy not enjoyed by the servants who lived inside the house.

He was also sympathetic when he witnessed Seb's fight for breath after one particularly bad bout of coughing. A widower, the head groom had brought up a crippled daughter, now fifteen years old, who was particularly sensitive to her disability.

When Seb paused from unloading the Quilter furniture to admire a pair of cart-horses being returned to the stables from the fields, the groom said, 'You like horses then, do you?'

Seb nodded as he stroked the nose of one of the horses, talking to it in low, soothing tones.

'Know much about 'em?'

'Not as much as I'd like, though I've helped out in stables in London once or twice.'

Tom made a derisive sound deep in his throat. 'You won't have learned anything about horses in *London*. Why, I hear there are horses up there ain't so much as tasted grass, let alone able to tell good grass from bad. No, my son. If you want to learn about horses you come and help me whenever you gets the chance. *I'll* teach you all there is to know about horses.'

As they spoke Seb heard the clattering of hoofs on the cobbles leading from the road to the main entrance of the manor. A few moments later a voice called impatiently for Tom Hanks.

'Talking of which, there's someone who ought to be taught a thing or two about horses . . . Coming, Mr Meredith! Be right with you, sir!' The last words were shouted for the benefit of the unseen caller as the groom disappeared in the direction of the main door of the manor house.

When he returned, Tom was leading a beautifully

proportioned horse with a gait as dainty as that of a deer. The horse was glistening with perspiration.

'This is Vulcan,' said the groom. 'He needs a good rub-down and a blanket thrown over his back. You can help me, if you've a few minutes.'

Seb looked pleadingly at his mother. There was still a great deal of work to be done in the rooms above the stable, but she waved her hand for him to go with the groom. 'Off you go, but don't be too long. We'll need to get a fire going if you want to eat tonight.'

Dolly did not complain about Seb leaving her alone to carry on with the hard task of cleaning up. Seb was looking very tired and probably could not have contributed much, and Dolly felt sure Tom realised Seb was a sick boy. He would not allow him to work too hard and it would be good for Seb to do something he enjoyed.

Inside the stable, Tom said, 'Fetch some water for Vulcan from the butt outside the door – but only give him a little. While you're doing that I'll begin rubbing him down. I don't know what Meredith Putt does to his mounts. No horse with this one's breeding should arrive back here in such a state. It's a pity Sir Nelson doesn't spend a bit more time at home, and less gallivanting around the world. If he learned what was going on he'd soon put a stop to it, I'm sure of that.'

Bringing a bucket of water to the horse, Seb said, 'I saw Vulcan earlier today. He was being ridden at full gallop through the woods by a young, dark-haired gent. He almost bowled over a blind gipsy girl.'

'That would be young Meredith. He's as wild as they come. I don't know what Sir Nelson was thinking of when he put him in charge of the estate. I wouldn't trust him to look after my cabbage patch. All the same,

Mr Meredith is the one with the power of hiring and firing on the manor lands. If you want to stay around you'll learn to doff your hat when he goes by and to say, "Yes, sir, sorry, sir," when he calls you a fool for doing something he ordered you to do only the day before. You'd best warn your mother about him, too.'

Rubbing down the horse was warm work. Removing his hat, Tom wiped perspiration from his forehead with a sleeve of his shirt.

'Now, get a couple of handfuls of oats from the bin over there. The horses will be coming in from the fields soon. If he had his way Mr Meredith would have me spend all my time taking care of this horse, but we've some of the finest working-horses in the county here. I'll not let them take second place to that popinjay's pet.'

CHAPTER FOUR

Dolly Quilter began work before sunrise the next morning, even though it was the height of summer, and dawn came early. Her first task was to clean out the kitchen hearth and light the fire which provided heat for the range and the ovens, then she had to bring in logs from the yard at the rear of the manor.

Coming down the outside steps that led from the rooms above the stable, Seb saw his mother struggling with the wood and went to her aid. He carried an armful of logs to the house only to find the sour-faced maid, Florence, standing in the kitchen doorway.

Barring his way, Florence said, 'You just stay outside this house, young man. Cook won't have you coughing over everything in the kitchen. You might have done it in London, but it's not the way we do things here.'

Behind the maid's back Dolly signalled for her son to hold his tongue. Seb set down the logs outside the kitchen door without a word.

Even this did not please the kitchen-maid. 'That's right, make a mess out here . . . Not that I should care. It's your mother who'll have to scrub the step – after she's done the floor inside. She'd better not be all day about it, either. Cook likes to make an early start and she's not one to pick her way around pails of water or walk over sopping-wet floors.'

On his way from the kitchen door, Seb thought it as

well the unhelpful kitchen-maid knew nothing of the freshly killed rabbit Tom Hanks had found at the foot of the steps leading to the Quilters' rooms.

Handing it in through the doorway to Seb, the head stableman had said, 'You mentioned that a gipsy girl might have been hurt by Mr Meredith if it hadn't been for you. Unless I'm mistaken this is a gipsy's way of saying "Thank you". But don't speak of it to anyone else. They wouldn't understand.'

The cook, a very large woman, proved far less formidable than had been suggested by the kitchen-maid. She was the only member of the kitchen staff who did not keep criss-crossing the flagstone floor while Dolly was down on her knees scrubbing. The cook eventually admonished the others for continually treading on the partly dried floor.

When Florence complained that Dolly was too slow, the cook retorted, 'I don't ever remember anyone praising *you* for your speed when you was scrubbing kitchen floors, Florrie Shaw. If you don't stop walking backwards and forwards over what's already been cleaned you'll find yourself down on your knees showing Mrs Quilter how it should be done.'

Cook reigned supreme in the kitchen. There was no more to-ing and fro-ing until the floor was finished. When Dolly tried to thank the woman, she was told, 'I wasn't doing it just for you, dear. I've got work to do. It won't get done with everyone in my kitchen and a wet floor beneath my feet.'

Nevertheless, while Amelia Putt and her son were eating breakfast, Cook handed Dolly a jug of hot milk and a plate on which was some bread and two small pieces of fat bacon, saying, 'Here, take this to that boy of yours while Mrs Putt's busy doing something else. He looks as though he could do with a bit of fattening up. As for this cough they're all talking about . . . I went up to London once, a few years ago. The river stank so much I'm surprised anyone up there can breathe at all. A bit of good food and a month or two of country air will work wonders for him, I don't doubt.'

Dolly could have wept. There had been few kind words spoken to her since leaving London.

As though embarrassed at her own kindness, the cook said, 'Hurry now. Mrs Putt will be down here soon and I've a sight more work for you to do before then.'

For three months Dolly was kept working hard from dawn until well after dusk for six days of the week. On the seventh day she was able to turn her back on the manor, although she saw Mrs Putt and the servants in Swinbrook Church, and no one washed up in her absence. The pots and pans were piled high to blight her morning when Monday came.

Seated beside his mother on the hard wooden bench-seats inside the small village church, it seemed to Seb that the congregation spent the whole service staring at the small family who had come to the village from far-off London. Although such curiosity was not unkind, it made Seb squirm. He wished he and his mother possessed Sunday-best clothes to wear to church, like the others in the congregation.

Although being employed at Swinbrook Manor meant that Dolly needed to work harder than she ever had before, life was very much enriched for Seb. Chief among his new pleasures was the opportunity to work with the horses of the manor's farm.

Pride of place in the stables was given to Vulcan and the Fettiplace string of hunters. It was on animals such as these that generations of gentlemen had learned the skills they had put to use on the field of battle as cavalry officers.

Lean, highly strung animals, they were pampered by the grooms and admired by visitors. However, Seb much preferred the giant cart-horses whose days were spent performing a variety of duties about the farm.

He admired their infinite patience and felt able to relax when he was helping with the slow, ponderous animals. He would speak to them softly as he dried them down at the end of their long working day, enjoying the rich, sweet smell that was so much a part of them.

One morning, when the last of the working-horses had left for the fields, Tom Hanks said to Seb, 'It won't be long before it's hunting season again. We'll need to get the hunters in trim if they're to do credit to us and their riders – whether it be young Meredith or Sir Nelson himself.'

'What do they hunt?'

Seb asked the question in all innocence, but Tom looked at him with a suspicion that swiftly turned to disbelief.

'Bless my soul! Don't they teach folk anything at all in London? They hunts foxes, of course. Nasty little creatures that wouldn't leave a lamb or chicken alive anywhere if the gentry didn't hunt them with their dogs and their horses – or so 'tis said. I've never been quite convinced of the truth of it, myself. Many a time when I was courting up on Handley Plain me and my late wife would watch a vixen and her cubs playing about at the edge of the woods. Pretty sight it was. Whatever the rights of it, we need to get the horses fit for the hunt. Right now they're so fat a man could do himself a mischief trying to get his legs around 'em.'

'Who'll have the job of exercising 'em?'

The casual manner in which Seb asked the question did not fool the Fettiplace head groom.

'I don't rightly know. Can't be me, that's for certain. I've far too much to do getting the other horses ready to bring in the harvest. I'll likely get someone in from the village . . .'

'I'll take 'em out for you.' Seb was unable to keep up his indifferent pretence any longer and his eagerness brought a brief smile to the older man's lips.

'Well, now . . . These aren't farm-horses, or your weary old London nags, you know. They're high-spirited hunters who can't so much as look at a hedge without wanting to jump over it.'

'I'll manage 'em.'

Tom looked at Seb's frail build. There was not much of the London boy, but he *did* have a remarkable ability to handle horses. 'Aye, I reckon you might at that.'

Twenty minutes later, wearing a pair of decrepit riding-boots discarded years before by a visitor to the manor, Seb rode from the stable yard, mounted on the most elderly of the Fettiplace-owned hunters.

It mattered not that the boots were several sizes too large for him. Seb was riding a saddled horse for the first time. To add to his moment of glory, his mother paused as she scrubbed the kitchen step and gazed after him with a look of sheer astonishment on her face. Seb waved to her and passed by close enough to recognise the pride in her expression as she waved in return.

That day marked the beginning of a new era for Seb. A natural horseman, he enjoyed the sense of exhilaration and unaccustomed freedom that came from riding a spirited horse along the narrow country lanes, with not another person in sight.

Occasionally, Seb would need to pull up the horse and allow a coughing fit to take its course, but the bouts were occurring less frequently now. In spite of the difficulties of her own situation as a servant in the manor house, Dolly knew she had been right to bring Seb away from London and she was prepared to put up with any amount of harassment if it would give Seb a new lease of life.

'Sir Nelson's going to be very pleased with his hunters when he returns to the manor. You've done well with those horses, young Seb. I can't remember when they've ever been in such fine fettle for the hunting season.'

Tom's praise came while he and Seb were sharing the bread and cheese the groom had brought from home for his midday meal. The shared meal was a ritual that had begun soon after the Quilters' arrival in Swinbrook. In those days Seb had eaten no more than a bite or two of the food the Fettiplace groom passed to him. Now he ate so much that Carrie, Hanks's crippled daughter, had complained just that morning that he was eating them 'out of house and home'.

'The only horse that ain't getting any exercise is Vulcan.' Seb spoke past a mouthful of bread and cheese. 'He's nearly as fat as old Bluebell.'

Bluebell was a cart-horse mare, due to foal any day now.

'If Mr Meredith doesn't return soon and exercise him, Vulcan will be waddling to the first hunt meeting.' Seb gulped down the food in his mouth, at the same time reaching for the last piece of cheese.

'It's sad to see a fine horse so sadly in need of exercise,' agreed Tom Hanks. 'Do you think you could ride him? He's a handful, mind.'

'I could ride him all right.' Seb was so excited his hand paused *en route* to the last piece of cheese and Tom beat him to it. 'But I thought Mr Meredith gave orders no one should ride Vulcan but him?'

'And so he did, but the horse is owned by Sir Nelson and I'm *his* head groom. I say the animal needs exercise. Besides, Mr Meredith's in London and what he don't see won't hurt him. Give Vulcan a run this afternoon – but don't take any liberties with him, mind. He's a wilful horse, that one.'

'He's bad-tempered all right, but I can manage him. There's no horse I couldn't handle, given time.'

Seb's statement sounded like a boast, but Tom had watched Seb working with the horses. His way with them was almost uncanny. It was as though he understood what they were thinking. Tom had looked after horses all his life. He believed he knew their ways better than any man in the district, but his skills had been learned. Seb's were instinctive.

'All right, you can take him out – but remember, it's my job that will go as well as yours if anything happens to him.'

CHAPTER FIVE

For the next few days Seb concentrated his efforts on bringing Vulcan to a peak of fitness. A superb animal, the stallion was everything Tom Hanks had claimed him to be. Seb worked hard exercising the horse and felt a thrill of achievement when his efforts began to bear fruit.

When he believed the animal to be capable of a sustained gallop, Seb took Vulcan to the forest where he had first seen Meredith riding at high speed. He too galloped along the woodland path, but at a more controlled pace. He had ridden for about a mile when a bout of coughing forced him to pull the horse to a halt until he was able to bring the spasm under control.

As he sat astride the horse waiting for his breath to return to normal he saw something small and red among the undergrowth on the ground. It looked remarkably like the strawberry his mother had brought him from the kitchen yesterday. It was the first time Seb had eaten such a fruit and its taste had been like nothing he had ever enjoyed before.

Dismounting from the horse, but keeping a tight grip on the reins, Seb peered more closely at the woodland plant. The fruit he was looking at was no larger than the nail on his little finger, but it *was* a strawberry and now he was dismounted he could see many more dotted about the woodlands.

As Seb bent down to pick the miniature fruit, a figure suddenly appeared from among the nearby trees. It was the blind gipsy girl. In her hand she swung a basket – and it was this that startled Vulcan. Snorting in fear, the horse reared up, pulling the reins from Seb's hand.

Leaping at the horse, Seb made a desperate attempt to catch the dangling reins – and missed. A moment later the horse was cantering off along the track, heading away from Swinbrook.

Seb watched the horse with a feeling of utter dismay. To have shouted or run after it would have destroyed any faint chance there might be that Vulcan would come to a halt of his own accord.

Suddenly a figure sprang to the track in front of the horse, waving his arms and shouting. It was the brother of the gipsy girl, Anna. Beside him a dog joined in the game, barking excitedly.

Vulcan slowed and stopped. Then, turning abruptly, he began trotting back the way he had come. In no mood to be captured just yet, the wilful horse stopped short of Seb and tossed his head defiantly. From farther along the forest path the gipsy let out a low whistle and his dog hurtled through the forest well to one side of the horse.

Vulcan looked about him uncertainly. With men on the track behind and to the front, and now a dog to one side, there was only one way left open to him. Tossing his head, the stallion turned into the forest. Within moments the undergrowth had become too thick for even such a strong horse to pass through. When Vulcan was forced to a halt he had two men and a dog behind him preventing any escape.

As the horse stood quivering uncertainly, Seb called softly to the gipsy, 'Stay where you are. Don't try to go near him.'

Instead of replying, the gipsy gave another whistle, much lower this time. The dog crouched on its haunches, quivering with excitement and giving the horse a 'run-if-you-dare' look.

Seb advanced slowly. Very slowly, talking quietly and gently to the highly strung horse. It took a great deal of patience. Whenever the horse showed the least sign of nervousness Seb would come to a halt, continuing to talk in soft, soothing tones.

It must have been fifteen minutes before Seb was close enough to reach out a hand cautiously and stroke the horse's neck. It was with a feeling of indescribable relief that, moments later, his fingers closed around the reins. Now he moved in, continuing to talk in a bid to keep the uneasy animal calm.

Seb had been aware that the gipsy brother and sister were close behind him, but he was so engrossed with the horse that it made him start when Anna spoke to him.

'I knew it was you, even though you've come up in the world since we last met.'

There was no hint of apology in the gipsy girl's aggressive statement of fact. Seb was to learn this was common to all gipsies. They never felt it necessary to make an apology, whatever might have occurred. 'If I hadn't caught the horse I'd have come down in the world with a bump,' said Seb heatedly as anger took the place of relief. 'This is the most valuable horse in the whole of Sir Nelson Fettiplace's stables. I shouldn't even be riding him, by rights.'

'If staying out of trouble's so important to you then you'd better stay somewhere where you *can't* do anything wrong,' retorted Anna. 'Just hang around the stables, waiting for an opportunity to bow and scrape when the lord of the manor comes by. Slavishness like that wouldn't help a gipsy, but it might do you some good – at least, for as long as it pleases Sir Nelson Fettiplace, or that nephew of his.'

Seb's anger disappeared as swiftly as it had come. 'It doesn't matter, I've caught Vulcan again now.'

Turning his attention to the gipsy, he said simply, 'Thanks.'

Looking at Anna once more, he asked, 'How did you know it was me, anyway?'

'I heard you coughing. It's not so noisy as when you last came this way, but I'm glad I haven't got a cough like it.'

As they talked, Anna's brother walked around Vulcan, occasionally reaching out to trace a muscle or run his hand down one of the horse's legs.

'T'ain't a bad animal, this. Do them up at the manor race 'en?'

'He's won at Burford Races these last two years.' It was an accomplishment of which Tom Hanks was happy to tell anyone who would listen. 'And he's hardly in his prime yet.'

'Will he run this year?'

'There's no reason why not. I've got most of the fat off him now.'

The gipsy looked at Seb thoughtfully. 'Think yourself good with horses, d'you?'

Seb shook his head. 'I like working with 'em, but I don't know enough about 'em yet.'

'Reckon you know as much about horses as most gorgios do, whether they call themselves grooms, stable-boys, or whatever, but none of you gorgios will ever know as much as a Romany.'

'D'you have horses?'

The young gipsy nodded. 'A few. One of 'em would give this horse a good run, for all its fancy breeding.'

Seb was sceptical, but he said amiably, 'I'd like to see your horses. Especially one that could come close to Vulcan.'

The gipsy grunted and without another word turned and walked away, the dog that had helped catch Vulcan trotting, rib-thin, at his heels.

The sudden departure took Seb by surprise and he said, 'Have I offended him? I didn't mean to . . .'

'Boz goes his own way. Take no notice, he's all right. He'll take you to see our horses in his own time. What are you doing here? You weren't riding when I came along.'

'No, I saw some strawberries growing wild and stopped to pick some. I'd never tasted them until yesterday.'

'Never tasted strawberries?' Anna's expression was one of disbelief. 'What sort of place is this London you come from? Surely they sell fruit, even if there's nowhere to grow it?'

Seb shrugged. 'I dunno. They never sold strawberries in our part of London. Not that we'd have had money to buy 'em, even if they did.'

Seb's words told Anna far more than he realised and she said suddenly, 'I've got a bowl here, in my basket. Help me fill it with strawberries and I'll give you a *real* treat.'

Seb knew he should be returning Vulcan to the Swinbrook Manor stables, but he was curious – and merely remembering the taste of the fruit he had enjoyed the day before was enough to make his mouth water. Putting his hand through the loop in Vulcan's rein he wrapped the leather strap securely about his wrist and helped Anna pick the small red berries.

In spite of her blindness, Anna was far quicker than he and when the bowl was half full she set off surefootedly along the path in the direction of Swinbrook, calling for Seb to follow.

When he caught up with her she resumed her questions about his life in London. It was not long before he found himself telling her more about himself and his family than he had ever told anyone. He asked his own questions too and although Anna never replied at any length he learned she had lost both her parents, although she evaded his question as to the cause of their deaths. Boz, her brother, had brought her up, helped by other gipsies in their group, all of whom seemed to be related to them in some way.

'It must be hard for you . . . being blind, an' all,' Seb said sympathetically.

'It's hard being a *Romany*,' declared Anna with a bitterness that took Seb by surprise. 'For most gorgios, "gipsy" is just another word for "thief". Especially gorgios like that Meredith Putt, up at your manor.'

'Have you met him?'

Almost before Seb could complete the sentence Anna reached out a hand and touched his arm. 'Stop here!'

'Why? What is it?'

'Can you see some goats nearby?'

'Goats? No . . . Yes! There are some over there.' He had detected them with difficulty among the trees. 'How did you know?'

She turned sightless eyes on him and there was an expression of scorn on her young face. 'Can't you *smell* them?'

Seb could not, but he would not admit it to Anna. 'Of course. You can smell goats from a mile away.'

'Well, come on, then. Take my hand and we'll get there a lot quicker. Old Barnard always puts his goats out where there's plenty of brambles for them to eat. Once when I tried to find them I got so tangled up that I had to stay where I was until Boz came to get me out.'

'Why would you want to find Old Barnard's goats?'

Old Barnard was a gamekeeper employed by Sir Nelson and a man notorious for his bad temper. Seb had met him once in the yard at the manor and the gamekeeper's scowl had been sufficient to terrify him.

'You'll see. Take my hand now – and don't lead me into any brambles.'

Anna's hand was warm and her grip firm, but she was not used to being guided anywhere. More than once Seb needed to tug hard to prevent her walking straight into a bush.

When they reached the tethered goats Anna released his hand and went with uncanny accuracy to the nearest animal. Gently stroking it, she ran her hand along its body, beneath its belly, and to its udder.

'This one will do. Give me the bowl.'

When he handed it to her she held it beneath the goat and skilfully milked the creature until the tiny strawberries were almost all submerged. Holding out the bowl to Seb, Anna said, 'Here, this is the way strawberries should be eaten.'

A strong aroma of goat lingered about the bowl, but it did not affect the taste and Seb had to admit that Anna was right. Strawberries in goat's milk *were* delicious.

When he thought he had eaten half, he passed the strawberries back to her. As she ate, he asked, 'How many times have you done this?'

Her mouth half filled with strawberries, Anna mumbled, 'Enough times to bring Old Barnard looking for me with his gun if he found out, but not often enough for him to become suspicious.'

'Doesn't it bother you to steal his milk?'

Anna spluttered indignantly. 'T'ain't stealing. Not *proper* stealing, anyway. Does Old Barnard pay anything for the brambles his goats are eating?'

'No, but—'

'Does his wife have milk for her needs and still some left over to sell?'

'I suppose so, yes.'

'Well, then.' Anna spoke triumphantly. 'We had a missionary come bothering us last year. He said you gorgios live your life by the Commandments. Not stealing's just one of 'em. Ain't there another one which says you mustn't be greedy?'

'I dunno.' Seb's attendance at the Swinbrook parish church every Sunday had not yet provided him with the answer to such a searching theological question. 'I . . . I expect there is.'

'Well, then, for Old Barnard and his wife to want more milk than they really need would be breaking one of your Commandments – and that's just as bad as stealing. Anyway, you've had as much milk as I have today.'

Seb was not certain Anna's logic would have stood up in a court of law, but he lacked the knowledge to counter her argument. And she was quite right: if they were caught he would be deemed as guilty as Anna – and had Seb not glimpsed a sudden movement far down the path through the woods, the matter might have been put to the test before a magistrate.

'Somebody's coming along the path. It's Old Barnard!' Seb had recognised the gamekeeper's green waistcoat.

'What do we do?' Momentarily, Anna was as concerned as Seb.

'I'll find somewhere for you to hide then come back for you when Old Barnard's gone.'

'If you can keep him talking and looking in another direction for a few minutes I'll be able to make my own way through the woods. I know more or less where we are.'

Seb marvelled yet again at the blind girl's confidence. Many fully sighted people would have been at a loss in the forest. 'All right. I'll ride down to the track and make sure he keeps his eyes on me. Hide yourself until you hear me shout for Vulcan to "Whoa". It'll be safe to make your escape then.'

As Anna crouched low beside the goats, Seb hurriedly mounted Vulcan and rode the horse in a wide arc downhill to the track.

'Whoa!' When Seb brought the horse to a halt it was between the gamekeeper and Anna.

'What d'ye think you're up to in these woods – and making a racket enough to frighten every animal and bird for miles about?'

'I was exercising Vulcan when I saw something up

among the trees. It was your goats.'

'I hope for your sake you haven't scared *them* too. Goats is sensitive animals. I've known a tiny storm to curdle their milk so 'tis undrinkable. If you have I'll be up at the big house tonight calling for you to fork out some of your wages to make up for what I've lost.'

As they were talking, Seb moved the horse until the gamekeeper had his back to Anna, but Seb could see her until the moment she disappeared among the trees.

'I don't get paid for my stable work up at the house. I do it to help out Tom Hanks.'

A malicious grin touched the gamekeeper's face as he said, 'That's just as well, I reckon, 'cos I wouldn't expect you'd be kept on after today.'

For a moment Seb thought the gamekeeper must have seen Vulcan galloping free in the forest, but he quickly dismissed the idea. Old Barnard would have mentioned it immediately.

'What do you mean?'

'Mr Meredith returned to the manor an hour ago. I remember hearing him tell Tom Hanks once that no one but him was to ride that there horse you're on. Oh, yes, you'll be on your way all right – and lucky if you have any skin left on your back to take home to London with you.'

CHAPTER SIX

Seb galloped Vulcan back to Swinbrook Manor, slowing only when the tall chimneys of the house were in view. He walked the horse into the yard and for a few moments his hopes rose. If Meredith Putt was in the house, Seb might be able to return Vulcan to his stall without Sir Nelson's nephew knowing he had exercised the horse.

His hopes were dashed when Tom Hanks came from the stable, pale-faced and unsmiling. Behind the unhappy groom, Putt emerged from the shadows, his cheeks flushed and angry, contrasting sharply with those of the other man.

Pushing Tom to one side, Putt glared up at Seb. 'Get down off that horse before I knock you down.'

'There's no call to talk to the boy like that, Mr Meredith . . .'

Putt rounded on the head groom. 'When I want your opinion I'll ask for it – and you and I will take this matter up later. Right now I want this boy off my horse.'

Seb slid to the ground. Standing uncertainly, holding the reins, he spoke to Tom, 'Shall I take Vulcan in and rub him down?'

'You'll have nothing more to do with the horse – no, nor with any of the others. I don't ever want to see your face about these stables again.'

Seb looked at Tom in dismay and the head groom protested, 'The boy isn't to blame, Mr Meredith. He's good with horses. Thanks to Seb, Vulcan's in better form than I've ever seen him. By the time you take him to the Wychwood Forest Fair for the races there won't be a horse to touch him.'

'I told you before, I don't need your opinion, Hanks. As for blame . . . I know where it lies and I've a mind to get rid of you too. My orders have been blatantly disobeyed and if I ever see this boy around the stables again he'll answer to a magistrate.'

Tom opened his mouth to protest further but Seb said quickly, 'It's all right, Tom. I'll go. I'm sorry you've got in trouble because of me.'

Seb remembered Tom's family circumstances. Doubtless his house belonged to the manor. Dismissal would be catastrophic for him. Putt's face was heavily flushed and Seb thought he had probably been drinking heavily. The chances were that by tomorrow he would remember little of what had been said. If so, Seb could resume his work with the other horses when Sir Nelson Fettiplace's nephew went away once more.

Seb greatly underestimated both Meredith Putt's sobriety and the depth of his anger. Dolly was dismissed from her lowly post as scullery-maid later that same evening. The reason given by Mrs Putt was Seb's 'unauthorised use of Fettiplace horses'.

Dolly broke the news to her son when she returned to the rooms above the stables that evening, a couple of hours earlier than usual.

'That's not fair!' Seb was indignant. 'Tom *asked* me to take Vulcan out. Anyway, she shouldn't sack you for something I've done. I'll go and see her.'

'It wouldn't do any good. Not now.'

'What do you mean "not now"?' Something in his mother's voice caused Seb's indignation to seep away.

'I couldn't go back, not after what I've said to her. I told her what I thought of her, her house, and the job of scullery-maid. As far as I'm concerned, Florrie Shaw's welcome to have it. She and the job deserve each other.'

'How long have we been given to find somewhere else?' Seb felt deeply depressed. He had enjoyed working with the Fettiplace horses more than anything else he had ever done in his young life.

'Mrs Putt wants us out by morning.'

Seb's eyes widened in dismay. 'But . . . where will we go? What are we going to do?'

'We'll have to go back to London. There's nowhere else.' Dolly was aware there was no place for them in the capital city either, but at least they knew a few people there and would be in familiar surroundings.

'We can't possibly be out by morning! Arrangements need to be made for our furniture. We can't just leave it here, it's all we've got in the world.'

The furniture had been bought by Dolly and Arthur Quilter in happier times and Seb knew it would break his mother's heart if she were forced to part with it now.

'I'll go and see Mrs Putt. After all, it's *me* who's the cause of this mess.'

'No!' Dolly put herself between the door and her son. 'She's been looking for a reason to get rid of us ever since we arrived here. If it hadn't been you it'd have been something else. Besides, "Mr" Meredith has been drinking heavily since he came home. He's not right in the head after too many, that one. You keep yourself well clear of him.'

A bout of coughing such as Seb had not experienced for many weeks solved the immediate question of whether or not he should go to the manor house to speak to Mrs Putt.

He was still fighting for breath when there was a soft knocking at the door and Tom Hanks entered the room, swiftly closing the door after him.

After a brief but sympathetic glance at Seb, the Fettiplace head groom spoke to Dolly. 'I'm sorry that Mrs Putt's put you out. It doesn't help knowing I'm more to blame than anyone. I should have known how Mr Meredith would react to someone else riding his horse.'

'You were being kind to Seb and I'm grateful to you for that. As for leaving here . . . it wasn't much of a way to earn a living, but it gave us a roof over our heads. I don't know what we'll do now.'

'I think I've found an answer for you. That's what I've come to tell you about.'

Seb had control of his breathing once more and Tom nodded in his direction. 'This concerns you in particular, Seb. It's work tending horses. Good horses, right here, in Swinbrook.'

'No one in Swinbrook would dare give us work after what's happened here, Tom. The Putts would see to that.'

'Ah, they might if you were going to work for anyone else but Christian Timms. He wouldn't take too much notice of the Putts, even if he and they were talking to each other – but they're not, and never have been.'

'Tell us about him, Tom,' said Seb eagerly, '. . . and the horses.'

'Most of what folk have to say about Christian Timms is gossip – though I don't doubt but it's true. His ma was parlour-maid up here at the manor many years ago. She had to leave when she found she was expecting Christian. That was more than forty years since. She wouldn't say who the father was, but everyone knew. It was old Sir Neville, the father of Sir Nelson Fettiplace. He sired more children in his time than did King Solomon, but after Christian was born she never needed to work again.

'When Sir Neville died about twenty years ago, he willed Handley Farm to Christian. It served to confirm what everyone had always said, but it didn't please the Fettiplace family – especially the Putts, because Sir Neville left nothing to them. It seems he knew them better than does Sir Nelson.

'Anyway, Christian has a cottage belonging to the farm that's been empty these last three or four years. You probably saw it by the side of the lane soon after you left the forest and entered the village. I went to see Christian tonight and told him what had happened here. As soon as I spoke of your way with horses, Seb, he said you could not only have the cottage – Fern Cottage, 'tis called – but he has a job for you, if you want it. You'd be helping him out on the farm, but in particular taking care of his horses. Christian's built up a reputation in the county for breeding strong, working horses. The old chap who's been helping him for years has suffered dreadfully from the rheumatics. It's got so bad lately that his daughter came over from Asthall only this week and took her father off to live with her there. He won't be coming back, that's for certain, and it's left Christian desperate for someone to work for him.'

As Dolly looked at her son, concerned about whether his strength would stand up to a full-time job, Tom continued, 'That's not the end of it. Christian's a widower, like me. He could use someone to do a bit of work and cooking in the house. He has a young tinker of about Seb's age who helps him about the farm and in the dairy, but she's always complaining of having too much to do, what with the milking, harvesting and suchlike and she can't do much in the house. If you ask me, he'd have been better off getting someone in from the village, but Christian's always had a soft spot for gipsies, and the like.'

'I've no doubt I can help about the farm as well as keep things right in the house for him. I've never done farm or dairy work, but I'm not too old to learn.'

'That's what I told Christian. He said the two of you might have been sent to Swinbrook by the Good Lord especially for the benefit of Handley Farm.'

The delight of Dolly and Seb brought an embarrassed smile to Tom's face. Taking off his ancient and battered felt hat, he scratched his head and said, 'You'll like Christian. He was given the right name, I reckon, though he can be a bit too religious for me, at times.'

'There's nothing wrong with you either, Tom Hanks. If it wasn't for you I don't know what we'd have done. But how do we move our belongings? We're supposed to be out of here by morning.'

'And so you shall be. Christian will be bringing a cart any time now. I must go before he arrives, in case anyone comes out of the manor. I'd rather it wasn't known that I had anything to do with finding you a place at Handley Farm. I'll no doubt be meeting you all again before too long – it isn't far from my place and he and I have been friends for a long time. Remember all I've taught you, Seb, and Christian will never regret taking you on.'

CHAPTER SEVEN

Christian Timms was well aware he was not welcome on manor property, but he was not a man to resort to any form of subterfuge. He rode into the yard of Swinbrook Manor farm singing the words of a Charles Wesley hymn as though he had not a care, or an enemy, in the world.

'Hail the Lord of earth and heaven!
Praise to Thee by both be given.
Thee we greet triumphant now . . . Whoa, there!'

This last addendum to Wesley's words of praise brought the giant cart-horse to a sliding, clattering halt on the wet cobble-stones of the stable yard.

'Hello! Mrs Quilter?' Christian called up the stone steps to where the light from an open doorway ventured out timidly from the home of the departing family. 'I'm here to take you to Fern Cottage.'

Flustered, Dolly appeared in the doorway, clutching a blanket-wrapped bundle. 'I'm sorry, Mr Timms. We should have had everything down ready for you, but it came on to rain. I didn't want it getting all wet.'

'The Lord's been kind to you and stopped it raining for a while so we'll be able to bring everything out in the dry. By the time it comes on to rain again you'll both be snug inside your new home. I called in at the cottage on the way here and dropped off a couple of pieces of furniture. I don't need them up at the farm any more. I lit a fire in the cottage while I was there. It'll take the damp off the air.'

As the farmer clasped hands with Seb, telling him how much he was looking forward to having him work at the farm, Dolly came close to tears. 'You're every bit as kind as Tom said you were. We'll never be able to repay either of you.'

'It's a neighbourly community here, Mrs Quilter . . . although I'll admit there's some more neighbourly than others.'

The remark was accompanied by a glance in the direction of the manor house. No lights could be seen at the windows on this side of the building and it seemed none of the occupants either knew or cared that their late scullery-maid was moving out.

Christian Timms was a big man and with his help it did not take long to load the cart with the few possessions owned by the Quilter family.

There was to be one more surprise in store for Dolly that evening. As the horse and cart clattered from the farmyard, a stout, bonneted figure stepped from the shadows beside the road. It was the manor's cook. In her hands she bore a large basket. Handing it up to Dolly, she said, 'Here, I doubt you'll have had all you're due from Amelia Putt. There are a few bits of food here, and a couple of pies I've baked myself. They'll come in handy, I dare say . . . although if that's Christian Timms I see up on the seat beside you, you'll not want for much.'

The cook was gone before Dolly could thank her, but Christian said quietly, 'It seems you've made friends as well as enemies while you've been here, Mrs Quilter. It's my belief that it's worthwhile making fifty enemies if it brings you one good friend.'

Fern Cottage was as charming as its name implied. Quite small, it was tucked away in the valley beside the road, about a half-mile from the cluster of houses forming the main village and within sight of the great Wychwood Forest. Inside it was snug and warm. Informed by Tom Hanks that the Quilters owned few worldly possessions, Christian had placed more than 'a couple of pieces of furniture' in the house.

When Seb left the cottage in the early morning, a low ribbon of mist hung above the small stream that flowed through the valley and a flock of raucous crows winged their way northwards in search of food. On the slope of the hill opposite the cottage a whole colony of rabbits hopped aimlessly in and about a warren that tunnelled deep beneath the roots of a giant elm tree.

Seb breathed in deeply but despite a freshness in the morning air he coughed only lightly. This was in itself a great relief after the severe coughing bout he had experienced the previous evening. Christian had told him to take a few days to settle in at the cottage, but Seb was eager to begin work with the horses of Handley Farm.

The animals were magnificent even when judged by the high standard of those kept at the manor farm. Descendants of the great black horses of medieval England, they stood higher than Seb, yet they possessed a gentle steadiness that soon had the boy enthusing about their qualities.

Watching Seb's face as he spoke to the great animals

and helped his new employer feed them, Christian knew Tom Hanks had not exaggerated the London boy's feel for horses. Seb would fit in well with the farmer's ambition to breed the finest working animals in the whole of the country.

There was some ploughing to be done on the farm, but Christian did not want to tax Seb's strength until the boy had put some more meat on his bones. For a day or two he would be content to attend to the work on the farm himself while Seb took care of the stables and got to know his charges.

Half-way through the morning, Seb was cleaning out the stall occupied by a mare and foal when the door to the stable opened. He looked up, expecting to see Christian. Instead, it was a girl of perhaps a year younger than himself. She was dark-haired and wearing a threadbare dress that had been intended for someone considerably smaller.

'Hello, are you the new hired farm-hand? What's your name?'

'Seb. Who are you?' It was an unnecessary question. The girl obviously knew her way around and Seb remembered Tom talking of a tinker-girl who worked at Handley Farm.

'I'm Melody. I work in the dairy. Hasn't Mr Timms told you about me?'

'No . . . but Tom Hanks has.'

'Oh! I don't suppose he had anything good to say. He doesn't really approve of me.'

'Tom's a good man.' Seb sprang to his friend's defence. 'He was kind to me and my ma when we first came to Swinbrook – and there's no one knows horses as well as he does.'

'Perhaps. But there's more to life than horses,' retorted the girl. She kicked the straw at her feet for a while before looking up at him with an expression on her face he could not fathom.

'Where do you come from?'

'From Hoxton, but you wouldn't know where that is. It's in London.'

'Tell me about London. I'm going there one day to see the Queen. Have you ever seen her?'

'Of course. Everyone in London's seen the Queen. She lives there.'

It was a lie. Seb had never seen any member of the royal family and knew no one who had – although he had once met a boy who *thought* he might have seen her.

'Is she beautiful, like on a halfpenny?'

'Better than that. Much.'

'Was she wearing her crown?'

'Of course. No one would know she was the Queen otherwise, would they?'

Seb wished he had never entered into this conversation. It seemed that one lie led straight to another – and he was not by nature a liar.

'Why did you come to Swinbrook?'

'My ma came to work at the manor.'

'I'd like to work in a big house. Is she still there?'

'No, she'll be coming to work here tomorrow, to clean in the house and help you in the dairy.'

'Why would she want to leave the manor and come to work on a farm?'

'Because this is a nicer place than the manor.'

Seb realised he should have nipped this conversation in the bud.

'Anyone who knows about horses would be only too pleased to work here,' he declared. 'Anyway, I had no choice about leaving. Meredith Putt gave me the sack for riding his special horse.'

'The big black one? I've seen him galloping through the forest on it sometimes. He looks handsome on a horse.'

Seb found such admiration for Meredith Putt hard to take. 'Ma says handsome is as handsome does.'

'That's the sort of thing my ma would say.'

A scheming expression crossed Melody's face. 'I need to get some hay down from the loft for the cows. Will you help me?'

'I'll be happy to do it when I've finished my work here.'

Melody pouted. 'It wouldn't take you more than a few minutes.'

Seb closed the door of the stall he had been cleaning and followed Melody. She led him out of the stables to a flight of stone steps that went to the loft.

There was the sweet smell of hay here and it was warm, lulling Seb into a false sense of well-being.

He was in the centre of the loft, shin-deep in loose hay, when the door swung slowly shut behind them.

'How am I supposed to see— Where are you, Melody?'

'I'm here, Seb. What do you need to see for? Come here.'

Afterwards, Seb wondered how he could have been so gullible. Melody closed with him. Whether he fell over something or Melody tripped him, the result was the same. The next moment he was lying with her in the hay. Somehow, in the few seconds after the door closed, she had shed her dress and was naked.

'No, Melody! The horses . . .'

'They're not going to run away. Come on, take your trousers off. I'll help you.'

Seb stumbled into the daylight and the door closed behind him, cutting off Melody's mocking laughter. He hurried down the steps, plucking hay from the waistband of his trousers and hoping Christian would not return from the fields until he had recovered some of his composure.

Resuming his tasks with a new-found vigour, Seb heard the stable door open but did not look up because he sensed Melody was looking at him over the low door of the stall.

'You've never been with a girl, have you?'

'That's none of your business.'

'You haven't, I can tell!'

From the corner of his eye Seb could see her looking at him as though he were a circus freak.

'I've never met a boy who's never done it . . . Not one as old as you. You're all right, aren't you? I mean, there's nothing wrong with you?'

'Of course I'm all right. More all right than *you*.'

Seb thought the stalls had suddenly become extremely hot. He was perspiring freely.

'It's going to be fun doing it with you . . . and I *will*, you know.'

Seb worked even harder, his shovel scraping noisily on the flagstone floor of the stables. Melody laughed again and then she was gone, but Seb never slackened. It embarrassed him even to pause and think about what had almost happened. Melody would not catch him out like that again.

For the remainder of the morning Seb worked feverishly hard. Farmer Timms was a deeply religious man, Tom had said so. What if he had seen something from the fields, or if Melody made up some story about him?

Seb heard the two plough-horses enter the farmyard from the fields. When he looked out from the stables, Christian and Melody were engaged in a deep conversation by the door of the house, and Seb's heart sank.

When the farmer brought the two horses to the stable, Seb expected him to demand an explanation for what had happened. Instead, Christian beamed, declaring Seb had done a grand job of cleaning the stables, and informing him that lunch would be ready when Seb had fed the two working horses.

In the house, Seb sat down to a poorly prepared meal of boiled pork, potatoes and cabbage, all swimming in the water from the meat, which Melody insisted was 'gravy'.

As they ate Christian chatted happily, seemingly oblivious of Seb's silence.

When the silence had lasted for many minutes, Melody said, straightforwardly, 'The cooking has put me a bit behind today. Could Seb help me get some hay from the loft when he's finished eating?'

'I'm sure he won't mind,' declared Christian failing to notice the flush of colour that jumped to Seb's cheeks. 'But . . . no, Old Harry Agg from the village is coming this afternoon. He can do that.'

To Seb, Christian explained, 'Harry's over seventy and as deaf as a gate-post, but it makes him feel useful, as well as earning him free milk, a few eggs and his meat.'

Seb looked accusingly at Melody, but she avoided his

eyes and spoke to Christian, 'It's time Harry gave up working here. He spends much of his time getting in my way. I'd have things done twice as quickly if he wasn't around.'

Christian smiled at Melody. 'If I believed that I'd find Harry some other work to do. But he's worked for me since the day I married my poor, dear wife. I could never get rid of him now.'

Turning again to Seb, Christian said, 'My wife, Harriet, was a wonderful woman with a needle. Her tapestries would take pride of place on the wall of the greatest house, but she baulked at farm work. Housework too, at times, and she pined away if she had no one to talk to for any length of time.'

'She would have been happy with Ma around. She's happiest when she has someone to talk to. She's looking forward to taking on the work in the house. It's the least she can do after all you've done for us.'

'I believe it's an arrangement that's going to work out well for everyone, Seb. Now, if you've finished eating we'll take out two more horses and I'll teach you something of ploughing. Until you've walked behind a plough you'll never appreciate just how strong one of my horses is compared with any other you've seen . . .'

CHAPTER EIGHT

'It's no good, Christian, the foal just isn't going to come.'

Tom Hanks, his arm bloody from shoulder to finger-tips, sat back on his heels, perspiration running in streams down his face and neck. He looked tired, and with good reason. Together with Christian and Seb, he had been in the Handley Farm stables for the whole night while one of the great shire mares struggled unsuccessfully to give birth to a foal.

'I must do *something*, Tom. Even if it means losing the foal. She's one of my best mares.'

There was good reason for Christian's anxiety. The mare had been in labour for more than twenty-four hours and had become noticeably weaker during the last two.

'I've done everything I know, Christian, and I must go home and clean up before going to work. Your only hope is to call in that gipsy lad who's so good with horses. The one with the blind sister.'

'You mean Boz. Boz Buckland.'

Both men looked at Seb in surprise. 'You know him?'

'I met him when we were coming through the forest on our way to Swinbrook from London. I've seen him a couple of times since. I'll go and ask him to come – if you know where he can be found.'

Seb was eager to help. Inexperienced in this aspect of animal husbandry, he had been able to do little more than soothe the mare during the long night and occasionally provide a mug of tea or coffee for the two men.

'If they haven't moved you'll find 'em about a half-mile to the north of the gibbet oak. That's the great tree that forces the track to curve around it, along the road to Leafield. There's a path from there that you'd probably not see unless you were looking specially for it.' The sun was up, but it was still gloomy in the forest.

•

The first path from the gibbet oak taken by Seb ended at a badgers' sett. He needed to turn his horse, return to the tree, and try again. He quickly found another path, but it was so faint he doubted it was the right one until he smelled wood-smoke. A few moments later he entered a small clearing, and found the gipsy encampment.

The dwellings of the gipsies were many and varied and spilled from the clearing into the forest on all sides. There were two wood-built caravans, four or five lighter, canvas-covered vehicles and a number of shelters constructed of blankets, saplings, ferns and grasses. Horses grazed among the trees, dogs roamed free, or were tied beneath the wagons, and there was a general appearance of untidiness about the camp.

Two of the dogs snapped at the air behind the legs of Seb's horse and their excited barking set up such a commotion among the others that within moments there could have been no one left sleeping in the encampment.

As Seb rode from the forest into the clearing, two burly, unsmiling men stepped into his path, and he pulled the horse to a halt.

'What are you wanting here?' There was no welcome in the man's question.

'I'm looking for Boz Buckland.'

'What do you want with my brother, Seb?'

Turning in the direction of the voice, Seb saw Anna coming down the steps at the rear of one of the canvas-covered wagons.

Relieved to see the blind gipsy girl, Seb said, 'We've a mare having serious trouble foaling. I was asked to come and find Boz. They think he's the only one who might be able to help.'

'Them at the manor have no love for gipsies. Why should they send you to find him?' A suspicious expression crossed Anna's face.

'I'm no longer working at the manor. I've come from Christian Timms.'

The suspicion cleared immediately and there was some conversation between Anna and the other gipsies before she turned back to Seb. 'What sort of trouble is it?'

'We all reckon the foal's probably turned the wrong way but neither Christian nor Tom Hanks have been able to shift it.'

'Boz won't be able to come. He broke his leg when a pony he was working fell on him. But come and see what he suggests.'

A small gipsy boy took the reins of Seb's horse from him. Seb followed Anna to the back of the wagon where Boz lay on a narrow, crumpled blanket bed, an expression of pain on his face and the injured leg bound rigidly between two straight saplings. It was cramped inside the vehicle, but apart from the bed everything was neat and tidy. There was even a small table set with plates and a tea-pot. The front section of the wagon was hidden by a hanging blanket and Seb assumed this was where Anna slept.

'What's going on? The dogs were making so much noise I thought the army had come in to move us on.'

Seb repeated the purpose of his mission, and Boz lay back and grimaced. 'There's nothing I can do to help while I'm like this . . .' Observing Seb's distraught expression, the gipsy fell silent for some moments. 'There's a man who might be able to help you, but he's being sought by the police – for a little misunderstanding. If they take him he'll hang, so he won't agree to leave the forest. The only other person I know who's capable of doing anything is Anna.'

'But Anna's . . .' Seb bit back the remainder of his retort.

'You were going to say, "But Anna's blind," isn't that right?' Anna rounded on him. 'Does that mean I can't do anything worthwhile?'

'I didn't say that.'

Boz interrupted the argument. 'Look, do you want to do something about this mare of yours? If you do, I'll have some of the women gather a few plants. We'll need two different potions. If it's one of the Christian Timms's farm-horses it'll be a big animal. That'll mean more potion than we usually use. Anna, get a pot on the boil. Gorgio, sit down and tell me exactly what the horse has been doing.'

It was a full hour before Seb was ready to leave. Various plants had been gathered from the woods and after being crushed and boiled together the resulting brew was poured in two water bottles, both of which looked as though they were relics of the Napoleonic wars.

'Do you want to ride while I walk?' Seb was not sure how the blind gipsy girl would cope with riding, but he did not invite further scorn by voicing his thoughts.

'I thought you were in a hurry?'

'I am.'

'Then get on the horse and give me your hand. I'll ride up behind you.'

A few minutes later they were trotting through the woods with Seb very aware of two slim arms encircling his waist.

'You've never had much to do with girls, have you?'

The straightforward question took Seb by surprise. 'I . . . why . . . of course I have.'

'Have you got a sweetheart? Someone in London, perhaps?'

'I don't see that it's any of your business.'

The memory of the way Melody had behaved was still fresh in Seb's mind, and his very indignation gave him away.

Anna smiled behind Seb's back, but it was a kindly smile. 'You're not a very good liar, Seb Quilter. What about that girl up at Handley Farm? Christian Timms's dairy-maid. She's an attractive girl, I'm told. Don't you have a fancy for her?'

'What do you know about Melody?'

'Being blind doesn't mean I don't hear things – and folk have a lot to say about Melody Pardoe.'

'I wouldn't know. I don't know enough people in the village to hear gossip, and Melody doesn't have time to waste talking to me.'

'Melody doesn't waste her time *talking* to anyone.

But perhaps she's growing fussier as she gets older. I've heard she's aiming to settle somewhere – and I don't mean as a dairy-maid, neither.'

Lost for a reply, Seb urged the horse to a faster gait that made talk more difficult. The only trouble was it caused Anna to cling more tightly to him. But he had to admit it was a very pleasant feeling to have her leaning against him with her arms about his waist.

When they reached the farm Seb helped her to slide to the ground. Before he dismounted, and while she still retained a hold of his hand, Anna said, 'I'll tell you something for nothing, Seb. There isn't too much of you for a girl to cuddle up to. You'll need to get Melody to fatten you up a bit.'

The mare was still down and no closer to producing her foal when Seb and Anna entered the stable. Christian was taken aback at having Anna in attendance instead of her brother, but Seb assured him that Boz had every confidence she could do what needed to be done as well as Boz himself.

While they were talking Anna was whispering quietly to the mare and running her hands over its body. Then, after calling for both the men to be quiet, she laid her head against the animal's bulging stomach.

Sitting back on her heels, she said, 'Well, the foal's still alive. All we have to do now is get it out. Pass me one of the bottles. The larger one. I'll need a tube too. Can you find me something? A stalk of cow parsley would do. See if you can find a piece that's not too brittle.'

'Seb, there's some cow parsley growing behind the pigsties. It's a tall plant, with a hollow stem. Here, take my knife to cut it.' Christian handed over a wicked-looking clasp-knife and Seb hurried away.

When he returned, Anna had her cheek against the mare's face, talking soothingly in a language that Seb thought must be that of the gipsies. Still speaking softly, she took the plants and knife from him and swiftly cut off a section of stalk about the thickness of a man's thumb and the length of her own forearm. Inserting it inside one of the bottles she had brought from the camp, she sucked up the contents until the hollow stem was filled with the potion, then pinched the end closest to her mouth before withdrawing the tube.

'Both of you hold her head up. She has to swallow this.'

Dosing the mare was not easy. Had the animal not been deadly tired after a full night in labour it would have been impossible. As it was, Anna eventually succeeded in dosing her with the entire contents of the bottle before resuming her soft talking, her mouth close to the horse's ear.

'There, she's at peace with the whole world for a while. You men can go out of the stable until I call you. When I've felt her stomach and found out which way the foal is lying I'll need to reach inside and move it. To do that I'll have to take my dress down to my waist if it's not to be ruined. Leave me a bucket of water to wash down with when I'm done.'

'Would you prefer me to move the foal?' Christian volunteered. 'It's going to take someone with a lot of strength.'

'It's going to take skill, first of all. Now your mare's relaxing nicely it'll be easier to move the foal. Once I've got it round the right way I'll give you a call and you can help me dose her with the second potion. That will send her into spasms and help push the foal out. All right, out you go.'

Outside in the farmyard, Christian said, 'That girl sounds very sure of herself – I wish I had the same confidence in her ability.'

'Her brother has faith in her. That's why he sent her and not one of the men.' Seb decided it might be politic to say nothing of the man who *might* have come in Boz's place had he not been wanted by the police.

Seb and Christian waited with increasing impatience for the best part of half an hour before Anna called to them. Hurrying inside they found the blind gipsy girl in a state of near-exhaustion. There were blood-stains on the floor and the water in the wooden bucket was stained red, but Anna was smiling.

'Help me give the last of this potion to the mare – and you'll have your foal within the hour.'

'Are you sure? Quite sure?' Christian looked at Anna disbelievingly.

'Hold her head while I give her this and you'll soon see for yourself – but I don't think you'll ever be able to breed from her again.'

Anna was no more than fifteen minutes out in her estimation and by the time she left Handley Farm the foal was standing uncertainly on long, spindly legs.

On the way back to the gipsy encampment, Anna rode behind Seb in silence. Her head resting against his back was an indication of the weariness she was feeling. It had been a difficult birth and only she knew how hard she had worked during the time she was alone in the stable.

When they turned off the track by the great oak tree, Anna suddenly raised her head and said, 'You'd better leave me here, Seb.'

'Why? You're tired out. I'll take you all the way—'

'No. When we left we were in a hurry to get to Handley Farm so nobody said anything about me riding behind you. Coming back the same way will start some of the women talking. Romany girls, *nice* Romany girls, don't get too friendly with gorgios – as one or two of the women have pointed out to me lately.'

Seb felt a sense of disappointment when Anna slid from the horse.

'Well, whether they like it or not, you've made a friend of Christian Timms.'

'How about you, Seb? Have I made a friend of you too?'

It was a light-hearted question, but Seb hoped his reply might be of some importance to her.

'I thought we were already friends.'

Her hand reached out to the reins and followed them up until she grasped his hand for a moment. 'I'm pleased about that, Seb. You're the only gorgio I've ever wanted to have . . . as a friend.'

CHAPTER NINE

In the September of 1853, accompanied by his mother, Christian and Melody, Seb set off for the Wychwood Forest Fair, held near the village of Charlbury. There were still stars in the sky when they left and dawn had not yet reached out to paint the eastern skyline.

Seb and Christian had been up for some hours, plaiting ribbons into the mane and tail of each of the six horses they were taking to sell at the fair.

Melody had arrived at the farm at the last possible moment and now sat huddled in the back of the wagon beside Dolly, trying not to shiver in the cold of the early morning and occasionally yawning noisily.

Although it meant an early start, Melody would not have wanted to miss the fair. In spite of, or perhaps because of, its reputation for rowdiness and drunkenness, it was the highlight of the year for all the young people of the surrounding district.

Two of the horses being taken to market for sale were handsome four-year-olds, steady and capable. The others ranged from eighteen months to three years. All were great cart-horses of the type bred by Christian for years, and strong enough for any task on a farm.

The two older horses would be bought for Swinbrook Manor farm by Tom Hanks and had already been chosen by him.

Seb thought it was ridiculous to take them all the way to Charlbury, five or six miles distant, for Tom to bring them back to Swinbrook again the same day. He voiced this opinion to Christian.

'It is ridiculous,' agreed the farmer. 'But as the manor will have nothing to do with me, this is the only way Tom and I can do business. I get paid a fair price and Tom has the horses he wants. All that's involved is a bit of extra walking for the horses.'

'So Tom will be at the fair too?' Dolly was pleased. She had seen little of the manor's head groom since she and Seb had left the rooms above the stables at Swinbrook Manor.

'Anyone for many miles around who has anything to do with horses, cattle and sheep will be there. So too will everyone with something to sell. There'll also be a great many others hoping to get rich without buying or selling anything at all, so be sure to keep your money where no skilful thieving fingers can take it, young Seb.'

Seated at the back of the cart, keeping a watch on the six horses secured to the tailboard, Seb grinned. 'They'd be disappointed with my pockets. All that's there is a penny-halfpenny and a piece of spare ribbon for the horses.'

'I've more than two shillings,' said Melody, surprisingly. 'Take me around the fair and I'll spend some of it on you.'

Seb was taken aback that Melody had two shillings to spend and embarrassed that she should suggest spending some of it on him. He was also aware that his mother was waiting with considerable interest for her son's reaction to the unexpected offer.

'That's very kind of you, Melody, but there's work to be done on the horses. I need to black their hoofs and brush them down, and then help Christian to show them off to the buyers.'

Melody shrugged, the movement just visible in the approaching dawn. 'Please yourself, I'm sure.'

On the wagon seat Christian tried hard not to chuckle and Dolly hid a smile.

'I'll need Seb to help me, Melody, but it should only take a short while. The horses are too good to be on offer for very long. There'll not be an animal to match 'em at the fair. If I get my price I'll put some money in Seb's pocket and he can take *you* around. Until then you'll have Tom Hanks's girl to keep you company.'

'Carrie Hanks is a *cripple*! Anyway, she doesn't enjoy fairs. She'll spend her time sitting by herself on the manor cart until it's time to go home. It's what she always does.'

'Well, she'll be there if you need company and don't want to wait for Seb.'

'He needn't bother himself. I'll find someone I know. I usually do.'

Seb wondered about Tom's crippled daughter. He had never met her. The only occasion on which he had gone to the Hankses' house had been when he was sent to bring Tom to Handley Farm to help the mare. Tom was in the garden then, but the girl was nowhere in sight. If she was as badly crippled as Melody's words suggested she would be a great responsibility for the manor's head groom. Seb was glad his mother had been able to come to the fair. She would be happy to spend part of her time with Carrie.

Dolly had originally intended remaining at Handley

Farm, carrying out Melody's duties as best she could while the others were at the fair. Although it was new to her she thoroughly enjoyed dairy work. However, Christian had insisted that she accompany them to the fair. The aged Harry Agg, assisted by his married daughter, was carrying out the farm duties for the day.

The fair was held on high ground, across the valley from Charlbury village, but it would have been impossible for even a stranger to lose his way today. The roads leading to the fair were packed with people, carts and animals, all heading in the same direction.

Almost every girl was wearing a bonnet tied under her chin with coloured ribbon and was dressed in a high-neck, printed cotton frock that had most probably been made specially for this occasion. Some girls wore boots beneath their dresses. Others carried shoes ready to be slipped upon aching feet when the fair came in sight. A few, and Melody was one of these, went barefoot.

It seemed to Seb that most of the population of Oxfordshire must be on its way to the Wychwood Forest Fair.

Long before they reached the site of the day's sales and festivities they joined a long line of slow-moving wagons. Many of the farmers hoped to sell produce at the fair and their carts were laden with vegetables of every description, together with baskets containing protesting chickens or squealing piglets. These men were intent upon entering the already crowded site of the fair. Others, and Christian was among their number, intended leaving horses and wagons on open land beside the road and taking their animals to join the others parading for sale.

While they were waiting in line with the other wagons, a group of gipsies came past. Their clothes added a great deal of colour to the day. Most of the women wore gaily coloured scarves, some covering their black hair, others flung carelessly about tanned shoulders. The gipsy men too were equally noticeable among the crowd with bright neckerchiefs and floral waistcoats.

Some of the gipsies rode horses or ponies, others walked. Among those mounted on horses was Boz, his leg not yet fully healed. Anna walked at his stirrup.

Seeing Seb's wave, Boz turned his horse away from the others and rode towards him. Anna came with him.

Before greeting Seb, the gipsy looked approvingly at the horses tied behind the cart and spoke to Christian. 'You have some fine horses. They should fetch a good price today.'

Christian looked pleased. 'I doubt if you'll see any finer horses in Oxfordshire.'

'Depends what you're looking for. This animal I'm riding, now. It won't pull a cart and it might be beaten on a sprint, but there's not a horse in the country will keep up with it over a distance.'

Standing beside her brother while he was talking, Anna had her head tilted, as though listening for something. Now she said, 'Is Seb there? Ask him what he thinks of the horse.'

'Well?'

Boz looked at Seb questioningly.

'It doesn't look anything special to me, and yet . . .' When Seb looked at the animal more closely he had to admit there *was* something about the horse.

Scrambling from the wagon, Seb answered Anna's

smile, even though he knew she could not see it.

Small-headed and wild-eyed, the horse did not stand as tall as the hunters kept at the manor stables and there had been no attempt to groom the animal, yet Seb could see it was superbly muscled.

After running his hand over the horse's legs and flanks, Seb looked up at Boz. 'This is a great horse. Where does it come from?'

Boz grinned. 'From a lot farther away than you, gorgio. Come to the racing this afternoon if you want to learn more about him.'

'You're racing him?'

'Come and see.'

Boz turned the horse away, but Anna did not follow him. 'I'll stay with Seb and make certain he doesn't miss the big race.'

For a brief moment a frown crossed Boz's face, but it went equally as swiftly. 'All right, but don't get lost.'

'Do you mind if I come with you?' Belatedly, Anna asked Seb the question. 'If I stay with Boz I always end up holding the horses while he and his pals go off together drinking. They think that because I can't see I'm not interested in what's going on at the fair.'

As Seb helped Anna to climb on the cart, he said, 'I'll not be able to go around the fair until we've sold the horses.'

Settling down beside him, Anna said, 'I don't mind. Tell me about the horses you've brought here for sale. Tell me so I can see each one of them in my mind.'

Melody snorted loudly as she moved to make space between her and the gipsy girl. On the wagon seat, where she now sat beside Christian, Dolly looked from Anna to Seb and her frown lasted far longer than had that of Boz Buckland as Seb began to describe the great cart-horses to the gipsy girl.

Before they reached the fair, Christian pulled his wagon and horses out of the line and drove into a field. There were only a few other wagons here. On one, Tom Hanks sat with his daughter, eating a belated breakfast.

Bringing his cart to a halt beside that of the other man, Christian said, 'Here you are, Tom. I've brought you the two horses you chose yourself. Young Seb here's seen to it that you're getting 'em in prime condition.'

As Melody rushed off to greet a tinker acquaintance, Tom nodded a greeting to Seb and Dolly. His glance lingered on Anna for a moment before passing on. 'I don't doubt it, Christian. Manor Farm has never regretted any of its purchases from you – and the Putts are no worse off for not knowing where they came from.'

Returning his attention to Seb, Tom said, 'You've never met my daughter Carrie, have you?'

'No, but I tasted her cooking often enough when you shared your meals with me up at the stables.'

Carrie looked up at Seb very briefly, and he caught a glimpse of alert blue eyes in a rather pinched face before she returned her gaze to her lap once more.

Seb busied himself with the horses, tying the big shires behind Tom's wagon while the two men settled the monetary side of the transaction. When it was done, Tom said he had to go to the fair in town to purchase a pony to draw the trap used by Mrs Putt. He asked Carrie to go with him. Although Seb could not hear her reply he saw her shake her head.

Melody had gone off with her friend and Seb was brushing the colts that were to be taken into town, when he had a sudden idea. Crossing to Carrie, he said, 'I ought to have introduced you and Anna. I've promised to go around the fair with her when the horses are sold, but that might not be for some time. Why don't you take her? You'd be company for each other.'

'She wouldn't want to come with me. I don't get around very fast. I'm a cripple.'

'You could still describe what's going on for her. Anna would enjoy that. You see, she's blind.'

'Oh! I'm sorry . . . I couldn't tell.'

'Of course you couldn't, any more than she can see you have a crippled leg. Will you take Anna off until the horses have been sold? I'll come and find you then.'

For a few moments it seemed Carrie would refuse. Then Anna, who had heard the conversation, said, 'It doesn't matter, Seb. I don't suppose Carrie wants to be seen with a gipsy girl.'

Her statement took Seb by surprise. The fact that Anna was a gipsy hardly mattered to him. It seemed it was equally unimportant to Carrie. Suddenly defiant, she said, 'It's usually *me* that people don't like to be seen with, as one of the village girls once told me. Come on, we'll go round the fair and I'll tell you what's happening.'

As Carrie limped away, hand in hand with her new-found friend, Seb spoke anxiously to Tom. 'I hope you didn't mind. I didn't think . . .'

'Mind? You've worked a small miracle, Seb. It worries me that Carrie spends so much time brooding about that leg of hers. It's the first time for months I've got her to leave the house. To see her go off to look around the fair is more than I dared hope. I'm not one of those who condemns gipsies out of hand and I live a lot closer to 'em than most. Mind you, I wouldn't let my hens stray too close to their camp but I've never yet heard of 'em doing any harm to a young girl. When you've sold the horses I'll buy you a drink for what you've just done. This is a day I'll remember for a long time.'

CHAPTER TEN

Christian Timms sold all his horses within an hour of his arrival at the Wychwood Forest Fair. Resplendent in their red, white and blue ribbons, with hoofs blackened and polished, each fetched his asking price with only a minimum of dickering. For Seb, the parading of the impressive great animals provided him with some of the proudest moments of his young life.

Dwarfed by the horses, Seb led them up and down the area set aside for horse sales, watched by every dealer and prospective buyer at the fair. First walking and then running, he showed off the fluid gait of the powerful animals to the approbation of everyone watching.

True to his word, Christian handed Seb a bright new sovereign to celebrate his highly successful first visit to the forest fair. Keeping the hand clutching the gold coin firmly in his pocket, Seb hurried off to find Anna and Carrie.

It took him almost as long to locate them as it had taken to sell the Handley Farm horses. It seemed incredible to Seb that so many people could have crowded into the one small area. He had never seen so many gathered together, not even in London.

All were sampling the many pleasures on offer for the fair-goers. Looking for them, Seb passed booths with criers calling on people to sample the delights of a Wild West Show, a menagerie of animals collected from the darkest, most dangerous corners of the world and a shooting-booth, the sounds of which startled Seb.

He paused for a while to listen to the music of a militia band and thought the splendid uniforms were far more impressive than the music the bandsmen were producing. But nobody cared. Everyone had come to the fair to have a good time.

Seb eventually located the two girls among the crowd surrounding a small dancing troupe which was performing to the music of a fiddle and tin whistle. Carrie was clutching a handful of 'broadsides', printed sheets giving the reader news of the day, details of recent executions, lurid court cases, and articles by a number of the authors of the day.

Forcing a way through the great throng, Seb led them to a small stall from which there drifted the mouth-watering aroma of hot meat pies.

Seb bought three pies, telling Carrie it was a return for the many meals he had shared with her father. For Anna it was a 'thank you' for the strawberries and milk enjoyed with her in the forest.

They ate the meal huddled together on a log of wood which served as a seat, close to the food-stall, before mingling with the crowds once more.

Seb was purchasing a tortoiseshell hair-comb and a purse for his mother when the church clock struck the hour of one, and Anna reached out and touched his arm. 'We should be making our way to the races.'

'I don't even know where they're being held,' confessed Seb.

'I do. I used to go to them every fair day . . . before I became crippled.' Carrie was not in the habit of talking about her infirmity, but she spoke eagerly, pleased to be able to contribute something. In truth, she could not remember another day like this, when she had enjoyed the company of someone else of her own age.

'How long have you been lame?' Anna asked the question in a perfectly natural way. She knew, more than anyone else could, how Carrie felt.

'Since I was nine. More than six years. I never hurt it, or anything. It just happened.'

Carrie did not feel it necessary to add that nothing would ever erase the loneliness of those six long years, not even the love of her father. Her mother had died while Carrie was still struggling to come to terms with the knowledge that she would never walk like other people and it had served to increase her isolation.

'Were you born blind?'

'No, I must have lost my sight at about the same time as you went lame. No one could ever tell me why. Things just started getting blurry. Then one day I couldn't see at all.' Anna shrugged. 'I had no mother *or* father to talk to. No one to tell how frightened I was. Only Boz. He didn't always understand, but he's been everything to me. He still is.'

Carrie reached out and took hold of the gipsy girl's hand. For a moment they walked hand in hand together, then Anna said, 'We'd better hurry. We don't want to miss the racing.'

Many of the men had drifted from the fair to the open common land where the horse races were to take place. Horse-racing was popular here and there would be two or three races during the afternoon.

The stakes were usually quite small for each event but today there was a buzz of excitement in the air. A purse of two hundred guineas had been offered for a special race, to be run over a six-mile course. This was more than twice the usual length race, but the high purse ensured there was no shortage of entries. Remembering what Boz had said about his horse, Seb wondered how much the gipsies had to do with having such a race run.

It was not hard to find them. The gipsies formed a noisy and colourful group, at the heart of which was Boz and his horse.

It seemed to Seb that Boz had been awaiting his arrival and that of the two girls. Long before the trio reached the chattering group, Boz had handed the reins of his horse to someone else and was limping his way through the crowd towards them, followed by many of his fellow gipsies.

Thinking Boz was concerned for his blind sister, Seb smiled his reassurance. 'It's all right, Boz, I've brought her back to you safe, sound and well fed.'

Boz's glance rested on his sister for only the briefest of moments. 'We've been waiting for you. We need a favour.'

'From me?' Seb could think of nothing he could do for the gipsies. 'What is it?'

'We want you to ride our horse in the big race.'

'Me?' Seb could not believe the gipsy was serious. 'Why *me*? There are all your own people . . . ?'

'If it wasn't for my leg, *I'd* be riding. We had another jockey to take my place but he's got himself so drunk he couldn't sit on a rock without falling off. Everyone else who rides well is too heavy. This is a distance race. We need a light rider, someone like yourself.'

'But . . . I've never raced a horse in my life.'

'You've galloped the manor's hunters hard. I've seen you. Riding our horse will be no different. All you have to do is guide him around the course. He'll do the winning.'

The gipsies nodded their agreement. Boz added, 'We'll pay you. Five guineas for the ride, another five when he wins.'

Seb's mouth sagged in disbelief. It was as much money as Sir Nelson Fettiplace had given his mother to enable her to bring Seb to Swinbrook and begin a new life. It was enough to take them back to London.

'When's the race due to start?'

'In half an hour.'

Seb made up his mind quickly. This was too good an opportunity to miss. 'All right, I'll ride him.' His statement was greeted with wide smiles from the gipsies as he asked, 'Does the horse have a name?'

'Grye.' Boz grinned too. 'It means "horse" in our language.'

'I'd like to sit him before the race.'

After a momentary hesitation, Boz nodded. 'Fair enough – but don't do more than walk him. Rumour has it that Meredith Putt's wagering a whole lot on his horse to win. We don't want to scare him off.'

'I'll be riding against Vulcan?'

'Does it worry you?'

Seb shook his head. Meredith Putt had returned to Swinbrook a week before after a lengthy absence. Vulcan was a horse that took a long time to come to full fitness. A week was not long enough, even though he might *look* fit.

'You should have told me I'd be racing against Meredith Putt before you offered to pay me. I'd have ridden Grye for nothing for the chance to beat him.'

'That's what I hoped to hear you say! Come on, gorgio. Let's introduce Grye to his jockey.'

Seb knew as soon as he sat on Grye's back that Boz was right. This was a quite exceptional animal. When he walked him he could feel that the horse wanted to *run*. There was a fluidity about its movements that promised speed and an easy power.

The race was to be run for the first couple of miles along a valley beside a small river. After this the course doubled back and the horses would turn into part of the estate of the Duke of Marlborough, one of the county's great landowners, and circle the park before returning through the forest to the fair.

Seb was aware as he walked the horse that gambling men were discussing the horse's merits, but one group of men he passed were dressed in sharp contrast to the majority of the fair-goers. These men wore everyday working-clothes. Most had taken the trouble to don *clean* ones, but a few looked as though they had simply dropped pick and shovel and come to the fair.

These men were 'navvies', tough labouring men employed digging culverts and tunnels to extend a network of railway lines over the land. They had come from the railway line advancing northwards along the valley of the river Evenlode, where the horses would be running. A section of the railway had recently been opened with a great deal of ceremony and celebration.

As Seb rode past them, one of the men said disparagingly, 'Nah! Not this one. Compared wiv that nob's 'orse, this one's a donkey.'

Stung by the remark, and recognising the accent, Seb

pulled Grye to a halt. 'I reckon a cockney navvy knows as much about picking out a good horse as I know of digging tunnels.'

'Lumme! The donkey's got a talking monkey on its back!'

One of the navvy's companions elbowed the speaker out of the way and stepped up to Seb's stirrup. 'You're from the same part of London as us, unless I'm mistaken. Do you think that horse you're riding stands a chance in the big race?'

Remembering Boz's words, Seb looked about him quickly. There was no one standing near who was likely to be a friend of Meredith Putt. The county gentry – and most other countrymen – kept well clear of the tough and frequently rowdy railway builders.

'You're looking at the *winner* of the big race.'

'Says you! What about the big black over there?'

The navvy nodded to where Vulcan was being walked by Tom Hanks. Meredith Putt stood nearby, surrounded by a dozen or so of his friends.

'I've ridden Vulcan. He's fast – when he's fit. He'd probably win over half the distance, but he won't stay for six miles.'

'You sure?'

'As sure as anyone can be when talking about horses. I'm riding to win.'

'That's good enough for me, son. What's the name of your horse?'

'Grye. It's a gipsy horse.'

'Ride him well. Our money'll be riding along with you.'

CHAPTER ELEVEN

By the time the eleven horses lined up for the start of the six-mile race excitement was running high among the spectators. Helpers had been positioned across the countryside to mark out the long course and ensure the race was run in a fair and sportsmanlike manner.

Before Seb went to the start with the others, Boz took him to one side and told him how he should ride the race. 'Don't let Grye take off too fast, but make sure Putt doesn't get more than five or six lengths ahead during the first three or four miles. Keep on terms with him and you've got him. After that you can let Grye have his head. He'll romp home.'

Seb hoped the gipsy knew what he was talking about. He had seen a great deal of money change hands between the navvies, the gipsies and professional 'bookmakers' who earned a lucrative living touring the fairs of England and Wales, offering odds against runners in the local races. There was far more than prestige involved in this race.

Vulcan was favourite to win. Next came a tall grey hunter that Seb dismissed as being too 'leggy'. Grye was well down the list and Seb knew this was due in no small measure to his horse's absence of grooming.

Dolly was most concerned about Seb riding in the race and it showed in her expression as the jockeys and their mounts set off for the starting line. Tom and Dolly had come to the races with the intention of collecting Carrie. Tom's work at the fair was at an end now. Meredith Putt had booked a room at an inn. After the race Vulcan would be housed in the inn's stables while his owner celebrated his anticipated win.

Carrie Hanks waved to Seb as she limped away but Anna was the last to offer him good wishes. Back with her gipsy friends, she called, 'You can win, Seb. I *know* you can.'

As Seb rode past Meredith Putt's cheering friends he saw Melody standing nearby and she waved to him. There was no sign of Christian.

Vulcan behaved skittishly at the starting line due to the proximity of the other horses. The big hunter was not a sociable animal and emphasised the fact by sinking his teeth into the flank of a horse being ridden by a uniformed militia officer. The officer's horse was a rank outsider, entered for the sole purpose of allowing his owner to show off his newly awarded militia commission.

'Damn it, sir,' snapped the immaculately uniformed young man. 'Learn to control your horse, if you please. Starter, if you don't hurry and send us off, this damned black horse will have *eaten* the opposition.'

The uniformed rider was a nephew of the Lord Lieutenant of the county and the race starter was a man with ambitions of political office. As a result the ill-tempered request was treated as though it were a command. The race was started so swiftly that the militia officer was taken by surprise, his horse left standing when the others leapt into action.

At the outset Seb found himself in a group, boxed in by all the other horses, unable to steer Grye clear. At the end of the first few furlongs, Vulcan had taken an impressive lead, while the other riders were bunched so closely together it was impossible for Seb to bring Grye through. Eventually, trusting in his horse's stamina, he eased Grye back and gained the space he wanted on the outside.

It was a gamble Seb felt he had to take, but for more than a mile he feared he had made a serious blunder. Grye was making no ground on the other horses, while Vulcan and Meredith Putt were increasing their lead.

Then one of the horses in front of Seb fell back, providing an example that the others followed one by one. By the time the half-way mark was reached Grye was lying second to Vulcan – but the big black horse was many, many lengths ahead. Far more than Boz had decreed.

The course was marked out over gently undulating countryside, part forest, part meadow, with occasional glimpses of a large manor house among the trees and a sprinkling of spectators here and there. But Seb had little time to take in his surroundings.

For a further mile Grye was able to do no more than hold his own against the bigger horse, maintaining the same distance between them.

When three-quarters of the irregular-shaped course had been covered, Seb saw Putt look over his shoulder before bringing his heels and whip to work on Vulcan.

With a sudden thrill, Seb realised that the unfaltering pace of Grye was finally narrowing the gap between them. Resisting the excited urge to coax more speed from his horse, he allowed Grye to maintain his own pace.

They were making up ground rapidly now, and

above the pounding of hoofs and the creaking of the leather saddle beneath him, Seb could hear the excited shouts of the crowd lining the approach to the finishing line.

For the first time in the race, Seb shook out the reins and urged Grye to greater speed. The horse responded magnificently and with some five furlongs still to run they drew level with Meredith Putt and Vulcan.

Putt glanced to his side and his expression contained both shock and desperation. The two horses were close together now, drawn in by the narrowing funnel of cheering spectators on each side of the finishing line, still well ahead.

Unexpectedly, Putt's hand shot out and the whip he was holding came down across Grye's face. The smaller horse immediately veered away from Vulcan – and Putt forged ahead once more.

It had all happened so fast that Seb could not be certain whether Putt had struck the gipsy horse deliberately, or merely been careless in his use of his whip.

Fortunately, although Grye had run wide, the horse did not break its rhythm and now Seb urged him on with voice, heels and the flat of his hand.

The incident made no difference to the outcome of the race. Vulcan was tiring – and Grye now showed his incredible stamina. The gipsy horse passed its rival from Swinbrook Manor with a furlong and a half to run and was still pulling ahead when Seb rode him over the line with the roar of an appreciative crowd in his ears.

The race was won!

Seb could remember few details of the next minutes as men crowded around to congratulate him. Not all had put money on the horse but many congratulated

Seb because they had been thrilled by the manner of his winning. Among these were some who had been close enough to witness Meredith Putt's actions, but Seb did not care now. He had won the race and he felt only intense relief and exhilaration.

Seb was rescued from the crowd by Boz and some of the gipsies. Their acclaim was even more boisterous than that of the others, and Seb was convinced his back would be bruised for weeks as a result of their fierce pummelling.

When he and the gipsies finally broke free of the crowd, Anna came forward and rewarded him with a kiss. On any other day it would have met with the displeasure of every gipsy at the fair but, on this day at least, Seb was one of their own, and he enjoyed the unique experience.

There were rewards of a more practical nature to come.

Unable to restrain his joy, Boz returned when the crowd about Seb was thinning, and counted not ten but *twenty* gold sovereigns into his hand. When Seb pointed out the gipsy's error, Boz shook his head. 'The extra ten is a present from the other Romanies. You rode a brilliant race and we've all won a lot of money. It's only right you should have a share.'

'But . . . this is more money than I've ever had in my life!'

'And it's gipsies' money. It'll bring you luck if you spend it wisely.'

Seb could not tell whether Boz was being flippant, or serious, and the gipsy was too happy to care.

'When will you race Grye again?' Seb asked.

'I won't. The story of how he beat Meredith Putt's

horse will be known throughout Oxfordshire and the surrounding counties tomorrow. He'd be favourite in any race in which he ran. There's no money to be made in that. He'll be sold to one of our people far from here. Up in the border country of Scotland, probably. He'll fetch a tidy sum. But I think there's someone else coming to speak to you. One of your London friends.'

When Boz moved on, Melody hurried to Seb with a warning. 'Steer clear of Squire Putt, Seb. He backed himself to win and lost far more money than he could afford. Word's gone around about his use of the whip on Grye and some of his kind are not happy with him. Knowing the sort of man he is he'll be blaming all his troubles on you. Don't give him any chance to get his own back.'

Melody left just as the Cockney navvy pushed his way though the crowd to reach Seb's side. Hot and happy, he shook Seb by the hand, then thrust a small roll of bank-notes at him. 'Here, this is for you, from all of us. Thanks to your tip, we won a packet on the race – and shouted ourselves hoarse cheering for you. Five pounds of the money we won is yours. If you ever need a favour done, there's a dozen of us'll be happy to oblige. Jacob Brailey's my name, boss of the best gang working on the Great Western Railway. Don't forget the name, boy, I owe you. We all do.'

Seb remained at the fair for another two hours. Recognised wherever he went, he had his hand shaken and his back slapped more times than he could remember.

Eventually he went in search of Christian, only to find the Swinbrook farmer's cart was no longer in the field!

Carrie Hanks supplied the explanation. Limping to him from the manor cart driven to the fair by her father, she said, 'Fairs – people getting drunk and enjoying themselves – aren't for Christian. He decided to go on home. He asked us to bring you back and said perhaps you'd help Dad with the two horses he bought for the manor. Here comes Dad now with your ma. She almost burst with pride when you won the race. We all did, but there was no getting near you then.'

When Tom and Dolly arrived Tom was leading the two great horses.

After Dolly had hugged her embarrassed son, Tom said, 'That was a fine ride of yours, young Seb. Mind, it brought me a tongue-lashing from Mr Meredith. He blamed me for not having Vulcan in peak condition.'

Seb's indignation gave him an excuse for escaping from the embraces of his mother. 'It's *him* who's to blame. If he hadn't given me the sack for riding Vulcan the horse would have been fit and he'd have had the race won in the first mile. Someone ought to tell him.'

'No one will, but don't fret yourself, young Seb. I've a jingle in my pocket that wouldn't be there but for you.' Grinning at Seb, he said, 'You're not the only judge of a good horse, you know. I only had a couple of guineas in my pocket, but I put them both on you and that gipsy horse. I got a quicker return than I'll ever have working up at the manor – but I don't think I'll tell Mr Meredith of my luck!'

It was a pleasant ride back through the forest to Swinbrook. Although the sun was low in the sky and there was an autumnal chill in the air, everyone was in a happy frame of mind. Two miles from their destination Tom stopped at an inn he called Dore's Lodge, sited in a gloomy part of the forest. Talking quietly when they were all seated at a corner table, Tom pointed out two men who were drinking apart from the others.

'Don't flash your money about in front of the likes of them, young Seb. They're highwaymen and either one of them would kill a man for less than you have in your pocket right now.'

Seb looked over the brim of his tankard at the two men, one of whom nodded in Tom's direction. Carrie stared at the highwaymen, wide-eyed, the whole time they were inside the inn. Beside Seb, Dolly's expression showed her disapproval of both the men and also the less than salubrious surroundings in which they were all drinking.

When they were once more back on the wagon, Seb asked Tom how he knew the two men were highwaymen.

'I've met up with them before, and I've known the younger of the two since he was a boy. You and your ma have both met his mother . . . Florrie Shaw, her who gave your ma such a hard time when she came to Swinbrook to work.'

'I didn't realise Florrie was married. I thought she lived in at the manor.'

'I didn't say she was married,' said Tom enigmatically. 'Matter of fact, it's always been said that young Will – him we left back here at the inn – is another of Sir Neville Fettiplace's bastards. If he is, Sir Neville refused to recognise him. They say that's what turned Florrie so bitter with the world. Sir Neville did well by Christian, but ignored young Will. They say that's the reason Will takes it out on the gentry. It's certain there's none of 'em safe on the roads for miles around here, after dark.'

'Why has he never been arrested?'

'It's one thing *me* knowing all about him, it doesn't mean others do. Mind you, he came close to being arrested a year or two back when two men who rode with him were taken and hanged at Oxford.'

They were riding through dark forest now. When Carrie shuddered Dolly put an arm around her and her father stopped talking about the highwaymen, leaving Seb to his thoughts.

The whole party lapsed into silence until they left the forest behind and reached Fern Cottage.

As Seb climbed from the cart, Carrie surprisingly asked him if he would call in to see her if ever he had the time. It was dusk, but there was enough light left for Seb to see the expression on Tom's face. It was a plea for Seb to accept.

'Of course I will. I'll probably come next Sunday. Perhaps my ma will come too, I think she's enjoyed having you to talk to. Christian isn't over-talkative – and Melody seems to enjoy talking to men more than to women.'

'That'll be nice. I'd like to see Anna again too. We got on well together.'

'I'm not sure about bringing Anna along,' said Seb doubtfully. 'When I say goodbye to her I never know whether I'll ever see her again. She and Boz seem to come and go pretty much as they please.'

'You'll see her again,' said Carrie with a smile. 'She's very fond of you, Seb. You'll meet her again.'

Behind them, Dolly frowned. She was very happy

that Seb would be seeing Carrie again and pleased she would have another opportunity to spend time with Tom and Carrie Hanks, but Seb and Anna?

Dolly had not brought her son all this way from London just to have him become involved with a gipsy girl. A *blind* gipsy girl at that!

CHAPTER TWELVE

Christian seemed uncharacteristically surly and morose the morning after the fair. Seb was surprised and not a little hurt. When they had been working together in the stables for an hour without a word passing between them, Seb decided the silence had lasted long enough.

Throwing a pitchfork-load of straw to the floor, he said, 'Have I done something to upset you, Christian?'

Christian frowned. 'You might as well know now, as hear me say it later . . . I don't hold with gambling. It's a sin in my book – aye, and in the Good Book, too.'

'But I haven't done any gambling.'

'You rode in that race yesterday. Because of it a great many men gambled away their money.'

'They'd have gambled it away no matter who was riding. I rode because Boz Buckland offered me five guineas to ride his horse – and another five if it won. I'd have been a fool to refuse.'

Seb's statement shook Christian out of his sullen mood. 'A gipsy gave you *ten* guineas, just for riding a horse? Why, that's almost a half-year's wages for a farm-worker.'

'By the end of the day I'd picked up a *full* year's wages. Boz doubled my money when the race was over.' Seb thought it wiser to say nothing of the extra five pounds donated from the winnings of the navvies.

'*Twenty* guineas. Bless me, boy, I'd never had such a

sum of money in my hand when I was your age. I hope you've given it to your mother to keep safe for you.'

'No, Christian, it's here, in my pocket. I brought it to work with me today because there's something I want to do with it. I talked it over with Ma, and although she doesn't really understand, she agrees I should put it to some good use. But you've been in such a mood this morning I haven't been able to say anything to you about it.'

Christian looked abashed. 'I'm sorry, Seb. To be honest, it's *me* that's out of sorts. Nothing to do with anything you've done, at all. But enough of that for now.' His surliness and opposition temporarily forgotten, the farmer said, 'Tell me the plans you have for all this money you've come by.'

'I'd like to buy one of your foals, Christian. The one that Anna helped bring into the world. I'd work for its feed and train it in my own time. When it's old enough I'd like to breed it back to one of your stallions. Perhaps one day I'll be able to rent a field of my own and keep one or two more. I wouldn't let it interfere with my work here and it won't be taking money from your pocket. A good horse will always sell well. I realised that yesterday when we were at the forest fair.'

Christian Timms gazed at Seb approvingly. 'There's a shrewd brain inside that head of yours, Seb, my lad, and I can see you've got ambitions. I like to see that in a young man. I'll need to watch my step or you'll be putting me out of business as a horse-breeder.'

'I wouldn't do that, Christian. Not after all you've done for me.'

Christian's heavy hand on Seb's shoulder brought his protestations to a halt. 'I'm joking with you, Seb. Like you said, a good well-bred horse will always find a buyer and I'm not afeared of fair competition. The foal is yours and you've made a good choice. Unless I'm very much mistaken she'll be worth all the trouble we had to bring her into the world. How much were you thinking of paying me for her?'

'She is good so I'd think it a bargain if you sold her to me for twenty guineas.'

'That's a fair price, Seb, even a little on the high side, perhaps, for such a young foal. Make it fifteen. As for the cost of keeping her, she can feed alongside my horses for now. I'll take the extra five guineas from you on the day you sell *your* first foal. There's my hand on it.'

Seb's elation was even greater than it had been when he'd passed the winning post on Grye the day before. He wanted to run to the house and tell his mother that he, Seb Quilter, the East-End London street urchin, now *owned a horse*.

But even in this moment of unspeakable joy, he remembered Christian's earlier mood. 'What's put you out of sorts, Christian? Is there anything I can do to help?'

Some of the pleasure left the farmer's expression, and he shook his head. 'It's young Melody. She's too wild, that girl. She and I had words yesterday, before I left the fair. When I was walking around I saw her with some of Putt's friends. I suggested she should come along home with me but she wouldn't. She said there was too much to see and a lot more friends to meet. I didn't want her to stay, but I couldn't force her to come home to Swinbrook with me and humiliate her in front of her friends. I'm worried about that girl. I fear she has bad blood in her veins. I know it's not very charitable of me to say such a thing, but it hurts me to see her trailing around after the likes of Mr Putt and his friends. No good can come of it, I'm certain of that.'

'I think you'll find Melody can take care of herself, Christian.'

'She *thinks* she can, Seb, but she's only a young girl. She's not a *bad* girl, either – over-generous with her favours, perhaps. While she's working for me I can't help having a feeling of responsibility towards her.'

'I'm sorry you had such troubled thoughts on a day that was the best in my life, Christian. As for your views on Meredith Putt, I must admit I share them. I would have ridden to beat him had I not been paid a penny for doing it.'

'You wouldn't be human if it were otherwise, Seb, and you mustn't blame yourself for causing Melody and me to fall out. I don't like her way of life and she knows how I feel. Hanging around Putt and his friends will lead to trouble and I've told her so. Anyway, that's an end to it for now. I've told her my thoughts before but it's made no difference. Perhaps you'll say something to her if she ever speaks to you about her way of life?'

'I will if she comes back to work here.'

'She will, Seb. I speak my mind to her and that's an end to it. I hope one day to show her the way to a better life, but I can't do it if she's not here. She knows she can come back to work for me, come what may.'

Meredith Putt had far more on his mind than the waywardness of a tinker-girl whom he had hardly noticed. He had wagered a great deal of money on the outcome of the forest fair race. It had been a desperate bid to stave off financial ruin – but he had ended up far worse off than before.

It had been a disastrous year for him. Some unwise investments, coupled with heavy gambling with his London friends had brought him to the edge of disaster.

An expert examination would also disclose a considerable deficit in the finances of the manor farm. If he could not make good the money before Sir Nelson Fettiplace returned to his home, Putt would undoubtedly lose the comfortable post he held at the manor. With it would go the very generous allowance paid to him by his baronet uncle.

Something needed to be done – and quickly. If only that damned boy had not stolen the race from him he would have earned a brief breathing space.

Putt had recognised Seb the moment they lined up for the start of the race. He had known instinctively that he was the one who needed to be beaten. He and a gipsy horse that should never have been allowed to race against gentlemen's horses in the first place.

He was still deep in troubled thought when he arrived at the gloomy Dore's Lodge inn soon after Seb and the others had left. He had been late leaving Charlbury and it would be dark within the hour. He had intended to stay at the inn, but he had no heart for celebration and as Swinbrook was not more than a twenty minutes' trot for Vulcan he decided to head for home. But first he turned in on the path that led to the forest tavern, ducking beneath the branches that hung low enough to unseat an unwary rider.

The inn was noisy this evening, the occupants ruffians for the most part. Putt was not concerned. He knew many of the customers by sight, if not by name – and he carried a loaded double-barrelled personal pistol in his pocket.

He sat talking to a Wychwood Forest keeper for about half an hour. When the keeper left, he sat alone for perhaps an hour more. By now the inn was less busy. Many of those who lived on the fringes of the great forest that surrounded the inn preferred to be home behind locked doors after dark. Others had left to pursue nocturnal activities, some lawful, a great many less so.

The Wychwood Forest was occupied by a shifting army of homeless men and women who lived among the trees with their families. Times were hard in the countryside and many found the forest preferable to the stringent disciplines of the workhouse.

They shared their shadowy world with gipsies, tinkers, recluses and criminals seeking to evade the justice of the courts. Most existed by poaching the animals of the forest. Deer, rabbits and sometimes squirrels and hedgehogs. For vegetables they would raid the fields and common lands of the villages in and about the great forest.

Once on the forest path Vulcan was eager to get home to his stable, but Putt held him in check. Clouds were drifting across the moon and on occasions it was difficult to see the way. Fortunately for the baronet's nephew, the moon emerged from behind a cloud as he was approaching the edge of the forest. Moonlight glinted on the metal buckle of a man standing beneath a large oak on the far side of a patch of deep shadow. Someone was lying in wait.

Meredith Putt had a great many faults, but he did not

lack courage, as two would-be footpads were quick to learn. Vulcan entered the area of shadow – but failed to emerge again immediately.

By the time the two men realised something had gone wrong with their planned robbery, it was too late. Meredith Putt had dismounted, looped Vulcan's reins around a low-hanging branch and slipped behind them.

'Both of you stay exactly where you are. I'm holding a two-shot pistol on you, and I won't hesitate to use it.'

The would-be highwaymen started in alarm, but did as they were commanded. 'We're not doing anything. We were on our way home and stopped here to talk.'

'You were unusually silent for talking men. No doubt you'll also deny that the poles you are both carrying were meant to knock a mounted man from his horse? It's me you're talking to, Will Shaw. I've known you for a long time. Too long, perhaps. You, the other man. What's your name?'

'Charlie . . . Charlie Fosset.' The hesitation was too long.

'A very good name too. Now I'll have your real name, if you please.'

'Harry Gaunt.'

The man sounded resigned to his fate and Putt made a whistling sound through his teeth. 'You're keeping exalted company tonight, Will.' Harry Gaunt was a highwayman who had once terrorised the roads and lanes over a wide area between Oxford and London. Little had been heard of him of late, but Putt thought there was probably still a small reward on his head. However, the baronet's nephew was not interested in paltry sums.

CHAPTER THIRTEEN

On the second Sunday after the Wychwood Forest Fair, Seb paid a visit to the house on the edge of the forest, the home of Carrie Hanks and her father. It was farther out of the village than Fern Cottage, and the garden backed on to the forest trees.

Tom Hanks had not returned from morning service in the village church, a duty that was imposed upon each of the manor's employees. Carrie was excused by reason of her lameness and Seb found her preparing a midday meal.

Carrie still retained her shy and reserved manner, but she was genuinely pleased to meet him once more. She would not hear of him leaving, although she was alone in the house.

'I hope you don't mind if I carry on with the cooking while we talk.' Carrie sliced a turnip as she spoke. 'It's a specially good dinner today. Morgan Edginton killed a pig this week and Dad was able to buy a whole leg with his winnings from the fair. We haven't had such a feast since last Christmas.'

Smiling at Seb, Carrie said, 'My dad says folk who were at the fair are still talking about your ride that day. There's not a man or woman in the village who isn't pleased that Mr Meredith Putt got his come-uppance.'

'He doesn't seem to be the most popular man in Swinbrook.'

As Seb was speaking he absent-mindedly ran his finger down the page of a book standing open on the kitchen table.

'I bought that at the fair,' explained Carrie. 'Do you read?'

Seb shook his head. 'I wish I could. The only school near us in London wouldn't take me. I tried once but my cough disturbed everyone else and I had to leave.'

'My dad's told me about your cough. He was worried about you for a long while. I'm glad it's getting better.'

Pausing in her cooking, Carrie looked up at him. 'I could teach you to read and write if you'd really like to learn.'

Seb had wanted to learn to read and write for as long as he could remember. 'I would . . . but there's a lot of work to do up at Handley Farm.'

Without looking at him, Carrie said, 'Winter's coming on. There's not much work can be done on a farm after dark. You'll have plenty of time then.'

'All right.'

Seb was secretly delighted with Carrie's offer. He had learned to recognise a few of the letters of the alphabet, but without any schooling it had never been possible to progress any further in London.

'It's strange.' Carrie chattered happily now, unlike the shy, unspeaking girl Seb had first seen sitting alone on the manor cart at the fair. 'I haven't had anyone call to see me for as long as I can remember, yet today I've had two visits.'

Looking to where Seb was running his finger down a page of the book, identifying the letters he knew, she added, 'Anna's brother brought her to say goodbye to me.'

The book suddenly forgotten, Seb asked sharply, 'She came to say "goodbye"? Why, where's she going? For how long?'

'Oh! I thought you'd know all about it. Anna and her brother are travelling north, somewhere. I don't know for how long.'

Seb was hurt that Anna had said nothing to him. She had not come to Fern Cottage or to the farm to tell him she was leaving.

'I'm sure you could still catch her if you really wanted to. She was here no more than an hour ago and I doubt if she and her brother will have left their camp yet.'

Entering the gipsy encampment Seb saw many of the men who had been at the fair. Men who had slapped him on the back and contributed money to his purse, but they displayed no friendliness today. No smiles. It was almost as though he had walked into a camp of complete strangers. Suspicious strangers.

Boz and Anna were nowhere to be seen and their canvas-topped caravan was not in the spot where Seb had last seen it. Stopping by a fire around which were hunched half a dozen gipsy men, he asked if they knew where he could find the brother and sister.

'Gone,' said one of the men, without looking up.

'Gone where? How long ago?'

'You might be lucky and find them down by the pond, over that way.'

Another of the men jerked his head towards the east. It was all the information Seb was going to get.

As he headed in the direction the gipsy had so surlily indicated, he wondered what could have happened to sour the gipsies' attitude towards him so quickly. He found it difficult to believe they were naturally so changeable.

Seb found the Bucklands' canvas-topped caravan by following fresh wheel tracks. They led to a small pool of dark water, hidden among bushes downhill from the encampment. Boz was sitting on the shaft of the cart whittling a stick. Tied to the rear of the caravan was Grye. Another, older horse was standing listlessly between the shafts. There was no sign of Anna.

Boz's greeting was hardly propitious. 'What you doing here?'

'Carrie Hanks told me you'd been to say goodbye to her. I wondered why you hadn't come to see me. I thought we were all friends?'

'Romanies don't make friends with gorgios . . . especially not Romany women.'

So that was it! Seb had sensed for a long time that Boz did not approve of the easy relationship that had grown up between himself and Anna. Before he could think of a reply, Anna appeared at the entrance flap of the wagon. Her long black hair was wet and her clothes adhered to her body as though she had just bathed and had not dried properly.

Looking at her aroused emotions in Seb that went far beyond the friendship he had just proclaimed.

In their own language, Anna said to Boz, 'That's no way to speak to Seb. If it hadn't been for him you wouldn't have had a horse to sell that'll likely make you the richest man in Wychwood.'

'He was paid well.'

'Would you have asked any other gorgio to ride the horse for you?'

Throwing down the stick he was whittling, Boz rose

from his seat on the shaft of the caravan and unhitched the horse. When the animal was free he walked it to the pond, limping badly. Once there he stood with his back to the others while the horse drank.

'You mustn't mind Boz. He has a lot on his mind right now. Selling the horse is not his only reason for leaving. You heard about the robbery on the Fulbrook road last evening?'

'No.' Gossip about such happenings would be exchanged at church or chapel on a Sunday morning. Seb had not attended church since leaving the manor and he rarely attended chapel. He would be among the last to hear such news.

'The owner of Widford Manor Farm was robbed on his way back from Burford after a settling meeting. It's said he had more than two hundred guineas stolen from him by two men. When things like that happen it's always the Romanies they look to first. Boz says we'll have a magistrate out here as soon as they get enough constables together. He wouldn't be surprised if they tried to make us move on – away from the forest. That would bring trouble for everyone. We knew that sooner or later we'd need to go north to sell Grye. Boz thought it'd be better if we went now.'

'You were going without telling me?' Seb spoke accusingly.

'Would that have upset you so much?'

'Yes.' The reply said far more than Seb had intended. Glad she could not see his blushes, he added, 'I wanted to tell you what I'd done with the money Boz gave me for riding Grye. I bought a foal from Christian Timms. The one you helped the mare with.'

'I'm glad for you, Seb. That foal will grow into a fine

mare. You know how to choose a good horse. There must be some Romany in you. What do you intend doing with it?'

'Breeding from her. I'd like to have a whole lot of horses one day, riding-horses as well as big work-horses.'

'And so you will, I'm certain of it. There's an air about you of getting things done.'

Boz led the pony from the pond and backed it between the shafts of the caravan.

'How long will you be gone?'

'As long as it takes.'

Boz called to his sister. 'Come, Anna, if you don't want to follow behind.' To emphasise his words, the gipsy slapped the long reins on the pony's back and shouted for it to move.

Unexpectedly, Anna stretched out her hand and touched Seb's face. 'Will you miss me, Seb?'

'I . . . Yes. But Carrie's going to teach me to read during the winter months.'

Seb did not know why he said it. The news had no relevance.

'Carrie's a nice girl. Clever, too. She'll be good for you – and you for her. Take care of yourself, Seb. Keep your chest warm and don't let the cold bring that cough back.'

'You sound like my ma.' Seb was glad to find something at which he could smile.

'I expect that's because we both care for you.'

Suddenly Anna moved forward and putting both hands to his face she kissed him.

'I'll miss you too, Seb, but I'll be back. Look for me in the spring.'

* * *

Despite his threat, Boz went no farther than the ridge above the dark pond before bringing the small caravan to a halt and waiting for his blind sister. He helped her to the seat beside him and as the caravan creaked and swayed its way between the tall trees of the forest, heading northwards, he said, 'You shouldn't lead Seb on, Anna. Gorgios have enough strange ideas about Romany women as it is. It isn't a good idea to give them more.'

'What makes you think I'm leading him on?'

Boz looked at his sister sharply. 'You have to be. He's a gorgio – and you're a Romany. The two don't go together any more than fire and water.'

'He's a gorgio, yes, but he's no more one of the villagers than we are. I suspect he never will be. As for leading him on . . . I'm fond of him, Boz. More fond of him than I've ever been of anyone else, except you.'

Reaching out, Anna found Boz's hand and gripped it tightly. 'I don't want to upset you, or any of our people, but times are changing for all of us. Every year something happens to squeeze us tighter. Perhaps it's time us Romanies started building bridges instead of digging ditches around ourselves.'

'I'm not digging ditches – or building bridges either. I'd be perfectly happy if the gorgios just left us alone to live our own lives.'

CHAPTER FOURTEEN

Boz Buckland's prediction of the response by the authorities to the highway robbery was uncannily accurate. Two days after the gipsy and his blind sister set off to take their horses northwards, a search party arrived at Swinbrook on its way to the forest encampment of the gipsies.

Oxfordshire had no county police force. For the maintenance of law and order it still relied upon the ancient, out-dated system whereby each parish was responsible for appointing its own constable.

This ancient system had many inherent faults. Swinbrook, for instance, had no constable. There had been no crime in the parish for so long it was not deemed necessary to appoint such an official.

Twelve constables, gathered from parishes in the Wychwood Forest area made the uncomfortable journey from the nearby town of Burford crammed inside a hard-sprung prison van. Accompanying them, on horseback, was Magistrate Arnold Peck.

Christian Timms's land ran along the forest edge and the magistrate chose the yard at Handley Farm as a suitable place to leave the prison van while a search was carried out of the gipsy encampment.

As the constables stretched cramped limbs in the farmyard, Dolly Quilter brought home-made bread and cheese, and drinks of milk or water for them.

Melody was nowhere to be seen.

'Come along now, I didn't bring you all this way from Burford for you to enjoy a picnic. We've work ahead of us, and it might well prove to be dangerous work, so I want your batons checked before we enter the forest.'

Seb thought the magistrate's words were more intended to impress Dolly, the only woman at the farm, rather than as a serious directive to the men he had brought with him.

'You'll not need weapons if you approach the gipsies in the right way, any more than you're likely to find the men you seek among their number.' Christian spoke scornfully as the constables drew their long, hardwood truncheons to reassure the magistrate. 'The gipsies in Wychwood do their best to stay clear of trouble.'

'Oh? And can I take it you're an expert on gipsies, Timms? Most farmers I know would be only too happy to see the back of these troublesome rogues and vagabonds – and this is what they are according to the laws of this land.'

'I'm as much of an expert as any man can be who's not of their own kind. As for trouble, they've given me none. Indeed, they've helped me on many occasions in the past to search for a lost animal, or cure one that's been sick.'

'You've been more fortunate than most, Timms. Mr Putt at the manor has often complained to me of their idle and dishonest ways.'

'If Meredith Putt behaves towards them as he does towards ordinary folk it's hardly surprising they give him trouble. So would others if their homes and livelihood didn't depend on him and the manor.'

'Be that as it may, Timms, as you're such an expert on these people perhaps you'll guide me to their encampment in order that I might carry out my duty.'

'I'll do no such thing! When you've stirred them up and gone on your way I'll still be living here. The gipsies have always been good neighbours – but I wouldn't care to make enemies of them. You'll need to find your own way to their camp.'

'I find your attitude most unhelpful, Timms. I might point out that it is the duty of every law-abiding citizen to help a magistrate to uphold the laws of this land.'

'I've never yet broken any laws and nor do I intend doing so, but my Christian beliefs won't allow me to help persecute innocent people.'

'It's all right, sir. I know where the camp is. I'll lead us there.'

'*You* know where it is, Constable . . . ?'

'Aplin, sir. Constable at Burford. I've been in the forest a time or two and spoken to the gipsies. Mr Timms is right. The gipsies are not as bad as they're made out to be. They have their own laws. They may not be quite the same as ours, but they abide by them. The ones who cause all the trouble are the tinkers and the *real* vagabonds who use the forest as a refuge. They cause the gipsies almost as much trouble as they do us.'

'I'm obliged for your offer to guide me to the gipsies' camp, Constable Aplin, but please leave speeches in their defence to the lawyers in a courtroom. Quite apart from any other consideration they're paid far more than you for doing it. I regret you are unable to offer me *your* assistance, Timms. I only hope your faith in these itinerant people will not prove to have been misplaced – but I fear it must. I agree with Mr Putt at the manor. The forest will be a better place when we rid it of gipsies.'

With a curt, stiff bow in Christian's direction the magistrate walked to where he had left his horse in the care of one of the constables.

'It seems our magistrate does not share your tolerant attitude towards gipsies, Mr Timms.' The Burford constable addressed Christian.

'Magistrate Peck's views on gipsies, in common with so many others, are based not on knowledge but on prejudice, sir. Now, if you'll excuse me, I have farm business to attend to.'

When the magistrate had led his small band of constables away to the forest, Melody came from the house and asked Seb why they had come to Swinbrook in such force.

When Seb had told her, she said, 'I heard the magistrate and Meredith Putt talking at the forest fair, before the races. The magistrate said Romanies are a blight on the countryside, parasites who exist by thieving and poaching. That's what he said.'

'They don't sound like the words of a man who should be looking at others with an open mind.'

'What's it matter what words are used, or who speaks them? What he said is what most gorgios believe. They don't try to understand. Sometimes I think they don't *want* to. They'll not be happy until there's not a Romany left in the world and everyone thinks and acts the same as you gorgios all do.'

With this remark Melody went on her way, leaving Seb to ponder on her words. Melody had repeated the words of Meredith Putt, words that had been echoed by Magistrate Peck, and no doubt most of the gentry in the country. Seb was happy that Anna and Boz had already gone from the forest and would not be subjected to the harassment of the magistrate and his constables.

Seb's relief was short-lived. The magistrate and his party were in the forest for almost five hours. When they returned along the road the whole encampment of gipsies was with them, together with their caravans and wagons and the women and children.

They brought a number of tinkers too, but many of their number had disappeared hurriedly when the detachment of constables entered the encampment.

As the long, sad convoy moved through the village on its way to Burford, two constables came to Handley Farm to collect the prison vehicle. One was Constable Aplin who had guided the magistrate to the encampment.

Christian was out working in the fields when the constables arrived in the farmyard, but Seb was there and he greeted them unsmilingly.

'I see you got what you came for. Do you get paid extra for women and children?'

'I'll get nothing – neither would I want it. Arresting them was Magistrate Peck's idea. No doubt it'll be popular among the county's gentry. As for connecting them with the highway robbery, we found nothing, and neither did I expect to. This raid wasn't my idea, friend.'

Remembering what Constable Aplin had said to the magistrate before the raid on the forest encampment, Seb's anger ebbed away.

'If you found nothing then why are they being arrested? They were harming no one in the forest.'

'You know that, and so do I, but Magistrate Peck

organised the raid. I suppose he needs to justify himself.'

'What will happen to them now?'

'They'll be charged with various vagrancy offences. The men will probably go to prison for anything from one to six months, as will some of the women. The remainder will get off with a fine or a warning. In a day or two's time the women and children will start moving back to the forest again to wait for their men to be released from prison. If there's another highway robbery in a year or two's time the same thing might happen again. If not . . .' Constable Aplin shrugged.

Seb turned away, angry with the injustice of it all. The gipsies were being arrested for no other reason than the fact that they had a different way of life. It was the same attitude he and his mother had encountered from the servants at the manor.

'Aren't you the lad who rode the gipsy horse when it beat Meredith Putt's horse at the Wychwood Forest Fair?'

'That's right.'

Seb would have ended the conversation there, but the Burford constable said, 'Is the owner of the horse a young gipsy with a blind sister?'

'That's right . . . but they weren't in the forest today.'

'It might have been better for them if they had been. Magistrate Peck was particularly interested in whether anyone had left the camp since the night of the robbery. None of the gipsies would say anything, but one of the tinkers who'd been camping nearby told him of the gipsy with the horse. Peck's raising a hue and cry for him – on suspicion of highway robbery.'

CHAPTER FIFTEEN

That evening, when every gipsy from the Wychwood Forest encampment was in custody, there was another highway robbery. This time the target was the mail-carrying coach from Burford to the railway station at Shipton-under-Wychwood.

It was a daring attack carried out in daylight at a spot where the coach toiled up the hill not far from its departure point. Two men stepped from the shadows of the forest and called upon the coachman to halt. The driver whipped up his horses, only to have one of them shot dead by a highwayman.

The passengers were relieved of their money and valuables and a box removed from the coach. Despatched from a Burford solicitor's offfice, the box was believed to contain more than five hundred pounds.

The return of the coach to Burford, pulled by only three horses and with the passengers in a state of near hysteria, caused great excitement in the small town. The local militia, mustering for drill, were immediately volunteered to join in a search for the highwaymen. Giles Aplin, Burford parish constable, accepted their offer. Accompanied by a growing number of outraged and public-spirited townsmen, they set off to scour the forest.

The party searched until dark and succeeded in retrieving the stolen box, but the lid had been torn from its hinges and was empty. They also caught two poachers – one the son of a militiaman with the search party – but not a trace of the highwaymen was found.

This latest outrage convinced everyone except Magistrate Arnold Peck that the gipsies arrested on his orders had nothing to do with the crimes attributed to them.

Arraigned before one of his fellow magistrates, the gipsies were dealt with harshly. Young men were imprisoned for a month, older men for three. Three gipsies who had been convicted of the same offence some years before were deemed to be 'Incorrigible Rogues' and remanded to a higher court for more rigorous punishment.

Two gipsy women found to have been convicted of minor offences some years before were committed to prison. The remainder, after being given a stern warning about their way of life, were released.

The women who had been set free with their children could make no decisions about the future without their menfolk, and most returned to the only place where the men would know they could be found – the Wychwood Forest.

Christian Timms brought the news of the magistrate's findings to Handley Farm on the evening of their court appearance. He had gone to the Burford magistrate's court with the intention of providing a character reference for the gipsies, but he was not allowed to speak.

'It was all cut and dried long before they were brought in to court,' the farmer said bitterly, as Seb cleaned up in the farmhouse kitchen after his day's work. 'I believe Peck and his fellow magistrates had decided among themselves what they would do long before the cases against the gipsies were heard. Possibly even before they were arrested, although if they'd bided their time the problem might have been solved for 'em.'

'How?'

Seb was hardly listening. The 'justice' dealt out to the gipsies at Burford magistrates' court came as no surprise. Constable Aplin had warned him what to expect. Seb was more concerned whether Anna and Boz would have travelled far enough away from the Wychwood Forest to avoid being taken. If not, Boz was likely to suffer the same fate as the other Wychwood gipsies and Anna would be left with no one to take care of her.

'Meredith Putt and some of his friends have petitioned parliament to have large areas of Wychwood deforested and enclosed. There's little doubt that they'll succeed. It seems to be a fashionable thing to do throughout the country. Enclosure will add a great deal of land to the estates of the larger landowners at a cost of next to nothing.'

Seb paused in his ablutions as the full import of Christian's words sank in. 'What will happen to the gipsies if they cut down the forest?'

Christian shrugged. 'Their way of life is as doomed as the forest itself, Seb. Either they adapt to *our* way of life, or they'll end their days rotting in some prison cell.'

While the gipsies from Wychwood Forest were in prison, Christian Timms provided their families with grain from his store. Twice a week Seb took a sack to the forest, carried in front of the saddle on one of the farm's riding-horses.

Apart from the absence of mature men, there seemed to be as many gipsies in the encampment as before the raid. They were hungry, not having menfolk to poach for them, and they would pour blessings upon Seb and Christian for the kindness being shown to them. They vowed that their men would not forget the farmer when they were free once more.

Every time he went to the camp, Seb hoped the gipsies would have some news of Boz and Anna, but he always received the same reply to his questions. They had heard nothing, although there was more than one knowing glance cast in Seb's direction because of his concern for the young blind girl.

At a time like this, when Seb was acting as a provider – and Anna was too far away for such an attachment to offend age-old prejudices – the women could tolerate a gorgio's affection for a Romany girl. If ever Anna returned to the Wychwood Forest it would be another matter.

Almost three weeks after the raid on the forest encampment, Seb was returning to Handley Farm with a wagon-load of hay, purchased from a farm situated between Swinbrook and Burford. Walking at the head of the cart-horse he was overtaken by Giles Aplin, the Burford constable.

Giles Aplin reined in alongside Seb and gave him a warm smile of greeting. 'You've saved me a longer ride – Seb, isn't it? Do you mind if I tie my horse behind the wagon and walk with you for a while?'

Seb looked at the constable's horse critically, it was old enough to have seen more indifferent days than better ones. 'Do you think your nag will be able to keep up?'

Seb's mild sarcasm provoked another smile. 'The horse came with the post of constable. I've ridden more lively animals, but this one gives me time to think while I'm riding.'

'You'll be in need of thinking time, with what's happening in your parish right now.'

'You're talking of the recent highway robberies?' There had been two more in the past five days. 'Yes, they're posing a few problems and no doubt they will for some time to come, but right now I'm rather more concerned about two friends of yours . . . the Bucklands.'

'Anna . . . and Boz?' Seb's cry startled the great horse and it threw up its head in alarm. 'You've found them?'

'Boz is in custody in Burford. He's due to appear before Magistrate Peck tomorrow for committal proceedings on a charge of highway robbery.'

'Boz never robbed anyone. He couldn't even if he'd wanted to. When he went away he could hardly walk because of his broken leg.'

'I'm inclined to agree with you – but Magistrate Peck thinks differently. Boz had almost five hundred pounds on him when he was arrested. Peck is convinced it's the proceeds of crime.'

'It's nothing of the sort. Boz carried off the owner's prize when I won the race on his horse at the Wychwood Forest Fair races. He won a lot more on wagers.'

'If you're prepared to stand up and give evidence on his behalf – and can find one or two more prepared to do the same – he might be found not guilty. Otherwise he'll go to prison, for certain.'

'I'll go to any court – and I'm sure Christian will do the same. But if Boz is in gaol, where's Anna? Is she in Burford too?'

'I don't know. I've spent the last three days at the Assizes in Oxford. I only learned of Boz's arrest when I returned to Burford today. I haven't even spoken to him yet. I came straight here to speak to you as soon as I heard he'd been arrested.'

'Why should you want to help a gipsy?'

'I became Burford's constable because I believe in the laws of this country. But the laws aren't made just to punish those who do wrong. They're there to protect the innocent. I can't persuade Magistrate Peck that Boz is innocent, although all my instincts tell me he is, so we need to use the processes of the law to prove it.'

Seb's thoughts returned to Anna. He was extremely concerned for her. With Boz in prison she would have no one. 'Can I see Boz?'

'I can't see any reason why not. He's in the lock-up in Burford. When you speak to him try to persuade him to engage a lawyer to act on his behalf. James Price is as good a man as any, you'll find his office in the High Street.'

Giles Aplin broke away and a few minutes later reappeared leading his horse. 'I'd rather not come all the way to Swinbrook with you. If word ever got back to Magistrate Peck that I'd been speaking to you on Boz Buckland's behalf I'd lose my job – and I enjoy it too much to want that to happen. I wish you luck. Remember, if you need my help anyone in Burford will tell you where you can find me.'

A few moments later Constable Aplin was riding

back the way he had come and Seb was trying to urge the great cart-horse to an unaccustomed speed. The longer he thought about Anna the more concerned he became. He intended borrowing one of Christian Timms's horses and going in search of her after he had seen Boz.

Christian was thoroughly angry about the arrest of Boz. When Seb brought the news to him, the farmer had returned to Handley Farm for the midday meal, which had been prepared by Dolly. Both agreed that Constable Aplin had been courageous to pass on his information to Seb.

'Magistrate Peck is making a mockery of English law.' Christian rose from the table and began pacing the length of the farmhouse kitchen. 'Aplin is right, it's not there to be used as a weapon for one man's prejudice. I'll go and see lawyer James Price first thing in the morning. He and I have done business before. James is a good man, a Methodist lay preacher like myself. He fears God – but no earthly magistrate.'

'I'm more worried about what might be happening to Anna. I'd like to go to Burford this afternoon and find out from Boz where she is.'

'She's probably with some of her own people in the place where they arrested her brother, but by all means go and see Boz. Tell him I'll be in Burford myself, in the morning. Once we've set Price to work on his behalf I'll be perfectly willing to stand up in court and say what a nonsense the charge against him is.'

'Tell the lawyer I'll give evidence too. I rode the horse in the race and have a good idea how much money was won by the gipsies. I also know that unless one of the highwaymen had a very bad limp then it couldn't have been Boz.'

'Do you think you're wise getting mixed up in something like this, Seb?'

Dolly expressed the deep concern she felt at the thought of Seb opposing someone in authority – especially a man who administered the law. Dolly had been brought up, in the East End of London, to regard the law as an instrument of the rich. Something from which the poor would be well advised to steer clear.

'I'll be all right, Ma. I wish I could be certain Anna was too.'

CHAPTER SIXTEEN

Seb arrived at the Burford clink soon after two o'clock that afternoon, but it then took him half an hour to locate the gaoler. He eventually found him in the Bull Inn where he seemed to have spent much of the day. Red-faced, ancient and bent, the gaoler grumbled all the way back to the lock-up.

'I don't know why you couldn't have waited until I'd finished drinking. He's only a gipsy, and he's not going anywhere. At least, not until he comes before the judge at the Oxford Assizes. It'll be transportation for him then, I've no doubt – and good riddance, I say. Man was put on this earth to work, not to tramp around the countryside looking for mischief.'

Breathing heavily beside Seb, he said, 'Slow down, young man. You'll not be able to speak to him until I get there with my keys and my legs won't move as fast as yours. That's the trouble with you youngsters today, too impatient by far. Now, when I was a boy . . .'

The clink was a small ground-floor extension to the ancient building that was used as a parish council meeting house. Divided into two tiny cells, it was dark and damp inside. Neither cell contained any furniture and Seb found Boz lying on the floor on a heap of straw.

The gipsy jumped to his feet when he saw Seb and greeted him eagerly. 'I never thought I'd be so pleased to see a gorgio! Do you have news of Anna? Is she all right?'

Seb's own hopes plummeted. 'I was hoping you'd be able to give *me* the answer to that question.'

'But if Anna didn't get word to you, how did you know I was here?'

'That doesn't matter just now. Christian Timms will be in to see you in the morning after he's spoken to a lawyer on your behalf – but I came to ask after Anna. Where did you leave her? Where is she now?'

'Send some of the men from the forest camp here to see me. I'll tell them and they'll know how to find her.'

'There's not a man left in the Wychwood camp. Magistrate Peck rounded them all up and sent them to gaol. If you know anything of Anna's whereabouts you'd better tell me because if I don't go looking for her no one else will. This isn't the time to come that "we're gipsies and you're a gorgio" on me. Tell me where I can find Anna and I'll bring her back to Wychwood. Is she with friends? Did you leave her with someone you can trust?'

Boz's face twisted in sudden anguish. 'I never had time to make any arrangements for her. We'd made camp close to the river and I left her cooking a meal while I rode into Byfield to buy one or two things we needed. I never went back. A Byfield constable stopped me and asked my name. I had nothing to hide so, like a fool, I gave him my right name. He said there was a hue and cry out on me and I was arrested. I didn't tell him about Anna at first because I didn't want them arresting her and I thought I'd be able to persuade them there'd been a mistake. By the time I realised they were going to bring me back here it was too late. No one would listen to me. They just heaved me inside a prison van and drove me down here.'

'When were you arrested? How long has Anna been on her own?'

'This will be the third day.'

Boz's statement thoroughly alarmed Seb. The thought of Anna being alone and sightless in a strange part of the country for so long did not bear thinking about.

'How far is this place Byfield, where you were arrested?'

'Not much more than forty miles away. We'd have been farther on but we broke a wheel on the cart.'

'How do I get there?'

'You're going to go looking for her?'

'Of course. Being left alone would be bad enough for a girl who can see. She'll have been frantic when you didn't return. I only hope she's found someone to help her.'

'Take Grye. They brought him to Burford with me and put him in stables behind the Lamb. But there'll be stabling fees to pay.'

'I have some money left from my earnings at the forest fair. I've brought it with me. Now, tell me where I have to go and how I get there.'

Seb rode Grye hard but it was dark long before he reached Byfield. Leaving Banbury he had taken a wrong road and wasted a full hour returning to the route he had memorised from Boz's instructions.

Travelling alone in this manner was a new experience for Seb and it would have been a great adventure had he not been so worried for Anna's safety. He thought it a great waste of money to pay one shilling and sixpence for a bed, and the same for a meal, but it gave him an unaccustomed sense of importance to hand Grye over to an inn's ostler and be addressed as 'Young master' when he gave instructions for the horse's welfare.

Once his horse had been settled in the stable, Seb made enquiries for the town constable, intending to ask him about Anna, only to learn the constable had been in Northampton for two days. He had gone there for the Assizes, to give evidence in the trial of a woman accused of murdering her husband.

The story of the murder dominated the conversation of the turnkey at the Byfield lock-up too. Seb had to tell him very firmly that, fascinating though the details of the murder might be, he was interested only in learning the whereabouts of a blind gipsy girl who might have found her way to Byfield, searching for her brother.

'Gipsy *girl*, you say? We had a gipsy *man* in here some days ago. Wanted down in Wychwood Forest for highway robbery. Nasty, *dangerous*-looking cove, he was. Only had to look at him to know he was guilty, all right. But a *girl* . . . ?'

The turnkey suddenly became crafty. 'Mind you, it's been a long and tiring day. I'll be 'anding over me keys in a short while. Sit me down in the beer-house over the way with a tankard of ale in me hand and I might remember all manner of things.'

Seb produced a shilling from his pocket. 'I've no time to waste in beer-houses, but here's a shilling for you to spend there if your memory should return a bit quicker.'

'Make it two, young sir, and I could likely tell you a thing or two.'

'I'll wait to speak to the turnkey who's coming on duty later. His memory might not be as expensive as yours.'

'It's come back to me now, young sir.' The turnkey snatched the shilling from Seb's palm before he had time to close his fingers on it. 'I heard it said that a young girl *did* come looking for the gipsy. A girl in some state, I believe. Blind too, so I heard.'

'That's her. That's Anna! Where is she now?'

'It would take far more than a shilling for the answer to that, 'cause I don't rightly know. She was taken to the workhouse, but I doubt if she'll still be there now. Horace Pilcher's the workhouse master and he won't feed more mouths than he's obliged to. They say he was the meanest man on Wellington's commissariat in the Peninsular war and has grown meaner over the years. He's more than seventy now, and well liked by those gentlemen who are obliged to contribute to the poor rate.'

'Where is the workhouse?'

'Along this same road, out on the edge of the village. But you'll not find anyone up or about there after dark. Horace Pilcher don't waste no money on candles or heating. When it's too dark to see, the inmates are sent to bed and the door's locked. Everyone inside stays in. Anyone outside, stays out.'

In spite of the turnkey's words, Seb made his way to the workhouse. The large, grey-stone building was in darkness and for all the response to Seb's hammering on the door, it might have been empty. Finally, Seb was forced to give up his efforts. If Anna was inside, he could not see her tonight. If she was not, he would need to search for her in the morning. Nothing more could be done tonight.

Seb was making his way along the gravel of the short driveway, when he sensed rather than saw someone standing in the shrubbery to one side.

'Who's that? Who's there?'

'Shh! Keep your voice down. If Poverty Pilcher hears us we'll both be in trouble. But I don't recognise your voice. Are you looking to find a place in the workhouse tonight?'

'No, I wanted to ask Pilcher about someone who's supposed to have stayed here earlier in the week. Are you staying here?'

'Yes, thanks to an enclosure order – and my lack of thrift.'

'What does that mean?' Seb was curious in spite of his great concern for Anna. Meredith Putt's preoccupation with obtaining an enclosure order in respect of the Wychwood Forest had often been spoken of by both Christian Timms and Tom Hanks. Seb had never understood what it meant, but here was a man who had experienced such an order, at first-hand.

'It means I gave up my claim to a piece of land for a few pounds doled out by my landlord. Now the money's gone – like my home and my livelihood – me and my family are guests of Horace Pilcher esquire, workhouse master, and if I want to visit 'em I need to climb in through a back window in the rooms where the women stay. But who have you come looking for?'

The other man leaned his face closer to Seb as he spoke and the smell of alcohol bridged the remaining gap between them.

'Anna Buckland. She's a gipsy girl. A *blind* gipsy girl.'

'Oh, *her*.' The man spoke contemptuously. 'Yes, she was here, but only for the one night. Pilcher wouldn't have her for longer because she wasn't the responsibility of Byfield parish. She was turned out with a warning from the constable to clear out of the parish or face arrest as a vagrant.'

'Do you have any idea where she went?'

'No, though just a minute . . . I heard someone at the beer-house laughing about some fun some boys had been having, teasing a young gipsy woman, over Charwelton way. Seems they thought she was some sort of witch.'

CHAPTER SEVENTEEN

As the canvas-topped cart lurched and swayed its way from the Wychwood Forest, Anna needed to concentrate hard to avoid being thrown off the rough wooden plank that served as a seat at the front of the vehicle. It was more than two hours before they reached a reasonable track. The going here was still uneven, but at least Anna found it possible to talk without upper and lower teeth jarring together painfully.

Boz too heaved a sigh of relief. The rough ground in the forest had caused him great pain in his recently broken leg.

'I thought you quite liked Seb?' Anna put the question to Boz.

'So I do. He's all right – but you can't alter the fact that he's a gorgio.'

'The way you spoke to him back there didn't sound to me as though you liked him. I don't suppose he thought so, either.'

'I wouldn't worry too much about that, even if it mattered what he thought.'

'It matters to me. I like Seb.'

'So I've noticed – and many others have too. Be careful, Anna. You know what our people think of girls who run after gorgios.'

'Who cares what they choose to believe? What do *you* think?'

'I think it's a good thing we're going away from Wychwood for a few months. It'll give you time to forget about him – and he about you.'

'He's not like any of the other gorgios I've met. It's probably because he and his ma don't belong among the villagers any more than we do.'

'Maybe not but they're not likely to be arrested just for walking down a road. There are good gorgios and bad ones. But when you get down to it they're all gorgios – and we're Romanies.'

Boz lapsed into a brooding silence leaving Anna to her own thoughts. Unable to see the distractions of the forest, now thinning out about them, Anna's explorations took place within the confines of her own mind.

She tried to picture Seb. She knew the contours of his face, but that was no more than a tracing of the real person. There was no colour to it. She could not picture his eyes, his hair, his teeth, his skin. She would dearly like to be able to see his smile – and she knew he smiled often, she could tell by his voice. He was kind too. She wondered whether this was the only reason he showed so much interest in her? She hoped not, even though they could never be more than passing friends. She was a Romany and he a gorgio. And she was blind . . .

A wheel broke on their canvas-topped wagon when they were on the outskirts of Banbury, and little more than twenty-five miles from Swinbrook and the Wychwood Forest.

They were fortunate enough to fall in with a small party of gipsies and they made a camp together until Boz was able to repair the wheel.

The Banbury gipsies were a sociable group and Boz

spent a great deal of time in the beer-houses of the district. Consequently it was a full week before he and Anna put the camp of their new-found friends behind them and headed northwards once more.

Two days of steady travelling brought them to the small village of Charwelton. After following a river bank for a while, Boz found what he described to Anna as a secluded spot for them to stop. Hidden by the trees in a thinly wooded copse close to the bank of the river Charwell they would be bothering no one.

Usually the river was an indifferent sluggish stream, skirting the village. However, there had been a great deal of rain in recent weeks and the river was swollen, the waters swirling high up its banks.

Anna awoke the next morning to the sound of bird-song. Boz, who had slept beneath the wagon, was already abroad and had a fire going. After washing her face and hands in the river, she took on the task of cooking some eggs and a piece of fat bacon for breakfast. No one watching would have known she could not see.

During the years of sightlessness Anna and Boz had worked out a routine to enable her to cook. He laid out the cooking utensils in a set order at a certain distance from the fire, and it never varied, no matter where they were. As a result, Anna cooked with an astonishing confidence.

'We could do with a few more stores.' Boz spoke as he ate. 'I'll take Grye back to Byfield this morning. It shouldn't take more than a couple of hours.'

'Unless you meet up with those Banbury gipsies again.'

'If I do I promise that this time I'll bring you back a jug of ale.'

When Boz had departed, Anna washed the dishes and laid them out in preparation for the next meal. She also washed some clothes in the river and hung them on a nearby bush to dry. There was a fishing line in the caravan and, baiting the hook with stale bread, she spent a while fishing unsuccessfully close to the camp.

When Boz's 'couple of hours' had passed, Anna smiled ruefully to herself. Boz had either met up with some fellow gipsies, or had found a beer-house where they did not mind serving a gipsy.

She did not begin to worry over Boz's absence until a drop in the temperature told her that it was evening and night was approaching.

The fire was burning low and she had used all the available wood. Carefully, she began a methodical search of the area for more fuel and managed to find enough to keep the fire burning into the night hours. It would serve as a small beacon in the darkness for Boz, should he not return before dark.

Anna realised night had come when the day sounds ceased and noises of the night made themselves heard. The most persistent was the tremulous hoot of the tawny owl. It was a sound that struck fear in the hearts of the superstitious and timid. Later, as she lay fully dressed on her blanket bed inside the canvas-topped caravan, Anna heard the cough of a dog fox as it passed through the copse on its way to the river bank.

She must have been half dozing when she heard a heavier sound from outside. Sitting up, she called hopefully, 'Boz, is that you?'

The only response was the surprised snuffling of a badger and as Anna lay back on the bed she could hear the sound of its clumsy retreat through the undergrowth, heading away from the caravan.

Anna was seriously worried now. Even if Boz had been drinking throughout the day he should have been back by this time.

She slept fitfully for the remainder of the night and when the outside sounds changed to those of the day she rose from her bed and made her way outside. She knew she needed to find out what had happened to her brother. He had set off for Byfield, so that was where she had to commence her search – but how was she to get there? Her mind went around and around the problem but she could find no solution. Still undecided, Anna located the fire of the previous evening and ran the palm of her hand over the ashes. There was still some warmth left in it. Gathering a few bundles of twigs she relaid the fire and blew new life into the warm embers.

There was some comfort to be found in the familiar and Anna decided she must have something to eat before she set off. It would also allow Boz time to return home if he had found something – someone – to keep him out all night.

There was little food left in the wagon – but there was the fishing line. Taking it from the caravan Anna mixed a paste from the remains of the bread they had been eating the previous evening and made her way to the river bank.

It required a great deal of determination when her instinct was to set off and search for Boz, but eventually she was rewarded with two small trout. Spearing them on wooden skewers, she cooked them over the fire and ate them quickly.

She was washing her plate in the river when she heard a sound from among the trees on the far side of the caravan. It was the direction taken by Boz when he rode to Byfield.

'Boz . . . is that you?'

She heard a sound once more – this time as though someone had fallen over something.

'Boz? Are you all right?' Perhaps he was still drunk and had collapsed. What if he had been lying there all night, or had come home during one of the very brief moments when she had dozed off? Her imagination ranged rapidly over the possibilities.

Arms outstretched, Anna began running in the direction from which the sound had come. She tripped twice, but so convinced was she that she was running to Boz and that he was in need of her help, she did not care about her own bruises and grazes.

'Boz, where are you? Make some sound . . . Please – Boz?'

She heard a sound, not in front but behind her – and this was not Boz. It was the creaking of a caravan in motion and it was suddenly accompanied by excited shouting and nervous laughter.

'Who's there? What are you doing? Leave that caravan alone, do you hear me?'

Anna shouted as she began running in desperation, back towards the river bank. But there was no need to ask questions now. She could tell from the sounds exactly what was happening. The caravan was being pushed down the slight slope that led to the river and it was evidently gathering speed.

Anna's feet found the same obstacles as before and she was sprawled on the ground after another fall when she heard an almighty splash and knew the caravan had been pitched into the river.

Her voice rose in an anguished shriek as she swore in vehement Romany at the unseen hooligans who had thrown everything she and Boz possessed into the water along with the caravan.

The response from her unseen tormentors was a jubilant cheer. It was followed by a chorus of jeers and Anna realised the cruel prank, if prank it could be called, had been carried out by a group of boys, or young men.

Scrambling to her knees, Anna held out her arms in a plea to them. 'Why? Why?'

Her answer was a stone which thudded into the soft ground of the copse not an arm's length away. It was the signal for a hail of missiles to come flying through the air. Stones, sticks and one of her own plates were hurled at her.

Some of the missiles missed, but a great many more hit her on the head, arms and body, and she felt blood trickle down her face when a particularly jagged-edged stone caught her on the cheek.

'Don't get too close to her. She's a witch, she might put a spell on you.'

There was a momentary lull, as the words gave her assailants pause. Then the stones rained down on her once again, some of them hurled with considerable force and Anna raised her arms to protect her face and head.

The nonsensical accusation had gained Anna only the briefest of respites from the attentions of her tormentors, but it gave her a desperate idea.

Struggling to her feet, she lowered the arm shielding

her face and pointed in the direction of the boys. 'Yes, I'm a witch, and I curse you. I curse you as only a Romany can. I curse you . . . and you . . . and you.' Anna jabbed her finger at three of the unseen stone-throwers and hoped the direction came close to *someone*. 'For every drop of blood you see on me, you'll see ten times as much pour from one you love. For every stone you've thrown there'll be a tragedy in your lives.'

It was all nonsense, but Anna was aware of the beliefs held by many gorgios about Romany powers – and her ruse worked. There were no more stones for the moment, and then she heard the boys racing away, no one wanting to be the last to leave the scene of their cruel adventure, and the final subject of the gipsy woman's 'curse'.

When the noises of retreat died away, Anna's knees suddenly felt weak, but this was no time to break down, or to congratulate herself on a fortunate escape. She was in a desperate situation. Everything left to Anna and Boz by their late parents had been lost in the river. When she called to their horse without result, she knew the boys must have run the animal off too.

Her need to find Boz was desperate now. She prayed he had not run foul of gipsy-hating countrymen like those who had just attacked her.

She hoped too that no one had suspected that about Boz's waist was a money-belt containing all the cash he had won at the Wychwood Forest Fair.

Anna felt as though she wanted to sink to the ground and weep at her misfortunes, but self-pity was a luxury she could not afford right now.

CHAPTER EIGHTEEN

Anna had frightened off her tormentors, but she knew she must get away from the copse. It was probable the boys would summon up new courage and return. She needed to find Boz, but it would be stupid to strike off across country in the hope of finding a road. She tried to remember the course she and Boz had taken to reach the place where they had camped. They had approached the copse by following the river. She would have to retrace this route and find her way to Byfield.

Before leaving, Anna felt around the ground, hoping she might find one or two pots and pans, but the boys had been thorough in their destruction. They must have kicked everything into the river after the caravan.

She made only slow progress along the river bank. When she tried to hurry she slipped and fell waist-deep into the water. It did not help her when it began to rain, turning the path to mud. There were many bramble bushes alongside the path too and the barbed branches caught on her dress and scratched her bare ankles and feet.

When it seemed she had been walking for hours Anna paused to make a meal from the blackberries growing on the bushes that had done so much to hinder her progress along the track. When she had eaten she sat on the river bank for a while, dangling her scratched and bloody feet in the water as she attempted to make a logical appraisal of the predicament in which she now found herself.

Time and distance had lost all meaning to her already and she thought she must have missed the track that Boz had taken in order to reach the copse. It might be sensible to retrace her steps, but if she did there was no guarantee she *would* find the route he'd taken. Furthermore, there was always the chance she would meet up with the stone-throwing boys once again. She decided to carry on beside the river bank. Somewhere along the way she would surely find someone to help her with directions.

After another couple of hours the path seemed to have disappeared altogether and she was encountering great tufts of coarse grasses that stood proud of the ground and tripped her more than once. It was marshier here too and her feet occasionally squelched in yielding, ankle-deep mud.

Anna had been walking with the river on her right, but now she heard the sound of fast-running water on her *left*!

It took her only a few minutes to ascertain that she had reached a junction where a swollen stream joined the river. It *might* have been possible to cross the stream, but it was carrying flood-water. When Anna lowered herself tentatively into it she sank to her thighs in mud and water and was almost knocked off her feet by the current. She could not swim and to attempt a crossing would have been exceedingly foolish.

Anna decided to follow the bank of the stream, but before long she found herself floundering through thick, cloying mud that brought her down, time and time again. She tried skirting the area of marshland but tripped and fell. Caught in a mud-trap she floundered around wildly until she began sobbing aloud in a desperate combination of fear and frustration.

Anna attempted to take a firm mental grip on herself, and gradually brought her breathing under control. It took a determined effort on her part. Even when she stood quite still it was easy to imagine she was sinking deeper into the morass.

When her breathing was almost normal once more Anna could hear the sound of the fast-running stream and gauge its direction. She had wandered farther from it than she had thought, but at least she had regained her bearings now.

Very slowly, determined not to fly into a panic, she chose a diagonal route to the stream bank. It took her a very long time but, once there, she was relieved to find herself standing on firm ground once more.

The effort of freeing herself from the area of marshland had brought her close to exhaustion and she was forced to sit down and rest for a while. The rain had stopped now, but it was cooler and she shivered. The trembling was not entirely due to the drop in temperature. Anna was desperately frightened.

After resting for about fifteen minutes, she set off once more but when she had travelled no more than another half-mile she was brought up short by a thick blackthorn hedge. It extended right across the route she had set for herself.

The hedge was an even more formidable barrier than the marsh had been. For a few defeated moments Anna almost gave way to tears – but she told herself it would solve nothing. There was no returning the way she had come, she had walked too far. There was nothing for it but to follow the course of the hedge and hope to find a gate before too long.

There was no gate. The hedge had been grown to keep farm animals from straying on to the dangerous marshland and it continued until the sound of running water had disappeared before gently altering course to her right.

Anna followed the hedge for another half-mile. Then, much to her relief, the hedge ended and a wall took its place. Built of Cotswold stone, no mortar had been used in the wall's construction and Anna was able to use the many irregular gaps as finger- and toe-holds as she clambered over, dropping into a meadow on the far side.

She set off in a direction that she hoped was parallel to the stream, but by now she was both tired and hungry and sensed that darkness was falling. It had also begun to rain more heavily than before. When Anna wandered into the shelter afforded by a large tree growing up in the hedgerow, she decided this was where she would spend the night.

Cold, wet and hungry, Anna felt very alone and vulnerable. She was also very, very tired. In spite of her predicament she slept the whole night through, undisturbed by the stoats, hedgehogs and badgers, which passed within feet of her during the hours of darkness.

When she woke she felt hungry and dirty, but there was nothing that could be done about either condition for the moment. Far more important to her well-being were the sounds of cows, pigs and cackling hens she could hear from somewhere nearby. They were farmyard noises and the most hopeful sounds she had heard for twenty-four hours.

The presence of a farm helped Anna resolve her course of action. She had been wandering around the countryside for so many hours, hopelessly lost. To carry on as she was without seeking help was not only futile, but dangerous. Although it went against all the principles of gipsy teaching, she would have to ask for assistance from gorgios.

Continuing on the course she had been following the previous evening Anna reached another wall. The farmyard was somewhere beyond the wall, no more than the width of a small field away. Clambering over the wall, Anna made her way towards the source of the sounds.

She had almost reached her goal when she heard a woman shout, 'What are you doing in that field, girl? Come here, quickly.'

Anna stopped, uncertain whether the words were intended for her. 'Are you mad, girl? Run! Run, I say, if you value your life – can't you tell a bull from a cow?'

Anna ran, imagining she could hear the hoofs of a bull pounding on the turf behind her. She tripped once on a mole-hill but scrambled to her feet again quickly. When it became alarmingly apparent that the hoofs were not merely in her mind she was grabbed by the arm. After colliding heavily with a gate-post, she heard a gate slammed shut behind her.

'What in the world did you think you were doing, girl? That bull has already killed once. That's why we were able to get it cheap. It almost killed you too – and look at the state of you! What have you been doing? Are you a gipsy?'

Suddenly the tone of the woman's voice changed. 'Why, bless me . . . you're blind, girl, aren't you?'

'Yes, and I'm lost . . . and hungry.'

'A blind girl, in the same field as that old bull . . .' the woman's voice carried disbelief. 'If I'd looked out half a minute later you'd have been dead by now . . . but come over here to the dairy, I've a glass of milk and a piece of cheese you can be putting inside your belly while you tell me just what you're doing here.'

The farmer's wife found a piece of coarse bread to go along with the cheese and milk and Anna ate as though she feared someone might come along at any moment and take what was left away from her.

As she ate she explained that she had lost her brother and told the farmer's wife of the boys who had pushed her caravan into the river.

'I don't hold with that sort of thing, my dear,' said the farmer's wife. 'But we've had a deal of trouble with gipsies in these parts. Mrs Elliot, up at the big house, lost her small boy only a year or two back. 'Twas said he'd been taken by some of your people who'd just passed through the village.'

'He'd more likely fallen into the same river as I did, or the marsh alongside it,' retorted Anna indignantly. 'Romanies have no need to steal other folks' children. Most have too many of their own to feed.'

'I'm not saying I agree with *what* was said, only that *'twas* said, but there's many folk around here believe it – and my husband is one of 'em.'

'Can I clean up a bit?' Anna asked the question past a mouthful of bread and cheese.

'You can swill off at the pump in the yard but there are one or two nasty cuts on your face and feet. You'd better come across to the house with me and we'll see what we can find to put on 'em. I doubt if we can do anything about that dress of yours. You've more mud on it than will ever come out – and it don't smell none too sweet, neither.'

Taking a hold on Anna's arm the woman led her from the dairy but they had not taken many paces before a man's voice shouted, 'Sally, who's that you've got there? She looks like a gipsy. Send her away from here this minute, before I turn the dogs on her.'

'It's a blind girl, Arthur Mott, and you'll keep those dogs locked in the shed until I've tended to her needs, or they'll feel the heavy end of my broom.'

Anna heard the footsteps of the farmer approaching across the cobbled farmyard as his wife pulled her to a halt.

'Blind, is she? Then how'd she find her way here?'

'You may well ask. She was in the field with that old bull of ours. If I hadn't pulled her through the gate she'd have been lying as dead as the farmer whose wife you bought him from.'

Anna felt the farmer's hot breath in her face before he said. 'Blind she may be, but I doubt she's lost any of her thieving ways because of it. There's some bad 'uns about right now. I heard tell only last night that the constable over at Byfield arrested a young gipsy villain who's wanted in Burford for highway robbery. Had five hundred pounds on him, they said, all stolen from honest folk.'

'That'll be Boz . . . my brother. He never stole anything. Where is he now?'

'There, what'd I tell 'ee? She's a bad 'un, right enough. I'll tell you what they did with him, my girl. They sent him off to Burford in a prison van, and if you ask me that's where you ought to go too.'

'You tell me when you've heard of a blind highwayman, Arthur Mott – especially a girl, and I'll agree with you, but not until then.'

'I'll not have you talking to me that way in front of a gipsy girl, Sally. I'm master in my own house and I say I'm entertaining no thieving gipsy here. Unless I'm very much mistaken you've already fed her from the dairy. That's Christian-enough duty towards the likes of her. She goes down the lane to Constable Dack. What he does with her is up to him.'

The farmer's wife protested, but Arthur Mott took a painful grip of Anna's other arm and pulled her from the grasp of his wife. He marched Anna from the farmyard, and the protests of his wife grew fainter as he propelled her along the lane. 'You don't need to hold my arm so tight,' she protested, 'I'm not likely to run off anywhere.'

'I'll make quite sure of that,' agreed the farmer. 'Lucky for you there ain't far to go. Constable Dack lives in the next cottage down the lane but I warn you right away that he has no more time for gipsies than I have. Unless I'm mistaken he'll have you out of the parish before you know you've even been here – and good riddance to you, I say.'

CHAPTER NINETEEN

Constable Alan Dack *was* of the same mind as Farmer Mott, but he was fairly new to his duties. Not at all certain what he should do with a blind gipsy girl, he took her to the home of the local magistrate and sought his advice.

General Sir Charlemagne Pope was a kindlier man than either the constable or the farmer. His answer to the problem was to order Constable Dack to take his charge to the workhouse, which was on the road to the next village along Anna's way.

The constable looked doubtful about obeying the magistrate's instruction. 'Horace Pilcher's not going to like having to take in a gipsy girl.'

'Pilcher will do as he's told if he wants to remain as workhouse master. He's to take the girl in for one night and have her clean herself up. Tomorrow she's to be shown the road to Burford, where she says she's heading. That should be the last the parish will see of her.'

Shifting his attention to Anna, the magistrate said, 'I hope you'll take this as a warning, young lady, and not regard it as weakness on my part. If you're seen here again you'll be brought up before me and I'll have no compunction about committing you to prison, is that fully understood?'

When Anna agreed that it *was* understood, the General dipped into his pocket and gave her a shilling to see her on her way, and Constable Dack escorted her to the workhouse.

Horace Pilcher hated gipsies even more than did Farmer Mott. Had it been anyone else but General Sir Charlemagne Pope who had sent the girl, he would not have allowed her inside the building. As it was, he was determined she would not *enjoy* her stay.

Bathing, Anna was informed, was allowed only in the evening. It would be a cold-water bath and could be taken while the others were eating. When Anna said if it was to be a choice between a bath and a meal she would take the meal, Pilcher made a careful entry in his daily journal against Anna's name. Refused to take bath.

Had she tried the food first, Anna might have preferred the bath. Supper was watery potato soup with a hint of cabbage and a hunk of coarse bread without butter. However, Anna was hungry and wiped her dish clean with the bread. She could have eaten much more, but knew better than to ask.

It was still early, but when supper ended it was time for the inmates of the workhouse to go to bed. Pilcher would light no candles for paupers. Neither would there be any form of heating. A threadbare blanket and a biscuit-thin mattress stuffed with straw was allocated to each inmate. Any attempt to provide more comfort would have been frowned upon by the Board of Guardians of the workhouse. It was intended that a workhouse should be looked upon by the poor of the parish as a last resort, not a haven, and only the barest necessities of life were provided.

That night was one Anna would remember with revulsion for the remainder of her life. Declaring he was not going to put a 'filthy gipsy' where others might be expected to sleep afterwards, Anna was taken to a room occupied only by an insane woman. Extremely violent, the woman was chained to a wall. As she broke furniture and tore up bedding, she slept, ate and carried out every other function on a thick bed of straw which was changed by two men from the village once a week. The smell in the room was nauseating, but when Anna protested, the workhouse master snapped, 'I've been ordered to provide you with lodging for the night, but even a magistrate can't dictate how I board those in my care. This is good enough for the likes of you, my girl. If you don't like it I'll show you the door and tell Constable Dack you'd prefer to see the inside of the lock-up.'

Remembering the magistrate's warning, Anna bit back the retort that she would as soon sleep in a cell as here. Boz had been arrested and needed help. She could do nothing if she too was committed to prison.

'I knew you'd see sense if you thought about it for a minute or two,' said Pilcher. 'You'll find your mattress against the wall on this side of the room. I suggest you don't stray from it. Lily can't reach you there, and it's just as well. She'd kill you for certain if she could.'

As if to prove his words, the mad woman screamed her fury at Anna and leaped across the room only to be brought up short by the chain. As the scream died away, Anna heard the door close behind her and a bolt rammed home on the other side. In common with the other inmates of the workhouse, she was locked into her room at night – but the others did not have to share their room with a mad woman.

Anna slept only fitfully through the night. Her room-mate had a wide variety of noises. Screams came intermittently, at other times there were moans, incoherent babbling and tears.

It seemed an interminable night and Anna felt incredible relief when she heard the bolt drawn on the door and Pilcher's voice say, 'So you didn't stray into Lily's part of the room after all.' He sounded disappointed. 'Come on out – unless you'd prefer to share your breakfast with her.' He chuckled. 'It's a pity you're blind. Watching what Lily does with her food is an experience men would pay to watch. Move yourself now. There's gruel if you want it, then you can be on your way – and good riddance, I say.'

Outside the workhouse, Anna took a deep breath of clean, sweet-smelling air. It was the first night she had spent inside a house of any description. She had not enjoyed the experience. On the road with Boz there had been the occasional night when extreme weather had forced them to find a barn in which to sleep, but a barn was somehow different from a house.

Anna was on a road that led southwards, away from Byfield and heading in the general direction of the distant town of Burford. She had travelled no more than a mile when she heard the sound of a horse coming from her left, while the squeak of a light, wheeled cart, or something similar, was coming towards her from the right.

A quick exploration with her bare feet indicated that the road forked here – and it presented her with a dilemma. Horace Pilcher had told her tersely that the road would eventually lead her to Banbury and that she would need to ask to be directed to the Burford road when she reached that busy market town, but he had said nothing of such a junction.

The horseman came on at a leisurely canter and Anna called out, hoping he would tell her which road she should take. He rode past without a break in the horse's gait, leaving her no alternative but to await the arrival of the squeaking vehicle.

As it drew nearer, Anna decided the vehicle was most probably a handcart and her hopes soared. Handcarts were the stock-in-trade of tinkers – and gipsies and tinkers trod the same paths.

As the handcart, for such it was, drew level with her, Anna called a greeting in the Romany language, and the cart came to a halt.

'Why, bless me if it ain't a Romany girl – and on her own too. Where are your folks, girl? We'd enjoy a little Romany company for a while.'

The speaker was a man, but Anna's keen hearing had picked up the footsteps of a companion, probably a woman.

'My folk are a long way from here and I'm trying to make my way to them. Would you tell me which of the roads will take me to Banbury?'

'What sort of Romany are you that you can't find your way around? And how d'you come to be so far from your family?' This time the speaker was a woman.

'I was travelling with my brother, but he was arrested a few days ago and taken to Burford. I'm making my way there now but it isn't easy. I'm blind.'

Anna felt no shame in confessing that Boz had been arrested. Gipsies and tinkers were arrested on the flimsiest of pretexts. It was an accepted fact of life for both communities.

'She's blind . . . did you hear that, Ted? The girl's blind.'

'I heard . . . and your luck's in, girl. Me and Serena were saying only this morning that it's time we paid another visit down Burford way. A nice part of the world, that is, with some very pleasant people. Well, would you believe it now.'

'You'll take me to Burford?' Anna asked the question eagerly. 'Boz – that's my brother – will pay you for helping me.'

'Then that settles it, it's Burford for us – but we can't set out until tomorrow. Right now we're on our way to the foresters just past Charwelton. You can't see this handcart I'm pushing, but I'm a knife-grinder by trade, this here's my stone, and I promised I'd be up there today to do some work for 'em.'

Anna's hopes sank. 'I don't want to go to Charwelton again. I . . . I had some trouble with a crowd of boys there. The constable will arrest me for vagrancy if I pass through Byfield again.'

'Well then, we'll need to take a path I know that'll lead us past both places without us being seen by a soul. You can trust Ted Stallard, girlie.'

Anna was unsure, but the woman said, 'He's right, lovie. You put your trust in Ted and you'll be in Burford two days after tomorrow, for sure.'

It was far quicker than Anna would make the journey to the Cotswold town on her own and she made up her mind.

'All right. Boz will see you're paid well for helping me.'

'Don't you worry yourself about that, lovie. If we don't help each other when we're in trouble, who will?'

CHAPTER TWENTY

As Anna walked with the two tinkers they questioned her about her background. In return, she learned something of her new-found companions. They were not married, but had kept company together for more than fifteen years. Travelling the length and breadth of England, they seemed not to remain in any particular district for longer than a few days.

Both tinkers went out of their way to be pleasant to Anna, yet she was not completely at her ease with them. They were, if anything, *too* pleasant. She felt as though they were putting on an act for her benefit. She also believed they were communicating with each other as they walked along, using some form of sign language.

They would occasionally stop and twice Anna remained with Ted while Serena went off to a nearby cottage. Ted said she was asking if the occupier wanted any knives sharpened. Anna wondered why Ted did not go himself, but she made no comments, even when she heard the chink of coins as Serena returned on the second occasion.

When they stopped for the third time, Anna was asked to remain with the handcart while both tinkers went off. She heard them whispering as they walked away, but she could not hear what they were saying.

Both were away for only a few minutes. Ted

returned first. Placing something in the handcart, he said, 'Come on, step lively, girl. Let's get on.'

'What about Serena?'

'She'll catch up with us in a minute or two. Come on, take a hold of my coat and keep up.'

Ted went so fast for a couple of minutes that more than once Anna had to trot in order to keep up with him.

The knife-grinder slowed suddenly when they turned a bend in the narrow lane and a few minutes later Serena arrived, breathing as heavily as her man.

'All right?' Serena put the question to Ted and he must have nodded, for Anna heard no reply.

As though feeling it necessary to give Anna an explanation, Ted said, 'They had a damn great dog back there. I thought they were going to turn it loose on us. Nasty-looking animal. I didn't want you getting hurt, girl.'

Anna had heard no dog, fierce or otherwise, but she kept her thoughts to herself. She had arrived at the conclusion that the tinkers were thieves. No doubt Serena kept the occupier of a house busy talking at the door while Ted went to the other side and stole anything that was immediately available. It was a simple but oft-used and effective ploy.

She tried to dismiss the thought. If this was what they were doing, why would they bother with her? The answer came to her when they stopped at another cottage and Serena went to the door leaving Anna with Ted once more. This time Anna was close enough to hear what was being said. Serena was begging, using Anna and her blindness to excite pity.

At first, Anna was angry, but the anger did not last

long. There had been occasions when she and Boz had made use of her blindness to persuade gorgios to buy from them. The thieving was another matter. If the tinkers were arrested by the police, she would be taken as an accomplice.

Stopping suddenly, Anna said, 'I've been thinking. Why don't you leave me somewhere on the road? You'll travel much faster without me. Then when you return we can go on to Burford together.'

'Leave you alone around here? We wouldn't dream of it, lovie.' Serena linked her arm through Anna's, reinforcing her statement. 'I'd never forgive myself if we left a pretty little thing like you on your own and something happened to you, and neither would Ted. No, you stay with us and we'll get you to Burford to find that brother of yours.'

Anna was aware that while Serena was speaking to her she was looking elsewhere, probably towards Ted. She wished yet again that she knew what their exchanged glances were saying.

'We'll be at a village in a few minutes,' said Ted. 'It's a fair-sized place and there'll be a market there today. I'll look around for something to eat then we'll take a path I know which comes out not far from Charwelton.'

Anna had hoped to be far away from Charwelton by now, but the two tinkers had promised they would head for Burford the next morning. She would decide then what action to take if they failed to fulfil that promise.

'Can we stop at a stream or a pond somewhere? I'd like to get cleaned up before we enter a village.'

'There's no need for that, lovie. You look all right just as you are. We'll make a camp by the river this afternoon while Ted goes on and does his little bit of work. You can have an all-over wash then – if that's what you want. I don't see the need for it meself, but I know some folks put a lot of store by bathing.'

Anna realised from the tinker-woman's words that she intended begging when they reached the market in the village. A *dirty* blind gipsy girl would arouse more pity than a clean one.

It all went very much as Anna had thought. There was a market in the main road of the village and with crowds all around them Anna was left standing beside the road holding the handcart while the other two went off together. Neither went very far and Anna could hear the wheedling tones of Serena's voice soliciting money from passers-by for 'A poor, blind gipsy girl with no one in the whole world to take care of her but a sick tinker-woman who isn't long for this life'.

Anna must have stood by the handcart for about half an hour when suddenly Ted was by her side. 'Quick, let's get out of here.' Pushing the cart one-handed he took Anna's arm and propelled her through the crowd, ignoring the protests of the men and women they bumped into along their way.

'What's the hurry?'

'Save your breath for running, if need be. Let's just say there's someone I don't want to meet if I can help it.'

Serena must have seen them leave because she had caught up with them by the time they had cleared the crowded marketplace.

Serena asked Ted the same question as Anna, and received a similar response.

When the sounds of the village and its market were far behind, Ted told Serena to push the handcart for a while and he dropped behind, but not so far that

Anna's sharp hearing did not catch the sound of coins being counted.

Once again Anna put her own interpretation on what was happening about her. She believed Ted had lifted someone's purse and either he thought he had been seen, or the weight of the purse had frightened him.

There was no evidence of pursuit and Ted's good humour grew as the distance between the three travellers and the village market increased, convincing Anna her surmise was right.

Before long Ted led them off the road and along a path that twisted and turned through woods and wasteland. Eventually they reached a river bank and here Ted said they would make camp while he went on alone with his handcart to fulfil his contract.

As he was speaking, Anna was listening to a sound from farther away and suddenly she said, 'We're close to Charwelton.'

'How'd you know that? I thought you was supposed to be blind.' There was menace in Ted's voice, but Anna waved him to silence.

'Listen! Can't you hear those rooks? There's a rookery in Charwelton. I could hear it when I was camped by the river with Boz. This must be the same river. You've brought me back even though I told you I didn't want to come here.'

'You're a bright girl, lovie. A very bright girl. That's Charwelton all right, but don't worry about being found. We must be a good mile from the place where you were camped with your brother. No one will find you here.'

Anna had told the tinkers of her ordeal at the hands of the Charwelton youths.

'Off you go now, Ted, but leave me that fowl you've got on the cart. Anna and I'll have it roasting nicely by the time you get back – and don't come empty-handed, mind. I'll expect to have the taste of "blue ruin" on me tongue by tonight.'

'You will, Serena, I promise you that. You too, girl. I won't forget you.'

Anna suspected that the dead chicken from Ted's handcart had been stolen from a hen-run belonging to one of the cottages they had called at along the way. However, she was not going to let such a thought spoil her anticipation of the meal it would provide and she was quite happy to help prepare the chicken, plucking the bird while the tinker-woman started a fire.

While supper was being cooked, Anna enjoyed her long-awaited bath in the river. Later, as the aroma of a spit-roasting chicken rose from the fire, Anna's spirits rose too. The tinker-woman's chatter was inconsequential, but it was friendly enough and Anna began to think her earlier misgivings about their intentions towards her might have been misplaced.

'It's getting late, Ted should have been here by now. If he doesn't get here soon he'll need to make do with cold chicken. It's done to perfection now. I'll give him a few more minutes and then we'll have ours.' Serena expressed her concern as she raised the spit clear of the fire.

'Is the place he had to go to very far away?'

Serena hesitated. 'I don't question anything he does, girl. That's something you'll need to learn if ever you get a man of your own. There's times when he goes his own way and I go mine. When we're back together we neither of us asks what the other's been up to. It's best that way.'

'Have you and Ted never thought of getting married?'

'I've thought of it. I doubt if he has.'

'I think if I spent most of my life with a man I'd want him to marry me.'

'You're young, girl. You don't know much about life yet awhile. When you find a man who's right for you then it won't matter who he is, or what he does. You'll be content to go along with him, no matter where it takes you, or how bumpy the road. God knows what me poor old mum would have said had she seen the man I've ended up with. She didn't do much better herself, but she always had high hopes for me . . .'

Anna was only half listening. She was thinking of what Serena had said about it not mattering who a man was if he was the *right* man. She found herself thinking about Seb. He was a gorgio and as such would never be accepted by her people. Yet her own blindness set her apart from her people too, in exactly the same way as coming from London meant that Seb was not accepted by the villagers of Swinbrook.

'Here, lovie. Have a piece of this chicken while it's good and hot. There's no reason why *we* shouldn't enjoy it while it's at its best. For all I know we might not see Ted again for a day or two, or even a week.'

Anna thought that if Ted had met up with a constable, or the man whose purse he had lifted earlier in the day, it would be considerably longer than a week or two before Serena saw the tinker again.

CHAPTER TWENTY-ONE

It was close to midnight when Ted returned to the riverside camp. He did not have his handcart with him and his blundering progress through the nearby undergrowth was accompanied by many curses and frequent crashes as he tripped and fell. When he bypassed the camp and seemed to be heading for the river, Serena called out to him and hurried to his rescue.

The tinker was reeling drunk when he arrived within the ring of flickering light cast by the fire, but he shook off Serena's supporting arm.

In his hands he carried two bottles of gin, one half consumed. Placing them unsteadily on the ground, he reached inside his pockets and produced two more.

'Here you are . . . one for each of us – and a drop extra for anyone still on their feet when they're gone.'

Standing swaying above Anna, who squatted close to the fire, he thrust a bottle at her. 'Take it, girl – but I shall expect a kiss in return. Go on, take it.'

'She can't see you, you drunken fool. Sit down afore you fall in the fire. I can see you've had a skinful of gin today, and no mistake.' Serena reached out and steadied him as he took an involuntary step backwards.

'And why shouldn't I?' Ted looked at Serena belligerently. 'I've done some good business today. *Good* business. Old Solomon said it's a long time since he's been offered such good stuff. He gave me a good price for everything too . . . better than last time.'

'Your tongue's longer than a hound's tail, Ted Stallard. It'll hang you one day, you mark my words. Now give those bottles to me and *sit yourself down*. I'll give the girl some blue ruin, not you.'

Instead of sitting down, the tinker crashed back through the undergrowth and moments later could be heard relieving himself beyond the firelight.

'You needn't bother giving me any gin. I don't like it. I never have.'

'Don't like gin, and you a *Romany*? It's the only pleasure given to the likes of us that'll make us forget all the misery in our lives. I couldn't go on if I didn't have an occasional bottle of blue ruin to look forward to.'

Using her teeth, Serena pulled the cork clear of one of the bottles she was holding and Anna heard the sound of liquid being poured from the neck of the bottle down Serena's throat.

'Ah! That's better.' Serena spoke hoarsely as the fiery alcohol snatched at her breath. 'You sure you won't have some, lovie?'

'Certain.'

'That's a pity. Like I said, it helps the likes of us to forget – and you'd do well to forget everything Ted said just now.'

'I don't know what he was talking about, and I don't care to know. All I want to do is find Boz. When that's done I doubt if I'll set eyes on you or Ted ever again.'

'You've got a sensible head on your shoulders, lovie. You'd have made someone a good wife had you not been blind.'

'Where's that gin? What have you done with the

bottle, woman?' Ted staggered back to the fire, his gait no more certain than before.

'It's where you left it, on the ground over there. Here, let me lead you to it. How you found your way back here I don't know. As for your handcart and sharpening wheel – we'll need to go and look for it tomorrow, that's if you've sobered up by then.'

'Who needs a handcart? We've got enough money to keep us drunk for a month – a year! But why isn't the girl drinking? Give her the bottle I brought for her, or have *you* kept it for yourself? Have you, you thieving shrew?'

'Oh, shut up, you drunken fool. The girl doesn't like blue ruin. Go and sit down before you fall down and I'll find some cold chicken and bread for you. It might help soak up some of that gin inside you.'

'I think I'll settle down to sleep now. Did you say you had a blanket I could use?' Anna decided to leave the tinker couple to their drunken evening. She had a great deal of thinking to do.

'That's what I said – but it's in the handcart, along with most other things we own, which ain't very much. The only thing I've got to warm you up is gin – or Ted.'

Serena's cackle of laughter suggested the gin she had drunk was beginning to have its effect on her too.

'At least show me somewhere that'll keep the night wind off me.'

'Course I will, lovie. Like I said, it's easy to forget you can't see. You're almost the same as we are. Come on now, you come over here.'

Serena led Anna to a spot where the coarse, dry grass had been partly flattened by the winds of autumn. 'This should do for you, lovie.'

Behind her Ted was calling drunkenly, 'Bring me some grub, woman. Where's my grub?'

'Shut your gob, you noisy bleeder!' Serena shouted her reply before saying to Anna, 'I'm going to have trouble with him tonight. Pouring gin in him has the same effect as feeding lettuce to a randy rabbit.' She laughed. 'All it does for me is send me to sleep!'

Serena made her way back to the fireside and Anna lay awake for more than an hour listening to their drunken talking, singing and occasional arguing. She was also thinking. It was apparent to her that the tinkers had no intention of heading towards Burford tomorrow. If they had enough money to keep themselves in drinks it was possible they would not move away from the area for the foreseeable future – and she could not wait. Boz was in a police cell in Burford and needed her help.

If she remained with the tinkers, Anna was convinced she would end up in gaol like her brother.

Anna was awakened suddenly by a heavy weight pressing down upon her. She opened her mouth to shout but a hand clamped down upon it with such force that her bottom lip was crushed on a tooth and she tasted blood.

'Stop struggling, girl. Don't tell me you haven't taken a tumble before. I wouldn't believe you. Open your legs!'

As Anna continued to struggle she felt Ted's knee force her legs apart. Then he reached down and lifted her skirt. His hand, rough and callused, scratched the soft skin between her thighs.

She had been pummelling him without effect but now she brought up her hand and gouged one of the tinker's eyes with her finger. He slackened his grip on her mouth and she bit him hard. His yell was almost as loud as her scream, but his was of pain, hers contained as much anger as fear.

Anna had succeeded in diverting the drunken and amorous Ted from his intent, but she had angered him beyond reason. Her body still trapped beneath him, she could only move her head from side to side, screaming in fury at him as he rained blows upon her face.

Suddenly there was another raised voice, that of Serena. A half-filled gin bottle crashed against the side of Ted's head and his body sagged on Anna.

Throwing the tinker from her, she rolled clear, and continued rolling. In the darkness she scrambled up and began a stumbling run that took her away from the tinkers as the gradually fading sounds indicated that Serena was still attacking her man with hands, bottle and feet.

Anna had sustained a number of cuts and she could feel blood on her face, but she did not stop running until the shouts and blows of the angry tinker-woman were no longer audible.

Along the way Anna crashed into trees, tore through thorn bushes and fell to the ground on numerous occasions. She knew her dress was torn, as was her skin – but she had escaped from the tinkers. They would not come after her in the darkness, even if they were sober enough to remember she had been with them in the first place.

When Anna stopped running she found to her distress she was shaking violently. Nothing like the attack by the tinker had ever happened to her before. The life of a gipsy was not an easy one, but within her own community she had never had to fear attack from any Romany man.

Anna took in great gulps of air, and gradually she regained control of her breathing. With her back against a tree and her knees tucked beneath her chin, she waited for morning, hoping she would hear sounds and find someone to put her on the road southwards. To Burford and the safety of the Wychwood Forest.

CHAPTER TWENTY-TWO

It took Anna a moment or two to recognise the sound that had woken her. It was the noise of someone chopping wood. She could hardly believe she had been able to sleep after the experiences of the night, but she must have slept until well after dawn.

She rose to her feet to discover she ached in every limb. Her face was stiff, swollen and painful and the area around one eye felt tender to her exploratory touch. She realised she must look a dreadful sight.

The axeman was at work layering a hedge. An old man, he reacted to Anna as though she were an apparition. Had his legs been younger he would have run away. He gave her directions to the road in a querulous voice, but was incapable of resuming work until she had passed out of his sight.

Anna found the road and took the direction suggested by the man, but she had been walking for no longer than twenty minutes when an unwelcome sound brought her to a halt. It was the noise of birds – in a rookery. The rookery of Charwelton! The sound had been in her ears for some time and she would have recognised it earlier for what it was, had she not been deeply immersed in her own thoughts.

Anna realised she required more detailed directions if she were to reach Burford, but she was unlikely to find anyone outside of a town or a large village with sufficient knowledge to give them to her. Byfield was out, so too was the village where the market had been held. She was convinced Ted had been on a pick-pocketing expedition there and she might have been seen with the two tinkers and reported to the village constable.

The knowledge that she was so close to Charwelton greatly alarmed her. She had no wish to repeat her frightening experience at the hands of the village youths. Yet if she retraced her footsteps she would be travelling in the wrong direction – and was likely to meet up with the tinkers once more . . .

As Anna pondered her dilemma she heard another sound, closer than the Charwelton rookery. It was the sound of a hen which had laid an egg and was proclaiming its achievement to the world. It meant there must be a house or farm somewhere nearby.

Following the sound of the triumphant fowl, Anna located a cottage at the side of the lane. She could tell it was not a farm by the absence of other animal noises. A woman was talking somewhere inside the house, the sound reaching her through an open window.

'Hello! Is there someone there?'

At the second call, a woman's voice replied, 'Who are you? What do you want?'

'I'm trying to find the Banbury road, but I want to avoid Byfield if it's possible.'

'It ain't possible, as far as I know, but I've never been farther than Byfield, myself. You'd best ask in the village. Who are you, anyway, and what you been doing to yourself?'

Before Anna could give an account of herself there was another voice, that of a small boy, who was in the room with the woman.

'Ma . . . that's her! That's the witch. The one who put the spell on Timmie Cooper.'

'A spell? What are you talking about, boy? What spell?'

'The curse she put on him. We saw her down at the river bank but she chased us away. While we were running she called out that we'd see the colour of our own blood before long. Last night Timmie was chopping kindling when the axe slipped and cut his leg wide open. It was her doing. Her and the curse . . .'

Anna had heard enough. The boy had been one of her tormentors – and now they really *did* believe she was a witch. She half walked, half ran along the road from the cottage, veering back on the lane whenever one of her feet strayed on to the grass verge.

Suddenly her feet were brushing through old leaves. A quick exploration revealed she was passing through a copse, or a small stretch of woodland. Anna decided she would leave the road here.

The words of the boy had frightened Anna badly. If the same story was circulating in the village she was in danger of being attacked once again, this time with far more serious consequences than before. She decided to find somewhere to hide and wait for darkness to fall. She would pass through the village of Charwelton at night.

At least she was certain now that if she stayed on the road she would be travelling in the right direction. The problem of avoiding Byfield could be dealt with once Charwelton was behind her.

The wooded ground dropped sharply away from the road but Anna had felt her cautious way hardly more than fifty paces before she came upon a combination of brambles and dried fern. Unable to find a path around the barrier, Anna dropped to her stomach and wriggled carefully and painfully into the thick of the tangled undergrowth.

She had no way of knowing if her refuge was secure, or whether she could be seen by anyone passing nearby, but it was the best she could do.

It must have been midday when sounds from the road proved that Anna had been wise to go into hiding. There were voices – many voices. Among them she recognised some of those who had stoned her after her caravan had been pushed in the river.

This time there were many more people than before and she could hear men as well as boys. They seemed to be moving along the lane, coming from the direction of Charwelton and Anna did not doubt they were looking for her.

The Charwelton men and boys passed by the copse where Anna was hiding but she wondered how long it would be before they returned. At that moment her stomach complained noisily, reminding her she had not eaten since the previous evening. The sound was so loud she was certain it would have been heard had the villagers been closer.

Almost two hours passed before she heard the voices again. Ominously, the men were shouting now, and she could hear them thrashing the undergrowth with sticks. It sounded as though they were searching a wide swathe of land on either side of the lane. There could be no doubting now that they were searching for her.

She hoped she was far enough from the road for them to pass her by without seeing her, but as the voices drew closer she heard the excited whimpering of dogs, coursing through the undergrowth ahead of the men. Anna realised she must move far lower down the slope before the men and their dogs reached her.

Wriggling on her stomach, she forced her way through the briars, trying to ignore the thorns that scratched her face and pierced the skin of her hands, arms and knees.

The brambles hurt, but it was preferable to the fear she felt when she encountered a space free from them. She had no way of telling whether she was still hidden, or leaving her cover behind and emerging in full view of those who sought her.

Suddenly she realised all the voices were on the slope above. Her hopes rose as she realised she was probably beyond the end of the advancing line. Then she heard a movement in the bracken nearby. The next moment a dog began barking furiously, little more than an arm's length away.

'Here, over here! One of the dogs has found something!'

There was an excited hullabaloo from the beaters as they crashed through the undergrowth heading towards the barking dog and Anna knew it was no use trying to hide any longer.

The sound that rose from the throats of the beating men and boys reminded her of the baying of a foxhound pack in sight of its quarry. She rose from the ground and with arms outstretched broke into a clumsy blind run away from them.

It was a hopeless attempt to escape. Anna realised before she had gone twenty paces that there was no way she could outrun her sighted pursuers. Her only chance was to stop running and plead to be allowed to go on her way.

When she stopped, so too did the sounds of immediate pursuit. Only those farther away continued to crash through the undergrowth towards her.

'Don't get too close to her. Remember what happened to Timmie Cooper!' The cry was in a boy's voice and came from one of those nearest to her.

The cry brought a babble of sound from the other villagers and the word 'witch' could be heard repeated more than any other.

'Witch she may be, but let's see her put a curse on this!'

A large stone followed the words, bouncing off the trunk of a large tree only feet away.

It was the signal for a barrage of stones and sticks which flew through the air all around her, some striking their target, but most fortunately missing.

'Leave her to me. I know exactly how to deal with a gipsy witch. Stand back and let me come through.'

The young voice rang out and, as the last missiles fell to the ground about her, Anna dropped the arms that had been shielding her face and stood frozen in a state of shocked disbelief.

'All right, stand back and let me deal with her. Don't get too close in case something goes wrong.'

Someone advanced through the undergrowth towards Anna and she heard the sound of creaking leather harness, as though from the saddle of a horse.

She stood absolutely still until she felt the heavy breathing of a horse brush her face. Then the voice of the last person she had expected to hear in this place said, in a whisper, 'I'm reaching down to you, Anna.

Take my hand and when I pull scramble up behind me and cling as tight as you can. We'll need to ride like hell because at least two of the men are carrying hunting guns. Are you ready?'

Reaching up quickly, Anna found his hand. Taking a firm grip on it, she nodded.

'Now!'

For a desperate moment Anna hung between the horse and the ground, and then she swung her leg over its back and clung to Seb as the animal took off as though it were taking part in a five-furlong sprint.

The men and boys let out a howl of fury when they realised how they had been tricked and a shotgun was fired after them, but the gun was well out of range.

By the time the gun-owner reloaded, Seb, Anna and Grye were pounding through the narrow village street. They scattered women who were gathered together in small groups along its length, waiting for their menfolk to return with the news that the young gipsy witch of Charwelton would cast no more spells over their children.

CHAPTER TWENTY-THREE

'But how did you manage to arrive in time to rescue me?' Anna and Seb sat beside a stream not far from the road. Byfield was ten miles behind them and Charwelton farther still. Anna was bathing her scratched and bruised face while Seb was cutting chunks of ham and laying them on the grass beside a loaf of bread. Both items of food had been purchased in a small hamlet through which they had recently passed.

'I was with the searchers for almost an hour. I'd met someone on the road who told me the Charwelton men were out searching for a gipsy witch in the woods behind the village. I feared it was you they were hunting. It wasn't hard to find the men, they were making so much noise they could be heard for miles. It sounded to me as though they were frightened they *would* find you.'

Seb handed Anna a hunk of bread upon which was balanced a large piece of ham. 'When I reached them they told me you were last seen heading towards the village from a small cottage farther along the road. All I needed to do was stay with the men until they found you.'

'What would they have done with me if you hadn't carried me off?'

'I don't know.'

Seb lied. The Charwelton men had boasted that

when they discovered the witch they intended driving her to an area of dried bracken and dead and broken twigs at the lower edge of the woods and then setting fire to the whole area.

Finshing what he was doing, Seb said, 'You'd better let me clean up the side of your face, you've set it off bleeding.'

Taking off his neckerchief, Seb soaked it in the river and after wringing it out wiped the blood from Anna's cheek before cleaning the many scratches she had on her face.

'You've a very nasty bruise by your eye – and *that* wasn't done today.'

'No.'

It was evident that Anna was not going to amplify her terse statement and Seb continued to clean the face she turned up to him.

As he worked, Seb could not help comparing the differing colour of their skins. Although he had been in Oxfordshire for some months his skin had not entirely lost the pallor of London's East End. Anna's was the colour of the dried fern among which she had nearly come to such a violent end.

'There, that's an improvement. Now we'd better eat up and get on if we hope to find somewhere to stay before it becomes dark.'

'Is it that late already? Where are we?'

From the river bank, Seb could see the rays of the setting sun striking fire from the windows of a fair-sized town a couple of miles away along the flat and shallow valley.

'We're not far from Banbury. I'm sure we'll find an inn there.'

'I'm not staying at an inn, Seb – not even if we *did* find one to give me a bed, which I doubt. I've spent one night in a workhouse and it's the only night I've ever spent beneath a roof. I intend it to be the last. Is there any woodland around here where we can camp, or even a good, stout hedge?'

Seb looked about him uncertainly. 'Nothing in particular. Most of the hedges about here seem to have been trimmed recently. There's a haystack . . . or at least a part of one.'

'Why didn't you say so before? A haystack is one of the best beds anyone could wish for. It's not too close to a farmhouse?'

'Two fields away, at least.'

'That sounds perfect for what we want. We'll wait here until it's too dark for anyone to see us, and then you can lead the way.'

When Seb led Anna to the haystack he was thoroughly chilled. Autumn was far advanced and with a cloudless sky above them it was likely to be a cold night. Using the rein, Seb tethered Grye nearby and then helped Anna make up their 'beds'.

The haystack consisted of the remains of the previous year's harvest but, although it smelled musty, a good thatch had ensured it remained dry. More recently much of the stack had been cut away, forming a wall of hay which kept off the prevailing wind but left enough loose to ensure the softest of beds.

The prospect of sharing a haystack bed with Anna stirred a great many unfamiliar emotions in Seb, but any hopes he might have entertained were quickly dashed. Anna shaped two hollows in the hay, an arm's length apart and separated by a wall of loose hay about two feet high.

'Is this all right for you?' Anna asked the question, sensitive to his silence.

'Yes, fine.'

The tone of his voice confirmed what his silence had hinted.

'Were you expecting more from me, Seb?'

Seb's cheeks flared into life in the darkness. 'No, of course I wasn't.'

'Yes, you were, and if anyone has a right to me, it's you. You've ridden all the way from Swinbrook to find me and today you've saved me from being killed. Any man who does that has every right to expect something in return. I have only one thing to give, Seb, but once given it will have no worth for anyone else – and neither will I. Most gorgios think all Romany women are *loudnies* – whores – but it isn't true. No Romany woman who lies with another man before she's married will ever find herself a husband among her own people. I'm sorry, Seb . . .' Anna broke off.

'Anna, it's me who should be saying that. Yes, I was hoping, but not because you owe me anything. It was . . . for the same reason I came looking for you. I . . .' Seb made a confused wasted gesture. 'I think I love you, Anna.'

'Seb . . . that's the most wonderful thing anyone has ever said to me.' Stepping towards him, Anna's hands found his arms and moved up to cradle his face. 'I'm very fond of you too . . . but it can't change what I've just said.'

'That's all right. I can wait until you feel the same way as I do.' Anna's admission that she was fond of him, although less than he hoped for, had lit a warm glow inside him that nothing would cool tonight. He drew her to him and she made no attempt to resist. Indeed, when he kissed her she clung to him, only breaking away when his body, pressed against hers, became too demanding.

'No, Seb. I . . . These last few days are catching up with me. If I don't sleep soon I shall start shaking. If that starts I don't think it will ever stop.'

'You're not sorry that we're both out here like this . . . together?'

'Of course not, but there are others who wouldn't be so pleased.'

'Your people, you mean?'

'Yours too. They find it easier to accept someone from a foreign land than a Romany. Even one born right here in England.'

'Well, we needn't trouble ourselves about them tonight. Settle down to sleep now.'

'Yes, my gorgio. I'll sleep all the better for knowing you're here with me.'

Seb had been lying still for a few minutes when he heard a rustling in the hay between himself and Anna and her voice said softly, 'Are you asleep yet, Seb?'

'No.'

'I don't think it would be thought wrong if we held hands.'

The rustling was repeated and, pushing through the hay barrier that separated them, Seb's fingers found Anna's hand and held it tightly.

'Seb?'

'Yes?' They had lain side by side for perhaps ten

minutes, communicating silently through tangled, never still fingers.

'Have you ever spent a night like this before? Just lying out in the open, waiting for sleep? Are there any stars?'

'Millions of them, and no, I've never slept in the open before.' He doubted whether he would sleep much that night. He wanted to savour every moment of just lying there, holding Anna's hand.

'I'm glad I'm here with you for the first night. I hope it won't be the last.'

They were both silent for a long time until Anna's fingers relaxed in his grip and her steady breathing told him she was asleep.

Seb lay for a long time looking up at the star-filled sky. Anna was right, there was something magic about the night. Especially this night. Somewhere in the far distance a cow bellowed noisily for the calf that had been taken from her only that day. From the farmyard a bad-tempered sow complained about nothing in particular and just before he dozed off Seb was frightened by the wing-beats of a night-flying swan, heading for the silver ribbon of river that tied Banbury to the valley.

Seb must have dozed off because he was awakened by Anna's cries of terror. For a moment he thought they had been found by the Charwelton men. Then he realised Anna was having a nightmare, a frightening dream that resurrected all the fears and horrors of the past few days.

As she began to thrash around, making pitiful, puppy-like noises, Seb swept away the flimsy hay barrier between them. As Anna started up, he took her in his arms. She was shaking as though she was in a fit.

'It's all right, Anna. You're safe. I've got you.'

'Oh, Seb . . . I dreamed . . . I thought the tinker had caught me.'

'It's all right, Anna. Don't think about it any more. You're here safe with me and tomorrow we'll be in Burford and you'll be with Boz.'

'I was so frightened.' Anna clung to him and he rocked her in his arms, soothing her as though she were a baby.

After a while she stopped shaking and lay back. Seb went with her, still holding her to him. Suddenly she turned to him and hugged him with a ferocity that took him by surprise.

'I want you to hold me tonight, Seb. Hold me close, but without . . . doing anything else. Whatever happens to me in the future I want to be able to look back to tonight and remember that you held me like this . . . because you loved me. Please, Seb . . . It's very important to me.'

Seb pulled her close and as she clung to him he could feel her whole body shaking. He realised he would probably never know how much she had suffered during the last few days and nights.

Twice more during the night, beneath the star-spangled sky, in the warmth of the haystack, she cried out and he held her close until she stopped shaking. For these few hours Seb believed that no one could ever have loved anyone the way he loved the girl who lay in his arms.

Eventually, he too fell asleep, still holding Anna close, knowing the world would never be quite the same for him ever again.

CHAPTER TWENTY-FOUR

Awakened by Anna's stirring, the first sound Seb heard was the crowing of a rooster in the farmyard, two fields away. It seemed Anna heard it too.

'Seb, it must be daylight. We have to move on before the farmer finds us.'

One of Seb's arms was trapped beneath her and he put the other about her. 'It's only just after dawn. Can't we stay like this for a while?'

'The night's over. We have to get to Burford and find Boz. Let me get up, Seb.'

Anna seemed to feel no embarrassment at waking in his arms, but neither was there any intimation that she remembered anything that had been said by either of them during the night. Seb felt hurt. He had hoped she would say something to set the seal on their new relationship.

'Are you sorry I spoke to you as I did, Anna?'

Sensing the hurt in him, Anna reached out and pressed her hand against his chest.

'I'm not sorry, Seb. I won't ever forget you holding me last night and I'll never want to. You made me feel safe again. But it can't make me a gorgio, or you a Romany.'

'Does that matter so very much, Anna? It didn't stop me telling you I love you – or you saying you're fond of me.'

'No, Seb – but would you be content to spend every night of your life in a haystack or a hedgerow? You know you wouldn't. Any more than I could spend the rest of my life caged inside a gorgio house.'

Even as Seb opened his mouth to dispute Anna's argument they both heard a shout of anger from the direction of the farm where the cockerel had finally ceased challenging the dawn.

'You! What the 'ell d'you think you're doing on my hay?'

Squat and bow-legged, the farmer let himself out of the farmyard and advanced across the fields, brandishing a stout blackthorn stick.

'Quick! We've got to get out of here.' Grabbing Anna's hand, Seb dragged her from the haystack and pulled her to where Grye was patiently grazing. Expediency had temporarily replaced injured romance.

Mounted on Grye, Seb and Anna made good their escape while there was still half a field between them and the irate farmer. The farmer's dog, noisily snapping at the heels of the gipsy horse, kept up the illusion of a pursuit until they reached the lane and the dog was called off.

The brief chase left Seb and Anna laughing, the tension between them blown away, Seb was content for now to have Anna riding behind him, arms encircling his waist, her voice in his ear.

It began to rain within the hour. A cold, miserable drizzle that remained with them until they reached Burford early in the afternoon. For the last few miles Anna continually asked Seb where they were. She could scarcely contain her agitation when he told her they were approaching the bridge across the river

Windrush which marked the northern boundary of Burford.

As Grye side-stepped to allow a carriage-and-four to pass on the approach to the narrow bridge, Anna squeezed Seb's waist to gain his attention.

'Seb, it might be as well if you said nothing to Boz about where we spent last night. He might not understand.'

'What is there for him to understand? Besides, last night wasn't important to anyone but you and me. Mind you, we haven't finished talking about us yet. Not by a long way.'

They found the Burford turnkey in the clink. He was cleaning out the empty cell where Seb had last spoken to Boz.

Looking up as Seb entered, the old gaoler said grumpily, 'Oh, it's you.' Then the turnkey saw Anna standing behind Seb. 'I don't want the likes of her in here. I had a tinker-woman in here yesterday and I doubt if I'll ever clean out the lice and bugs she's left behind her.'

Ignoring the man's outburst, Seb said, 'What's happened to Boz Buckland? The gipsy? Has he been set free?'

'Set free?' The turnkey chuckled. 'Not he, not with Magistrate Peck on the Bench. If you want to speak to Gipsy Buckland you'll need to ride to Oxford – but I wouldn't leave it too long if I was you. He's been sent to the gaol there. Come the Winter Assizes he'll no doubt be chained in the hold of a transport ship bound for Australia.'

Despite Anna's protests that she wanted to go straight

to Oxford, Seb took her to Swinbrook. He explained that even such a big-hearted horse as Grye could not make the long journey to the city where Boz was housed in gaol, after carrying them both from Banbury.

It had been Seb's intention to ride to Handley Farm to ask Christian what had happened at the Burford magistrate's hearing, but as he passed Fern Cottage, his mother came running out to call after him.

Reining in, Seb's first question was to ask why she was not at work.

'Work? You go off to visit someone in gaol and three days later you still haven't come back! How do you expect me to be able to work? I haven't slept for worrying about you since you left. I got myself into such a state Christian sent me home. Anyway, Melody's up there and it won't do that little madam any harm to do some hard work for her keep. She can get on with the milking and do her share of the housework. It'll do her good.'

Seb had turned Grye so little could be seen of Anna but the arms about his waist, and her black hair, tangled by wind and rain. Nodding disapprovingly in Anna's direction, Dolly said, 'I see you've managed to find your gipsy girl. No doubt that's why it's taken you so long to come back home.'

'Anna's had a very bad time, Ma, and we've ridden a long way today. We could both do with something to eat.'

'Could you now? Don't you think you ought to take her back to her own folk first?'

'Anna has no one but her brother – and we've learned today that he's been taken to Oxford gaol. We could *both* do with some food.'

'Then you'd better come in and I'll see what I can find.'

Dolly was not overjoyed at the thought of having a gipsy girl inside her house, and she sniffed her displeasure, but as she turned to go inside the cottage, Seb lowered Anna to the ground from the horse and Dolly saw her injuries and the torn dress.

'Look at the state you're in, girl. What on earth's been happening to you?'

In spite of her earlier misgivings, Dolly moved closer. She saw a slim, slight, dark-skinned girl with a dress in tatters and a badly bruised and scratched face.

'I told you, Ma, Anna's had a rough time. A *really* rough time. If I hadn't found her when I did she'd be dead now.'

'You poor child, come on inside with me.' Her earlier disapproval forgotten, Dolly put an arm about Anna's shoulders. 'We'll get you something to eat and clean you up. We're going to have to find a dress for you, although from where I don't know. Everything I've got would go round you twice over.'

Seb smiled at the picture of his mother walking away with her arm about Anna. Calling after them, he said, 'I'm taking Grye to the stables up at the farm. I'll be back as soon as I've had a word with Christian.'

Anna stopped and turned sightless eyes in his direction. 'Ask him what he knows about Boz, Seb. Try to find out when I can visit him.'

Dolly saw the expression of tragic pleading on Anna's face and it came as a great shock to her to realise how much Anna relied upon Seb. He was not old enough to have to carry such a burden.

'Seb'll sort out everything with Christian, don't you

worry. You just come inside with me and tell me something of what's been going on. I'm sure I don't know what the world's coming to. We never had things like this happening when we were in London. And they try to tell me things are quieter in the country!'

When Seb arrived at Handley Farm, Christian was in the stables, settling down the two horses that had been working in the fields that day.

He was delighted to see Seb but his first question was of Anna.

'I found Anna and brought her back – but she's worried sick about Boz. The turnkey at Burford said he'd been taken to gaol in Oxford. I thought we were arranging for a solicitor to have the case against him dismissed?'

'Magistrate Peck was too quick for us. He sat earlier than usual the day after you left. By the time I reached Burford Boz had already been committed to the Assizes.'

'Why should a magistrate want to do that?'

'I think he suspected that we intended speaking up for Boz.' Christian grimaced ruefully. 'Peck and Meredith Putt are as thick as thieves at the moment. It seems they both share a great many business interests.'

Seb was angry that Putt should have helped add to Anna's anguish, but he was also puzzled. 'Why would Meredith Putt go to such lengths to have one gipsy put away?'

'There are a number of reasons, Seb. It was Boz's horse you were riding when you beat Putt at the Wychwood Forest races. Putt lost a lot of money – and he doesn't forgive easily. But there's far more to it than this, that's why you too must be on your guard against him.'

Christian stroked his chin thoughtfully. 'There's another reason. Putt wants to have the forest cleared and an enclosure order made on the land. The manor stands to gain a great many extra acres should that happen. If Boz is convicted of a serious crime it will strengthen Putt's argument that the forest is inhabited by dangerous criminals.'

'But Boz is innocent!'

'We both know that, Seb, and fortunately James Price believes us. His brother is a barrister in Oxford and he's agreed to represent Boz at the Assizes. If you and I are there to give evidence he should be released – and there's likely to be harsh words said about Magistrate Peck by the judge.'

'I hope you're right this time, Christian. Anna was desperately upset when she learned Boz had been taken to Oxford gaol. I'd like to be able to reassure her about him. She's had a bad time while she and Boz have been separated.'

Seb gave Christian an outline of all that had happened to Anna in Charwelton and the farmer listened with increasing disbelief.

'They intended to *burn* her as a witch? Surely they wouldn't really have gone that far, Seb. Such things died out in the Middle Ages.'

'Not for any gipsy girl unfortunate enough to be close to Charwelton.'

'Where's the girl now?'

'She's at Fern Cottage, being cleaned up by Ma.'

Christian began pacing the stable. 'The gipsies are a persecuted people, Seb. Persecuted in a way that would have the sympathy of Our Lord. I've felt for a very long time that I was being called to take the Word to them. Now I'm quite certain – and it's *you* who has finally shown me the path. I'll build a chapel on that piece of land close to Fern Cottage and spread word that gipsies are especially welcome there. Yes, that's what I'll do.'

Embarrassed by Christian's religious fervour, Seb said, 'I'd like to get back to Ma and Anna now. Can I leave Grye in the stable for a while? I'll tend to him, of course.'

'Yes, yes. There are plenty of spare stalls.' Christian was hardly listening. Gripped by the fervour of his new resolve, the chapel was already taking shape in his mind.

On his way across the farmyard, Seb met Melody. She was carrying two buckets of skimmed milk from the dairy to mix with the pigs' food. Welcoming an opportunity to put down her load for a while, she seemed genuinely pleased to see him again. 'You've been gone a long while. You've had your ma worried sick about you. Where have you been? Did you find Anna?'

'She's down at Fern Cottage, recovering from her experiences. She's been badly beaten and is cut and scratched from wandering around in the woods.'

'Poor Anna. I'll go and see her when I've finished my work. I'll see if Mr Timms will let me take her some of those roses he's got growing at the back of the house. They smell lovely, she'll like them.'

Seb walked away, deeply touched by the simple, warm-hearted reaction of Melody to Anna's plight. He could not help comparing it with the barbaric behaviour of the Charwelton villagers.

As he walked across the farmyard he suddenly realised how much he felt he belonged here, in Swinbrook. London was no longer his home.

CHAPTER TWENTY-FIVE

Much to Seb's disappointment, Anna remained at Fern Cottage for only a few hours. The gipsy girl's pleasure when she heard Seb's voice on his return from the farm confirmed Dolly's suspicions about the young couple's relationship.

When she turned and saw the same expression on her son's face she knew something had to be done. She did not know what had occurred between the young couple on their journey back to Swinbrook, she did not *want* to know, but she was determined it would go no further. Anna was a beautiful young girl, but she was blind – and a gipsy. She was not the girl for Seb.

Seb had found himself in many ways since leaving London in the middle of the year. His cough troubled him only rarely these days. He owned a horse, and was well thought of by Christian Timms. Seb had come far. Dolly had no intention of watching him throw it all away on a gipsy girl, however nice she might be.

Yet none of the gipsy men had returned to the forest and the women were constantly on the move. It would not be safe for Anna to return until Boz's release had been secured. Explaining that the only girl she knew of Anna's size was Carrie Hanks, Dolly took Anna off to the Hankses' cottage while Seb was eating – and she returned without her.

Carrie had insisted that Anna remain at the cottage,

Dolly said. Everyone was aware that Anna would not be happy staying within four walls, but she would be better off with Carrie than staying anywhere else.

During the time Anna was staying at the Hankses' cottage, the most daring highway robbery to date was committed. A carriage occupied by a cousin of the Duke of Marlborough and his wife was held up in broad daylight in the forest near Asthall Leigh, no more than a mile and a half from Swinbrook.

As with other recent robberies, it was impossible to blame this outrage upon the forest gipsies. Yet it added force to the outcry against those who used the forest of Wychwood to evade justice. There were renewed calls for the forest to be cut down and the land converted to productive farmland.

While Anna was in Swinbrook Seb spent most of his spare time at Tom Hanks's cottage. His excuse was that he was taking advantage of Carrie's offer to teach him to read and write. He fooled no one and no matter how much time he spent there it was never possible to get Anna to himself for longer than a few moments.

Anna herself did not help. She always seemed pleased to greet him, but she complained about being confined within the cottage and she was increasingly concerned about her brother.

Eventually, Seb approached Christian with a suggestion. The farmer had been saying ever since the Wychwood Forest Fair that he should have offered two more of the great Handley Farm horses for sale. Both were ready for work and selling them at the beginning of the winter would leave more fodder for the others. Seb suggested they should take the horses to the market at Oxford, adding, 'Many of the inquiries we had at the forest fair came from that side of the county. We might do well. Anna could come with us too and visit Boz in gaol.'

'We couldn't both go. This wet weather shows every sign of breaking. As soon as it does we must get on with the ploughing or we'll be behind.'

'Oh!' Seb tried hard to hide his disappointment. 'All right, I'll stay here and you can take Anna. If she doesn't get to Boz soon I can see her setting off to make her own way to Oxford.'

'The first field to be ploughed is on too much of a slope for anyone without experience to attempt it. I think it's a good idea to try to make a sale in Oxford – but it will have to be you who takes the horses.'

Seb tried hard to hide his delight. This was even better than he had hoped. He and Anna going to Oxford without Christian accompanying them.

Christian rested a hand on one of Seb's thin shoulders. 'I'll tell you something else, young Seb. I'll give you the price I expect the horses to fetch. If you can't make it, you can bring the price down. Make my price, and every penny above it is yours. You've proved to me you know horses – now's your chance to show you can sell 'em.'

Dolly did not share her son's enthusiasm for the forthcoming journey to Oxford with only a gipsy girl for company.

'Oh! And how many days do you think you might be away this time?'

'We'll be there and back the same day. I'll take Grye

and Anna and I can ride him back together.'

'Very cosy, I'm sure. Supposing I said *I'd* like to see Oxford too?'

Trying hard not to show disappointment, Seb said, 'I'd say it's a grand idea. Of course, it does mean we'll need to take the cart and that will take us longer. We'll need to leave the afternoon before, and not be back until midday the day after the market. But I'm sure we can find somewhere to sleep for the two nights we're away. Anna favours haystacks.'

'Does she now?'

As colour flooded Seb's cheeks, Dolly added, 'One day you can tell me a bit more about that remark, young man. All right, you go off to Oxford with Anna, but remember I'll be waiting up until you get home, so don't get finding any excuses for not coming home that same night.'

Seb and Anna set off for Oxford before dawn on market day. They made good time with Anna on Grye and Seb riding one of the great cart-horses without the aid of saddle or stirrups.

Outside the city, Seb drew on his experience at the Wychwood Forest Fair and spent half an hour grooming the two horses and plaiting ribbons in their manes.

Grumbling at the high cost of putting Grye up at the stables attached to an inn for no more than a half-day, Seb guided Anna to the Oxford gaol and made certain she was allowed inside before continuing to the market.

Seb had been fortunate in his choice of market days. Today was one of the city's special days for the sale of livestock and horses were being sold along the whole length of the great space of St Giles.

There was immediate interest in Christian's two horses and, in his turn, Seb was extremely interested in a number of horses being sold by a gipsy. He had three animals on offer. One mare had an ugly-looking skin disease, but it was this animal that particularly interested Seb. She had lines not unlike those of Grye and Seb felt that if the skin disease could be brought under control she would be a fine horse.

But soon Seb was surrounded by a number of prospective buyers who were attracted by the sheer bulk of the animals from Handley Farm.

So keen were the men to buy that, far from having to drop his prices, Seb put the horses on offer for a high price – and then found himself conducting an auction. When one man finally walked away leading the two great horses, Seb had made sixteen pounds for himself on the deal. This, added to the five pounds he had brought from home gave him twenty-one pounds in his pocket.

On the way to Oxford gaol he took another look at the horse with the skin disease and was more than ever convinced the horse was worth considering. However, he heard the gipsy owner tell a prospective buyer he had scorned an offer of twenty-seven pounds and Seb decided it would be a waste of time even to express an interest.

Boz was lodged in a communal cell in the gloomy interior of the ancient prison. Anna was with him. He was sharing it with a number of the Wychwood Forest gipsies who had been sentenced for vagrancy offences by Magistrate Peck, at Burford.

Boz showed little pleasure at receiving a visit from

Seb and there was no enthusiasm from the other gipsies when he offered to take messages back to their camp on his return.

Anna explained this by telling him that many of the gipsy women had moved from the forest to the Oxford area to be close to their husbands.

After spending a difficult hour trying to make conversation with Boz, Seb suggested it was time he and Anna left, in order to find something to eat before returning to Swinbrook.

'Anna won't be coming back to Swinbrook. At least, not yet.' Boz's statement was as brusque as it was surprising.

'What do you mean? She can't stay in Oxford alone.' Seb thought Boz had taken leave of his senses.

'She won't be alone. You heard her tell you that the wives of many of the Romanies sentenced by Magistrate Peck are here. She'll be among friends.'

'She's among friends at Swinbrook,' Seb persisted. He had been looking forward to the slow ride back on Grye, much of it in darkness, with Anna's arms encircling his waist. 'She and Carrie are getting along well.'

'You're gorgios at Swinbrook. She'll be among Romanies here. You'll find our people in a quarry at Cassington, about five miles outside Oxford on your way home. Leave Anna with them there.'

Once again Seb was faced with the assumption that he would do exactly as Boz wished. No 'please' or 'thank you'. It was a form of arrogance Seb had always found hard to accept from Boz.

'Perhaps you'd prefer not to have gorgios giving evidence for you at your trial? There were plenty of your own people who saw as much as me and Christian.'

'Give me a Romany judge and I won't need to call any witnesses at all. He'll know I'm telling him the truth.'

'Will you take me to Cassington, Seb? Please?'

After only a moment's hesitation, Seb nodded. 'All right, but we'd better go now if I'm to travel on to Swinbrook afterwards.'

Seb turned to leave without another glance in Boz's direction, but he had taken only a few paces along the corridor, heading towards a door guarded by a turnkey, when Boz called to him.

'Gorgio . . . Anna told me what you did for her at Charwelton.' Yet again there was no hint of gratitude. 'Where's Grye?'

'He's safe enough. Anna rode him to Oxford today. I put him in stables here in Oxford while I sold Christian Timms's mares. Do you want me to deliver him to Cassington too?'

'No. Take him back to Swinbrook with you. He's yours.'

Boz's astonishing offer shook Seb out of his mood of resentment. 'I can't take Grye from you. He's worth a small fortune.'

'Is he worth more than Anna? I've told you, he's yours now, gorgio. Any debt I owe to you is settled.'

Seb still could not believe his incredible good fortune when the gates of the gaol clanged behind him. As he guided Anna through the crowded streets, he asked, 'Do you think Boz really means it, Anna? Or will he change his mind when he's out of prison?'

'Boz doesn't change his mind in that way. He meant

everything he said. By rescuing me you put him in your debt. Deeply in your debt. Boz doesn't like to owe anyone anything, whether they're Romany or gorgio. He owes you nothing now and he'll be all the happier for it. Grye is yours.'

'I'd give Grye back to him in exchange for having you return to Swinbrook with me.'

Seb had a hold on Anna's arm and she reached up and gripped his hand. 'You mustn't say things like that, Seb. Boz is right. You're a gorgio and I'm Romany. We're different people. You'll see me soon enough. After Boz gets out of gaol we'll be returning to the forest above Swinbrook and Grye will still be yours. We'll talk some more then.'

'Carrie's going to miss you too.'

'I'll miss her, but tonight I'll go to sleep in the open, breathing good, clean, fresh air. I'm Romany, Seb. Nothing can ever change that.'

'We'll see. After the way my own life has changed in recent months I know that nothing's impossible.'

As they walked together, talking, they passed within sight of the St Giles horse-market and Seb brought Anna to a sudden halt.

'Anna. There's a mare I'd like to look at again. It's in a poor condition, covered in sores, but I think that it has some of Grye's breeding in its background.'

'Is it a Romany horse?'

'Yes.'

'Hmm! Then perhaps it's as well you spoke to me before buying it.'

The gipsy had sold the other two horses he had brought to market and was left with only the sore-covered mare.

When Seb asked him the price, the gipsy replied, 'Thirty-five pounds, and not a penny less.'

Seb was dismayed by the gipsy's words. He had anticipated beating him down from twenty-seven pounds, not from thirty-five, but Anna was talking to the man in his own language.

After a lengthy conversation between the two, the man glanced at Seb. 'The girl tells me you're a friend of Boz Buckland. Then the horse is yours, for thirty pounds – and you've got a bargain.'

'I heard you offering it to someone earlier for twenty-seven.'

'So? Since then it's become a seller's market. But, all right, twenty-seven pounds it is.'

Once again Anna took over the conversation and this time the argument between her and the horse-seller was more heated. Waving the man to silence, Anna ran her hand over the horse's legs, flanks and head. Finally she coaxed the animal to open its mouth and felt inside, fingering its teeth.

Her inspection completed, she rounded on the gipsy and this time the conversation was entirely one-sided. When she was done, she took Seb's arm and said, 'Come. We'll look for another horse for you.'

As they began to walk away, the gipsy called after them, 'All right – you can have it for twenty-two pounds, but it's less than it cost me!'

'Twenty.'

Anna threw the offer over her shoulder before Seb could pull out the money he carried in his pocket.

The gipsy horse-dealer mouthed something that would have sounded like an oath in any language.

'Do Romanies have robbers for friends now? All

right, the horse is yours for twenty.'

'Buy it, Seb. It's a good horse,' Anna whispered urgently, but her words were unnecessary – he already had the money in his hand.

As they walked away with the horse, followed on their way by the grumbling of the horse-dealer, Anna cut through Seb's excited stammer of gratitude. 'You've got a good mare, Seb. She and Grye should produce some wonderful foals. Don't worry about the sores. When we reach the camp at Cassington I'll have someone mix an ointment that will clear them up in no time. What will you call her?'

'I haven't thought of it yet. D'you have any ideas?'

'She's going to be the wife of a Romany horse, so why not call her that. *Romni* is a wife.'

'I like that. Right, Romni it is.'

They walked along in silence for a few minutes, but Anna sensed Seb was looking at her and, eventually, he found the words he wanted to say.

'What is the gipsy word for a Romany who marries a gorgio, Anna?'

'I'd be a *moola*, Seb. A ghost. Someone my people would look at and not see. Would you wish that on me?'

CHAPTER TWENTY-SIX

The months that preceded the Christmas of 1853 were happy ones for Dolly. Each day reinforced the wisdom of her decision to make a home in Swinbrook for herself and her son. Only when Seb became very excited, or exceptionally angry, did his cough return to bother him.

Seb had changed in other ways too. Gone was the sickly street urchin. He put in a full day's work at Handley Farm and Christian Timms was fond of saying he did not know how he had managed before Seb came to the farm. In addition, Seb was now the owner of *three* horses and ownership had brought with it a new-found pride in himself.

Many of Seb's long, early winter evenings were spent at the Hankses' cottage where Carrie was continuing to help him with his studies. Recently, Dolly had got into the habit of going to the cottage with him.

While the two young people worked together in a corner of the kitchen, Dolly and Tom would sit on either side of the fire, talking of London, of Swinbrook gossip, or of nothing in particular, simply enjoying each other's company.

Sometimes Tom would offer her a glass of ale. On other occasions she would bring a cake she had made. It was a cosy end to each day and Dolly felt more content than at any time since her late husband had gone abroad with his regiment.

Dolly was happy working at Handley Farm and in the house of Christian Timms. The Methodist farmer was a very kind employer. In fact, there were times when she found him *too* kind. *Too* holy. Dolly had just told Tom her thoughts, adding she would prefer to wait until she went to heaven to learn to live with a saint.

'Your pa and my ma get along very well together.' Seb spoke softly to Carrie, as the couple by the fireside laughed together at her remark.

'It's good to see Dad laughing again after so long. He used to laugh a lot when Mum was alive, but not so much since.'

'I don't suppose either of you have had very much to celebrate in recent years. Meredith Putt isn't an easy man to work for.'

'No, and he's getting worse. Dad says there's something funny going on up at the manor. Mr Meredith's taken to going off on long rides on his own and then denying that he's ever been out. Dad wonders whether there's anything mentally wrong with him.'

'It's no secret that he's got serious money problems. Christian says the whole village knows he's sunk far more money than he can afford into some scheme to bring the railway through Witney to Burford and on to the west.'

'Why should he want to do that?'

'That's what I asked Christian. He says it's to do with getting wool, lamb and corn to market, and bringing in coal for the blanket factories in Witney. If it came about Mr Meredith would make a lot of money as a shareholder in the railway company.'

'And if it doesn't?'

'Mr Meredith will *lose* a lot of money – more than he has already.'

'I hope he does lose it. I've only met him a couple of times, but he scares me. Even though I'm a cripple I sometimes feel he's stripped all the clothes off me when he looks at me.'

'Why do you say, "Even though I'm a cripple", Carrie? Having something wrong with you doesn't mean you stop being a person. You take Anna, now—'

'Ah! I wondered when we'd get around to talking about her.'

Seb looked at Carrie uncertainly, wondering what she meant. 'She doesn't let her blindness stop her from doing any of the things she wants to do.'

'So I've noticed!' Carrie grimaced in an embarrassed manner. 'No, that's an unkind thing to say, and I like Anna far too much to want to be unkind to her. But she's a special sort of person, Seb. We can't all find the strength to shake off our afflictions as she does.'

'But it doesn't mean that others can't find you attractive. You have lovely blue eyes, you're far cleverer than any girl I've ever known, and when you smile you're really very pretty.'

Even as he spoke Seb realised it was the first time he had ever looked really closely at Carrie. He felt vaguely guilty.

'I bet there are a lot more things you could do too, if you really wanted to. Riding, for instance. Have you ever ridden a horse?'

'Not for a long time. When I was little, Dad used to take me up to the manor sometimes and give me a ride on the farm-horses, but that was before I lost the use of my leg.'

'I mean *really* ride, Carrie. With a proper saddle . . . perhaps not astride, the way Anna does, but if we could get an old side-saddle I could teach you. I've got two riding-horses now. I could take you out for a ride some time, perhaps on a Sunday.'

Tom and Dolly had paused in their own conversation to listen to Seb. Now the ostler said, 'We've a couple of old side-saddles up at the manor that will never be used again. I'll ask Mrs Putt if I can have one. I can't see her refusing.'

'There you are, then, Carrie! We can go riding and you'll be able to travel farther and faster than anyone with two good legs.'

The trial of Boz Buckland was due to begin at the Oxford Assizes in mid-November. Late in October James Price, the Burford solicitor, rode to Swinbrook to ask Seb and Christian to attend and give evidence on Boz's behalf.

'There's little doubt that he'll be found innocent,' the solicitor assured them. 'But it's as well to be certain in matters of this nature, especially as Magistrate Peck's had a hand in the case.'

James Price, Christian and Seb were standing in the farmyard and the solicitor nodded in the direction of the Wychwood Forest, dominating the skyline to the north and east for as far as could be seen. 'When the forest is cleared and the land is enclosed I don't doubt you'll end up a land-wealthy man, Mr Timms.'

Christian frowned. 'Why should that be? The forest doesn't belong to me.'

'Not at the moment it doesn't, but you *do* have grazing rights?'

'Of course.'

'Then when the trees are cleared and the enclosure order goes through – and I don't doubt it will go through – you're entitled to a grant of enclosed land to compensate you for your loss of grazing rights. Surely you've discussed the matter with someone – the enclosure commissioners?'

'Until a moment ago I thought all this talk we've heard of enclosure was no more than mere rumour, spread by people like Meredith Putt.'

'Oh no, it's much more than that, Mr Timms. I'll take a few details from you before I go and ensure your claim is registered. We can't have all the enclosed land divided between manorial rights and the Crown. Both are renowned for their greed.'

'What about the rights of the gipsies? They've lived in the forest for as long as I've farmed Handley – and for very many years before that. Who'll be taking care of their rights?'

'I regret that an itinerant has very few rights in the eyes of the law, Mr Timms. His way of life precludes him from a great many of the benefits afforded to those of us who engage in honest toil.'

'What does that mean when it's put into everyday language?' Seb asked.

'It means that the gipsy has to change his way of life or be persecuted into extinction. Life is changing for all of us, Seb. Who'd have dreamed a few years ago that we'd have trains running on rails and able to take us from one end of the country to the other in the matter of a few hours? We need to bend to the shape of the changing world in order to exist. Your present-day gipsy is unbending, so he will break. I'm not saying this is the way it *ought* to be, I am merely stating an irrefutable fact.'

'They'll soon have the chance to find their way to a better life in the world to come,' said Christian to the Burford solicitor. 'I'm building a new chapel alongside Seb's cottage. It's my intention to go among the gipsies and invite them to worship with us. I feel it's a mission that's been thrust upon me. The Lord is offering me a challenge I shall gladly meet. Come down and let me show you what's been done so far. If all goes to plan we'll be worshipping there this Christmas Day.'

Seb watched the two men leave the farm. Then he set about his tasks in the stables with an angry zeal. Talking of a better life for gipsies in the next, uncertain world was all very well for Christian. Seb believed Boz, Anna and the other gipsies would find something tangible in this life preferable to a promise given to them by a gorgio preacher of a better life to come when they were dead.

CHAPTER TWENTY-SEVEN

The party that left Swinbrook, bound for the Winter Assizes at Oxford, was larger than Seb had anticipated. The two defence witnesses and solicitor James Price were accompanied by Dolly, Melody and Carrie.

Under Seb's tuition, Carrie had mastered the art of side-saddle riding and she was overjoyed with the new mobility it afforded her. She, Seb and James Price were riding, while Christian drove Dolly and Melody in a small gig he had recently purchased from one of his Methodist minister friends.

Dolly had saved all the pay she received from Christian and was going to Oxford to purchase some urgently required winter clothing. She had invited Carrie to accompany her and was both surprised and delighted when the invitation was accepted. Dolly had become very fond of Carrie and was pleased that the young cripple was beginning to leave her cottage more often. Dolly considered Carrie to be a good influence on Seb.

Melody had made a last-minute surprise plea to be included in the Oxford-bound party. Dolly believed it was made in order to avoid having to remain behind working on the farm, but she said nothing. Melody had the morals of a farm cat, but she was a kind-hearted girl and posed no threat to Dolly's plans for Seb.

It had been arranged, as before, that Harry Agg, the aged helper, should come in with one of his daughters to take care of the farm while the others were away.

In any other circumstances Melody would have enjoyed the opportunity to give orders to someone new about the farm. However, she became easily bored with work and saw this excursion as an opportunity to relieve such boredom and accompany Seb.

Contrary to Dolly's belief, Melody *did* have designs on Seb, but she was not looking for a long-term commitment. Her ambitions did not extend beyond an occasional half-hour in the warm privacy of the hay-loft – or anywhere equally convenient.

The weather for the journey was cold and uncertain, with a hint of early snow in the air as the party travelled to Oxford on the day before the trial was due to begin. They were to spend the nights before and after the trial at an inn owned by a former client of James Price. Here they would meet Calvin Price, brother of James, and Boz Buckland's defending barrister.

For Seb, the most exciting aspect of the long ride was the opportunity to see Anna once more. He thought about her a great deal during the time they were apart, but he was unable to discuss his thoughts with anyone.

Any mention of gipsies to Christian prompted the deeply religious farmer to launch immediately into great detail about the chapel alongside Fern Cottage, which was now nearing completion.

Dolly's reaction to discussion about Anna was to become tight-mouthed and to inform her son she had more to do than think about a gipsy girl. She frequently advised him to 'forget all about her'. Even Carrie, usually so ready to talk about anything that interested

Seb, would change the subject as soon as Anna's name entered into their conversation.

When the party had left the town of Witney behind, Seb reined in beside the gig and spoke to his mother. 'I'm going to ride on ahead. I'll meet up with you again on the outskirts of Oxford.'

'I'll come with you.' The unwelcome offer came from Carrie who had ridden up to the gig with Seb. James Price was some way behind the others, engaged in conversation with a traveller they had met on the road.

'Do you think you'll be able to keep up? You've never ridden such a distance as this before.'

'I'll keep up. If I don't, I'll know where to find you. I'll simply ask my way to the gipsy camp in the Cassington quarry.'

Seb was eager to see Anna again, but Carrie had no sense of urgency and Seb was obliged to curb his impatience at her leisurely pace, keeping Grye moving at a speed that enabled Carrie to stay with him.

When they eventually turned off the road into the quarry, Seb was surprised to see many more gipsies here than there had been on his earlier visit. Caravans, canvas homes and makeshift shelters covered the whole of the quarry floor. In between the temporary homes was an accumulation of rubbish that seemed to typify a gipsy encampment.

Seb recognised many of the gipsies as being among those who had made the Wychwood Forest their home and it was from one of these that he asked after Anna.

Raising his voice, the gipsy called in Romany, 'Anna! Your gorgio champion has arrived to rescue you from us.'

The gipsy's cry raised a laugh from those about him.

However, the laughter was not unkind and the glances that were thrown in Seb's direction were friendlier than at any time since he won the race at the Wychwood Forest Fair. Anna had told the story of her rescue by Seb and it had been repeated many times to newcomers, in the caravans and about the evening fires.

Seb's dogged search for Anna, his guile and daring final rescue, had lost little in the repeated telling.

Anna appeared from somewhere amidst the crowded encampment and seemed delighted that Seb had come to see her. He had been hoping she might greet him with a kiss. Instead, she grasped his hand and clung to it affectionately. Seb told himself she could hardly kiss him, a gorgio, in front of so many of her people, and consoled himself by telling her how much he had missed her.

Anna *did* kiss Carrie, but Seb realised this would be acceptable to her people.

'I am so happy that you have at last managed to travel so far from your cottage,' said Anna. 'Have you and Seb ridden from Swinbrook together?'

'There are a whole lot of us on our way to Oxford,' explained Seb hurriedly. 'Christian, my ma, Boz's solicitor – and Melody too. Carrie and I rode on ahead of the others to see you. I didn't expect to find so many of your people here. Is this a regular camping place for them?'

'Our people have come from all over the country to be in Oxford for Boz's trial. If he's convicted the authorities are going to have to deal with a lot of angry Romanies on the streets of Oxford.'

'James Price says Boz is bound to be found not guilty and released.'

His words brought a return of the warmth he had hoped Anna would show towards him. 'You've given me new hope, Seb, I hope you're right. A great many Romanies here say there's no justice to be found in the courts of England for our people, no matter who we have on our side. But there's someone here I'd like you to meet. Come with me.'

As Anna threaded her way carefully through the crowded quarry encampment, Carrie limped after her with Seb bringing up the rear. Along the way Seb acknowledged the smiles and greetings from many of the Wychwood gipsies he had met before. Eventually Anna stopped before a magnificently carved and painted caravan.

'Nahum! Alamena! Come out and meet two friends of mine.'

The caravan had stable doors, the top one standing open. At Anna's call a woman's face appeared at the open door and quickly withdrew. A moment later the other half of the door opened and a man stepped outside, closely followed by the woman who had looked out.

In his early twenties, the man was dressed in a far more elaborate fashion than any of the other gipsies in the encampment. Over his white shirt he wore a black waistcoat, elaborately embroidered with gold and silver thread. Black pantaloons were tucked inside tasselled Hessian boots, the whole conveying an impression of elegance, rather than foppishness.

The girl who followed him was dressed more simply, but she wore a colourful shawl about her shoulders. Tall for a woman, she was as dark-skinned as Anna and had wide dark eyes that sought out and found Seb.

Listening to the tread on the steps from the caravan, Anna waited until both girl and man had stepped to the ground before saying, 'I'd like you to meet Alamena. She's to marry Boz as soon as it's possible.'

The news took Seb by surprise and he said, 'I never knew Boz was likely to be married soon.'

Anna smiled. 'There's a lot you don't know about us, Seb.'

'But there is much I know about you, gorgio.' Nahum Plunkett advanced towards Seb with an outstretched hand. 'You are the one who rode to Charwelton and rescued Anna from the villagers who would have burned her as a witch. We are very grateful to you.'

Seb grasped the gipsy's hand but he resented the proprietorial attitude the man seemed to have towards Anna. Nevertheless, the gipsy had such an honest, open face it was difficult not to like him on sight.

'This is Nahum,' explained Anna. 'He is Alamena's brother. He is also a second cousin to Boz and me. He can not only read and write, but he's been to a university!'

Nahum smiled. 'There is always pride among our people when they can point to one of their own and boast that he has some learning.'

'I can understand why,' said Seb. 'Carrie has been trying to teach me to read and write. Anyone who has mastered both and gone on deserves the praise of others.'

'This girl has *learning*?' Nahum's eyes went to Carrie and he did not miss the awkward way she stood on her crippled leg. 'Who are we to be so pleased with ourselves when here is someone who has not only beauty, but learning too?'

Smiling at Carrie's sudden confusion, Nahum said gently, 'Anna has told me of your great kindness to her. Such things are never forgotten by our people. I would like to offer you my personal thanks.'

Carrie blushed in a manner Seb had never seen before, and he wondered what there was about this man that made everyone to whom he spoke pleased to be noticed by him.

Nahum carried a natural air of authority that did not accord with his status as a member of the lowest stratum of life in the kingdom. He also seemed to be assuming a great deal of personal responsibility for Anna, which Seb resented.

'You'll meet another friend of your people tomorrow. Christian Timms will be giving evidence for Boz too. He's just built a chapel next to our cottage. He hopes to persuade the Wychwood gipsies to attend services there. He'd be absolutely delighted if Boz and Alamena were to be married there.'

'Ah yes, Christian Timms. I met him once, many years ago when I was a boy, but I doubt if he'll remember me. Yes, he has the reputation of being a good and honest man.'

Nahum gave Seb a direct look. 'I understand Boz rewarded you with a horse for finding Anna and returning her to us?'

'That's right. I rode it from Swinbrook today. It's tied over there.'

'Boz was on his way to sell it to *me* when he was arrested. However, it was his to give and no reward is too great for the return of kin. Would you mind if I had a look at the horse?'

Nahum went with Seb to where Grye was tied and

once again he observed the deference shown to Nahum by the other gipsies.

When they reached Grye, Nahum walked around the animal making appreciative noises. 'Yes, it's certainly a superb horse. I can't remember when I've seen a finer animal. Would you take two hundred for him?'

'Two hundred *pounds*?' Seb looked at the other man in disbelief. He could not believe he was serious, and yet . . . 'No, I don't think I would.'

'All right, two hundred and fifty.'

Seb gulped painfully. He could not help feeling his mother would have him locked away if she knew he was turning down such an incredible sum of money for a horse, but he shook his head.

Nahum shrugged. 'You're a good judge of horses, gorgio. A man could found his fortune with a stallion like this, if you could only find a mare to put to him.'

'I believe I already have. She's the mare Carrie rode here. I bought her in Oxford when she was in a poor condition. Anna helped me choose her. She's tethered over there.'

Nahum examined the mare and turned back to Seb with an expression of envy on his face. 'The Buckland family owe you a great deal for all you've done to help both Boz and Anna, but you'll never be sorry. With these two animals you have the chance to breed horses that will make you the envy of every knowledgeable horse-dealer in the land. To ask you to sell the mare after you've refused to part with the stallion would be like asking you to cut off your left hand instead of the right. But I ask for first refusal when a foal is born to the pair of them. Is it a deal?'

The gipsy held out his hand and after only a

moment's hesitation, Seb shook it.

Seb and Carrie remained at the camp for an hour, during which time Nahum flirted openly with Carrie, bringing a sparkle to her eyes that Seb had not thought possible.

Seb angled to get Anna away from the others for a while so he might speak to her, but there was no way it could be achieved. Anna did not leave the fireside once during the hour Seb and Carrie were at the camp, and Alamena was always close when he tried to speak privately to her.

Eventually the time came when Seb told Carrie they must leave the encampment and set off to rejoin the others.

Only now did Anna display any untoward affection for him by holding his hand for longer than was necessary when they said goodbye.

'Thank you for calling in to see how I am, Seb, and for coming all this way to help Boz. I'll be at the court tomorrow too.'

This was as much as she had said directly to him during the whole time he had been at the encampment and he rode away with a feeling of disappointment. He hardly said a word to Carrie along the way, but she was so full of talk about Nahum, he doubted whether she noticed.

They met up with the others on the road to Oxford and Seb told his mother and Christian of the gipsy's offer for Grye. As Seb had anticipated, his mother thought he was insane not to have sold for such an unheard-of price. She even suggested that Seb should take the horse back to the gipsy in the hope he had not changed his mind.

Christian agreed with Seb. He *did* remember Nahum and, what was more, he was *very* impressed that Boz should be marrying Nahum's sister. As he explained to Seb, 'You'll hear a lot of rot spoken about gipsy kings and queens and the gipsies themselves will scoff at such talk. No one among them has the right to such a title – but if they *did* have royalty, then the man you've just met would be the heir to the throne – and his sister a royal princess. They both belong to the most influential gipsy family in the country. It's even said their father had the ear of King William the Fourth. If Nahum's coming down here has anything to do with the enclosure of Wychwood Forest, then Meredith Putt might well find he's involved in more of a fight than he ever bargained for.'

CHAPTER TWENTY-EIGHT

The street outside the Oxford Assize Courts was thronged with gipsies, most dressed in their colourful Sunday best. There were so many of them that the heavily out-numbered constables ringing the court building were looking decidedly nervous.

Few of the gipsies attempted to enter the high-ceilinged courtroom. Those who did were firmly and not always politely turned away by the tall-hatted city policemen. Only three of Boz Buckland's people were allowed to take a place inside it: Nahum, Alamena and Anna.

Their admittance had been secured by Calvin Price, Boz's barrister. He insisted that Anna was required as a defence witness and he wanted her to be where he could see her until her brother's case began. The others would remain to look after and guide her to and from the court, as required.

Seb and Christian took their places in the same row of pew-like seats as the three gipsies and their presence was acknowledged by Nahum and Alamena. However, much to Seb's chagrin, he and Christian were separated from the gipsies by two men who smelled as though they had come to court direct from a farmyard.

The three women from Swinbrook had decided not to attend the court. Dolly and Carrie were looking around the shops and stalls in the Oxford streets. Melody said nothing of where she intended going, saying only that she was not going to court 'just to hear some old judge sentencing a Romany to prison'.

The first man to be brought before the Assize Court judge faced the accusation of raping 'a girl of simple mind'. The man, grey-haired and frail, had almost fulfilled his biblical life expectation of three-score-years-and-ten, and was scarcely less witless than his victim.

The old man pleaded guilty to the charge and thereby earned the judge's approbation. He also earned a sentence of a lifetime's transportation to Australia. It was doubtful whether he understood the meaning of the sentence and was led away smiling toothlessly and bobbing his gratitude to the judge.

During the to-ing and fro-ing that went on as court officials prepared for the next case, someone entered the court-room and took up a place in the row of seats behind Seb. Not until the new arrival leaned forward and whispered, 'Hello,' did Seb realise it was Giles Aplin, the Burford constable.

'What are you doing here? Have you come to listen to the case against Boz?'

'No, I'm quite confident you've tied that up securely with James Price and his brother. I'm more interested in the man who's coming up now – or to be more accurate, in his companions who still remain at large.'

Even as the Burford constable spoke a man was being led up the stairs from the cells to the court-room, escorted by two prison warders. He looked vaguely familiar, but Seb did not at first recognise him.

During a brief introduction to the case, it was

revealed that the man had been arrested by Giles Aplin in the forest near Shipton-under-Wychwood on a charge of robbery – highway robbery – with violence. However, once in custody it had been discovered that he was wanted in neighbouring Buckinghamshire for murdering a man during the course of a similar robbery. As this felony had taken place in an area that was included within the jurisdiction of the Assize Court judge, it was being proceeded with today.

When the prisoner was asked how he pleaded, he replied in a resigned voice, 'I'm guilty, just get on with it.'

During the buzz of interest caused by the accused man's reply, Seb leaned his head back and spoke to Giles Aplin. 'I've seen that man before.'

'Where? Was anyone else with him?'

When Seb hesitated, the Burford constable urged, 'It's important, Seb. So far they've shot and seriously wounded two of the men they've robbed. Sooner or later they'll kill someone in Wychwood, for sure.'

'I saw him at the Dore's Lodge inn, near Leafield, the night I was returning from the Wychwood Forest Fair. He was with Will Shaw, son of the kitchen-maid at Swinbrook Manor.'

'Will Shaw! I suspected as much, although I still have to prove they were working together. It doesn't help me find the third man either – and there *must* be another involved. Neither the man in court today nor Will Shaw has brains enough to execute some of the robberies that have been committed around the Wychwood area, let alone plan them.'

Giles Aplin glanced about the court-room and gave a start of surprise. 'Talking of men who've sadly wasted their education and breeding . . .'

Seb followed Aplin's glance and was as surprised as the constable to see Meredith Putt standing at the rear of the court-room.

As though talking to himself, Aplin said softly, 'I know Putt's friendly with Magistrate Peck, but I hardly think he's ridden such a distance merely in order to report back to his friend on the outcome of Boz Buckland's case. Peck would learn the result quickly enough through official channels.'

'Perhaps it has something to do with the gipsy who's sitting with Anna. Christian believes his father is probably the only gipsy alive who's capable of influencing the enclosures issue.'

'Is that so?' Giles Aplin cast a glance in Nahum's direction. 'I must see if I can have a talk with him afterwards. If he has such power he might be able to do something for *me*.'

Although the man in the dock had pleaded guilty to murder, the prosecution outlined its case against him. It seemed Harry Gaunt was suspected of a great many crimes and there were numerous warrants out for his arrest. The murder for which he was being tried had been committed during the course of a robbery, when he battered his victim to death with a stave of wood.

When the prosecutor had ended his summary, the judge looked at Gaunt over the rim of his half-moon glasses. 'You've heard what has been said by the prosecution. Is there anything you would like to say in reply?'

The prisoner shook his head.

The judge frowned. 'The court wishes to hear your reply, not surmise what is meant by a movement of your head. I repeat, do you have anything to say?'

'No, m'lord.'

'The charge is true?'

'Yes . . . m'lord.'

'Then I have no alternative but to pass the only sentence the law allows for such a crime. Harry Gaunt, you have pleaded guilty to a barbarous crime, committed on the Queen's highway, where all Her Majesty's subjects have a right to pass in safety. The sentence of this court is that you shall be taken from here to the place whence you have come. There, on a date to be fixed, you will be taken to a place of execution and hanged by the neck until you are dead. May the Lord have mercy on your soul, more mercy than you showed to your unfortunate victim. Take him away, please.'

The judge's words made Seb go cold. He was looking at a man who lived, who spoke and who had feelings, for all he was a convicted murderer. Yet he was to be taken away and in a matter-of-fact manner have a rope placed about his neck that would extinguish his life as though it were of no more importance than a candle flame.

As he was led away, the condemned man looked about the court, as though seeking someone. Giles Aplin turned, hoping the glance might fall on someone he knew, but Gaunt's glance never lingered upon any one person and when Seb looked, he saw that Meredith Putt had left the court.

The next case on the list was the one being brought against Boz – or, in the words of the court, 'The case against Boswell Buckland, of no fixed abode, charged with being concerned with others unknown, in robbing one Leslie Gunther, on the Queen's highway.'

Looking at Boz, the clerk of the Assizes said, 'You've heard the charge. How do you plead?'

'Not guilty.'

Boz's words rang out in the crowded court-room and as a sigh rose from the public gallery, one of the ushers raised his voice. 'All witnesses in the case against Boswell Buckland will please clear the court.'

As Seb and Christian edged their way along the line of seated people, Anna was being guided from the court-room by Alamena. Nahum remained behind.

Outside, in a crowded corridor, Seb managed to speak to Anna and tell her not to worry. 'It'll be all right, Anna. I know it will. Boz is going to be found not guilty.'

'That's what I've been telling her.' Alamena's thin-lipped statement was as much an expression of disapproval because Seb had spoken to Anna, as an attempt to reassure her.

It was half an hour before Christian was called to give evidence, leaving Seb feeling more nervous than ever. He had hoped to use this opportunity to talk with Anna. Now it had arrived he could think of nothing but trivia to say.

The door to the court-room opened. Seb's name was called in a loud voice that echoed along the corridor and he stepped back inside the court-room to give his evidence in defence of Boz.

Nerves threatened to overwhelm Seb completely when he stood in the high, pulpit-like witness-box and stared out over the well of the court to where the judge sat resplendent in his red robes and grey wig, staring at Seb over the rim of his spectacles.

Calvin Price was also wearing a wig, and a black

gown, but his smile was the same one Seb had seen the previous evening when the barrister had visited the inn where they were staying, and somehow he seemed far less formidable than the other court officials.

'Will you please tell the court, in your own words, what happened on the fifteenth day of September this year?'

'You mean the day I went to Wychwood Forest Fair . . . ?' Seb began to tell of travelling from the Swinbrook farm taking the horses for sale at the fair, but he was interrupted by the judge.

'Mr Quilter, this court does not need to know *every* detail of what you did that day. Will you please begin by telling me when you met the accused, and what happened thereafter?'

'He asked me to ride Grye, his horse, in the six-mile race being held at the fair . . .'

'Why you? Why did not he or one of the other gipsies ride the horse?'

'Boz couldn't ride, he'd broken his leg only a short time before and he could hardly walk, let alone ride in a race. He'd made arrangements for another of the gipsies to ride for him, but the gipsy got so drunk he wouldn't have been able to stay on the horse . . .'

The laughter in the court-room was silenced abruptly by yet another glare over the rim of the judge's spectacles.

'You won the race, I believe.'

'Yes, m'lord.'

'Do you know how much prize money was won by the accused?'

'Yes, two hundred guineas – but he won a lot more on wagers.'

'Hmm! I don't think this court will concern itself with such a matter. Thank you.'

Calvin Price smiled reassuringly at Seb. 'I have no more questions for the witness, my lord.'

Seb would have left the witness-box, but Price signalled for him to remain. Moments later another bewigged barrister stood up. Smaller than Price, he too had a smile, but there was little warmth in it.

'Mr, er, *Quilter*? You were paid to perform this ride, I believe?'

'Yes, Boz paid me ten pounds – but he gave me an extra ten when I won.'

'No doubt you also won a great deal of money as a result of wagers made by you on the result of the race?'

'Before Boz gave me money for riding Grye I never had any money to gamble with.'

'I see. You are friends with the accused, are you not?'

'I wouldn't say that. It's very difficult to get to know Boz.'

'You are saying you are *not* a friend of Mr Buckland?'

'Not really, I'm not.'

'Hmm! Can you put a value on the horse you call Grye?'

'I think so. I refused an offer of two hundred and fifty pounds for him only yesterday.'

'*You* refused? Are you telling the court you are now the owner of this very valuable horse, Mr Quilter? You, who had no money to back a horse, now *own* a horse valued at two hundred and fifty pounds? I suggest that is the price paid by the accused for you to come into court and tell a pack of lies today.'

Calvin Price sprang to his feet and protested at the

counsel's allegation, but Seb was giving his own heated reply to the prosecuting barrister.

'It's nothing of the sort. Boz gave me the horse for finding his sister, Anna, and bringing her back to Swinbrook.'

'Finding his sister . . . ?' The judge looked puzzled. 'Will you explain that please, Mr Quilter?'

'Boz's sister's blind. When he was arrested in Byfield she was left behind and didn't know anything of what had happened. She had the caravan and all their belongings thrown into the river, was beaten by a tinker and then set upon by some boys who were going to burn her because they thought she was a witch. When I'd found her and brought her back Boz gave me Grye. He said he could always buy another horse, but could never buy another sister.'

'That, at least, can be accepted as an irrefutable argument,' commented the judge, dourly. 'Can this incredible story be verified, Mr Price?'

'The girl in question is outside the court, my lord. She is to be my next witness. I have questioned her and can confirm that she indeed suffered a series of most harrowing experiences.'

'I see.'

When the judge returned his attention to the prosecuting counsel, the barrister was taken by surprise. He stood up in such a fluster that his wig was knocked askew and he never quite succeeded in settling it in its original position. 'Mr Parsons, I have listened to two defence witnesses. Both have given their evidence in an open and honest manner. Indeed, the first witness would appear to be a man of some substance and the second, having turned down an offer of two hundred and fifty pounds for a horse that was given to him as a gift, will undoubtedly one day achieve a similar status. You have called no witnesses to substantiate a case which, in my considered opinion, is based on nothing more than 'circumstantial evidence of the flimsiest kind. I have no doubt you would wish to avoid wasting any more of this court's time. Need I say more?'

'My lord's intimation is perfectly clear.' The barrister shut his leather-bound folder with a show of resignation. 'If it pleases the court, the prosecution wishes to offer no more evidence against Boswell Buckland and withdraws its case.'

'I thank you for wasting no more of my court's time, Mr Parsons. A formal verdict of not guilty will be recorded. I also wish notification of my displeasure be passed on to the magistrate who committed this case for trial. Mr Buckland, you are free to go and you take with you the apologies of this court.'

Someone at the rear of the court-room rushed outside to convey news of the verdict to the waiting gipsies. The roar of approval with which it was received could be heard in the court-room as Boz was being hugged by Anna and Alamena, who had rushed in to him, and pummelled on the back by Nahum.

'I think we've performed our duty satisfactorily, Seb. Shall we find the others and head back to Swinbrook?'

Seb looked to where Boz and his companions were being hustled from the court-room. In the doorway Wychwood gipsies were clamouring to congratulate the newly freed man.

'Yes, let's go.'

Seb should have felt delighted that Boz had been set free. He *was* delighted, but his feelings were not as clear-cut as they might have been. He had been looking forward to his reunion with Anna, here in Oxford, hoping he might re-establish the bond they had forged on the road back from Charwelton. He wanted an opportunity to recall the words they had said to each other.

Instead, Anna had succeeded in reminding him of the wide gulf that separated Romany and gorgio.

'Cheer up, Seb. Anyone would think you were on the losing side.' The words were accompanied by a slap on the back from Constable Giles Aplin.

Seb watched Anna and the others as they were swallowed up by the crowd of noisy and jubilant gipsies who spilled into the court-room, defying all the efforts of court officials to eject them.

'Yes – and they might be right.'

CHAPTER TWENTY-NINE

For more than a week after the Oxford court hearing the lanes around Swinbrook echoed to the cries of gipsy children, the creak of caravans and horse harnesses, and the disapproving muttering of the villagers. The gipsies of Wychwood were returning home – and with them they brought many others, arriving to attend the marriage of Boz Buckland and Alamena Plunkett.

Christian was probably the only man in the whole area who was unaware of the massive influx of gipsies. His chapel was nearing completion and he spent every daylight hour there, leaving the day-to-day running of Handley Farm in Seb's hands.

Seb was still being helped by Carrie with his lessons, but since returning from Oxford he had arrived at the Hankses' cottage later each evening. One night the hour was so late that Carrie had put away the books and was preparing for bed. He settled down to work, but looked so tired that Carrie found it impossible not to feel pity for him.

'I'm sorry,' he apologised, after making the same simple error for the third time. 'I've had a very busy day. There's been a lot to do up at the farm and this evening I had to put one of the mares to the stallion.'

Carrie's sniff gave no hint of her sympathy. 'That's what you say. I wouldn't be surprised if it didn't have something to do with Melody being up there to "give you a hand". You had more to say to her on the way back from Oxford than you said to me.'

This was not true. Seb had said very little to anyone. Melody had chattered to *him* almost non-stop, telling him about her day in the city. Seb remembered hardly any of what had been said. But Carrie's words reminded him of other incidents with the young tinker-girl.

Seb's blush took Carrie by surprise. 'Don't tell me she *has* added you to her long list of village boys?'

'I've got far too much to do up at the farm to bother with the likes of Melody.'

'That's not what I've heard.' Carrie had heard nothing, but she wanted his explanation for the blush.

'Are we going to stand here all night and talk of Melody, or get on with some writing? If it's just talk then I'll go home now and do something useful – like sleep.'

Seb had no cause to feel guilty, but he was on the defensive. Melody had come in the stables from the cow-shed while the stallion and mare were mating and suggested to him that he might prefer to be doing something similar with her instead of looking after a 'load of old horses'.

He was saved from making a decision when a noise from the cow-shed suggested one of the cows had broken free of the rope securing her to the milking stall. He was embarrassed by Carrie's questioning because he was still not certain in his own mind whether or not he would have accepted Melody's uncomplicated offer.

Carrie shut the book she had just opened with a force that added nothing to the life of the book. 'If that's what you want then don't let me stop you. I was just going to bed myself, anyway.' Her face was so tight and pale, it made her eyes appear unusually large.

Seb rubbed his chin ruefully. 'I'm sorry, Carrie. I *have* been working extra hard today. Old Harry Agg didn't come in to work and with Christian so busy on that chapel of his there's more to do up at Handley than I can rightly manage on my own. But I shouldn't take out my tiredness on you.'

Carrie reached out a hand and gave his thin forearm a squeeze. 'It's all right, Seb. I understand. My dad gets like it sometimes.'

'Where is he tonight?' Carrie's sympathy had moved Seb far more than had her anger.

'They're having a party at the manor to celebrate Sir Nelson's promotion to Brigadier. Dad's gone to help out with the stabling of the horses. He said I was to tell you to help yourself to a beer from the barrel in the outhouse. I think he knows how hard you're working up at the farm.'

Such was Tom Hanks's trust in Seb that he thought nothing of leaving him with Carrie if he needed to be absent on any evening.

Settling down at the kitchen table to follow Carrie's instructions, Seb laboriously copied words that she wrote for him. They worked mostly in silence and he paused only when she said suddenly, 'I saw Anna today.'

'Where?' It was a foolish question. Despite her recent outings, Carrie rarely left the vicinity of cottage and garden.

'She came here with Boz. They were on their way to the forest, but stopped to show off Boz's new caravan.

Nahum and Alamena were with them in their own caravan. Anna said she'd probably be seeing you soon when Boz comes to the farm to talk to Christian.'

The hopes that Carrie's remarks had raised were dashed again by her final words. Anna was not coming to see *him*, but Christian.

'Why should Boz want to talk to Christian?'

'It's something to do with his marriage to Alamena. They've heard about Christian's new chapel and I think they'd like to be the first to be married there.'

'That will please Christian, but it surprises me. I would have thought that Boz, more than most people I know, would have scorned a chapel wedding as being for gorgios.'

'I don't suppose he'll have changed his views, but he's marrying into the Plunkett family and even my dad knows how influential they are. If the Plunketts say it's to be a chapel wedding, then that's what it will be.'

That night when Seb went home to Fern Cottage there was still a lantern burning inside the chapel. He looked in to see Christian whitewashing a wall, while Dolly sat on a bench stitching kneelers and chatting to him.

'Well, this is a hive of industry, and no mistake. You'd better hurry and have the chapel completed, Christian. Anna and Boz called in on Carrie today. It seems he's hoping that he and Alamena will be the first to be married here.'

Dolly and Christian exchanged a glance that was filled with hidden meaning. Turning back to him, both spoke at the same time.

'Seb—'

Christian signalled for Dolly to speak first but she

was silent for many moments before looking up at her son uncertainly. 'Seb . . . Tom came in to see me on his way to the manor tonight. He . . . he's asked me to marry him, here in Christian's chapel, when it's completed.'

Seb was struck dumb as the full import of his mother's words sank in.

Watching him, Dolly's expression shifted from apprehensive expectation to dismay. Then Seb opened his arms and mother and son hugged each other, both too choked with emotion to say anything for a long time.

Finally, as she fought back tears, Dolly said, 'I've been so worried about what you would say, Seb. If you hadn't approved of him I don't know what I would have done. You're everything to me, and always have been, but Tom makes me feel so . . . safe. I know there have been lots of times when I've seemed to be strong. I've had to be, for your sake, but that's not how I feel for most of the while, Seb. There are times when I'm afeared I'll break down and show the world just how weak I am.'

'You don't have to explain that to me, Ma. I've watched you far more often than you know and I've often wished I was stronger so I could do something more for you. Soon I will be, but that don't matter now. You'll have Tom and he's a good man. You couldn't have chosen better.'

The tears were flowing freely now and Dolly clung to her son. 'You don't know how relieved I am to hear you say that, Seb. If you'd said you were opposed to me marrying Tom, I don't know what I'd have done.'

'There was never any fear of that.' A sudden thought

came to Seb. 'Carrie doesn't know anything of this, does she?'

'I don't know. I don't suppose so. When Tom left me he had to go straight on to the manor.'

'Can I go back and tell her?'

'I don't know, Seb. Wouldn't her pa want to be the first to tell her?' Even as she spoke, Dolly's thoughts were moving ahead. When she and Tom were married, Carrie and Seb would see much more of each other. Carrie's crippled leg did not prevent her from doing anything she really wanted to do and she was a bright, sensitive and kind-hearted girl. A girl who would be good for Seb.

'I'm sure Tom wouldn't mind if you really wanted to be the one to break the news to Carrie.'

The Hankses' cottage was in darkness when Seb reached it, but the flames of the kitchen fire traced a pattern of light and shadow upon the window. Thinking that Carrie might be sitting in the darkness beside the fire, Seb let himself in.

Carrie was not there, but as he made his way to the door, a voice from the top of the stairs called, 'Is that you, Dad?'

'No, it's Seb.'

The stairs creaked in protest as Carrie ran down awkwardly and collided with Seb in the darkness. 'What is it? Has something happened to my dad?'

'No, it's all right.' Seb was gripping Carrie's upper arms and he could feel her trembling. 'It's *good* news. At least, I hope you'll think so. He called in at Fern Cottage on his way to the manor. He's asked my ma to marry him. She's said she will.'

Feeling Carrie stiffen beneath his hands, he added, 'I

think they'll make each other very happy, Carrie. I really do.'

'I've never doubted it, ever since your mum started coming here. But . . . what do you think? Does it make you happy too?'

'Yes. Life's been tough for both of 'em, and I like your pa very much.'

Taking Seb by surprise, Carrie suddenly hugged him. 'It is wonderful news, Seb. I'm pleased. *Really* pleased, for both of them.'

Seb found holding Carrie pleasantly disconcerting and he made no move to release her. 'I'm pleased too, but I wasn't sure how you'd take it.'

Pulling away from him abruptly, Carrie said, 'We'll be step-brother and step-sister.'

'Yes, I suppose we will. I hadn't thought about it.'

'Will you come to live here?'

Seb realised there was more to his mother marrying Tom Hanks than he had realised.

'I don't think so. One of us will be quite enough for a couple of newly-weds to get used to. I'll probably stay at Fern Cottage.'

When Seb left the cottage Carrie was still bewildered and feeling a little apprehensive. She would have liked to have Seb beneath the same roof as herself . . . but *not* as a step-brother.

CHAPTER THIRTY

Tom Hanks's intended marriage to Dolly Quilter was known to every man, woman and child who lived in Swinbrook less than twenty-four hours after his proposal. At any other time the news would have proved a gift to the acid-tongued gossips of the village. They would have made much of the fact that both future partners lived so close to each other, in cottages far removed from the censorious eyes of the villagers.

But during the night an event had occurred to send a *real* sense of shock and outrage through the small community.

The highwaymen of Wychwood Forest, undeterred by the capture and conviction of Harry Gaunt, struck again. This time the outcome had been what Constable Giles Aplin had always feared and predicted. And the robbery had culminated in not just one death, but two.

The outrage had taken place much closer to Swinbrook than any of the earlier robberies, the victims being the elderly Sir Vincent and Lady Sybil Hammond. The titled couple had been robbed and murdered whilst returning to their South Lawn home, only two miles from the party they had been attending at Swinbrook Manor.

Two highwaymen had stepped from the forest and brought the light carriage to a halt. Threatening the carriage driver with guns, they ordered its occupants to step down.

Unfortunately for everyone concerned, Sir Vincent kept a loaded small-bore pistol in the carriage for just such an emergency. As he stepped out he fired the weapon, wounding one of the two robbers. The second highwayman returned the fire and Sir Vincent fell to the ground. As Lady Hammond went to the aid of her mortally wounded husband the highwayman callously turned the second barrel of his pistol upon her and shot her through the head at point-blank range.

Ignoring the terrified coachman who leaped from the carriage and ran into the forest after witnessing the shootings, the highwayman stripped Lady Hammond of the considerable quantity of jewellery she had worn to the manor party. Next, he robbed the dying Sir Vincent of his money and a valuable gold watch before riding off, supporting his wounded accomplice.

In Swinbrook the villagers stood at every doorway, and in small groups in the narrow lane. Others sat in the tap-room of the Swan Inn discussing the robbery. One word was common to every gossiping group. The word was 'gipsies'.

Giles Aplin called in to see Seb later that same day wearing a uniform that denoted a new status. The Burford man had been appointed Superintending Constable by the Court of Quarter Sessions. His appointment meant he was responsible for overseeing the police work of a wide area which included Burford, Swinbrook and much of the Wychwood Forest. The appointment was an attempt by the Oxfordshire authorities to avoid the example set by the majority of other counties.

'They've established properly organised police forces under a single authority,' Giles Aplin explained. 'Oxfordshire will need to follow suit eventually, but until they do I and others like me will have to do our best to maintain the law.'

'You're here to investigate the robbery and murder, I dare say.' Seb talked as he curried one of the big horses. It had been rolling in the mud of the field where the animals were turned out for exercise. 'Do you have any ideas yet?'

'A few,' was the surprising admission. 'However, unlike everyone else in these parts, I *don't* believe it has anything at all to do with the Wychwood gipsies.'

'You, Christian and I must be the only ones around here who aren't blaming them, but what we think isn't going to change people's opinions.'

'It is if I can prove them wrong – and that's where I could do with your help.'

'Me? I know nothing of police work.'

'No, but you know gipsies. When we were at the Oxford Assizes you pointed out a gipsy and told me he had a great deal of influence among the others. Has he come to Wychwood?'

'You're talking of Nahum Plunkett. Yes, he's here. His sister is to marry Boz.'

'Could you find him and bring him to the farm? I want to speak to him but if I were to go into Wychwood and find him I'd likely discredit him, and that would defeat my object.'

'What is your object?'

'Quite simply, to find these highwaymen before they

kill someone else. Unfortunately, it might prove even more difficult than before. The jewellery they stole from Lady Hammond is worth many thousands of pounds. The highwaymen might have made enough money from this robbery alone to lie low for a long while. Personally, I don't think so for a number of reasons. I believe this gipsy leader might be able to help me to speed things up.'

It was evident that Giles Aplin intended saying no more until he had spoken to Nahum Plunkett. After asking a few more questions that were left unanswered, Seb took Grye from his stall and set off for the gipsy encampment.

An air of apprehension hung over the whole camp. Seb realised they too must have heard of the two murders and were wondering what action the authorities were likely to take this time.

On this visit Seb did not find it necessary to ask for the Buckland caravan. When he stopped at a cooking-fire on which a plump Wychwood pheasant was roasting, a woman at the fireside immediately pointed to a pair of smart, colourfully painted caravans.

Anna was seated on the steps of one, stitching binding to the back of a rag rug. Dismounting, Seb walked Grye to the foot of the steps and said quietly, 'Hello, Anna. Carrie told me you'd come back to the forest.'

Seb's impression was that her thoughts were a long distance from the Wychwood Forest. This was confirmed when his greeting startled her. However, the smile that replaced the surprised expression made Seb's knees go weak.

'Seb! What a lovely surprise. I was just thinking about you.'

Rising to her feet she held out her hands and when he grasped them she squeezed his fingers tightly.

'What are you doing here, in the forest?' Releasing his hands abruptly, the smile disappeared. 'I hope it has nothing to do with the terrible business that happened on the South Lawn road last night?'

'No,' he lied. 'I've been trying to think of an excuse to come to see you and now I've found one. I want to speak to Nahum.'

'Nahum? What business do you have with him?' asked Anna.

Alamena had appeared in the doorway of the adjacent caravan as Seb arrived. He had observed her disapproval when Anna held out her hands to him and he knew she was listening to all that was being said between them.

'He said he'd be interested in any foal sired by Grye from a good mare. I've got one ready to put to him and I wanted him to see her, to know if he'd be interested.'

'Is this Romni, the mare you bought in Oxford?'

'No, it's another that Christian has had for some time. It'll soon be ready.'

'Nahum will be interested in any foal sired by Grye. He's always regretted not being able to buy him.'

'Then perhaps he'd like to come back with me and have a look at the mare now, while she's in tip-top condition.'

'Alamena, Seb would like to talk to Nahum.'

Anna hardly raised her voice to call to the other girl and Seb realised that Anna must have somehow realised Nahum's sister was listening at the doorway of the next caravan.

When Alamena disappeared inside, Seb said very

softly, 'I was disappointed that you didn't call at Fern Cottage, or the farm, to say you were back.'

'When I'm in a caravan with Boz driving I can only stop at the places he approves.' Anna's voice was as quiet as Seb's.

'Are you saying he doesn't approve of me?'

'He thinks more of you than of any other gorgio he knows. But you're not Romany . . . and I'm his sister.'

'Where's Boz now?'

'He's gone to Witney town, to have a special suit made for his wedding.'

The conversation came to an abrupt end when Nahum emerged from the next caravan. He, at least, seemed genuinely pleased to see Seb.

'How are you, Seb? It's good to see you again.' Advancing to shake hands, he looked from Seb to Anna and said, 'Of course, you two are old friends. That's reason enough for you to come visiting. But Alamena said you wished to speak to me. What can I do for you?'

Seb repeated his story and suggested Nahum return to Handley Farm with him and take a look at the mare.

'Of course.' Something in the way Nahum looked at him suggested to Seb that his story had not taken in the gipsy leader. 'I'll fetch a horse and be with you in a few minutes.'

Seb had exchanged no more than a few unimportant sentences with both Alamena and Anna by the time Nahum returned, leading a horse. With a sudden flash of inspiration, he said, 'Alamena, why don't you bring Anna to visit my mother and me at our cottage? You and my mother have something in common. She too will be marrying in the chapel shortly. She's marrying

Tom Hanks, the head groom at the manor.'

'That's wonderful news, Seb,' said Anna. 'Tell her I'll come and bring a present for her.' Turning her face towards Alamena, Anna added, 'Seb's ma was very kind to me when I returned from Charwelton.'

Alamena inclined her head to Seb. 'Then I too will bring her a present. A gorgio woman who is friendly towards us expecting nothing in return is even rarer than a gorgio man.'

On the way through the forest, Seb told Nahum the true reason why he wanted the gipsy leader to accompany him to Handley Farm.

Nahum seemed puzzled. 'You say this man is chief of all the constables in this area yet is kindly disposed towards Romanies?'

'He recommended the lawyer who defended Boz. He also once told me that laws are made to protect the innocent as well as to punish the guilty.'

'I've yet to meet a constable who believes that a Romany is entitled to protection under gorgio law.'

'Well, you soon will. Giles Aplin is an exceptional man, as I'm sure you'll agree.'

It was evident from the moment they met that Giles Aplin and Nahum Plunkett liked each other, even though a thousand years of divergent cultures had dug a deep chasm between them.

'It was thoughtful of you not to call on me in the forest,' said Nahum. 'Had you done so I could have done nothing at all to help you. As it is . . . what can my people do to convince the world that no Romany had anything to do with the murders you're investigating?'

'Help me find the guilty parties. The coachman says that before he was killed Sir Vincent Hammond shot and wounded one of the highwaymen. I visited the spot where it happened and found blood smeared on a large stone where the highwayman fell. I think he was hurt quite seriously. Both highwaymen escaped into the forest and my hunch is that one, or both of them, may still be there. Find them and the talk of gipsies being involved is scotched, once and for all.'

'Will it put an end to the talk of disafforestation and enclosure too?'

'I can promise you nothing – but finding the highwaymen *will* take away one of the main reasons why folk around here are demanding that the forest be cut down.'

'What if it's learned that those involved *are* Romanies?'

'If *I* find them, they'll be hanged. I doubt if I'll learn anything about it if they're discovered by *your* people. But I leave that to your conscience. I would, however, suggest that you consider the best interests of your people not only now, but for the future.'

'All right, I'll have a search carried out, but if anything is found I'll be the one to decide whether or not you should know about it.'

'That isn't the way I like to do things, but it's more than I'd expected. Get word to Seb if you need to speak to me again.'

Nahum nodded. 'I will. Now, Seb, you brought me here to look at a mare. I hope the story wasn't an entire fabrication. Where is she?'

Twenty-four hours after the meeting between Giles

Aplin and Nahum Plunkett, a young gipsy lad came running to Handley Farm as though the devil were after him. When he found Seb, he gasped out his message as best he could, the words tumbling over each other.

'Nahum Plunkett sent me . . . said you were to tell the constable. He's had . . . us looking about the forest at Knothook, close to where them . . . two in the carriage was murdered. We didn't rightly know what we was looking for . . . but we knew right enough when we found it!'

'Found what? Take a deep breath before you speak and you might get it out!'

'A body. One of them highwaymen!'

'So old Sir Vincent's shot was a good one.' Giles Aplin had been right. The highwayman had been badly wounded.

'Likely it was, but that weren't the shot that killed him. He'd had a pistol put to his head while he lay on the ground where we found him.'

Seb looked at the gipsy in horror. 'Are you sure of this?'

'No doubt about it. Someone fired from such a short range it caught some of his hair afire. Whoever the dead man is, he weren't much good at choosing his friends.'

Recognition of the dead man was not long in coming. The body was that of Will Shaw, son of the Swinbrook Manor kitchen-maid. The identification ended all talk of gipsy involvement in the crime, although many spoke darkly of the bad company the dead man had kept.

The circumstances of Will Shaw's death had dire

consequences for his mother. Stricken with grief for the death of her son, Florrie Shaw was dismissed from the manor by Amelia Putt. Ignoring the known facts of the hold-up, Sir Nelson Fettiplace's housekeeper declared she would not have the mother of a man who had murdered her friends working in the house.

There was no more talk against the gipsies, but with such a violent highwayman still at large, the villagers waited expectantly for another robbery to take place.

When a couple of weeks passed without further incident, they began to relax and, very gradually, life in the Wychwood villages returned to normal.

CHAPTER THIRTY-ONE

Christian Timms's chapel was opened two weeks before Christmas. It became part of the circuit of the Burford Wesleyan minister, with Christian as the principal lay preacher.

For the first service in the new chapel Methodists came from many of the surrounding villages and it was a grand occasion. However, after this day the regular congregation would rarely exceed thirty. The antipathy of the vicar of Swinbrook, coupled with a stern warning from Meredith Putt, ensured that many who might have attended stayed away.

Those who came to the services rarely left disappointed. Christian was a powerful preacher. His congregation left the chapel in awe of the Lord and fearful lest any of their human transgressions reached the ears of Christian Timms.

The marriage of Boz and Alamena took place on a December Saturday, eight days before Christmas. Christian was delighted to have the ceremony performed in 'his' chapel, but he was unprepared for the vast numbers of gipsies who attended.

It seemed to the bewildered villagers of Swinbrook that every gipsy in the land had descended upon them. Some arrived a full week before the celebrations were due to take place. Most camped in the forest with Boz's group of gipsies. Others set up their camps well away from their Wychwood brethren, a precaution made necessary by reason of long-standing family feuds.

As the numbers increased, so the apprehension of the villagers grew. Chickens cackled in futile complaint at being locked inside hen-houses by day and by night, while farmers took to counting the sheep and cattle grazing in the fields, morning and evening.

Only the landlord of the Dore's Lodge inn welcomed the gipsy inflow without reservation. His sales increased so dramatically that he was obliged to send a messenger to the Burford brewery that served him, requesting an urgent delivery of ale that same day.

Despite the fears of the villagers, the only loss was suffered by an elderly man who lived in the small village of Widford, scarcely a mile away, along the valley of the river Windrush.

The man's young wife went off with a handsome traveller who stopped to mend a pan for her.

Even this incident was found to involve not a gipsy, but a travelling tinker. Besides, the Widford husband was a notorious wife-beater. The general opinion was that his wife should have left him many years before.

The day of the wedding dawned crisp and cold, but beautifully clear. Although the service was scheduled to begin at 11 a.m., the gipsies began to gather long before this time. Seb, Dolly and Carrie were the only gorgios attending the ceremony as guests, although Christian and the Burford Methodist minister would be officiating. Tom Hanks had been invited, but he was working and thought it might be unwise to ask for time off to attend a gipsy wedding.

By 10.30 a.m. it would have been impossible for a horse to pass along the crowded road outside the chapel, but no one entered the building until the arrival of a middle-aged gipsy couple who accompanied the bride and bridegroom, and Nahum and Anna.

The older couple were as impressively dressed as anyone else attending the wedding. A heavy gold chain linked the waistcoat pockets of the man, while the woman was bedecked with an impressive array of jewellery.

The family likeness was such that Seb knew immediately the new arrivals must be Noah and Elvira Plunkett, the parents of Nahum and Alamena. The man and woman were shown a deference by their fellow Romanies that immediately set them apart from others.

Only when the Plunketts and their party were seated and the three gorgios had been ushered in after them, did the remaining gipsies jostle each other for a place in the tiny chapel.

When they were packed shoulder to shoulder inside the building there were still nine-tenths of their number left outside and their excited chatter proved a distraction during the whole of the service.

It was doubtful whether more than a handful of the gipsies present had ever been inside either a church or chapel before, and the proceedings were a mystery to them. Occasionally, when the coughing and whispering became too loud, Noah Plunkett had only to turn his head for all such sounds to cease immediately.

The fidgetiness of the congregation was quite understandable. The service lasted far longer than usual, mainly because Christian insisted upon giving a long eulogy, praising 'this auspicious occasion', and hoping it was only the beginning of an 'era of fellowship and understanding' between the two peoples.

During his long sermon, he made a statement which caused almost as much excitement as the wedding itself. He announced that school lessons were being arranged for gipsy children and would be held in the chapel on weekdays.

'The teacher is at this wedding today as a guest of the bridegroom. I am talking of Carrie Hanks,' said Christian proudly. 'She is a very talented young lady who will greatly add to the understanding that has been brought about by the happy event we are here to witness today.'

Seated on the other side of Dolly from Seb, Carrie kept her eyes cast down to her lap while Christian sang her praises. She had said nothing to Seb about her plans, but he reminded himself there was no reason why she should. He thought she would do well if the gipsy children could be persuaded to attend. She had proved her teaching ability with him. He could read and write with only a little help now. Of course, teaching undisciplined gipsy children would be very different.

Eventually, to everyone's relief, the ritual and eulogising came to an end and the marriage service began.

Standing at the altar rail, Alamena stood as tall as her bridegroom and was beautifully dressed in a green velvet dress and white apron. On her head she wore a white, tiara-like headband of cleverly made artificial flowers.

Anna stood behind Alamena as her attendant and she too wore a velvet dress, although hers was in blue.

Beside Seb, Dolly murmured, 'They both look so *young*, and they've got all life's troubles to face up to. Still, they'll be facing them together. That counts for a great deal.'

'You and Tom will be doing the same very shortly,' whispered Seb.

His remark brought a smile to Dolly's face and she squeezed his hand in acknowledgement.

When the Methodist minister pronounced Boz and Alamena man and wife not even a stern warning glance from Noah Plunkett could prevent the gipsy congregation from erupting in a loud cheer and breaking into prolonged applause.

The sound was taken up by those gipsies waiting patiently outside the chapel and it went on for so long that the Methodist preacher was obliged to bring the service to a close sooner than he had intended, much to everyone's relief. It had seemed for a moment that Christian was about to launch into another speech.

Seb found no opportunity to speak to Anna at the chapel, but there was to be a gipsy wedding and party in the forest afterwards and he hoped they would be able to speak there.

Seb was the only gorgio present at the gipsies' wedding celebrations in their encampment. Tom Hanks had drawn the line at Carrie going to the forest, even though Seb had promised he would take care of her. Christian too declined to attend, suggesting his presence at a primitive wedding ceremony would suggest approval of such ways and was not likely to further the cause of either Methodism or relations between their two peoples.

Many of the gipsies present had begun celebrating long before the wedding ceremony and when Seb reached the encampment he was quickly intercepted by a watchful Nahum and escorted to where Noah

Plunkett and his wife were seated upon sheepskins on the ground.

Before the ceremony began, Noah shook hands enthusiastically with Seb. 'I am very happy to meet you, young man. Had it not been for you there might have been no wedding today. Anna has also told me what you did to help her. Preacher Timms spoke of co-operation and understanding between our peoples. Kind words slip easily from the tongue and are pleasant to the ear, but deeds come harder. You have earned the respect of my people for what you have done. However, you are not yet known to everyone and tonight they are celebrating. Remain close to me or Nahum while you are here with us.'

The suggestion met with Seb's approval. Anna was with the Plunkett family group. This was where he wanted to be.

The gipsy wedding was as brief as the chapel ceremony had been long. When Noah rose to his feet and made an announcement in Romany, the men rushed to form two lines. The end two men in each line crouched with a broomstick held between them, little more than a foot from the ground.

As Boz walked between the lines of men, most had something to say to him, and many patted his back along the way. When he reached the broomstick he leaped over it with ease and turned to await his bride.

Alamena's dress prevented her from hurrying, but when she reached the broomstick, she hitched up her long skirt and also jumped over, to be caught in Boz's arms. He then kissed her and a great cheer went up from the men and women witnessing the ceremony.

Noah moved forward and he too kissed the bride.

Stepping back he motioned for Seb to come and do the same. Seb did so and stammered his congratulations to Boz before returning to sit beside the gipsy leader while every man in the camp lined up to pay his respects to the bride and groom.

When a fiddler struck up a tune the gipsies lined the perimeter of a huge space that had been cleared in the centre of the encampment. Clapping their hands in time to the music, Boz and his new bride led the dancing, followed by Noah and his wife. Seb thought he was at last going to have an opportunity to talk to Anna, but it was not to be. Nahum drew her to her feet and they too went off to join the dancing.

Seb remained on his own for perhaps half an hour, accepting the drinks thrust upon him by his gipsy hosts. Then a voice he recognised said, 'What you doing sitting here on your own? Come on, you can dance too.'

It was Melody. Seb had not seen her at the wedding celebrations before now and had forgotten that her home was with those who lived in the forest.

'I can't dance.'

'Then I'm just the one to teach you.'

Seb's protests were in vain. A number of gipsies thought Melody's idea a good one and they crowded around, helping Seb to his feet and pushing him towards the square.

The arrival of Seb among the dancers brought an outburst of rowdy applause and grins of approval from Boz and Nahum.

With Melody holding both his hands and leading him, Seb quickly picked up a passable version of the dance and soon there were far too many dancers crowding the clearing for any errors he made to be noticed.

'Are you enjoying the party?' The question came from Melody. 'You wait until it gets dark. That's when things really begin to liven up.'

'I look forward to it.'

Further conversation became impossible as they were both caught up in a circle of dancers. Arms about the shoulders of the men and women on either side, Seb was taught new and more complicated dance steps.

Seb danced for half an hour before the area was cleared for a solo from Alamena. It was an exciting dance which had its origins somewhere among the gipsy tribes of Europe and earned Alamena wild applause, not least from her new husband.

When general dancing resumed, Seb returned to the sheepskin-strewn area reserved for the wedding-party. Anna was there – but so too was Nahum. Seb tried to talk to Anna on many occasions, but somehow Nahum was always included in the conversations.

Seb accepted a few more drinks in a bid to fuel his courage to ask Anna to dance with him but, as though reading his thoughts, Nahum took Anna back to the dancing throng before Seb was quite ready.

Melody too was keeping a careful watch on the proceedings and no sooner had Anna and Nahum disappeared among the dancers than she was at Seb's side.

'You'll have no fun sitting here drinking alone. Come and dance with me again.'

It was growing dark now and, as Melody had predicted, the dancing was getting wilder.

'I'll think I'll sit here for a while longer.'

'No, you won't. Much more of that stuff you're drinking and come morning you won't know whether you've had a good time or not.'

Ignoring his protests and with a surprising strength, Melody hoisted Seb to his feet and dragged him, still protesting, to the dancing area.

The noise, the drink and the excitement had Seb's head in a whirl and he lost all track of time. He only knew it was quite dark when he collided with another pair of dancers and crashed to the ground with an unknown woman.

He rose to his feet first and helped the woman from the ground. His reward was a kiss on the lips that went much farther than a friendly 'Thank you'.

Seb was pulled away by Melody, and in the darkness the woman peered closely at her before muttering, 'Oh, it's you . . .' before being dragged away by her own partner.

'Who was that?' Seb asked the question as he put an arm about Melody's shoulders and they resumed the dance.

'She's what the gipsies here call a gorgio whore, because she left her own people and married a gipsy. Why do you ask? Would you like to have her?'

'No. I only wondered who she is, that's all.'

Melody stopped dancing and pulled Seb around to face her.

'She's *my mother*, that's who she is. Are you satisfied now?'

While Seb's befuddled mind was still digesting this information, Melody said, 'I've had enough of dancing for a while. Come on.'

Melody took a firm grip on his hand and led him

away, but they were not heading back to the place where he had been seated.

'Where are you taking me?'

'To get a drink. A real drink, not that rubbish you've had so far.'

If Seb had not drunk so much already he might have pulled away from Melody and returned to the Plunketts and the Bucklands. As it was, he followed her until they reached an area on the fringe of the encampment where the fires burned low and there were no caravans, only tents and makeshift shelters.

Melody stopped when they reached a small, bow-shaped tent. 'Sit down here while I find the bottle.'

Melody sat him on a corner of a blanket, just inside the tent. Rummaging farther back in the simple dwelling, she emerged clutching a heavy bottle. Drawing the cork with her teeth, she passed the bottle to Seb.

The fumes from the contents caught at the back of his throat and he was coughing before he took his first sip. When the drink reached his throat it had him gasping for breath and he could feel it burning a path all the way to his stomach.

'Whew! What is it?'

'It's good brandy. Have you never tasted it before?'

Seb shook his head. 'No, I've never tasted *anything* quite so strong.'

'Well, don't hog the bottle, I want some too.'

Melody put the bottle to her lips and tilted it, taking far more than Seb had. As she drank he observed that the clothes she was wearing were far more tattered than those worn by any other gipsy woman celebrating the wedding. He wondered vaguely why he had not noticed the fact before.

Removing the bottle from her mouth, Melody caught Seb looking at her. Passing it to him, she leaned back, supporting herself on her elbows.

'You met my mother back there and saw what she's like. Do you know what it is to be half-Romany, half-gorgio?'

When Seb shook his head, Melody looked sceptical. 'I would have thought it was something you and Anna would have talked about a lot.'

'Why?'

'Because she – and everyone else – knows you're sweet on her, that's why.'

While Seb was digesting this revelation, Melody said, 'Anyway, I doubt if you'd have believed her, but you've got to believe me because *I* know. I know what it means to have everyone treat you as a whore because that's what they believe you are. I'm a whore because I'm the daughter of a whore and she became one from the moment she married a Romany. If you ever married Anna that's what she'd be too. That's the way it is, Seb. That's the way Romanies think.'

Taking the bottle from Seb, Melody took another long draught and handed it back.

'Well, now you know what I am, do you want me? I'll learn you a thing or two, Seb, I promise you. Things you'll never find in all those books you get from Carrie Hanks.'

The perspiration Seb felt now had nothing to do with either drink or dancing.

'I . . . I'd better get back to the others. They'll be wondering where I am.'

Melody sat up suddenly and with a hand on his chest prevented him from rising.

'Why are you so keen to go back? Just so you can torture yourself by watching Anna dancing with her future husband?'

Melody laughed at the expression of disbelief on Seb's face. 'Hasn't she told you? But no, of course she wouldn't. She wouldn't want to hurt you. Not after all you've done for her. Well, *I'll* tell you. There's going to be another wedding between the Plunketts and the Bucklands before many months have gone by, Seb. Anna and Nahum are betrothed, and have been for years.'

CHAPTER THIRTY-TWO

Seb woke with the feeling that he had a cannon inside his head. When he opened his eyes he saw he was in a bow-shaped tent, low to the ground. He felt very cold and when he moved he discovered there were no blankets over him and he was minus his trousers.

Memories of the previous evening returned to him in sharp, painful snatches and he groaned. He located his missing clothes and as he dragged them on he remembered more.

He had not wanted to believe what Melody had told him about Anna and Nahum, but in his heart he knew she was telling him the truth. It explained so much that had puzzled him. He had tried to drown his anguish with the aid of the brandy, but Melody had taken it from him saying, 'If you want to kill yourself, wait until you get home. I didn't bring you here and serve you good brandy just to watch you drink yourself to death.'

He remembered far more . . . things he wished he was able to forget. He could not remember actually taking off his trousers, but there was a time during the night when he realised they must have been off.

'Oh, you've decided to wake up, have you?' Melody's face appeared at the entrance to the tent. 'Mind you, you're not looking as fit this morning as you thought you were during the night. Not that I'm making a complaint. You were every bit as good as I thought you'd be. What would you like to do now? Go back to the party? There's no hurry, it'll go on for days. They haven't even started fighting yet. Would you like some breakfast? I could borrow some fat bacon and eggs for you.'

Looking at the changing colour of Seb's face, Melody said, 'No, perhaps we'll forget about the breakfast. I tell you what, I'll come back in there with you for a while, and then we can decide.'

It was Sunday morning and as Seb trudged homewards, the picture of dejection, he met Tom Hanks who was about to leave his cottage on his way to church. The manor's head groom looked at Seb and grinned enviously. 'My word, it looks as though you've been to a good party, Seb, and no mistake. I've heard these gipsy weddings are memorable. The wedding of Noah Plunkett's daughter would need to be bigger and better than usual.

'Mind you,' the grin widened, 'I don't think you'd better go home to your ma looking like that, or she'll be up at the gipsy camp demanding to know what they've been doing to you. Come on inside and we'll see if we can make you look as though there's something alive in there.'

Seb found the thought of meeting Carrie in his present condition even more embarrassing than a meeting with his mother, but he felt in no condition to argue.

Outside the back door of the cottage, Tom pulled a bucket of water from the well and Seb stripped to the waist. Shivering, he plunged his head into the water. It was so cold it took his breath away and he straightened up gasping.

As he turned he was handed a towel. Ignoring the throbbing in his head, he rubbed face and hair vigorously in an attempt to warm himself.

'Phew! That's better. I had a lot to drink last night and must have fallen asleep.'

'By the look of those scratches on your back you must have rolled in a bramble bush while you were sleeping.'

The comment was made by Carrie and when his head emerged from the towel, Seb was dismayed to see it was she who had handed him the towel, and not Tom.

His face scarlet, Seb pulled on his shirt and said, unnecessarily, 'I've been to Boz's wedding.'

'I know where you've been, Seb Quilter – and now I have a pretty good idea of what you were up to there. I gather that you and Anna must have had a grand reunion. Congratulations!'

As Carrie turned to go inside the cottage, Seb said quickly, as though to justify himself, 'Anna's to be married. She's betrothed to Nahum Plunkett.'

Seb had half believed Carrie already knew about Anna's intended marriage, but when she turned towards him again it was apparent that his news had taken her by surprise.

'When did you learn this? Has Anna told you so herself?'

'No.'

'Then who told you?'

'Melody.' The name came out after an initial hesitation.

'That explains a great many things about your state this morning, but, whatever else she may be, Melody isn't a liar. It will be the truth. I'm sorry, Seb. I really am. I know how much you think of Anna – and she's fond of you. That's why I thought . . . but it wouldn't have worked out, you know.'

'Melody said that too.'

Seb looked at Carrie, his face contorted as he made a desperate effort to maintain a grip on his alcohol-eroded senses. 'It doesn't help, Carrie. It doesn't help at all.'

When Seb reached Fern Cottage he had to endure a scolding from his mother such as he had not known since they left London. Fortunately for Seb he felt too ill and miserable to care and most of it went unheeded.

The situation was not improved when Tom, who had accompanied Seb to the cottage, said with a mischievous twinkle, 'You've got the cleaned-up version, Dolly. You should have seen Seb when he arrived at our house. Our Carrie wasn't sure whether he should be washed or exorcised.'

'That's quite enough gloating from you, Tom Hanks, it wasn't your fault you didn't go to the gipsies' wedding party yourself and I don't doubt you'd have come back in just as bad a state. Be off with you now, or you'll be late for church and earn the disapproval of her at the manor. Come on, I'll see you on your way.'

Outside the house, Tom gave Dolly an affectionate kiss on the cheek and said, 'Don't be too hard on the boy, Dolly. He's worked hard enough since he's been here to deserve a good night's celebrations, and he'll have learned something of gipsy ways over these last two days.'

'Trust you men to stick up for each other! But I'm pleased you do, Tom. I'd be a very unhappy woman if I thought that you and Seb didn't get along with each other.'

'You need have no worries on that score, Dolly. Seb is just the sort of son I'd have liked to have for my own. He's a good, hard-working and honest lad – and yet he's not *too* good. I'll tell you something else too. Our Carrie thinks the world of him.'

When Tom called in at Fern Cottage on his return from church all his cheerfulness had disappeared and he was looking distraught.

Seb was at work at the back of the house splitting tough elm logs when his mother put her head out of a window. 'Tom's called in on his way home and I've made a jug of tea for us all. You'd best come in right away. Tom says he has some important news for us.'

Seb hoped the news had nothing to do with his exploits at the gipsy encampment. He reassured himself with the thought that Tom would hardly have met anyone at the village church who might have witnessed what had taken place in the Wychwood Forest, but he entered the house apprehensively.

Tom was hunched in a chair by the fireside, nursing a mug of tea in his hands and he looked more serious than Seb had ever seen him.

'What is it, Tom? Is it bad news? Has there been another highway robbery?'

'It's far worse than that, young Seb, especially for those friends of your'n up there in the forest. They're going to have to look to their ways now, and no mistake. I wouldn't be surprised if they had no place to live come this time next year.'

Tom took a mouthful of tea and gazed morosely into

the fire for some minutes before talking again.

'Mind you, I reckon it's going to affect every one of us in some way or another. There'll be changes, that's for sure. There's bound to be.'

'*What's* going to affect us all, Tom? What's all this about change? You're talking in riddles.'

'I'm talking of the death of Sir Nelson Fettiplace. It was announced by the vicar in church this morning. He was on his way with his regiment to some troubles they're having in Ireland. He had a stroke. There'll be no more Fettiplaces in the manor from now on. He was the last. No one knows who the new lord of the manor will be. But we all know who's in charge of the estate. Meredith Putt has a free hand now.'

CHAPTER THIRTY-THREE

The day after Sir Nelson Fettiplace's death was announced in Swinbrook church, Magistrate Arnold Peck, accompanied by a full company of local militiamen, rode through Swinbrook village – and no one was in any doubt about his destination.

Christian certainly was not. He was layering a hedge in one of his top fields when he saw the party riding along the road towards the forest. Arriving in the stables which Seb was cleaning out, he panted, 'Quick. Get up to the gipsy camp and warn 'em. Magistrate Peck's on his way there with a whole lot of militiamen. I don't know what he's up to, but it can only mean trouble.'

Seb hurriedly threw a saddle on Romni and rode off across country. The mare was not as fast as Grye but she had the edge on the stallion when it came to jumping, and Seb did not intend stopping to open any gates.

He crossed the road well ahead of the militiamen and rode into the encampment where the wedding was still being celebrated.

There were many bodies lying around, some gipsies were drunk, others simply exhausted. The dancing was still going on too, although Seb thought the playing of the fiddlers lacked the exuberance of the first night.

Seb rode to where Noah Plunkett still sat on his sheepskin 'throne', giving the impression he had remained in the same place since the wedding party began. Seb told the gipsy leader of the approach of the magistrate.

'How many militiamen are with him?'

'Somewhere between sixty and eighty, I'd say.'

'That's too many for us to frighten away with a show of force.'

A number of gipsy men had crowded around to learn why Seb had come galloping into the camp and now Noah Plunkett turned to them and began issuing orders in the Romany tongue.

The men and women lying around on the ground were roughly shaken awake. Those too drunk to stand were dragged away to their tents and caravans. When the fiddler leading the dancing stopped playing and asked what was going on, he was ordered to carry on, as though nothing was happening.

A rapid tidying up of the encampment was carried out. It seemed Noah wanted the magistrate to find nothing with which he could possibly take issue.

When the magistrate and his party from Burford reached the encampment, the militiamen took up positions virtually surrounding the celebrating gipsies. Peck, accompanied by an officer and two armed and nervous militiamen, rode to the centre of the clearing and Noah rose from his sheepskin to meet them.

'Who is the leader here?' Magistrate Peck asked the question whilst looking directly at Noah.

'There is no leader.' Noah spoke with the caution bred of years spent dealing with authority. 'But I'm willing to act as a spokesman if you feel one is needed.'

'I have an injunction declaring these festivities to be a public nuisance and ordering you to cease immediately.'

'A *public* nuisance in the heart of a great forest like Wychwood?'

'The death was announced yesterday of Sir Nelson Fettiplace, lord of Swinbrook Manor and a verderer of Wychwood Forest. To have a noisy celebration going on at such a time is causing considerable distress to the family of the late Sir Nelson.'

Arnold Peck looked about him. 'What's more, I see a great many men here whom I recognise as having already been convicted of vagrancy offences. You will all be taken into custody and escorted to Burford by the militia. There you will be charged with various offences against the Vagrancy Act—'

'You are Magistrate Peck, I believe?' Noah Plunkett interrupted the mounted man.

'I am. I don't think I caught your name?'

Peck was annoyed at the interruption, but there was something in the bearing of the man who stood before him which could not be ignored.

'My name is Noah Plunkett. I am well known in much of the country by various men of standing – including the Duke of Marlborough. He, as I am sure you know, is Ranger of Wychwood Forest, an office bestowed upon him by the monarch of this realm.'

Noah's statement and the manner in which he delivered it took Arnold Peck aback, but he said haughtily, '*I've* never heard of you, sir.'

Unconcerned by Peck's manner, Noah replied, 'Nor I of you until I came to Oxfordshire to attend the wedding of my daughter. I am told you were recently criticised by a learned judge for wrongly sending a Romany for trial to the Assizes in Oxford?'

'This is impertinence, sir! I uphold the law of this

realm – and the law states quite clearly that vagrants are rogues and vagabonds. The scourge of the countryside. As such they should be lodged in gaol.'

'I suggest that most of the sentiments you express so forcibly are your own, Mr Peck. The Act of which you speak states equally clearly that a rogue and vagabond is a person who wanders abroad *without any visible means of subsistence*. I wish to point out that such a definition applies to none of the people present in this forest today. I personally guarantee that every man, woman and child in this gathering has fifty pounds at his or her disposal.'

Noah's knowledge of the law applicable to gipsies surprised Arnold Peck, but now he glanced about him at the listening gipsies. Turning a scornful look upon the gipsy spokesman, he said, 'What you are suggesting is quite preposterous. There must be five hundred gipsies here at least.'

'There are seven hundred and sixty *Romanies* – making a total of thirty-eight thousand pounds, I believe. Do you doubt I have such a sum?'

'Your finances are no concern of mine.'

In spite of his continued haughtiness in speaking to the gipsy, Noah's authoritative manner had badly shaken the magistrate's confidence. 'I am here to ensure that the laws of the land are obeyed.'

'And so they shall be. We are gathered here to celebrate a marriage but, in deference to the family of the late verderer and lord of the manor, our celebrations will cease. However, if you attempt to arrest any man or woman here on a charge of vagrancy I will see they are defended in your court – and in any higher court to which they may be sent for trial. What's more, if I deem it to be necessary I shall call upon the Duke of Marlborough to give evidence on our behalf.'

'A . . . a *duke* give evidence on behalf of gipsies!' Arnold Peck spluttered his indignation. 'I have never heard of anything so absurd.'

'I doubt if you'll have heard of a Romany having a magistrate removed from office either, Mr Peck, but make one arrest here and you're very likely to be the first.'

Arnold Peck glowered at the man who stood before him. Noah Plunkett was as calm as though they were discussing the state of the weather. He was bluffing, of course, and yet . . .

The officer commanding the militia had been listening to the conversation between the two men with growing unease. The Duke of Marlborough wielded enormous power in the county. He could have a militia unit disbanded if he wished.

The officer regretted putting his men at Peck's disposal. He should have known better than agree to support a magistrate whose hatred of gipsies was so well known. What had begun as an amusing jaunt for the militia showed every promise of ending in disaster.

'I think you and I should draw aside and discuss this matter, Mr Magistrate.'

'You are here to assist me in upholding the law, sir. Nothing more.'

Having firmly put the militia officer in his place and redeemed some of his own wounded pride, Arnold Peck said to Noah, 'Do you agree to abide by the terms of the injunction I came here to serve upon you?'

Noah nodded. 'I have already said so.'

'Very well.'

Inclining his head to the militia officer, Arnold Peck said, 'We have performed the duty for which we came here. We may return to Burford.'

As the last of the militiamen were swallowed up by the forest a great roar of delight rose from the gipsies and they crowded around Noah to congratulate him on the unexpected victory he had scored over the Burford magistrate.

When the tumult died down and Seb was able to hear himself speak, he asked Noah, 'Do you really know the Duke of Marlborough?'

'We've met,' declared the gipsy Leader, ambiguously. 'I doubt if His Grace would ever stand up in a court-room to give evidence on my behalf, but I counted on Magistrate Peck being afraid to put it to the test.'

Smiling benignly at Seb, the gipsy leader said, 'One of the most important lessons to learn in this life is that if you wish to convince someone of anything you must first convince yourself. At the time I was talking to the magistrate I had no doubt at all that the Duke of Marlborough would give evidence for me, if necessary. The time for doubts would have come afterwards.'

Draping an arm about Seb's shoulders, Noah said, 'Thank you for warning us of the magistrate's approach, Seb. You've once again proved your friendship to the Romany people. You'll find it won't be forgotten.'

As Seb walked to where he had tied Romni his name was called and he turned to find Anna walking towards him. He thought her arms were outstretched for him, but realised with a pang of disappointment they were to ward off any obstruction that might be between them.

Behind her, Nahum was looking on with an unsmiling face.

'I'm here, Anna.' When Seb spoke to guide her, she came unerringly to him and reached out to take his hand.

'Were you going to leave yet again without saying goodbye to me, Seb?'

'I didn't think it would matter to you any more than it did before.'

'Of course it matters to me – but I thought you were being well entertained by others on the evening of the wedding.'

'I'd have enjoyed it more had you found time to speak to me.'

Anna looked unhappy. 'It's not easy being blind, Seb. I was dancing much of the time on the wedding day. When I returned I listened for you. When I didn't hear you I thought you must be dancing too.'

'You could have found out where I was by asking your fiancé.'

Anna released his hand. 'Oh! So you know about that?'

'It's true, then?'

'Yes, Seb, it's true. I should have told you myself, but somehow the opportunity was never there.'

'What you mean is, you hoped I'd find out from someone else. Well, you had your way. I did find out from someone else.'

'From Melody, no doubt.' Anna caught her breath and then said, very quietly, 'You're quite right, Seb. I didn't want to tell you. I didn't know how.'

'How long have you been betrothed to Nahum?'

'For so long it just didn't seem real any longer. I still

had my sight when the marriage was arranged between our families. I don't think any of Nahum's family realised I was blind until they arrived for Boz's wedding to Alamena. They were so shocked that for a while I was convinced they would go away and not only cancel our betrothal but probably the wedding between Boz and Alamena as well.'

'Well, Boz and Alamena are married now, so I suppose your wedding to Nahum is still on too?'

'Yes, Seb.'

Anna's reply came out as hardly more than a whisper.

'Will you be leaving the forest when Nahum and his family go?'

'No, I'll be staying here for a while, sharing the caravan with Boz and Alamena.'

'Then I'll be seeing you again – unless Nahum forbids it. He's watching us right now so I've no doubt he'll have *something* to say about it to you.'

'Nahum won't mind me talking to you. He understands we're friends, and he likes you. I'm more concerned about you, Seb. I'm sorry I've hurt you, truly I am. Can't we stay friends? I'd like . . . I *want* you as my friend, Seb.'

'No, Anna. It would only be possible if I didn't love you, but I do.'

Nahum was approaching now. He was not hurrying, but his attitude suggested he thought Anna and Seb had been talking together for quite long enough.

Without another word, Seb untied the mare's reins, mounted and rode away.

As he left the encampment behind, a slim, ragged figure emerged from the undergrowth to intercept him.

Melody was the last person he wanted to see at this moment, but he reined in when she called him.

'Hello, Seb. I saw you talking to Anna. Did she tell you about her and Nahum?'

'Yes.'

'You see, I wasn't lying to you.' Melody looked up at his drawn face and said, 'I'm sorry it was me that told you, Seb, but I'm not sorry about what we did afterwards, are you?'

Seb looked down at her and wished all the happenings of that night could be obliterated from his memory. But Melody had her face turned up to him eagerly and he remembered other details of Boz's wedding-night party: his meeting with Melody's mother and the small, shabby tent that was her home. He remembered their talk together and the bleak picture she had painted for him of her life.

Seb had an ache inside him caused by Anna that he believed would never leave him. Yet he had friends, the love of his mother and he lived a full life. Melody had nothing. She had never had anything, and her future was equally as hopeless as her past.

'No, Melody, I'm not sorry for what we did. You were very kind to me at a time when I needed comforting and I'm grateful to you.'

As he rode away, Seb thought it had been a very small lie, yet it had brought an expression of joy to Melody's face that he would never forget.

CHAPTER THIRTY-FOUR

Christmas was a happy time in Swinbrook for Seb and his mother. They shared the festivities with Tom, Carrie and Christian, dividing their time between the three houses and enjoying a spell of mild weather that did not last into January.

Seb saw little of the Wychwood gipsies during the hard winter months that followed Christmas. There were weeks of unremitting frost, occasional snowstorms, and periods of rain that seemed to soak right through the body to chill the bones.

Occasionally one or two gipsy women made their way to Handley Farm from the forest to buy flour. Others called at Fern Cottage to sell pegs or other wares, made during the short, grey winter days.

Melody still came to the farm to help out with dairy work, but these days, much to Seb's relief, she seemed content just to be near him, making no embarrassing demands. She brought with her news of the gipsy encampment – and of Anna.

It seemed the blind girl found living with Boz and his bride very restricting, but due to the bad weather she was not allowed to leave the camp for much of the winter.

Seb spent many of the long winter evenings at the Hankses' cottage and his reading and writing improved so much that Carrie was reluctantly forced to admit there was little more she could teach him in these two spheres of learning.

Then, almost overnight it seemed, Oxfordshire suddenly threw off the mantle of winter. With the advent of new life in the forest and fields about Swinbrook village, Tom Hanks and Dolly Quilter arranged to be married in the small chapel alongside Fern Cottage.

Amelia Putt had dropped her objection to the wedding of one of her employees taking place in chapel and not church when she learned the identity of Tom's bride-to-be. Had she insisted on the couple marrying in the village church she would have been obliged to attend the ceremony. Mrs Putt had no wish to acknowledge her former scullery-maid. For the same reason, Tom was informed he would not be obliged to attend Sunday services at the church with his new wife. He was free to follow his inclinations and join the worshippers at the Methodist chapel, if he so wished.

'It's an unexpected and welcome bonus,' declared Tom, happily, when he passed on the news. 'I rarely get away from church without someone finding something for me to do up at the manor. Mrs Putt might want a stall cleared out and fresh straw put in for some company she's expecting, or she'll want me to hitch up a carriage so she can go visiting. As for Mr Meredith! I dread going to church when he's home. No matter that I'm dressed up in my Sunday clothes. He expects me to carry on up at the manor as though it's just another working day.'

Tom was speaking when the Hanks and Quilter families were meeting with Christian in Tom's cottage to discuss details of the forthcoming wedding.

'Has young Meredith changed any of his wild ways

since he took over the reins at the manor?'

The question came from Christian, who sat astride a bench seat at the kitchen table, contentedly puffing on a smoke-blackened clay pipe.

'Not him! All it's done is to give him more money to gamble away up in London. The servants in the house say he and his mother have some dreadful quarrels about his ways. Last time he came home she said if things went on as they are for much longer he'd lose the manor and the farm on the turn of a card!'

'It's a pity you can't find work away from that place, Tom,' said Dolly, shaking her head in concern. 'I'd be much happier knowing you and I weren't at the beck and call of such a man.'

'Ah well, you never know,' said Tom, winking affectionately at his daughter. 'If young Seb can add to the three horses he's got now he'll soon be needing someone to help him out. He might find it useful having an old man like me around to give him a few tips on how to manage horses.'

'I'm working on it, Tom,' declared Seb. 'If things go well I hope within a twelve-month to double the number of horses I own.'

'There's ambition for you!' exclaimed Dolly, proudly. 'But you're not *old*, Tom!' She gave her future husband a playful dig in the ribs with her elbow. 'You're hardly older than me, and I've a year or two to go before I'm forty.'

'You'm right, Dolly. Why, we might even start another family!'

'Yes, and I might one day be Queen of England! We'll keep our feet firmly on the ground if you don't mind, Tom Hanks.'

'While we're talking of being practical' – Christian removed the pipe from his mouth – 'have you both given any thought to where you'll be living when you're married?'

'I'm sorry, Christian, Tom and I ought to have discussed it with you. We've talked about it and decided we'd move in here, in Tom's cottage. He has a lifetime's belongings here and we could hardly expect Carrie to move into Fern Cottage.'

'You'll both be moving into Tom's cottage, you and Seb?'

'Of course.'

Christian had been watching Seb while Dolly was talking and now he asked, 'Is this the way you see it, Seb?'

'Well, no, it isn't.'

'What do you mean it isn't?' Dolly demanded. 'You can't stay here on your own.'

'Why not? You'll still be working up at the farm and I'll be having my midday meals up there, same as I do now. Some evenings I expect I can come along and eat with you, Tom and Carrie.'

'But who'd do your washing, clean the house and make your bed for you?'

'You can carry on doing my washing, if that will please you – and knowing you as I do, I don't doubt you'll be in here at least once or twice a week clearing things up and telling me what a mess I'm living in – just as you do now. Besides, it makes sense, Ma. There are only two bedrooms at Tom's house. Where would we all sleep?'

'I don't know, Seb. I don't like to think of you in the cottage all by yourself.'

'I shouldn't worry yourself, Dolly,' said Carrie, with apparent innocence. 'I expect Melody will come and keep him company sometimes.'

'Melody in Fern Cottage with Seb, without me around to keep an eye on the pair of 'em? Oh no, my lad, you'll come with me, like I say.'

'Seb's idea makes sense, Dolly.' Christian came down on Seb's side when the laughter of Carrie and Tom had ceased. 'Tom might have been talking in jest a while back, but there's nothing to say you *won't* have another family between the two of you. If you do it would be a tight squeeze for you all in Tom's house. Besides, Sir Meredith Putt's not the most stable man these days. He might one day get it into his head to dismiss Tom. At least this way you'll still have a home to move into.'

'Um! All right, I'll think seriously about it.'

By the end of the evening there was only one person in the room who still felt strongly about Seb living in Fern Cottage on his own. Yet Carrie dared not speak out for fear they would question her reasons, and she was not clear about them herself. She only knew she was bitterly disappointed that she and Seb would not be living under the same roof.

The wedding of Tom and Dolly was as quiet as that of Boz and Alamena had been rowdy, although the chapel was far more crowded than Seb had anticipated. Dolly was still not very well known in the village but Tom was a popular member of the community.

It was a warm but simple ceremony and, as at the previous wedding, the Burford minister officiated, with Christian assisting him. Afterwards a small party was held at Christian's farmhouse, attended only by the bride and groom, Seb and Carrie, Christian and the minister, together with half a dozen villagers who were related to Tom.

The weather had been kind for Boz's wedding but it was less so for Tom and Dolly. Bitterly cold, it rained hard, although, once inside Christian's snug farmhouse, no one cared very much.

Seb was in the kitchen fetching ale for the men when, through the window, he saw Melody. Barefooted and bare-armed, she was bringing in the cows from the fields for milling. She wore no coat and was soaked through. When he took the ale into the warm farmhouse living room and saw everyone standing around the crackling log fire with food and drinks in their hands, he thought again of what he had just seen through the kitchen window.

Returning to the kitchen, Seb filled a pint pot with ale from the small barrel and shovelled a large portion of hot meat pie into a dish. Opening the door, he splashed his way across the farmyard to the milking parlour.

There was room for eight cows in here and every stall was full, but he could see no sign of the half-gipsy girl.

'Melody, are you in here?' Hearing a movement that sounded too quick for a cow, he called again, 'Where are you?'

'I'm up here, Seb. In the loft.' Melody sounded as though she was speaking through chattering teeth and he climbed the ladder, carefully balancing pie and ale.

'I've brought this for you.' His head rose above the floor level of the hay-loft in time to see a great deal more of Melody than he had anticipated as she slipped her ragged clothes back on.

'I just dried myself with some hay and wrung out my dress before putting it back on. It'll soon dry on me while I'm leaning against the cows, they're warm, they are.'

'And wet. You'll catch your death of cold if you're not careful. Here, take this. I saw you through the window and thought you could probably do with something to eat and drink.'

'You've brought it out here, specially for me?' Melody's delight and incredulity were genuine, but it did not prevent her from taking the food and drink from his hands and bolting it as though she were starving. From what Seb had seen of her body – and he had seen a great deal – he suspected it was not far from the truth.

When the pie had gone and half the ale been downed, she offered the tankard to him. 'It's good. D'you want some?'

'There's plenty in the house. I brought this for you. I'd better get back now. I can't have them all trooping out in their wedding finery looking for me.'

Seb had two feet on the ladder when Melody took him by surprise and caught him in a hug. Pressing herself close as she kissed him, she pleaded, 'Can't you stay here for a while, Seb? You and me in the hay, like that night in the forest . . . do you remember?'

Her body moved against his, leaving him in no doubt what she meant, whether he remembered or not.

'No, Melody. If I don't get back they'll miss me. They might even be on their way across here now. If Christian catches us he won't have you back on the farm again.'

Melody released him reluctantly – and only just in time. The door to the cow-shed opened and Carrie stood there.

'I saw you come over here and guessed Melody would be somewhere near. Can't you wait until you have a cottage to yourself and can do what you like with your life, Seb Quilter?'

'I saw Melody through the window. She was bringing the cows in and was soaked through. I brought her some hot pie and ale.'

When Carrie looked at Melody's dripping hair hanging all about her face and the sodden dress clinging to her body, she realised Seb was telling the truth and her face lost its tightness.

'Melody, you'll catch a chill if you stay like that. You must go back and change into something dry.'

'I've nothing to change into, but I'll be all right now I've had a drink, and something nice and hot to eat.'

'I suspect it's probably the first decent meal you've had for days, Melody. Isn't that so?'

Melody did not reply to Seb's question, but her face gave her away.

'You just wait here. I'm going back to the farmhouse to fetch my coat, then you'll come with me to our cottage.' Carrie's tone of voice brooked no argument. 'I've had to clear out lots of things to make room for Dolly, including a couple of dresses. They're not all that good, but they're better than that soaking wet rag you're wearing now. You'd better come back to the farmhouse too, Seb. They're calling for you to give some sort of speech.'

As Carrie limped back to the house beside Seb, she said, 'You'll need to watch yourself, Seb. Melody is a poor soul and I feel very sorry for her. She's never had a chance in life – but she trades on her ill-luck. One day someone is going to feel so sorry for her he'll end up marrying her. You're soft on those who've been treated badly by life – and if you're not very careful it might well be you.'

As she limped into the farmhouse behind Seb, Carrie thought of her own words. She wondered why Seb had never fallen for *her*.

CHAPTER THIRTY-FIVE

In April of that year, Seb took two of the Handley Farm horses to the Spring Fair at nearby Witney. Riding Grye, he led the cart-horses, tied to ropes behind him.

As was usually the way when the magnificent horses were offered for sale, they sold within the hour, leaving Seb to look around at the other animals and sample the pleasures offered to the fair-goers.

Towards noon, Seb went in search of something to eat before making the return journey to Swinbrook. As he walked through the centre of the town he saw a large group of navvies sauntering across the wide market-square, whistling at the women and calling out to any particularly young or good-looking girls – or those of any age who were careless enough to throw a smile in their direction. Among their number Seb recognised Jacob Brailey, the Cockney gang-boss whom he had last met at the Wychwood Forest Fair.

Jacob saw Seb at almost the same time. Breaking away from his fellow navvies he elbowed through the crowd to shake Seb vigorously by the hand. 'It's good to see you here, lad. Have you come to ride in the race this afternoon?'

'I didn't know there was one,' said Seb honestly.

'Didn't know . . . Why, damn me, boy. I thought that was why you was here. You've disappointed me now. The race could have been laid on especially for that horse you rode before. Four miles long and over some good country.'

'I own the horse now. I rode it to the market today.'

'Well, there you are, then! There's twenty-five guineas to the winner – and if you had some money to back yourself to win you could make as much as that again.'

Seb had ten pounds in his pocket, saved from his previous winnings. He had brought it in the hope of finding a second-hand saddle of his own. Until now he had been using one loaned to him by Christian. He reached a rapid decision.

'Grye's in good condition. As fit as he was at the Wychwood Forest Fair. If I enter him for the race will you wager ten pounds for me?'

'Ten for you, ten for me and as much as the others can add to it. You go and enter your horse for that race, lad, and I'll be there to cheer you on when you're first past the winning-post.'

Seb had no difficulty entering Grye for the race. There were only seven other runners. The organisers were eager to attract more entries. When someone there recognised Seb as the jockey who had won the previous year's race at the Wychwood Forest Fair it created a sudden surge of interest and betting became very much brisker.

There was no horse of Vulcan's calibre in this race and Seb went to the front half-way around the four-mile course. From this moment the gap between Grye and the remainder of the field increased with every stride until Seb passed the winning-post.

Jacob was not waiting there, but he put in an

appearance only a few minutes later, beaming cheerfully.

'I knew you'd do it, lad. I told me mates it was a sure thing and they emptied their pockets and put every last halfpenny on you and that horse of your'n. Here, the best I could get for you is evens, but with another fiver collected for you from me mates, and the prize for winning, you'll go home with fifty pounds in your pocket. That's not a bad day's work for a lad, I'd say.'

Seb grinned happily. 'It'll do – but talking of work, what are you doing in Witney? I know Meredith Putt's been doing a lot of talking about the railway, but I didn't know it was on its way.'

'It will be, lad. The railway will come at least as far as Witney, you mark my words. There'll be more rail than road in this country of ours one day. But we're not working on a line at the moment. We've been taken on as a whole gang with lots of others, to make roads for those who are chopping down the trees in Wychwood Forest. In little more than a year's time the forest will be gone and there'll be farms in its place.'

Seb and Christian spoke until well into the night about the changes that total disafforestation would bring to the area – and to the gipsies in particular. They agreed that nothing could be done until it was learned exactly what was taking place.

Christian set off early the next morning to ride to Burford. He was going to speak to James Price, the solicitor acting for him, to ask what information he had gained about the disafforestation.

Seb was repairing a fence in one of the fields when Melody brought the cows back to the pasture for milking. She came across to speak to him.

Seb always felt vaguely uncomfortable when Melody caught him on his own. This unease was not helped when she hitched her dress above her knees and squatted cross-legged on the grass to talk to him as he worked.

'D'you like my dress, Seb?'

'It's fine.' He spoke without looking at her, in case his gaze rested on her bare legs and gave her ideas. 'Better than the dress you were wearing on Ma's wedding day.'

'This is one of those Carrie gave me.' Melody smiled as she plucked at the material of the loose sleeves.

Her actions reminded Seb that Melody was really a very simple soul, her emotions straightforward and uncluttered.

'Carrie's nice. She's promised to give me some schooling if I can get to chapel in the mornings. Do you think girls should have schooling, Seb?'

'I think you ought to give it a try. The light mornings are coming along and the cows can be taken in for milking earlier. I'm sure Ma would help you with that, if you'd like her to. You should be able to spend at least two or three hours learning with Carrie.'

'Would you like me more if I had some schooling, Seb? Would you do things with me like you did when Boz got married?'

'Now, Melody . . . I've apologised many times for what happened that night. I don't want to talk about it any more. It shouldn't have happened.'

Melody shrugged her shoulders in a gesture of feigned indifference. 'I know. You were drunk and wouldn't have done it otherwise. Well, I haven't the money to get you drunk every time I want you to love me.' She hesitated before adding, 'I doubt if Anna would have to get you drunk afore you did it to her.'

'I've said I don't want you talking about it – or about Anna in that way, either.'

'Anna isn't very happy, Seb.' It came out almost reluctantly.

He stopped working. 'Why do you say that? What's making her unhappy? It's got nothing to do with me, I'm certain of *that*.'

'Are you? I don't think *she* is. But no, it isn't you. Alamena, Boz's wife, is making life difficult for her, telling her she's not to leave the camp and that she's too free and easy with everyone. She's making it very clear she doesn't believe Anna's good enough for that brother of hers. Everyone always said it wouldn't work having two women sharing a caravan. They were right.'

Seb felt guilty. He had not been in the forest since Boz's wedding. Had not seen Anna since then, but he said, 'Why doesn't Nahum do something about making things easier for Anna?'

'Nahum Plunkett isn't in the camp. He went back up north to be with his family. He's been gone a month or more.'

Melody looked speculatively at Seb. 'Are you still fond of Anna, Seb?'

It was a wistful question and Seb softened his attitude towards Melody.

'Yes, I suppose I am.'

'I think she feels the same way about you too, but Romanies and gorgios shouldn't marry. *I* should know if anyone does. Our lives are too different.'

Stretching her brown, barefooted legs out in front of

her and exposing half of her thighs, Melody gave Seb what he had come to think of as one of her 'looks'.

'You'll never get from Anna what you can have from me, Seb.'

With a stout and newly repaired fence between them, Seb felt he could afford to smile at her. 'Be off with you, Melody. If you stay here any longer it'll be time to take the cows in for their evening milking.'

As he watched Melody walking back to the farm, deliberately exaggerating the swing of her hips for his benefit, Seb was thinking of Anna. He wondered what was going to happen to her now the forest was actually being cut down. He could not imagine her living anywhere else but in Wychwood Forest.

Christian returned late that evening. He had spent much of the day with James Price. The Burford solicitor had confirmed what Jacob Brailey had told Seb. The forest, or much of it, was being cut down and the land enclosed. Most of that land had been allocated to those with forest grazing rights, whose method of running stock would be affected by the enclosures. The remainder was being retained by the Crown and would be used to form seven large, Crown-owned farms.

'Two small sections of Wychwood are to be left standing. The largest part is over by Charlbury, where the forest fair is held. That will become part of Cornbury Park. The other piece is right here, from Widley Copse to Stockley – that's the area where the gipsy encampment is now.'

'So they'll be able to stay after all?'

Seb's delight was short-lived.

'I doubt it very much. This part of the forest is being

allocated to the manor. Even though he'll not be allowed to cut it down, Putt will have the gipsies out.'

Seb's spirits sank. 'Meredith Putt will be overjoyed when he hears the news.'

'I shouldn't think so. He'd have been hoping for lots more land. Although he was one of the prime movers in having the forest cut down and enclosed, Putt's come out of it badly. That piece of forest is the only land allocated to the manor. Most has been given to farmers like me who have long-standing grazing rights. I've been given a hundred and fifty acres, Seb. The only condition is that fifty acres of it remain as woodland. If Boz and his people have to move their camp but wish to remain hereabouts they're welcome to camp there.'

'That's wonderful news for you and for them, Christian. Congratulations! It gives you an impressive land-holding – and offers a way out of their problems for Boz and his people. When will you go and speak to him about it?'

'The sooner the better, otherwise he'll be hearing any number of garbled stories about disafforestation from others. We could go now, if you wish – I presume you'll want to come with me?'

As Seb saddled Grye, his mind was working hard. By the time he set off with Christian he had half formulated a plan to help with the future he had in mind for himself.

As they entered the forest, Seb asked, 'What will you do with your extra hundred acres of farming land, Christian?'

'They'll need to be ploughed and planted with a root crop for the first year. Perhaps turnips, or mangels. Something like that.'

Seb nodded thoughtfully. 'How many other farmers hereabouts have been given similar awards?'

'Dozens. Most of those with lands bordering the forest.'

Seb's enthusiasm quickened. 'Do any of them own horses like ours?'

'I can name four farmers who own single horses. No more than that. Why do you ask?'

'It will take a team of at least three horses to plough such rough land – and even then it will be difficult going with all the roots that'll be left around when the foresters have moved on.'

'True. But what does that prove, except that you've learned something about farming since you've lived in Swinbrook?'

'If I use my own money to buy a plough, will you supply the horses and let me spend two or three days a week hiring out to those with new lands? We could share all the money I earn – and I believe we'd make a great deal.'

The idea took Christian by surprise, but he did not dismiss it out of hand. 'It makes sense, but why do you think they'll hire you?'

'They'll have to hire someone with good horses, and they won't find a better team of animals than we can supply.'

'Where will you get the money to buy a plough?'

'I've already got money that I've saved from Grye's winnings.' Seb did not amplify his statement. He had not forgotten that Christian disapproved of gambling.

Christian rubbed his chin as he looked at Seb and thought seriously about the plan he had put forward. Eventually he nodded twice. 'All right, Seb, I'm willing to give it a try. Mind you, you're not the only one who's thinking of the future. I've been giving it a great deal of thought myself in recent weeks. Once I'm absolutely clear in my own mind I'll put *my* plan to you – but here's the encampment and unless I'm mistaken that's Boz coming out to meet us.'

CHAPTER THIRTY-SIX

The circle of seated gipsies listened to Christian's account of his meeting with the Burford solicitor with growing alarm. There was also anger.

Before the Swinbrook farmer had finished talking to them, Boz leaped to his feet to say, angrily, 'We Romanies have been using the forest for hundreds of years. Except for one or two magistrates like Peck we've been left alone, and have never done anything to trouble those who live around the forest.'

When Christian tried to interrupt the angry outburst, Boz waved him into silence.

'Oh, I know a few Romanies have been sent to prison for poaching – but so have a great many gorgios. Why has no one bothered to tell *us* what's happening? Are they intending to cut the trees down all around us without any warning?'

'This particular part of Wychwood won't be coming down, Boz, but it will be passing into private hands – as part of the manor's lands. However, I'm able to offer you an alternative, in Faws Grove.'

Christian went on to tell the gipsies of the award made to him by the enclosure commissioners, but he was interrupted abruptly by Boz, who said, 'There's no water in Faws Grove.'

'Not actually in the wood, true. But there's water not too far away, on my land.'

As though Christian had not spoken, Boz said, 'There's also a road running across Handley Plain, alongside the copse. We'd have to cross it to get water.'

'That's so, but it shouldn't be too much trouble for you if you really want to stay in the area.'

'It would be no trouble for us, maybe, but it'd trouble those gorgios who pass along the road and they'd start complaining about us. When we're out of sight we can get by. If your people have to see us their imagination runs riot, and we get trouble.'

Boz's fellow gipsies nodded their unanimous agreement, but Christian pleaded, 'Give it a try, Boz. It's better than nothing and between us we can make it work.'

'You have nothing to lose if it doesn't work, Mr Timms. We have *everything* to lose. I expect some of us will be moving off soon, going to the places where summer work's to be found. The rest of us intend staying right where we are – and Meredith Putt will find he'll not move us on without a fight.'

Boz's defiant statement was greeted with applause and cheering from the gipsies.

As Christian continued to argue, Seb moved away. He walked first of all towards the place where he and Christian had tied their horses, but then changed direction to where he had noticed Anna seated on the steps of a caravan.

Edging to within hearing, he called softly, 'Hello, Anna. I haven't seen you in a long time. How are you?'

Seb thought she looked thinner and seemed to have lost much of the air of confidence that had always been so much a part of her. It hurt him to see such changes in her.

However, her face lit up in a smile when she heard his voice. 'Hello, Seb. Boz said you were coming. When you didn't speak to me straightaway I thought you'd go off again without a word to me.'

'It might be better if I did, but I couldn't do it, not once I'd seen you sitting here. You're looking tired, Anna. Are you unhappy?'

Instead of replying, Anna countered with a question of her own. 'Is it true what I just heard the women saying? That the forest is being cut down?'

'Much of it is, but Christian has been given fifty acres of forest land. He's offering to let Boz and the rest of your people stay there, but I don't think Boz is going to accept.'

'He won't. A year ago, perhaps – or he might have considered it as recently as six months since. But now?' She shrugged unhappily.

'What's happened to change him? He's made a good marriage. He should be a very happy man.'

At that moment the caravan door behind Anna opened and Alamena came out. When she saw Anna and Seb talking together, she said sharply, 'Anna! What do you think you're doing?'

The remainder of her conversation was in fast Romany and Anna replied with a note of anger in her voice.

Alamena's voice rose a full octave and increased so much in volume that many of the men seated about Christian looked their way. Suddenly, Boz sprang to his feet and strode towards the group outside the caravan, his face screwed up in fury.

Seb realised immediately that Boz was seeking trouble as a means of purging himself of the anger and frustration that was bubbling inside him.

When Alamena saw her husband coming towards them she raised her voice still more. Anna interjected with her own heated views, but when Boz reached them, he confronted Seb.

'What are you doing talking to my sister? Don't you know she's betrothed to Nahum Plunkett? Do you want to get her talked about?'

Thoroughly bewildered, Seb said, 'Boz, this is *me* you're talking to, Seb Quilter. I rescued Anna from a crowd at Charwelton and brought her back here to you and your people – remember?'

'I remember – and it's lucky for you no one asked any awkward questions about what happened along the way when you and Anna spent a night together.'

'Stop it, Boz. Stop it this instant.' Anna's voice shouted at her brother, but his words had angered Seb beyond reason.

'What "awkward" questions? You're singing a different tune now from the one you sang after *you'd* left her behind and got yourself arrested. Nothing "happened" – but that wasn't my fault and I don't think much of a man who's foul-mouthed enough to insinuate things about his own sister!'

Boz took a quick step forward and before Seb could raise his guard the gipsy swung a wild punch. It caught Seb high on his left cheekbone. The blow stung and Seb retaliated immediately, moving in with arms flailing.

As both young men threw punches the encampment erupted in a noisy outcry. Anna was screaming for someone to stop them, while the gipsies were urging them to fight to a finish.

Christian stepped in and called on both Seb and Boz to cease fighting. When he was ignored, the farmer reached out and grabbed both men by their hair. Drawing them apart he suddenly cracked their heads together.

Boz went to the ground like a felled tree and Seb dropped to his knees, thoroughly dazed. Before he had fully recovered, Christian hauled him to his feet and dragged him away from his groaning adversary.

As Boz rose unsteadily to hands and knees, Christian said to the watching gipsies, 'When Boz has calmed down a little, tell him my offer still stands. All of you are welcome to stay on in Faws Grove for as long as you wish. If you need to see me you know where I'm to be found. You're all welcome at Handley Farm, or in Swinbrook chapel at any time. Remember it.'

'Cor! That's a beautiful black eye you've got, Seb – but the one Boz has got is better. He can't see out of his.'

Melody expressed her admiration the following morning as she stood watching Seb currying one of the horses. He worked as though he was trying to remove every hair from the horse's hide.

'I don't care if Boz is as blind as Anna. He had no right to say what he did.'

'About you and Anna, you mean? Oh, I don't know. You two say you did nothing – and *I* believe you – but think how it must look to Boz. I doubt if any gorgio woman would still be a virgin the morning after spending a whole night with a *Romany* man.'

'You've not got a particularly delicate way of putting

things, Melody, but I take your point . . . Ouch!'

Seb turned a little too quickly and discovered yet another badly bruised part of his anatomy.

That same evening, after dark, Seb was sitting at the table in Fern Cottage, working by the light of a lamp. He was laboriously attempting to sort out the financial details of the scheme he had put to Christian. A double-furrow plough would take a great chunk of the money in his possession, and he had worked out it would need at least four great horses, not three, to carry out the intended task. On good soil he could probably plough two or three acres in a day, but on the more difficult land that had until recently been forest he would be lucky to manage half of this.

At two pounds and ten shillings an acre it would take only ten working days to pay for the plough, but he had promised Christian half his earnings. This meant he would need to double the time to twenty days. If he was working for only two days every week it would be ten weeks before he began to make a profit.

His mind reeling with the difficult mathematical equations, he suddenly heard a soft knocking at the door. He was only half-way across the room when the sound came again, louder this time.

'All right, I'm coming.' He spoke irritably, his mind filled with figures that still needed to be written down. Who could it be calling on him at this time of night? He could think of no one who would knock.

Seb opened the door to find Melody standing outside in the darkness. Surprised, and not a little alarmed to see her there, he opened his mouth to speak but Melody was quicker.

'I've brought someone who wants to talk to you. I'll wait outside.'

Moving away from the door, Melody pushed Anna from the darkness to the light of the doorway.

'Anna! What are you doing here? Is something wrong?'

He took the hand she held out to him and guided her inside the cottage. Before closing the door he looked outside but could not see Melody, or anyone else.

Seb guided Anna to a chair and sat her down, but instead of releasing his hand immediately she pulled him to her and her hand went up to his face, her finger-tips gently assessing his injuries.

'Poor Seb. You didn't deserve that, but Boz was upset. All the men were upset.'

'So was I – at what Boz said about us . . . about you . . . Er, would you like a cup of tea?'

It was a totally inappropriate thing to say, but she *was* a visitor, and the first since he had been staying at Fern Cottage on his own.

'No, I can't stay long. I was only able to come because all the men have gone off to a meeting with Romanies from other camps. It's the only good thing to come from this threat to cut down the forest. Old feuds have been forgotten for the time being. With Boz out of the caravan I was able to get away for a while. Alamena knows we can't stay in each other's company for longer than a minute or two without quarrelling.'

'Poor Anna. Life isn't treating you very kindly lately.'

'I didn't come here so you could feel sorry for me. I wanted to see how *you* are. I had a big row with Boz about what happened. It's the first time we've ever quarrelled like that. It's this business about the forest. It's going to change life for everyone. There are really two types of Romany, the forest Romany and those who spend the whole of their lives on the road. We've always been forest Romanies, but if Wychwood is to be chopped down Boz and the rest of us will have to take to the road.'

'That isn't really necessary, Anna. You're welcome to camp in the fifty acres of forest belonging to Christian – and there will be a lot more forest left around here. Enough to make your people feel at home, at least.'

'Few landowners are like Christian. We won't be welcome by many of them. If all the Romanies in the forest try to squeeze into fifty acres we'll be falling over each other all the time and there'll be fighting like no one's ever seen. It won't affect me, but Boz and the others will suffer.'

'It won't affect you?' Seb suddenly realised the full import of her words, 'You mean . . . you're going ahead and marrying Nahum?'

'Of course. It's been arranged for a very long time.'

'Do you love him?'

'He's very kind.'

'That doesn't answer my question. Does he love you?'

'He'll take care of me.'

'I'd take care of you *and* I'd love you. I *do* love you.'

'Don't say that, Seb. Don't make me sorry I came here to say "Goodbye".'

'Goodbye? You mean . . . when is this marriage to take place?'

'In two months' time, but it's two weeks' journey and

I'll need to get to know Nahum's family. We're leaving in a week and I might not get another chance to come and speak to you. I shouldn't have come tonight. I must go now.'

Anna stood up facing him, with no more than a hand's breadth between them. Reaching out he pulled her to him and kissed her.

'No, Seb!' She moved her head away from him, but he moved with her and his mouth closed on hers once more.

For a few moments more she struggled, but he felt her resistance weakening. Then her arms went about him and there was a heat in her that for a moment matched his own.

This was the moment when Melody chose to knock at the door and Anna's head jerked back, away from him. 'I must go now, Seb.'

'Don't go, Anna. Stay here. Stay with me.'

'I can't. Let me go, Seb.'

Anna attempted to break away, but he held her tight and tried to kiss her again.

'Don't, Seb. Please let me go.'

Suddenly she stopped struggling, and as the knocking came again she began to cry. 'I shouldn't have come. I *knew* it was wrong . . . but I wanted to. I couldn't leave without speaking to you, just once more.'

Seeing tears spring from Anna's sightless eyes made Seb feel thoroughly ashamed. Releasing her, he said, 'I'm sorry, Anna.'

Her finger came up and stopped the flow of his words. 'Don't say that, Seb. I'm not sorry, but I ought not have met you again. It makes everything so much more difficult.'

'You'll not still marry Nahum, Anna? Not now. You can't . . .'

'Nothing's changed, Seb. We've both known for a long time how we feel about each other and all the reasons why nothing can ever come of it. A kiss doesn't change the world around us.'

The knocking was repeated yet again, and it was more insistent now. Melody called softly, 'Come on, Anna, or I'll have to come in.'

As Anna stretched out her hand and moved slowly towards the sound, Seb made another plea. 'It *would* work for us, Anna. I'd *make* it work.'

Anna reached the door and as she fumbled for the latch, Melody opened it from the other side.

'Goodbye, Seb. Take care of yourself. You should marry Carrie. She'd make you a good wife – and she loves you too.'

With this revelation, Anna stepped from the cottage and was gone.

CHAPTER THIRTY-SEVEN

Seb spent the next few days wrestling with very tangled emotions. He felt he wanted to go to the gipsy encampment and tell Boz that Anna could not marry Nahum. Seb believed she loved *him*. Was certain she did. He was equally certain they could cross the barrier between gorgio and Romany together.

Seb realised his mother would be bitterly opposed to such a marriage. Despite this, he felt she would love Anna as a daughter when she knew her better.

Yet common sense – and Melody – constantly told Seb it would be not only futile but foolhardy to go to the encampment just now. Feelings were running high among the gipsies because of the imminent disafforestation of Wychwood. In addition, Seb's fight with Boz had made him a temporary focus for their anger.

As Melody put it to Seb when they were discussing the matter for the umpteenth time at the farm, 'You go up there and try to tell 'em Anna shouldn't be marrying Nahum Plunkett and they'll tear you to pieces and feed you to the dogs.'

'I know what you say is true, Melody, but I can't stand by and allow this wedding to go ahead. It's just not right for Anna.'

'You can't stop it now, Seb – and you mustn't even

try. It will be a very happy marriage, Nahum isn't like his sister.'

The knowledge that he was helpless to do anything about the forthcoming wedding made things no easier for Seb, and proof that the end of the gipsies' way of life in Wychwood was near at hand.

The road-builders, moving ahead of the woodcutters, approached Swinbrook from the direction of Leafield. Huge gangs of navvies, dealing with their new task in the same manner with which they had extended the railway lines the length and breadth of the land. Toppling trees and clearing the undergrowth as they moved inexorably forward, they carved a thirty-feet-wide gash through the forest.

Behind the road-builders trundled wagons laden with graded stone to be pounded and pulverised into place to make a road which was intended to last for centuries to come.

Horse-hoeing a field above part of the forest that would soon come down to form an additional hundred acres of pasture for Handley Farm, Seb listened to the growing hubbub. It was the sound of more than a hundred working men and it rose above the sounds of the countryside that had become familiar to Seb's ears.

There would be even more noise when the navvies moved to their next camp closer to Swinbrook and beside a stream that flowed through the village and on to the river Windrush.

Christian told Seb where the camp was to be. The farmer had taken his Bible beneath his arm and visited the navvies earlier in the week. It was doubtful whether his preaching saved many souls, but enough of the navvies gave him a polite hearing to satisfy his missionary urges.

Later that evening, when darkness was falling, Seb was working in the stables by lamplight. The next day he was due to take some of the big farmhorses to the blacksmith for shoeing. This meant he had to bring forward some of his morning chores.

Seb was forking hay from the loft above the stables when he heard his name being called from outside. At first he failed to recognise the voice and shouted, 'I'm here. In the stables.'

Then the door was flung open and Boz stood in the doorway, wild-eyed and angry.

Looking around the stable he at first failed to see Seb, until he looked upwards. Then he started towards him, crying, 'I want you, gorgio. Where is she? What you done with her? I'll wring your bloody gorgio neck when I get hold of you!'

'You come a step farther up that ladder and I'll run you through with this fork.'

Seb backed up his threat with a two-pronged pitchfork, jabbing it to within inches of Boz's face as the gipsy placed his foot on the first rung. Behind him, three more gipsies crowded in through the doorway.

'Who are you talking about?' Sudden fear gripped Seb. It could only be . . . 'Has something happened to Anna?'

'Don't try to make out you know nothing.' Boz's manner was still threatening, but Seb's response had taken him by surprise. He had been convinced Anna was with Seb. When he found Fern Cottage in darkness and Seb missing he had been doubly sure. Now a doubt was creeping into his mind for the first time.

'Don't do anything foolish, Boz. If something's happened to Anna you're going to need help. Has she gone missing?'

Finally convinced Seb knew nothing, Boz stepped back from the ladder. 'She went out before noon today with some trinkets to sell. She said she was going to take them to the men working on the road.'

'Have you been to their camp yet?'

'No. They don't like Romanies at the best of times. At this time of the evening they'd have been drinking for an hour. I'd get no help there.'

'I'll go to the camp. They know me. Meanwhile you begin searching in the forest. How many men can you call on to help you?'

'No more than eighteen. The rest have already left Wychwood.'

'Eighteen men won't be able to do much in the forest, but get torches and search from your camp to the South Lawn road. If Anna's not with the navvies I'll try to get some of their men to search between your camp and the new road.'

Boz left the stable without another word as Seb flung aside his pitchfork and climbed down from the loft to hurry to the farmhouse.

Leaving Christian pulling on his boots with the intention of going to assist the gipsies, Seb made his way to the camp set up by the road-makers.

The camp was almost as noisy as the point of work had been during the day. There were a great many men here – and some women too. Several fires were burning, the green wood being used sending clouds of acrid smoke swirling among the tents and make-shift huts.

Some of the navvies formed noisy groups playing cards, others sat around the fires, singing. There was some cooking being carried out by the women – and a great deal of drinking.

Seb asked the whereabouts of Jacob Brailey, the Cockney gang-boss, a number of times without receiving any coherent reply, when a voice from inside one of the tents boomed, 'Who's that asking for me?'

'It's Seb Quilter . . . the jockey.'

'Then come on in, boy. Come and have a drink and be introduced to Sophie.'

Seb ducked inside the tent and saw Jacob Brailey leaning back against a heavy, wooden chest, his arm about a well-rounded girl. On the box were a couple of well-filled tankards.

'Here, take this.' Without changing his position, Jacob reached between himself and the woman and picked up one of the tankards, holding it out to Seb. From the woman's protests, Seb assumed the drink was hers.

'I haven't come to drink with you. I'm here looking for someone. A gipsy girl . . .'

'You'll find no gipsy girls here. The last one went a week or two ago. At least, she *said* she was a gipsy. My men called her something else when they started going down with the "clap", but she was long gone by the time they found out.'

'Anna isn't one of those. She's a decent young girl.'

Seb's statement brought a chorus of derision from a couple of navvies who had entered the tent behind him and were listening to the conversation.

Jacob waved them into silence. 'Let the lad speak. Go on, Seb.'

'You might have seen the girl at the Wychwood Forest Fair, last year. She's the sister of the man who owned Grye – the horse I rode in the race. She's about my age, and blind. She's the girl I hope to marry.'

Now Seb had the men's attention he said, more hopefully, 'She left her own camp in the forest to come down here hoping to sell a few trinkets to your men. That was before noon today. Her brother just came to Handley Farm to say she hasn't gone back.'

'There's been no blind girl here. She probably got herself lost in the forest.'

'No, Anna's more at home in the forest than most sighted men. Something must have happened to her.'

'What do you want us to do about it?'

'You once said if there was anything you could do to help me I had only to come to you and ask. I need your help now, Jacob. I want your men to search the forest for Anna.'

One of the men behind Seb began to protest, but Jacob cut him short. 'A walk in the forest will be better for the men than what they're doing right now. We might even get a decent day's work out of 'em.'

The gang-boss rose to his feet, allowing the woman to drop back heavily against the box. She swore, but lay where she had fallen.

Jacob ducked outside the tent and began shouting for his men to gather around. Many of them grumbled, but other gang-bosses got their men on their feet and soon all the navvies in the camp were gathered about the tent.

Jacob wasted no time giving detailed explanations. 'A friend of mine – a good friend – has got trouble. The girl he's going to marry – a young blind girl – is lost somewhere in the forest. I've told him we'll help search for her. Some of you collect all the lanterns we can muster. The rest of you can light torches from the fire.'

Turning to Seb, he said, 'Where do you suggest we start?'

'Form a long line along the piece of road you've been making and search the forest to the north.'

'You heard what the lad said. Don't stray from the line and shout if you find anything at all. Right, off you go.'

Some of the men grumbled as they moved away, but all found some form of light and took a place in the line to join in the search. For many it was something to break up the monotony of camp-life. Soon they were calling and shouting to each other as they moved off into the forest.

They cursed the trailing brambles that caught at their ankles and set up shouts as rabbits and pheasants fled into the darkness before them. Once a stag caused a great hullabaloo by breaking from cover and bounding away noisily. Seb thought that if Anna was anywhere within this part of the forest she could not fail to hear the searchers.

The navvies beat their way through the Wychwood Forest for almost three hours by which time the initial enthusiasm had long since waned. Indeed, a number of men had already made their way back to camp, ostensibly to re-kindle their torches, but in reality to resume drinking.

Suddenly a cry went up along the line. 'Here! Come here! We've found her.'

Relief surged through Seb as he stumbled his way through the undergrowth towards the direction of the shouts. As he drew nearer his relief gave way to apprehension. Seb could see the growing knot of men and the light of their torches, but now the shouting had ceased and had been replaced by a low, angry murmur.

Seb pushed his way through the circle of men and in the dancing light of breeze-blown torches he saw Jacob kneeling on the ground. The still form of Anna was lying beside him. As one of the torches suddenly flared he saw blood on her face, hair and shoulders. She had been badly battered about the head. Fearfully, Seb drew closer and could see her dress had been ripped down from the neck to waist. Jacob's jacket had been used to cover Anna's body from the waist down and this act told its own silent and ominous tale.

'Is she still alive?'

Jacob nodded. 'Only just.' Trying to control the fierce anger he was feeling, the navvy asked, 'What shall we do with her?'

Seb thought quickly. The gipsy encampment was probably closer, but he decided against taking her there. 'Bring her to my mother's cottage. It's just along the Swinbrook road.'

'I'll send someone for a blanket and we'll get her there in no time at all.'

Standing up, Jacob laid an arm sympathetically across Seb's shoulders. 'I'm sorry we've found her in this state, boy. I only wish the man who did it had still been with her.'

'Who would do something like this?' Seb did not want to look, but his gaze kept returning to Anna's battered face.

'I don't believe this is the work of my navvies, Seb. They take their women as they come – good, bad or indifferent – but not like this. All the same, I'll check. If I learn that any man went missing today he'll need to satisfy *me* where he was.'

CHAPTER THIRTY-EIGHT

On the way back to the Hankses' cottage with Anna, Seb and the navvies met one of the gipsy women who had been enquiring after the missing girl in the village. After a brief glance at Anna, the gipsy hurried off to find Boz and tell him where she was being taken.

Dolly, Tom and Carrie had all gone to bed, but Seb's knocking brought Tom to the bedroom window complaining about being disturbed at such a late hour. Seb shouted up to tell him what had happened and it took Dolly no more than a couple of minutes to hurry downstairs and throw open the cottage door.

Anna was carried upstairs to Carrie's bedroom. Shooing the men from the room, the two women undressed her, examined the injuries she had sustained and began the task of cleaning her up. Waiting outside the room, Seb could hear the occasional moan of distress from his mother and he wondered what else they had discovered.

Dolly and Carrie were still working on Anna in the bedroom when Seb heard Boz at the door of the cottage. The gipsy was loudly demanding to be allowed in to see his sister.

Tom escorted the gipsy up the stairs to the bedroom, his face registering disapproval. 'He says he's here to take Anna back to the gipsy camp.'

'No one's taking the poor girl anywhere,' declared

Dolly firmly as she emerged from the room to confront Boz. 'You can come in to see her, young man, but she needs the attentions of a doctor – and that's what she's going to get. In the meantime she stays here.'

Boz made no reply but pushed rudely past Dolly and entered the room. He was inside for only a few minutes and emerged very badly shaken. 'Does anyone know who might have done this to her?'

Seb shook his head. 'Jacob Brailey's promised to question all his men, but he's pretty sure it wasn't any of them. I believe him. His men are as tough as they come, but they don't do things like this to women.'

'*We'll* find out who it was. When we do . . .' Boz left the fate of Anna's attacker to the imagination of his listeners. 'A doctor can see her. I'll be back again tomorrow.'

There was no thanks, no expression of sympathy for what Anna had suffered. Seb had grown used to gipsy ways by now – especially Boz's ways – but Dolly muttered angrily about 'gipsy ingratitude' and returned with Carrie to the room where the badly injured girl lay. Seb left the house and made his way to Handley Farm to fetch a horse. He would ride to Burford to get a doctor.

Not until he galloped Grye into Burford did Seb realise he had no idea where the doctor lived. Much of the town was in darkness, but there was noise coming from one of the inns in the High Street and he decided to make enquiries there.

As he passed through the light spilling into the inn-yard from one of the windows, a voice from a deep, shadowed doorway called, 'Hello, Seb. You've come a long way for a late-night drink.'

It was Superintending Constable Giles Aplin, accompanied by another of the town's constables.

'I've not come for a drink. I was going inside to ask the way to the doctor's house. We need him urgently at Swinbrook.'

'You'll never make yourself heard above the din in there,' commented the Burford constable. 'It's the inn-keeper's birthday. Come with me, I'll show you where Doctor Cheatle lives. On the way you can tell me what's happened to make you lather up that great horse of yours in such a fashion.'

Grateful for the Burford man's help, Seb told him of finding Anna in the Wychwood Forest, adding, 'It's lucky she didn't die before we found her. If the navvies hadn't been there to help she'd not have been found for days.'

Doctor Cheatle was preparing for bed, but he agreed to accompany Seb immediately. Giles Aplin decided he would go too.

'The gipsies won't appreciate my help and they'll do nothing to assist me, but this sounds as though it's a very serious assault. If the girl dies it will be murder and it's happened in my area.'

Seb was silent for much of the ride. He had not faced the possibility that Anna might die.

When they reached the house there was not a gipsy or navvy to be seen, but Dolly and Carrie were still sitting beside Anna's bed. The presence of Giles Aplin took Dolly by surprise, but she said, 'I'm glad you've decided to come along. I have something here that might help you find the man who attacked the poor girl. I found it clutched in Anna's hand when we cleaned her up. She was holding it so tight the hook was embedded in her flesh. If it hadn't been she would probably have dropped it on the way here. It looks as though it might be the fastening from a man's cape.'

Dolly handed the constable a piece of black chain on which was a hook, made to resemble a swan's neck and head. Giles Aplin examined it with some interest before consigning it to a buttoned pocket without comment.

When Doctor Cheatle left the room where Anna lay, his face was grim. 'The girl's been badly beaten. She was probably left for dead by her attacker after he had violated her. I suspect she has a fractured skull and her cheekbone is also broken. It's an appalling crime to happen anywhere, but it's unheard of in a peaceful village like Swinbrook.'

'Will she live?' Seb asked the question anxiously.

'I will do all within my sadly limited power to ensure she does. Unfortunately, in cases like this, God alone has the power of healing. I suggest you ask Him to do everything He can.'

Giles Aplin left Swinbrook for Burford with the doctor. Both men promised to return the next day.

Boz called at the Hankses' cottage early the next morning. He was mounted on a gipsy pony and had make-shift saddle-bags slung on either side. He looked in briefly at the unconscious girl. Outside the room, standing at the top of the stairs, he was told exactly what the doctor had said.

Boz nodded grimly. 'I thought as much. All right, I'll leave her here until she comes to, then we'll take her back to the camp.'

'Oh, no, you won't,' said Dolly, positively. 'She'll leave here when the doctor says she's fit to go, and not a moment earlier.'

As Dolly followed Boz down the stairs from the bedroom, she said, 'Seb met Constable Aplin in Burford and brought him back here with the doctor last night. He'll no doubt come to the forest to see you today.'

'He won't find me in the forest. I'm on my way to tell Nahum Plunkett and his family what's happened here. They have a right to know.'

Boz made the announcement as though expecting Dolly to argue with him, but she merely nodded acknowledgement of his statement. She would argue about moving Anna before she had fully recovered – *if* she recovered – but she would put nothing in the way of Anna's marriage to Nahum Plunkett.

'When the constable comes ask Seb to tell him we don't need his help. *We'll* find out who did this, and deal with it in our own way.'

'If you have any messages like that you can pass them on yourself – but I'd advise against it. Giles Aplin's a great believer in justice – but only within the law.'

'Romany law is as ancient as yours – and our justice is *seen* to be done.'

Anna was unconscious for a full week. During this time Doctor Cheatle came from Burford every day and Giles Aplin every second day. When Anna eventually opened her eyes Carrie was with her. Holding the gipsy girl's hand, Carrie answered as many of the questions that crowded Anna's confused mind as she could.

When Dolly arrived at Handley Farm and informed

Seb that Anna had regained consciousness he left his work and hurried to the cottage to speak to her. He found Carrie seated by the bedside, but was distressed to find that Anna would not talk to him.

Following the despondent Seb outside the room when he eventually left, Carrie said, 'You mustn't take it too much to heart, Seb. It's only natural that she shouldn't want to speak to you.'

'Why? I don't understand.'

'Think about it, Seb. Think of what some man's done to her. It's something a girl dreams she'll one day do with the man she loves. Now that dream's destroyed for ever for her. She doesn't want to talk to any man just now – you especially, I suspect.'

Seb remembered what Anna had said to him when they shared a haystack bed on the road back from Charwelton. She had told him then that her body was all she had to offer a man.

'I'd better go and tell someone up at the camp that she's come round.'

As a result of Seb's visit to the encampment a gipsy woman called to speak to Anna later that same day. She remained in the room for a long while but although Carrie went there twice with tea for them, she found them talking in the Romany language and did not understand anything they said.

When the woman had gone Anna was left in a very distressed state but she declined to say what had passed between her and the visitor.

Later that evening, Anna had another caller. Giles Aplin rode from Burford and was delighted to learn of the improvement in her condition. He too wanted to talk to her about the attack, but found her far less ready to talk to him than she had been to the woman from the gipsy encampment.

Giles Aplin remained at the Hankses' cottage until Tom returned from his work at the manor. Although the ostler's evening meal was almost ready to be served, the Burford constable asked him to accompany him to Handley Farm, where he was going to talk to Seb, and the two men walked along the road deep in conversation.

Standing in the farmyard, Giles Aplin also spoke to Seb at some length. He asked if Anna had mentioned anything at all about her attacker that might prove useful to him.

'Anna hasn't spoken to me at all,' confessed Seb unhappily. 'If I enter the room when she's talking to Carrie or my ma, she'll simply dry up and say nothing until I've left. She might have said something to them.'

'No, I've asked them already. It's made doubly difficult because of her blindness. Even if she did claim to know who it was we'd find it difficult to convince a judge, without far more proof than I have at the moment.'

'I hope you find the proof soon. Anna and the gipsy woman spoke together for a very long time. If Boz believes he knows who did it he won't wait to find the sort of proof that a judge would need. Revenge is a matter of honour for a gipsy.'

'Then I'll need to work at it even harder than I am at the moment.'

As Superintending Constable Giles Aplin mounted his horse he looked down at Tom and Seb. 'I have no doubt we'll be meeting again in the course of the next week or two. In the meantime, take care of Anna. That poor girl has been through a terrible ordeal, and if I know anything of gipsies, it's not over for her yet.'

'She's in good hands with Ma and Carrie to take care of her,' said Seb. 'I wish you luck with your inquiries and hope you find out who did it.'

'I believe I already know who did it,' came the Burford constable's astonishing reply. 'The difficulty I have is proving it.'

As the constable rode away, Seb turned an incredulous look upon Tom. 'Do you think he really does know who attacked Anna?'

'I don't know.' Tom Hanks was not a man who jumped to hasty conclusions. 'All I do know is that when we were on the way here he was asking me a great many questions about what went on in the village. He even asked me about them up at the manor. Wanted to know if I could remember whether Mr Meredith went off riding on the day Anna was attacked.'

'And did he?'

'I couldn't tell him for sure, but he's been taking Vulcan out most days. Wrote it all down, did Constable Aplin. Said that in future he'd be obliged if I kept careful note of when Mr Meredith took out a horse. He seemed especially interested in the times he had Vulcan out at night, as he did so often last year. Last thing he asked me was where he might find Florrie Shaw. Said he wanted to have a chat to her about her son's murder. I wouldn't think there's any connection between the attack on Anna and the killings of Sir Vincent, Lady Hammond and Will Shaw, would you? And what would any of this have to do with Mr Meredith?'

'I've no idea, Tom, but I wouldn't put such a question to anyone else, if I was you. Not if you value your job at the manor. Just do as Giles Aplin's asked you, and keep quiet about it. All I hope is that he gets whoever attacked Anna – and gets him quickly.'

CHAPTER THIRTY-NINE

Seb learned that Boz had returned to the Wychwood Forest when Melody came to the farm one afternoon to say goodbye to him and to Christian.

'What do you mean, "Goodbye"? Where are you going?'

'I don't know. Up north somewhere. Boz is taking us.'

'Is Boz back here in the forest?'

'He's been back for two days.'

'But . . . he hasn't been to the cottage to see Anna.'

'I don't know anything about that. I can't speak for Boz Buckland. Nobody can. If you want to know any more about what he's doing you'd better go up to the camp and ask him yourself.'

Seb entered the gipsy encampment warily, remembering the reception Boz and his friends had given him on an earlier visit. He wished he had Christian with him, but the farmer had ceased work at Handley Farm early that day. He was preaching that evening at a chapel a couple of miles beyond Burford.

Everyone here seemed busy and it was apparent that the few gipsies still remaining in this part of the forest were on the move. Even the tinkers camped nearby were packing up their few belongings and preparing to leave.

Seb found Boz tying some of the bulkier items of his

household to the rear of his caravan. The gipsy seemed embarrassed at Seb's presence.

'What's all this about, Boz? Where are you going?'

'Up north. That's all you need know.'

'But Anna's nowhere near fit enough yet to travel with you!'

'She won't be coming.'

Seb thought he must have misheard the gipsy. 'What about . . . the wedding? Surely you're coming to the cottage to tell Anna and us what's happening?'

'There's not going to be a wedding. Noah Plunkett and his family have come out against it. He says the Plunketts are having no gorgio's cast-off in their family.'

Seb should have been overjoyed at the news that Anna was not to marry the educated young gipsy, but he knew that unless Boz explained it to her – preferably in a more diplomatic way than the manner with which he had just broken the news to Seb – she would be devastated.

'Anna's nobody's cast-off, as well you know – and being attacked wasn't her fault. She was raped, for God's sake!'

'That isn't the only reason Noah Plunkett's called the wedding off. When he came here, he didn't realise Anna is blind. It happened after the betrothal. Then he began to hear rumours about you and her. He watched you both and saw how friendly you were. Far too friendly. Then someone told him you'd spent a night together on your way back from Charwelton.'

'Nothing happened between us then – or at any other time.'

'I believe it – now. Noah Plunkett doesn't. What

happened to Anna in the forest was the final excuse he needed to call off the wedding. Noah said everything – including the attack on her – has been brought about by her departure from Romany ways. He says Anna isn't the right wife for a Plunkett – especially one who's been given a university education so he can become a spokesman for our people. These are difficult times, he says. We need to unite our people and not risk dividing them.'

'How are you going to explain all this to Anna?'

'I'm not.' Seb thought he detected a brief flash of unhappiness in Boz's expression before the gipsy added, 'Noah wants me to take his daughter and the rest of our people north to a place he's found. It's best I don't see Anna. I'll only upset her. You tell her, gorgio. You've never made any secret of wanting her. Now you've got your wish.'

'She'll be absolutely heartbroken, Boz – and she's a very sick girl. You and Anna have always been so close. She thinks the world of you – and you're her brother. You can't just desert her like this.'

'You may not understand it, gorgio, but she will. She's a Romany.'

Although Melody had already said her farewells to Seb, she found time to visit Anna before she left with the others. She spent almost an hour in the room with Anna. At one time Carrie thought she heard Anna crying, but she could not be certain and Melody had insisted that she wanted to be alone with Anna for a while.

Seb arrived at the cottage as the half-gipsy girl was leaving and asked her what she had said to Anna.

'I told her what needed saying, Seb, for your sake as much as anything else. She's like me, now. Deserted by her people. On her own. An outcast.'

'That's totally unfair, Melody. She's done nothing to deserve this.'

'What did I do – except be born? I've never been forgiven for that.'

'She's still a very sick girl, Melody. This might well prove too much for her. Go back and tell her everythings going to be all right.'

'I can't, Seb. I've been many things in my life, but I'm not a liar.'

For twenty-four hours after Melody's visit Anna neither ate nor drank anything, and never spoke a word to anyone.

Seb was forced to watch her grow steadily weaker. He felt helpless at being able to do nothing and no matter how many times he tried to convince her everything would be all right, she did not respond.

Seb was in Anna's room the next evening, talking vainly in an effort to get through to her, when his mother came up the stairs and into the room.

Motioning for Seb to come to her, she stood in the doorway and in a low voice, said, 'There's someone downstairs to see Anna. He seems a nice enough young man, but I refused to allow him up until I'd spoken to you.'

'Who is it?'

'He says his name's Plunkett. Nathan . . . no, *Nahum* Plunkett.'

They had both forgotten Anna's exceptional hearing but suddenly Anna whispered her first agonised words for more than twenty-four hours. 'No! I don't want to speak to him – *ever*! Tell him to go away.'

'I'll speak to him,' Seb said to his mother. 'You stay here with Anna.'

Nahum was in the kitchen talking to Carrie. When Seb entered the gipsy turned and extended a hand in greeting. He looked tired and travel-weary and his first words confirmed he had been riding hard.

'I came as quickly as I could. I would have liked to beat Boz here but I gather he told Anna what my father had said?'

'Not personally, but I think that's what Melody came to tell Anna yesterday. She hasn't said a word since and refuses to eat or drink.'

'I was afraid something like this might happen if I didn't get here first. She's a very sensitive girl – but I don't need to tell you that, Seb. I think you probably know her better than anyone else. I suspect that you love her too.'

Seb felt as though the ground was opening beneath his feet. 'You mean . . . *you* love her? After what your father said about her? In spite of everything that's happened?'

'Anna has suffered a great deal already, yet nothing that's happened has been of her making. Do you believe you are the only one able to love her, Seb? As for my father . . . He belongs to the past. He had me educated so I could speak for the Romanies of today – and of the future. He's a good man who's done much for our people, but he can't quite let go of the life he and our forefathers have always known. Anna's offended against age-old Romany taboos, but after what's happened to her she needs to be helped, not rejected.'

'I can help her.'

'Seb, you've already helped her more than anyone else – more than any of her own people have – but right now she needs someone who understands Romany ways, and someone who cares for her too. My father thinks she's far too forward for a Romany girl, but that's merely her way of doing things. She, like so many of our young Romany people, is on the first step of the ladder to a wider, less restrictive world. But it's a long ladder and Anna isn't ready to go any farther. She still needs the security and familiarity of the world she's always known. You care about her, Seb, and I believe that in your heart you know what I'm saying is true.'

Seb *did* know. He had known for a long time, but had refused to admit it to himself. Neither was he ready to admit it to this assured young gipsy who stood before him. Yet Seb could not find it in his heart to dislike Nahum Plunkett.

'You'd better go upstairs and see her, Nahum. Try to persuade her that life is still worth living. That we *all* care about what's going to happen to her.'

Nahum was upstairs with Anna for more than two hours. Meanwhile, Seb waited in the kitchen, growing increasingly depressed. He knew he had lost Anna. He had lost her long before Nahum arrived. The time had come for him to be totally unselfish and think only of Anna.

Seb had hoped that rejection by her family and her people would make her turn to him and accept a gorgio way of life. He had honestly believed he could take the place of everything she had ever known if only she was willing to give him the chance. Now he was forced to admit he had been wrong.

Anna was in danger of dying because he had not enough to offer her to replace what she would be losing. She felt she had nothing to live for. His love was not sufficient. It was a bitter pill to swallow, but he took it and would try to act as a man should.

'If you move over I'll put some wood on this fire and make us a cup of tea.'

Carrie and Seb were alone in the kitchen. Tom was at Swinbrook Manor and Dolly had gone to the farm to prepare some bread she intended baking the next day.

The two young people had been sitting in silence for most of the time Nahum had been upstairs, Seb gazing morosely into the fire and Carrie reading at the kitchen table.

'What? What was that you said?' Seb started, as though his mind had suddenly returned from a very long distance.

'I said, move over. You've been sitting there for an hour watching the fire almost go out. I'll put on some wood and then make us a cup of tea.'

'It's all right, I'll put the wood on. You get the things ready for the tea. It might be an idea to make a couple of extra cups. Nahum would like one, I'm sure, and he might have been able to persuade Anna to drink something.'

'Nahum Plunkett coming here to see Anna is probably the only chance anyone has of pulling her through this crisis, you know that really, don't you, Seb?'

He nodded. 'Knowing doesn't make it any easier for me, but I hope he can give her a reason for living. I can't, yet God knows I've tried hard enough.'

'Seb, you've given her the *opportunity* to live, not once but *twice*. At Charwelton you saved her life and you did it yet again by organising a search for her after she was attacked. You've shown everyone how much you care for her and we all admire you for it. Now you've got to prove it yet again – this time to yourself and it's going to be the hardest thing you've ever done for her. You have to let her go.'

'You're not telling me anything I don't already know, Carrie. I've repeated it to myself a hundred times already. But, like I said, it isn't easy.'

CHAPTER FORTY

When Nahum came downstairs from Anna's room, Dolly and Tom had returned home and Christian had joined them from Handley Farm. Nahum's smile swept away the air of apprehensive gloom that had hung over the cottage since Anna's latest decline.

'Anna's going to be all right, thanks to all of you. She's complaining of feeling hungry. If there was something she could eat . . .'

The whole family and Christian crowded around the young gipsy, congratulating him as though he had just achieved some major feat.

Seb was somewhat less effusive in his acclaim, yet he was far more relieved than anyone else at Nahum's success. The news even managed to overshadow some of the heartache he felt at knowing he had finally lost Anna.

'What will you do now?' Dolly put the practical question to Nahum when the back-slapping and hand-shaking had come to an end.

'I'd like to stay in Swinbrook until Anna is fully recovered – that's if you don't mind having her in your home for a while longer?'

The nodding of heads gave Nahum his answer as Dolly said, 'I'd be deeply offended if you took her off anywhere else.'

'That's wonderful of you. When Anna's feeling well

enough I would like us to be married in the same chapel as my sister and Boz.'

Nahum looked at Christian. 'I believe you could arrange this for us?'

Christian beamed. 'I'll be delighted – absolutely delighted!'

With everyone in the room so happy, Seb tried hard not to let it show that he was the only one less than ecstatic over the forthcoming wedding. He had felt he should ask Nahum to stay at Fern Cottage with him, but was relieved when Christian insisted that the gipsy leader's son stay at Handley Farm for the remainder of his time in Swinbrook.

Christian was delighted when the gipsy accepted the offer. Nahum was a leader of the future. One of Christian's oft-repeated dreams was to establish a Methodist mission among the country's gipsies and Nahum's status could help him achieve this ambition.

When Tom produced a half-firkin of ale, saved from his own wedding, it became apparent the celebration was going to carry on far into the night. At the height of the party, when he thought he would not be missed, Seb slipped away to return to Fern Cottage.

His departure did not go unnoticed. As he reached the gate, Carrie's voice brought him to a halt.

'Seb! Wait!'

He stopped by the gate and waited as she limped towards him in the darkness.

When she reached him, she put out a hand to grasp his arm. 'Where are you going?'

'Home to Fern Cottage. I've got a lot of work to do tomorrow and I can't see Christian being up very early to help me. He'll have Nahum talking until dawn about his idea of a mission for the gipsies.'

Carrie's hand dropped away from his arm and there was relief in her voice when she said, 'I saw you leaving and was worried about you.'

'Worried? Why?'

'Well, with everyone congratulating Nahum and chatting about a wedding. I know how much you were hoping that everything would work out for you and Anna.'

'Were my feelings so obvious?'

'No, Seb, you hid them well – but you and I have talked a lot about Anna. I know how you must have been feeling inside.'

'The only really important thing is that Anna's going to be fine.'

'Yes. We've all been worried about her. She is going to be all right, Seb. She'll be happy with Nahum. He's very nice, and kind.'

Seb let himself out through the gate and Carrie was half-way back to the house when his soft call brought her to a halt.

'Carrie!'

'Yes, Seb?'

'Thanks for caring.'

The three words were not a great deal for Carrie to pin her hopes to, but she had a warm and happy glow deep inside her as she let herself in at the door of the cottage.

Seb's apparent resignation to the fact that Anna was to marry Nahum did nothing to ease the pain he felt whenever he thought about it during the next few days. He found it was at its worst in the late evenings when he sat alone in Fern Cottage.

Seb could have gone to the Hankses' cottage and perhaps worked on his learning with Carrie, but that would have meant paying a visit to Anna in her sick room and listening to his mother chatting about the plans for the wedding.

Dolly had taken the young gipsy girl to her heart once it was established she would not be marrying Seb. She was determined the wedding would be one for the young blind girl to remember, even though it was not likely to be attended by any of the Wychwood gipsies who had been at Boz's marriage to Nahum's sister.

One evening, Seb could put up with his own company no longer. Setting out from Fern Cottage he bypassed his mother's home and cut through the forest, heading for the navvies' camp. He knew he would be assured of company there with no talk of weddings, and they would no doubt offer him a drink.

It was growing dark when Seb reached the camp and the evening activities were just warming up. The camp had acquired a new 'amenity' since Seb's last visit: ale and spirits were being dispensed from a wooden-sided enclosed wagon by a leather-aproned vendor.

Jacob Brailey was standing by the wagon and when he saw Seb he called to him and thrust a tankard of ale into his hand, saying, 'Here, boy. It's good to see you. How's that blind gipsy girl of yours?'

Anna was the last subject Seb wished to talk about, but he said, 'She's recovered consciousness and the doctor says she's well on the road to recovery – thanks to you and your men.'

'The men will be pleased to learn she's going to be all right.' Raising his voice, Jacob bellowed, 'Listen to me, men. Seb says the young gipsy girl's going to be all right.'

A great cheer went up and Jacob beamed at them. When he turned back to Seb his expression had changed. 'Are they any closer to finding out who did it?'

Seb shook his head. 'No one's been arrested yet.'

'It wasn't anyone from here, I can assure you of that. I've spoken to every one of the men and we had that constable from Burford here asking a lot of questions. He's nobody's fool, that one.'

At that moment there was a commotion in one of the tents and a young woman emerged pulling down her dress. At the same time she handed off a man who was trying to prevent her from leaving.

'Who says Anna's going to be all right?'

The girl stood swaying slightly, but she stared about her in a belligerent manner, as though challenging someone to answer her.

'Melody! What are you doing here? You came and said good- bye.'

At the sound of Seb's voice Melody started guiltily and looked about her as though she might run away. Instead, she shrugged and said, 'Hello, Seb. I didn't expect to meet up with you.'

'I was about to say the same to you. I thought you'd gone somewhere up north with the others.'

'I did, but I came back.'

'Does your ma know where you are?'

'She's the reason I came back. You'll probably find her in the tent over there – or perhaps that one.' She nonchalantly waved a hand in a direction that might have included any tent in the camp.

'I didn't know you two knew each other,' said Jacob. 'Mind you, it doesn't surprise me. Both Melody and her ma make friends very easily. But come over to my tent and bring your drink – bring Melody too, if you like.'

Before Seb could decide whether he wanted to spend the evening in Melody's company she was following close behind the gang-boss. Seb grimaced, it was all the same to him. He fell in behind her.

Seb spent the evening drinking steadily, talking generalities, until Jacob was called away to intervene in a fight between two of his navvies.

When he was out of hearing, Melody asked, 'You going to marry Anna now she's on her own?'

'No – and she's not on her own. She'll still be marrying Nahum. He's here, in Swinbrook.'

'Nahum Plunkett's still going to marry her, after all that's happened?'

'I don't think he's got his pa's approval but, yes, he's going to marry her. They're to be married soon in the same chapel where Boz was married.'

'Oh, that'll be why Boz has come back to Wychwood. For the wedding.'

'Boz back here? No, Melody, you must be mistaken. He went north leading the party you should have been with.'

'He set off with them, but so did I. Now we're both back. I saw him in the forest a couple of days ago. It was when I went for a walk to our old camp. He was there with three of the others.'

'But he hasn't been anywhere near our place, or tried to see Anna.'

'Then I wonder what he's up to.' Melody's eyes

widened suddenly. 'It must have something to do with the attack on Anna. Boz told some of the others that he knows who attacked Anna.'

'How can he? Anna doesn't know.'

'Is that what she told you? But then, I suppose she would. It's the duty of one of her own to avenge her. Not an outsider. Not even a constable. It has to be a Romany from her own family.'

'No, Melody, that's *not* the way. If Anna were to tell Constable Aplin all she knows he'd make certain that whoever did it is brought to justice and sent to prison.'

'A gorgio sent to prison for attacking a Romany girl?' There was no humour in Melody's short laugh. 'He'd likely walk free and *she'd* be sent to gaol for being a whore. Anyway, he wouldn't even be arrested – not by any constable in Oxfordshire.'

'Who is he, Melody? Who is it who attacked Anna?'

Melody hesitated a moment or two, wondering whether to speak or hold her tongue.

Making up her mind, she said fiercely, 'It was him up at the manor. The one who rides that horse of his like a madman. Meredith Putt.'

CHAPTER FORTY-ONE

Seb tackled Nahum Plunkett the next morning. He told him Boz had been seen in the area. After suggesting the reason for his presence was revenge, he asked, 'Has Anna said anything to you about the man who attacked her?'

Nahum shook his head. 'She wouldn't. Boz is the only one she'd tell such a thing to, but she's already told me Boz hasn't been to see her since the attack.'

'He hasn't, but he sent one of the women from the camp. She went up to the bedroom to see Anna and they spoke together for a long time.'

'Anna would have told her who she thought it was – if she knew. If she did then family honour demands that he takes revenge.'

'You must stop him. You've said you want to bring your people out of the Dark Ages and into the nineteenth century. Well, now's your chance to prove you mean it. Order Boz to go to Constable Aplin and tell him all he knows. Or do you intend obeying only those laws you agree with?'

'I'm willing to abide by all laws – and I'll try to persuade other Romanies to do the same, but I'm not likely to succeed until my people can see these laws *protecting* as well as persecuting them.'

'If Boz goes ahead with his revenge there'll be no protection for him, or any hiding. Constable Aplin will know immediately who's done it.'

'From what you've told me this constable knows as much as Boz about the man who attacked Anna, but he's made no arrest yet.'

'There'll be an arrest when Aplin has the proof he needs to put before a court.'

'There you've touched on the major flaw in your argument about justice in this country. This so-called "one law for all" means one thing when it's applied to gorgios and something else when Romanies are involved. The slightest suspicion of having committed an offence is considered reason enough to arrest a Romany. Proof is sought afterwards – but then only if it's absolutely necessary. That's what Boz will tell me if I tackle him, Seb. Unfortunately, he'd be right. Nevertheless, I'll do what I can. Where was Boz last seen?'

'Close to the old camp in the forest.'

'You won't mention this to Anna?'

'Of course not.'

Seb would have little difficulty keeping this promise. He had not seen Anna since Nahum's arrival in Swinbrook and he had no plans to visit the Hankses' cottage in the near future.

As though Seb had spoken his thoughts aloud, Nahum said, 'Go to see Anna some time soon, Seb. What's happened to her has injured more than her body. One of her worst fears is that folk will shun her because of what's happened. Boz must take much of the blame for that. If I can find him I'll try to persuade him to visit her too.'

Seb told himself he really *did* intend calling at the cottage to see Anna, but it was easy to make excuses to put off such a visit. It would soon be time to commence hay-making in the Handley Farm pastures. Once this began all other farm duties would take second place. Seb and Christian were trying to complete all the tasks about the farm before then.

When the farm chores ended each day, Seb would often make his way to the camp of the road-building navvies. He enjoyed their company and more recently his 'relaxation' at their camp had lasted longer with each successive visit. At the end of each evening he would stumble home at an hour when most of the villagers were in bed asleep.

On two occasions, Dolly came to the cottage during the evening and left a meal on the table for him. When she had looked in to clean up the following day the meal was still on the table, untouched.

When Dolly tried to speak to Seb about his drinking, he refused to listen to her. As a result, she became very worried about him. She discussed the problem with Tom but he suggested she should bide her time, adding, 'The navvies will have finished the road by the time Anna's wedding comes around. Seb'll settle down again once they're gone.'

Dolly would have felt less reassured had she known Melody was staying at the navvies' camp. However, she took Tom's advice and busied herself preparing for Anna's wedding day.

During one of Seb's evening drinking sessions at the navvies' camp he told Jacob that Anna was to marry someone else. The gang-boss was suitably sympathetic, but his sympathy was expressed with pints, rather than words.

That night, Seb had so much to drink that when he tried to rise from the ground beside the camp-fire to return home his legs felt like rubber and he sat down again unexpectedly.

Melody was seated next to him. 'You've had a skinful tonight, Seb Quilter. You'd better stay here, with me.'

'Got to get back. Work to do on the farm . . . in the morning.' Having delivered this barely intelligible reply, Seb made it to his feet with difficulty, and stood swaying over Melody.

'If you try to get home in that state you'll wind up back in London. Stay with me, Seb. What have you got to lose that you haven't already given me?'

Seb shook his head slowly and very deliberately, 'Going . . . home.'

Melody sighed. 'Well, you're not going to make it in that state and that's for sure. I'd better come with you and help you . . . steady!' Melody grabbed Seb as he leaned to one side and began side-stepping towards the blazing wood-fire.

To the accompaniment of a chorus of ribald shouts and cat-calls, Seb weaved his way beyond the lights of the camp. Melody, her arm about his waist, was having to work hard to keep him upright.

They managed to stagger clear of the forest and emerge on Handley Plain before Seb dropped to his knees and was violently ill. Melody managed to raise him to his feet once more, but after only another fifty paces, Seb veered from the path and stumbled clumsily across broken ground for some distance before collapsing into a depression in the ground that was half-hidden by undergrowth.

Melody tried to raise him to his feet yet again, but Seb pushed her off. 'Go away! Let me sleep.'

As he lay face down on the grass of the hollow, Melody, who had also consumed a considerable amount of drink, sat down heavily beside him and spoke to herself. 'Your luck's running true to form, Melody. Here's you thinking you'll be lying the night in a comfortable bed with someone whose fingers aren't as calloused as a piece of old limestone, and what's happened? You've ended up dossing-down with a man who's as limp as a plucked dandelion and who'll probably snore like a hedgehog.'

Seb stirred irritably, imagining he could hear voices. When he opened one eye the light was so bright he closed it again hurriedly. Then he heard the voices once more – and this time he knew it was not his imagination. He moved and let out a groan as he discovered how stiff his limbs were. Beside him, Melody murmured in sleepy complaint. Memory returned to Seb in disjointed snatches and he hastily checked he was wearing his trousers.

Satisfied he was at least decently dressed, Seb raised his head cautiously and peered over the edge of the hollow.

'What you doing, Seb? Ain't it enough to keep me awake all night with your snoring?'

'Shh!' Seb reached down and put a hand over her mouth.

Silenced for a moment, Melody also heard the sound of voices. Sitting up, she peered over the edge of the hollow alongside Seb.

Two horsemen were riding past in a leisurely manner, skirting the forest. On one of the horses was a pair of bulging saddle-bags.

'It's the pay for the navvies, the contractors and the waggoners. It's always brought to them first thing in the morning. After it's been dished out the paymasters ride on to take the pay to the men cutting down the forest. There's a small fortune in those saddle-bags.'

As they watched, Seb said suddenly, 'Look! Over there, under the trees.'

As he pointed, a horse and rider emerged from the shadow of the forest. The rider had a scarf tied about his face and in his hand he held a double-barrelled pistol.

'It's the highwayman!' Melody clutched Seb's arm, squeezing it tight in a combination of fear and excitement.

As though they were seeing actors on a stage, Seb and Melody watched as one of the two riders suddenly kneed his horse forward. There was a puff of white smoke from the highwayman's gun, and the horse of the man riding towards him reared in the air. When it came down, its rider slumped in the saddle, clutching his shoulder.

The second man handed over his saddle-bags to the highwayman and both men were immediately waved on their way, the robbed man supporting his companion. Not until the two men were out of sight did the highwayman turn his horse and put it into a gallop along the track that passed near to the hollow where Seb and Melody were kneeling.

Melody dived to the bottom of the hollow and Seb crouched low until horse and rider passed by. When he raised his head again he was beside himself with excitement, all thoughts of his hangover and pounding head forgotten.

'That horse . . . it's Vulcan! Meredith Putt's horse! I'd swear it.'

As Melody stared at him wide-eyed, Seb said, 'Run to Jacob Brailey's camp. If the two men haven't gone straight there tell Jacob what's happened. I'll go to the farm and get a horse, then I'll ride to Burford and find Constable Aplin. He should know about this right away.'

Seb reached Burford in a state of high excitement only to find that Superintending Constable Aplin was in London. He was attending a conference which had been called to discuss the formation of a police force in Oxfordshire.

The constable left in charge of Burford was reluctant to take any action, even when Seb reported the highway robbery at Swinbrook.

Shaking his head doubtfully, he said, 'I'm not at all certain Swinbrook lies within my jurisdiction. In any case, I've never been called on to deal with anything like this before. As for this highwayman being the lord of the manor . . . !' He looked at Seb suspiciously. 'Would I be right in thinking you've been drinking, young sir?'

'That was last night. It has nothing to do with what I saw this morning.'

'Ah, so you say. Drink can play funny tricks on people, especially a young lad like yourself.'

'Look! I saw a robbery. Are you going to come and do something about it or not?'

'I'll tell you what to do, you go along and speak to Magistrate Peck. Tell him what you've just told me. If he says I should ride to Swinbrook, why, that's what I'll do.'

Seb never went to see Magistrate Peck, and he returned to Swinbrook a very worried young man. If word reached Meredith Putt that there had been witnesses to his crime Seb would be in great danger. If he was indeed the highwayman who had terrorised the area for the past year he had been responsible for the murders of a number of men and women already. One more would make little difference to him and Seb had first-hand experience of the man's anger.

Seb did not doubt at all that the man riding Vulcan was Meredith Putt, even though he had been masked. It all fitted neatly into place. Constable Aplin would agree, of this Seb had no doubt. Aplin had been asking many questions about Putt, not only in connection with the robberies but with the rape of Anna too.

It was this that made Seb resolve he would not let the matter drop. That evening, after a great deal of worried thought, Seb confided in Tom Hanks. Expressing initial disbelief, Tom confirmed that Putt went out riding on Vulcan most mornings. He also ventured the opinion that Putt was now dangerously insane.

'I'm not saying you're right, young Seb, but don't you tell anyone else what you've just told me. Keep it quiet – and stay out of the forest until Giles Aplin comes back from London. He'll know what's to be done about Meredith Putt.'

CHAPTER FORTY-TWO

The day did not begin well for the lord of Swinbrook Manor. The mail arrived early and he opened his letters as he sat at the breakfast table. Among may other bills was one from his London tailor. Meredith Putt read the letter enclosed with the bill with increasing fury.

It was not so much a letter, as an ultimatum. Either Mr Putt settle his long-standing and substantial account, or the tailor would take him to the debtor's court.

It was an almost unheard impertinence for a tradesman of such lowly status to threaten one of his customers in such a fashion. Putt resolved the man would have no more of his business.

He was still fuming when his mother entered the room. One glance at the letters heaped untidily beside her son's plate was sufficient to identity them for what they were.

'More demands for payment, I see.'

'What if they are? They're none of your business.'

'None of my business, you say? How dare you! Who do you think has to deal with the tradesmen and tell them there will be no money to pay their accounts this month – even though there was none last month, and it is highly likely there will be none next month either? None of my business indeed!'

'Well what do you expect *me* to do? I can't make money grow.'

'If you didn't fritter it all away with your high-living friends up in London you wouldn't need to make it "grow". The income from the farm and lands are enough for us to live in comparative comfort without going cap-in-hand to common tradesmen. I wish to God Nelson had put *me* in charge of the manor's affairs, and not a spendthrift like you. Another month of this and I'll not be able to put a meal on the table.'

'If it weren't for your penny-pinching ways I wouldn't be so eager to spend my time in London. At least my friends don't pass every minute of the day counting the cost of everything I do.'

'They have no need to count every penny. We do.'

'I'm not sitting here listening to your nagging. I'm going out riding.'

'That is your answer to every problem. To run away from it. I don't know where I've gone wrong in your upbringing. Perhaps if your uncle had only been home more often . . .'

The door slammed behind Meredith Putt and, still furious, he headed for the stables.

It seemed to Putt that life was a constant battle against debt. He had thought the death of his uncle, Sir Nelson, would bring about the end of his monetary problems, but Sir Nelson's wealth was in his land and livestock. There was very little hard cash. What little there was had gone to pay off Sir Nelson's own not inconsiderable service debts.

The argument with his mother left Putt in a foul mood. He worked off some of the anger by berating Tom Hanks for not having Vulcan ready more quickly when he ordered that the horse be prepared for a ride.

There was still enough ill-temper left in him to startle Vulcan into a gallop when two spurs were simultaneously jabbed into his body as they entered the straight stretch of forest track.

This had long been Meredith Putt's favourite ride. He used it even though there was now a good straight road running along the edge of the forest. This was the place where he had almost bowled Anna over many months before and where he enjoyed riding the horse at breakneck speed, disregarding anyone else who might chance to be on the path.

On this occasion, fate in the form of Boz Buckland stepped in before Vulcan had got into full stride. A limp rope, lying unseen across the track suddenly rose in the air and was pulled tight between two trees.

Putt saw the movement of the rope at the very last moment, but too late to do anything about it. As he tried in vain to jerk his head away to one side, shouting in fear, the taut rope caught him across the throat, cutting off the sound of his voice and throwing him backwards off his horse.

The force of the impact between rope and throat was such that it ruptured ligament and cartilage in Putt's larynx. He lay on the ground thrashing around in great pain, strange choked gurgling sounds escaping from his throat.

He struggled even more when four men pounced upon him and pinned him to the ground, but his frantic movements were more an attempt to breathe than to escape.

After the struggles had continued for some minutes it became clear to his ambushers that Putt was not about to die and they dragged him away through the trees to a spot out of sight of the track, where a small fire was burning low.

Putt was still making choking sounds deep in his throat, but he had recognised his attackers as gipsies and the fear he felt was greater than the pain. He knew why they had swept him from his horse and he was terrified of what they would do to him.

One of the men stood over him menacingly. 'D'you know who I am, Meredith Putt? No? Then let me tell you, I'm the brother of the girl you attacked in the forest not far from here. The *blind* girl. Remember her?'

Putt tried to reply but the result was a sound such as might escape from the lips of a choking man.

'I see you *do* remember. I'm glad, because now you'll know why we've taken you. It's for revenge, Putt. We're going to make quite sure you don't do the same to any other girl, whether she's willing or not.'

The fear in Meredith Putt's eyes became terror and his struggles increased in a frantic attempt to break free, but to no avail.

'Hold him while I take his trousers down.'

The hoarse noises from Putt's throat resembled the sounds of a broken whistle.

'Get to work, Isaac – and make a good job of it. I want him to live. To remember always . . .'

The inhuman whistle from the pinioned man's throat reached a new pitch as the sunlight filtering through the trees glinted on a knife blade. The gipsy put the knife to work and Putt's body arched as a pain unlike anything he had ever known spread from his groin to the whole of his body. His torso lifted from the ground for a moment then collapsed into unconsciousness.

'Get me that iron quickly.'

The gipsy discarded the knife, now discoloured with blood, and took the red-hot iron, fresh from the fire. As he applied it to Putt's body the sickening stench of burning flesh rose into the air and one of the gipsy men uttered a faint sound of revulsion.

Standing up, the gipsy threw the iron from him and, grim-faced, spoke to the others. 'It's done, and although I say so me'self, it's one of the neatest jobs I've ever performed.'

'He'll live?' Boz asked the question fiercely.

The gipsy nodded. 'Whether he wants to or no.'

'Then it's time to go. Clem, go down to the cottage where Anna's staying. Wait outside until you see the girl who lives there, the cripple girl. Give her a message to pass on to Anna. She's to tell my sister she can be married with honour now.'

Meredith Putt was discovered later that day by one of the forest gamekeepers. He was crawling painfully through the undergrowth towards the track, his horse nowhere to be seen. The ugly weal across his throat told its own story of why he was unable to say what had happened, although the gamekeeper believed he must have been swept from his horse by the low-lying branch of a tree.

Blood-stained trousers indicated that Putt had suffered other injuries and he made it clear that he was unable to walk.

The gamekeeper ran to the nearby camp of the navvies and with the aid of a sheep-hurdle Putt was carried through the village to the manor.

Shocked and distressed by the state of her injured son, Amelia Putt went in search of Tom Hanks and sent him to Burford to fetch the doctor.

However, by the time she returned to the house Putt had locked himself inside his room and he refused to open the door to her.

The doctor was no more successful in gaining entry to the room, and he told Mrs Putt that the fall had most probably affected her son's mind. However, he assured her that the fact Putt was conscious when he was brought back to the manor meant he had probably suffered no permanent damage. The doctor would return the next day and he had no doubt her son would be much recovered by then.

News of Meredith Putt's 'accident' quickly went around the village, together with various versions of his peculiar behaviour.

When Tom Hanks passed on the news that evening on his way home, Seb heaved a sigh of relief. It meant that Meredith Putt would not be going anywhere before the return of Superintending Constable Giles Aplin – and he would not come seeking Seb because of what he had witnessed on Handley Plain.

CHAPTER FORTY-THREE

On the eve of Anna's wedding to Nahum, Seb returned home to find Nahum lounging on the grass bank outside Fern Cottage, enjoying the late-evening sunshine.

Seb was slightly embarrassed at meeting the gipsy. He had not yet been to the Hankses' cottage to visit Anna, and it was of this the gipsy first spoke.

'I told Anna a week or so ago that you'd promised to visit her. She's disappointed you haven't called. She was hoping to speak to you before the wedding.'

'I've been busy, we've started hay-making.'

'That's what your mother told Anna. She said you'd call in as soon as you could. There'll not be time now. It's our wedding day tomorrow.'

Seb nodded without speaking. He needed no reminding of when Anna was to be married.

'Tom Hanks is going to give Anna away and Carrie will be her attendant. I'd like you to stand with me as my best man. I know you feel I've taken Anna from you, Seb, but it isn't true. Our marriage was arranged many years ago. If anything, I suppose I could complain that you've tried to take her from me – but I don't blame you for that. Even if our marriage hadn't been arranged I would have wanted to marry Anna. She's a fine girl, Seb, and she's had a hard time. I'd like tomorrow to be the happiest day of her life, with nothing to mar it at all. If I've read you aright you'll wish the same for her. Will you stand with me?'

Seb swallowed hard, then nodded. 'If it's what you really want.'

'Good man, Seb!' Nahum sprang to his feet and shook Seb's hand enthusiastically. 'It will make Anna very happy, I promise you.'

Nahum grinned. 'What I'd really like to do now is to go for a drink with you. Christian's a fine man, but I can only take so much religion in a week. Tonight I feel I'd enjoy a pint of ale more than a text from the New Testament. Will you come with me?'

'Why not?' Nahum's happiness was infectious and his gesture of conciliation had saved Seb from an embarrassing situation. He had not been clear whether or not he should attend the wedding ceremony. 'Give me a few minutes to clean up and we'll go to the Swan Inn.'

The Swan Inn was on the far side of the village from Fern Cottage, situated close to the bridge over the river Windrush. It was a warm evening, the sun was still in the sky and Seb enjoyed chatting to Nahum as they walked. They had never talked at any length before and Seb found the gipsy stimulating and amusing company.

They were still chatting happily together as they walked inside the inn and Seb called, 'Two pints of ale please, landlord.'

The inn was crowded and a sudden hush fell on the customers as the landlord said loudly, 'Gipsies aren't served at my inn.'

Seb was taken completely by surprise at the gruff announcement and he said, foolishly, 'I'm not a gipsy.'

'Mebbe not, but *he* is.' A thumb was jerked in

Nahum's direction. 'Like I said, I don't allow gipsies in here.'

Suddenly angry, Seb said, 'You'd refuse to serve a man who's had a university education, is respected by everyone he's met and whose father is acquainted with the Duke of Marlborough. Why? Nahum could buy this inn if he'd a mind.'

The landlord was taken aback by Seb's words, but he remained unmoving. 'I don't serve no gipsies here.'

'He's getting married tomorrow. Would you deny any man a pint of ale on his wedding eve?'

Seb was inclined to argue further, but Nahum had observed the inn's customers pressing closer about them, clearly prepared to take an active interest in the landlord's quarrel.

'Come on, Seb, let's go. As you say, it's my wedding day tomorrow, I don't want to arrive at the altar with my face in a mess.'

Seb was still angry as they walked away from the Swan Inn, retracing their footsteps through the village.

'I would never have believed that a landlord – *any* landlord – would refuse a man a drink the night before he was wed.'

'If you were a Romany you'd need to get used to such things, Seb. It's happened many times to all of us. I've learned to turn the other cheek in a manner that would make Christian proud. It's the way we have to be if we're to survive. If there's any trouble, it isn't the villager who finds himself before the court, but the Romany.'

'Well I know where we'll get a drink – and enjoy a sight better company than we'd have got back there.'

Only the nucleus of Jacob Brailey's gang remained at

the camp on the fringe of the Wychwood Forest. The road-building had been completed, but Brailey and his men had stayed to dig stone from a small quarry nearby for the wall-builders who followed them, enclosing the newly cleared land.

The remainder of the navvies had gone. Some would find work with the foresters cutting down the trees. Others would move on to wherever their skills were required to construct railways, roads or canals.

When Seb introduced Nahum as the man who would be marrying Anna on the following day, Jacob said, 'I thought *you* were hoping to marry the girl at one time?'

'So I was, but it seems Nahum and Anna were betrothed by their parents when they were still small. They're to be married in the small church that Christian built, next to my cottage.'

While Jacob was still shaking his head, Nahum said, 'I believe I owe you and your gang a debt of thanks for finding Anna and bringing her to safety. I know Anna would be delighted if you'd come to the wedding tomorrow. In the meantime, can I buy you all a drink – if the man who owns the ale-cart doesn't mind serving Romanies?'

As the drinks were being distributed, Seb told Jacob of the attitude of the landlord of the Swan Inn.

'That man's lucky he's still got an inn to serve drinks from,' said Jacob. 'He tried to prevent the ale wagon from coming up here to our camp. It wasn't until I threatened to bring my men down to discuss it with him at the Swan Inn that he had a change of mind. Perhaps I should have let them go.

'That reminds me, another friend came here today with a message for you. Melody's moved on with some of my men, but she said she saw Boz again a day or two ago. He was with some other gipsies. She said to tell you that one of the men with Boz is Isaac Cribben.'

Nahum drew in his breath sharply and Seb said, 'Does the name mean something to you?'

'Yes – but unless I'm mistaken it'll mean a lot more to the man who attacked Anna. Isaac is known among the country as an expert at gelding ponies. It's said he can geld and cauterise a pony so expertly and swiftly there's hardly time for blood to spill.'

The two men looked at each other aghast. It was left to Seb to put their thoughts into words. 'Meredith Putt! I'd like to know more about the nature of his "accident"!'

It was very late when Seb and Nahum left the navvies' camp. They had both drunk far too much, yet it had been a very enjoyable evening and on the way home each vowed eternal friendship with the other.

With arms about each other's shoulders and Seb singing a different song from Nahum, they followed an erratic course from the forest to the newly made road. They would probably have passed the cottage of Tom and Dolly Hanks without being aware of it had not a window been thrown open unexpectedly.

Dollys voice brought them to an abrupt halt.

'Is that you, our Seb? What on earth are you doing waking the whole world up at this time of night? Who's that with you?'

'It's my old pal Nahum. He's getting married tomorrow so we've been . . . and had a drink together.'

'You've had more than one, by the sound of you.'

There was sufficient moonlight for Dolly to see the

two 'pals' reeling about the lane as Seb raised his head to speak to her and upset his balance.

'By the state you're in I'd say you've both drunk the barrel dry!'

'Nahum's asked me to be his best man . . . I've said, it's . . . an honour. Isn't that what I said, Nahum?'

'You said it would be an honour and a privilege. That's what you said.'

'If you two don't get to bed soon it'll be a miracle if you're up and about in time for the wedding. All I can say is, I'm glad I'm not the bride tomorrow. She'll be lucky if she doesn't have to hold both of you up during the service. I've a mind to come down there, bring you in and dip both of your heads in a bucket of water!'

Beside her, Tom Hanks put an arm about Dolly and hugged her. 'Leave 'em be, Doll. It's the best thing that could have happened to the pair of 'em. They'll not be as lively as they ought to be come morning, but tonight will have got a whole lot of unhappy things out of Seb's system. He'll be all the better for it, you'll see. Come on, back to bed and let these two find their own way home.'

In the other bedroom, Carrie and Anna were listening at the open window, both doing their best to suppress giggles.

When Dolly and Tom returned to bed and Seb and Nahum went on their way, still singing, Anna suddenly and unexpectedly put her arms about Carrie and hugged her happily.

'You know, Carrie, if Seb and Nahum have become friends tonight it will be the best wedding present I could possibly have.'

'You *do* love Seb a little, don't you, Anna?'

'I love him a lot, Carrie. I always will. But it would never have worked for us. Our ways are far too different. Mind you, I love Nahum too, but in safer, more real way. Do you know what I mean? Do you think it's possible to love two men, in two different ways?'

'I don't know.'

Carrie spoke truthfully. She had only ever loved one man – and tomorrow the barrier that stood between them would finally be removed, when Anna married another.

CHAPTER FORTY-FOUR

The marriage of a blind gipsy girl touched the hearts of every woman in Swinbrook and all those who could attended the wedding in Christian Timms's small chapel. Jacob Brailey and his small gang of navvies were also there.

So too was a small group of half a dozen gipsy men. They had arrived earlier that morning bringing a brand-new caravan with gleaming paintwork. It was pulled by a fine horse and there was another tied behind the caravan. This was Nahum's wedding gift to his bride.

As Seb stood beside Nahum in the chapel, awaiting Anna's arrival, he glanced to where the six gipsies stood in the front pew of the chapel, brightly dressed, but decidedly ill at ease.

'It's a pity you couldn't persuade your family to be here today.' Seb spoke softly, as the atmosphere inside the chapel dictated.

'They are, in a manner of speaking. Every one of the men who delivered the caravan is a Plunkett. They're all my cousins. My father couldn't come because he's publicly declared his opposition to the wedding and my mother wouldn't dare come without him – but she's sent good wishes through one of the cousins. In a couple of years – sooner if a child is born – I'll be forgiven and Anna will be taken into the family. It will be easier for my father to change his attitude now that

Boz is known to have avenged the family honour.'

'Where will you and Anna live until then?'

'In Kent.'

At that moment there was a stir at the rear of the chapel and everyone stood as Anna entered on the arm of Tom Hanks.

The wedding between the two young gipsies was a moving ceremony, although Christian's lengthy sermon had everyone fidgeting on the hard bench seats before it was ended.

Christian spoke of Nahum as belonging to the new generation of his people, an educated man and a future spokesman for them. He predicted the young gipsy would rise to new and great heights now he had a wife beside him – a wife who had spent most of her life in the Wychwood Forest and whose trials had touched the hearts of all those who knew and loved her.

'Now her life has changed, as the forest itself is changing, bringing new challenges to the lives of both gipsy *and* villager. Nothing will ever be quite the same again. Gipsies must move towards us, become part of the community, contributing their skills to our daily lives as we offer our knowledge to them. We must be ready and eager to receive them into our lives. Welcome and help them . . .'

Seb and Nahum looked across at each other and both tried not to smile. The Swan Inn landlord's wife was in the chapel. She had been present at the incident involving Seb and Nahum the previous evening.

The long sermon eventually came to an end and shortly afterwards the young couple left the chapel as man and wife, to the applause of those who had witnessed the ceremony.

A reception was held at Handley Farm during which Nahum made an emotional speech, thanking everyone who had been so kind to him and Anna during their time among the 'gorgios' of Swinbrook.

When it was time for the newly-weds to say goodbye, Anna behaved in a most un-Romany manner by flinging her arms about Seb and kissing him. 'I'll miss you, Seb. I've always felt safe when you've been near. I wish you were a Romany and could come with us.'

'If I was a Romany I'd have ended up fighting Nahum,' said Seb, trying not to allow the emotion he felt to show. 'But he's a fine man, Anna. He'll take good care of you.'

Giles Aplin did not return to Burford from London until a week after the wedding. Accompanying him was Constable Gideon Eddy, a detective policeman from the newly formed squad based at Scotland Yard.

Aplin brought Eddy to Swinbrook and introduced him to Seb and Christian as the man 'who's come here from London to help me solve the problem of our murderous highwayman'.

'What about the attack on Anna?' asked Seb, indignantly. 'Isn't anyone going to investigate that?'

'From what Superintending Constable Aplin's been telling me along the way, if we can solve one, we're likely to find the perpetrator of the other. Where is this young gipsy girl now?'

'Gone,' said Seb, shortly. 'She got married a week ago and went off with her husband.'

'Did she make an official complaint to you about the attack?'

Detective Eddy put the question to Giles Aplin.

'No.'

Detective Eddy shrugged. 'Without a complaint we have no felony. I'd say that leaves the way clear for us to concentrate on the robberies.'

Aplin nodded, but he was looking at Seb. 'I thought you had ideas of matrimony with the gipsy girl – Anna?'

'She married one of her own people. Nahum Plunkett. You'll remember him.' Seb did not believe any further explanation was necessary.

Nodding his head, Aplin asked, 'Is that why you'd been drinking, the night before you saw the robbery on Handley Plain?'

'It had something to do with it, yes.'

'My constable in Burford is convinced you were still drunk when you rode in to speak to him.'

'Your constable in Burford was looking for an excuse not to take any action. I know what I saw.' Somewhat embarrassed by the presence of Christian, Seb repeated what had occurred.

When Seb's story came to an end, Giles Aplin cast a quizzical glance in the direction of the London detective. 'What do you think?'

'I believe Seb's story, and I think you do too – but it wouldn't convince a judge. The highwayman had a mask over his face during the robbery and kept it up when he rode away – and a horse is a horse. Whatever colour it is, you'll find a hundred or more with similar markings. It wouldn't be accepted in a court as conclusive evidence. The most damning fact of all is that Seb had been drinking. A defence counsel would tear his evidence to shreds on that fact alone.'

Seb was uncomfortably aware that Christian's

expression was one of censure, but Detective Eddy had more to say.

'It's like so many things you've told me about these murders, robberies and the rape. They all point to Meredith Putt – but we've no firm evidence to offer a court. If we are thinking of taking a lord of the manor to a Court of Assize we need to have a watertight case.'

'You mean Meredith Putt's going to get away – yet again?'

'No,' said the London detective, patiently. 'It merely means we haven't sufficient grounds for arresting him yet. The strongest piece of evidence we've found so far is that piece of chain, which ties in with the attack on the gipsy girl. It wouldn't convict our man, but it gives us an excuse to go and pay a call on the Putts of Swinbrook Manor.'

When they reached the village, the two men paused to speak to Tom Hanks first. He told them that none of the servants had seen Putt since the forest 'accident'.

'They're talking of little else,' said the head groom. 'He spends all day in his room and hasn't been heard to say a word to anyone. The servants say the doctor's been three times but been forced to leave again without seeing him. They've heard his mother hammering on the door, demanding that he open it to her. They don't think he ever has, but the trays left outside his door are always taken in. The only thing I can tell you with certainty is that Master Meredith hasn't been riding since the accident. I don't know anything about the rights of *that*, neither. It was forty-eight hours before we got Vulcan back. He'd galloped all the way to Leafield and we would have lost him for good if someone there hadn't recognised him.'

'Do you mind if I see the horse?' The London detective asked the question.

'No, he's over here – and a fine horse he is, too.'

Detective Eddy showed he was a man who appreciated horses as he ran his hands over Vulcan's body. 'He's a distinctive animal, taller than most.'

'That's right,' agreed Tom. 'And Seb's ridden him a few times. He wouldn't mistake any other horse for this 'un, you can be sure of that.'

'That's pretty much what Christian Timms told us. Thank you, Mr Hanks. I think the time has come to ask Meredith Putt a few questions.'

When Amelia Putt entered the room into which Constable Aplin and Detective Eddy had been shown by a manor servant, she looked pale and upset and her expression was strained. But she made it immediately clear that she regarded the two policemen as being of a social order little higher than the servants.

'I understand you wish to see my son. I am afraid that is not possible. He had a nasty accident when riding in the forest – a *very* nasty accident and is seeing no one.'

'I'm sorry about that, ma'am. I hope he soon makes a full recovery.' Detective Eddy was suitably sympathetic. 'Perhaps we needn't bother him at all. You see, we've picked up a thief who had a cape he admits to stealing. We've been making inquiries and learned that Mr Putt has been seen wearing one rather similar. It's a cape with a swan-neck fastening chain. Would you know whether he has had one stolen?'

'Meredith still has his cape. I can be quite certain because he broke the chain some time ago and my own maid replaced it. So I am afraid your time has been wasted.'

Outside the manor once more, Detective Eddy said to Giles Aplin, 'I think that Mrs Putt's admission concerning the cape is sufficient for us to obtain a search warrant.'

'You'll never get one from Magistrate Peck. He'd be more likely to tell Meredith Putt of our intentions.'

'A case of gentlemen sticking together, eh? Well, the cape would do no more than implicate Putt in the rape of the gipsy girl and it seems she's married and gone. From what I know of gipsies she'd never make an official complaint even if we caught up with her. So, supposing we *did* get a search warrant, what would we find? Certainly not jewellery. If Putt is in the habit of making frequent journeys to London he'll have already rid himself of such incriminating items there. No, Giles, we must try another tack. I think your highwayman is a cunning and resourceful villain. So we'll need to be twice as cunning and four times as resourceful. What's more, we'll need more than a fair share of luck.'

CHAPTER FORTY-FIVE

By the time hay-making came to an end it was impossible to work in any of the Handley Farm fields without hearing the sound of axes eating their way through Wychwood Forest. The noise of splintering wood became more commonplace than the singing of birds as saplings and lesser trees were crushed beneath the weight of falling forest giants.

Seb was working with Christian on top of a steadily rising haystack, the last of many. Around them women and men and children worked in the hayfield, gathering and loading, raking and stacking. It was a time of year when there was enough employment on the farms of the English countryside for everyone. Only the very old and infirm were excluded from the activities of the hayfields.

Resting gratefully on his pitchfork as they waited for a slow-moving loaded wagon to reach them from the far end of the field, Seb said, 'There'll be another hundred acres to work by the spring. Do you have any new ideas for them, Christian?'

'Nothing that can't be changed if you have a scheme that's worth thinking about.'

'It's not so much a scheme . . . I'd like to buy half of them from you.'

'Buy fifty acres! How would you find the money – and what would you do with so much land?'

'The forest fair isn't too far away, neither are Witney Feast, Burford Fair and a whole lot of other fairs. There'll be racing at each one. I'd like to enter Grye. Then there's the ploughing. The new plough will be ready any day now and already I've had farmers come and see me about turning over both new and old ground for them. I'll have money enough to pay you by spring, Christian – that's if you think three pounds ten shillings an acre is a fair price.'

'It'll do,' agreed Christian. 'And mind you, you're not the only one who's looking to the future. I've got a plan of my own I'd like to discuss with you. But here's the hay-wagon. We'll talk about it later.'

Seb and Christian had not found an opportunity to have their promised talk by the time the first of the local fairs came around. It was at the village of Bampton, and Grye had a comfortable win. Unfortunately for Seb, it was a small field with a prize to match and the only two bookmakers present made Grye a clear favourite.

It was the turn of the Witney Feast a week later and here the competition was keener. Tom Hanks had come to the fair with two ageing horses from the manor he wanted to sell and he brought Carrie with him, riding in a light cart behind which were tied the two horses.

It was a close result and as Seb passed the winning-post no more than a neck ahead of his nearest rival, he could hear Carrie's shrill voice above the noise of the crowd, urging him on.

The odds and the prize money here were considerably higher than at Bampton and as Seb was walking away from the race officials with his winnings, a voice in his ear said, 'Put that money somewhere safe, Seb. There are at least ten known pick-pockets here today – and probably as many more who aren't known to us.'

Seb turned to see Giles Aplin. A few paces away, Detective Eddy stood gazing out over the heads of the crowd.

'What are you doing here? Witney isn't part of your parish.'

'Detective Eddy has received word from London that someone he wants to see is expected to be here today. We haven't found him yet, but thanks to you and your horse we'll be going away from Witney richer than when we arrived. That's a good horse, Seb.'

'It's a gipsy horse – and I have a mare in foal to him.' Seb was still in high spirits after winning the race. 'In a couple of years I'll have an even better horse than Grye.'

'Giles. Over there – the weasel-faced man in a green coat!'

Before the Burford constable could reply, Detective Eddy was pushing his way through the crowd and Constable Aplin hurried after him.

'Seb, that was a *wonderful* ride.' Carrie, her face red and flushed as a result of the shouting she had done, hugged him enthusiastically. Behind her, Tom Hanks's happy face showed that he too had backed Grye to win.

'You've done me proud again, Seb. As a result of your win I can buy something special for your ma. Some really nice material for a dress, perhaps. Will you take care of Carrie for a while? I'll meet you back at the cart in an hour or so.'

'Dad's very fond of your ma, Seb. I'm so happy for them both.'

'So am I. In fact, life's been good to both of us since we came to Swinbrook.'

'Even though you didn't get the girl you hoped to marry?'

'Are you trying to spoil my day, Carrie?' Even as he asked the question, Seb realised that it no longer hurt in the way it had for a long time.

'I'm sorry, Seb, I shouldn't have said that.' Carrie could have kicked herself, even though she would have dearly liked to hear Seb say it no longer mattered.

'It's all right. Anna would never have settled down to marriage with a gorgio, I realise that now. Besides, she's got a good husband and I hope she'll be very happy with him. Life's been pretty hard for her up to now.'

Carrie felt a sudden surge of happiness. 'You're a good man, Seb. Because I'm specially pleased with you I'll let you buy me something to eat from your winnings and you can tell me what Constable Aplin was saying to you just before I came along.'

'Just a minute, Charlie. I want to have a talk with you.'

Detective Policeman Gideon Eddy put a hand on the shoulder of the green-coated man. Hurrying to catch up with his London colleague, Giles Aplin thought the surprised man was about to slip free of the garment and make a run for it.

'Gor blimey! Wot you doing 'ere, Mr Eddy? You ain't come all this way just to collar me, 'ave you? I ain't done nuffing, honest I ain't.'

'Be careful how you use words like "honest", Charlie.

They're likely to stick in your throat and choke you as surely as will a hangman's rope one day.'

'Now wot sort of talk's that, Mr Eddy? I've 'elped you in the past, you know I 'ave. I've been good to you.'

'You're going to help me again now, Charlie. Me and Mr Aplin here, who's the Superintending Constable for a large parish around the Burford area. Giles, meet Charlie Smith. He knows more ways to earn a dishonest living than any other villain I know.'

Charlie Smith began to protest, but Gideon Eddy brought his protestations to an abrupt halt.

'I'll do the talking for now, Charlie. It'll be your turn in a minute. It came as a very pleasant surprise to me when I learned that you were in the habit of spending some time in this part of the world. As I said to Mr Aplin, when we find Charlie Smith all our troubles are going to be over. He'll know exactly what's been going on and will be only too eager to help us. Isn't that so, Charlie?'

'Depends on what it is you're wanting to know, Mr Eddy. You know me, if it's possible I'll 'elp any way I can, but there's one or two things even I daren't open me mouth about.'

'You'll open it for this one, Charlie, because it's important to Mr Aplin – and that means it's important to me. A matter of murder – more than one murder, highway robbery and probably the rape of a young girl too. All committed by a man who has to be caught. You understand how important it is now?'

'You talking about them robberies and murders around the Wychwood Forest, Mr Eddy? Yes, course you are. That's why you're 'ere wiv 'im. It's about time they brought someone like yourself in to sort it out – no offence meant to you, Mr Aplin, but Mr Eddy 'ere's the best detective they've got up at Scotland Yard, make no mistake about that.'

'Less of the soft sawdering, Charlie. What do you know about what's going on?'

Charlie's face reminded Giles Aplin of a weasel as his eyes darted here and there before replying. 'Ave you paid a visit to the ale-house up at Dore's Lodge yet, Mr Eddy?'

Detective Eddy looked questioningly at Giles Aplin and the Burford constable said, 'It's a notorious ale-house in the forest. I can take you there.'

'You ought to go there and 'ave a word with the guv'nor.' Once again the small, weasel-faced man's eyes searched the crowd moving about them. 'The highwayman who got "topped" and the other one who was murdered in the forest used to meet there . . . with this nob.'

'Do you know who he is, this "nob"?' Aplin asked the question.

Charlie Smith shook his head. 'I never 'eard 'is name mentioned, but there's something crazy about 'im, I can tell you *that*. I don't frighten easy, but that geezer frightened me. Scared the landlord, too. One night 'e wanted money and 'e made the landlord buy a gold ticker orf 'im. Threatened to shoot 'im if 'e didn't.'

'This man was armed?'

'That's right. A two-shot pistol – and keen to use it, or so I've 'eard. Go and ask the landlord about the watch, guv. He'll still 'ave it stashed away somewhere. It's far too 'ot to try to sell, that much I'm sure of.'

Detective Gideon Eddy laid an arm across the shoulders of Charlie Smith in mock affection. 'I knew you'd be happy to help me, Charlie. Off you go now – and behave yourself, or I might feel obliged to tell a certain Whitechapel widow-woman where she can put her none-too-gentle hands on you.'

When the small, green-coated man had disappeared in the crowd, Giles Aplin asked, 'Can we believe what he just told us?'

'As though it were sworn in a court-room,' confirmed the detective. 'Charlie Smith knows better than to lie to me. Let's pay this Dore's Lodge a visit.'

The landlord of the Dore's Lodge ale-house was less eager to be helpful than Charlie Smith had been. When he learned the identity of his two customers, he said, 'I run a respectable ale-house here, even though many of my customers would be shown the door if they went to one of your big city taverns. If they learn who you are I'll lose more business than I can afford. So I'll be obliged if you two gents would drink up and leave.'

'Did you hear that, Giles?' Gideon Eddy gave the Burford constable a look of mock-horror. 'We're being thrown out of an *ale*-house, no less.'

'Not "thrown out",' said the landlord, looking decidedly uncomfortable. 'I'm just saying I'd like you to leave when you've supped your ale.'

'I'm sure you would, landlord, but I've taken rather a fancy to this ale-house of yours. I don't know what it is about it, but I find I have the urge to sit here and enjoy it. Perhaps it's the furniture that would send a splinter into a man if he didn't sit as still as a rock. Or the aroma from the half of a poached deer that's hanging behind your scullery door. Then again it might be the company you have here. Shall I ask their names, Constable Aplin, or would you like to do it?'

'Now, gentlemen,' the landlord had perspiration on his forehead and upper lip, 'I'm merely trying to earn an honest living . . .'

'I doubt that, landlord. I doubt that very much.' The glance that Gideon Eddy turned upon the perspiring landlord had struck fear into a whole generation of London criminals. 'Constable Aplin and I came here to ask you a few questions about a certain matter. Since you seem reluctant to help us in our inquiries it might be as well if I stayed here to keep an eye on you while Constable Aplin rides to Burford to swear out a search warrant.'

'What is it you want to know?' The landlord's voice was as faint as he felt. If a thorough search was made of the ale-house and its out-buildings he would go to prison for a great many years.

'That's better. Now, we're interested in a watch. A gold watch. It was given to you by a certain gentleman, as security against a loan.'

The landlord capitulated. Disappearing into a back room, he emerged carrying a gold watch and chain which he handed to the two policemen. A crude attempt had been made to erase three initials, but they were still plainly visible.

'V.G.H.' The London detective read them out to Giles Aplin. 'They mean anything to you?'

Giles Aplin nodded. 'Vincent Garland Hammond. *Sir* Vincent Hammond. He and Lady Sybil were murdered by the highwayman just outside Swinbrook.'

Turning back to the landlord, Giles Aplin said, 'I already know the name of the man who gave you this watch – but I want to hear it from your lips – and I want the truth.'

The landlord gave a half-hearted gesture of resignation. 'If you've got this far with your investigation, you'll know already. The watch was given to me as a surety by Meredith Putt, lord of Swinbrook Manor.'

CHAPTER FORTY-SIX

Tom, Carrie and Seb returned late from the Witney Feast. They had stopped at an inn close to Minster Lovell to buy a grand meal and sup a few tankards of ale.

They had enjoyed a happy day and it seemed to Carrie that Seb had noticed her, *really* noticed her, as a young woman for the very first time. She was still feeling pleased with life when they crossed the bridge over the river Windrush and entered Swinbrook village.

Lamps were burning inside the Swan Inn, but any drinkers still there were quiet as the trio made their way along the winding lane through the village. Seb was riding Grye beside the light wagon, discussing with Carrie the next race in which he intended running the horse.

They were talking as the horses climbed the low hill on which church and manor stood facing each other, when Carrie suddenly exclaimed, 'What's that light in the window of the manor, Seb?'

Seb looked up towards the manor house and saw a dancing orange light flickering erratically at one of the upstairs windows.

'It looks almost as though it might be a fire.'

Even as he spoke, a similar glow appeared at a window farther along on the same floor. This time there was no doubt what it was. As they watched in horror, they saw flames eating their way up one of the heavy curtains.

They had hardly digested the import of what they had seen when still more flames appeared at a third window.

'Someone's inside setting fire to the manor. Get across there and try to wake the Putts, Seb. I'll rouse some of the villagers.'

Tom handed the reins to Carrie and leaped from the light cart, heading for a nearby cottage. Meanwhile, Seb tied the reins of his horse to the back of the cart before sprinting towards the manor house. By the time he reached the front door there were flames at a fourth window and he could hear an ominous crackling sound from inside the house.

Seb hammered at the door and tugged at the bell-pull but without anyone answering. A few more attempts convinced him that nobody was going to put in an appearance. By now villagers in various states of dress were arriving on the scene, and each had his or her own idea of what should be done.

A few of the burlier men put their shoulders to the door, but it was built of ancient oak, heavily reinforced with iron and their combined weights failed so much as to cause the door to tremble on its massive hinges.

'Try a window,' shouted someone, and within a matter of minutes two men had stout stakes and were breaking in the ground-floor windows. At first, all attempts to gain access in this manner were as unsuccessful as those through the door. There were shutters inside each window and they too resisted all efforts to break them down. However, they were made of lesser wood than the door. When two men used one of the stakes as a battering ram, the shutter suddenly split apart – only to reveal an inferno raging inside.

'What about the servants?' One of the men voiced his somewhat belated fear and it was immediately taken up by others. Moments later a shower of stones was hurled at the attic-room windows of the servants' quarters.

It seemed an age before one of the windows was thrown open and a woman's head appeared, rag-curlers showing beneath a sleeping-cap.

'Wake the others and get out! The manor's on fire! Hurry! Quick!'

Advice was hurled up at her, but smoke began seeping from the window behind the servant and she needed no urging.

'They'll come down the servants' stairs and out at the back door. It'll give us a way in. Hurry, form a chain to the pond with as many buckets as you can lay hands on, and keep the water coming. I think we're going to prove too late, but we'll have to do what we can.'

Tom issued the orders to the watching villagers and, as they scurried to do as they had been told, he said to Seb, 'Go around to the stables. Take the horses out and lead them over to the tithe barn. They should be safe enough in there. Be quick now, Seb. It only needs a spark from here to land in the stable hay and we'll lose them all.'

As Seb reached the stables screams from the back of the house indicated that some of the servants, at least, had found their way to safety. Suddenly there was someone beside him. 'I'll give you a hand.'

It was Carrie.

Seb protested that it was no work for a girl, realising

that the horses might panic when they saw the manor burning, but Carrie said, 'I know the stalls even better than you. I've been here often enough with my dad. You take the hunters. I can manage the cart-horses.'

As it happened, Seb had far more problems with the highly strung animals than did Carrie with the steady, patient cart-horses. One or two of the gentle, giant horses snorted in fear, but they allowed her to lead them to the safety of the barn, while Seb was struggling to maintain control of the hunters.

When the stalls were empty, Seb took Carrie's hand and, with a brief 'Well done!', led her back to where the villagers were fighting a losing battle against the manor fire.

The chain of helpers worked hard swinging buckets of water from hand to hand between the village pond, fed by a small stream, and the burning manor, but their efforts were having little effect upon the fire.

Efforts to enter the building and find Meredith and Amelia Putt also proved futile and the would-be rescuers were driven out by the heat and flames.

When part of the roof collapsed and flames rose half as high again as the manor house, the firefighters drew back and restricted their efforts to keeping the outbuildings of the farm damped down.

It was about now that an ugly story began to circulate, originating with the manor's servants.

It seemed that soon after dark a rough-looking man wearing ragged clothes had appeared at the manor house, demanding to speak to Meredith Putt. Amelia Putt was called by the servants and told the man that her son was sick and seeing no one.

However, so insistent was the man, saying his message was a matter of life or death, that Meredith's mother finally agreed to go to his room to see if he would emerge and listen to what the messenger had to say.

He must have followed her upstairs, for when she knocked at Meredith's door the man pushed past her and hammered with his fist on the door, crying, 'It's the pot-man from Dore's Lodge, Mr Meredith. I've a very urgent message for you from Mr Norris. He says the game's up, sir. You're to get away, as far as you can.'

The door was flung open and Meredith Putt stood in the doorway, unshaven, unwashed and wild-eyed, his condition startling the messenger.

Ignoring his mother, Putt tried to speak to the pot-man, but could only utter unintelligible noises.

Gathering his wits, the pot-man said, 'The constable and a man from Scotland Yard in London came to Dore's Lodge today. They knew all about the watch . . . and they took it away with them.'

Putt's face contorted with an expression of such mad rage that the frightened pot-man fled. His mother rounded on him. 'What was that man talking about? Why should someone from Scotland Yard be making inquiries about you? Meredith, what have you been up to? I *demand* to know. Does this refusal to speak to anyone have something to do with it? Have you really lost your voice?'

Putt turned to go inside his room, but when he tried to close the door, his mother's foot prevented it and she pushed past him.

'Oh no, there's been quite enough of this nonsense. If you really *cannot* talk then you can write your replies, but I am not leaving this room until I have them. It feels as though my whole world is collapsing about my ears – and I intend to know why!'

The servant who passed the story on to the firefighters had been standing nearby taking in all that was being said until a glance from Meredith Putt through the partly open door sent her scuttling upstairs to complete her work, filled with apprehension by what she had just heard.

When the maid returned upstairs Mrs Putt was berating her son in a near-hysterical voice, the predominant words being, 'Why? For God's sake, Meredith, *why*?'

The maid fled to her room but could still hear Mrs Putt's shrill voice until there was a brief, muffled scream, followed by a whole series of sounds that might have been a fight.

When the servant had gone to investigate she came face to face with Meredith Putt in the corridor outside his room. Pointing upstairs, he left her in no doubt that she was being ordered back to her room.

Too frightened to tell the other servants what she had seen and heard, the girl went to bed and cried herself to sleep. The next thing she remembered was being woken up and told the house was on fire.

The villagers were still talking about the servant-girl's revelations when dawn broke on a grim picture. Windowless, roofless and with blackened walls, the manor house was still smoking and nobody dared go inside just yet.

Dolly was one of the assembled crowd. Indeed, she had been one of those in the chain passing water to the house from the pond. She had been in her cottage waiting for the return of Tom and Carrie when a villager ran past shouting news of the fire and she had turned out to help.

Everyone was black-faced and weary, and numbed as they contemplated their own futures. The manor was the heart of the village. The lords of the manor owned almost all the lands about the village and now nobody was sure what they should do.

When Constable Giles Aplin and Detective Policeman Gideon Eddy reached the smouldering remains of Swinbrook Manor, the villagers had discovered two charred and unidentifiable bodies among the ruins of the house.

The two policemen took statements from the servants about the last known moments of the occupants of the manor, and from Seb, Tom and Carrie, who described what they had seen as they approached the manor house the previous night.

'I think that should satisfy the coroner.' Giles Aplin patted the papers into order and placed them inside a leather document-holder.

'I would say it also closes the file on your outstanding murders and highway robberies,' suggested Gideon Eddy. 'It means I have no reason to remain here any longer. It'll be back to London for me tomorrow.'

'Do you really believe all those murders and robberies were committed by Meredith Putt?'

The two policemen were sitting in the kitchen of Handley Farm when Seb put the question to them.

'There was sufficient evidence for a magistrate to issue this.' Giles Aplin drew a carefully folded document from a pocket. 'It's a warrant ordering the arrest of Meredith Putt to answer to a charge of murder.

Well, he'll be tried by a higher court than we have in this life. I only wish there was some way we might learn the verdict.'

'Why should he, the lord of Swinbrook Manor, resort to robbery? He had everything a man could possibly want.' This time the questioner was Christian.

'As you know, Putt was a spendthrift and a heavy gambler. He owed money to numerous tradesmen, here and in London. He's not the first gentleman to turn to crime to pay off his debts, but I suspect that had we brought him before a court he would have been declared insane.'

'It's tragic that he and his mother should meet their end in such a fashion. Tragic for them, the manor – and, more especially, for the village.'

Later in the day, James Price rode to Swinbrook. The office of the Burford solicitor was responsible for the affairs of the Fettiplace family and Price informed the numbed and bewildered villagers that the solicitors had still not heard from Sir Nelson Fettiplace's next-of-kin. Unfortunately, the new baronet lived in India and no instructions from him were expected for many months.

In the meantime, the solicitor intended administering the estate on behalf of the family. He asked Tom Hanks to take charge of the day-to-day running of the farm, and hoped everyone else would continue to work as before.

The solicitor guaranteed they would receive payment for their labours as though the Putts were still alive.

James Price's words eased the immediate worries of the villagers but for many of the older ones the world they had always known had come to an end.

Not only was the great forest of Wychwood being felled, but they had lost their manor and the family who had governed their lives from time immemorial.

CHAPTER FORTY-SEVEN

On the Sunday following the manor fire, as Tom, Seb, Dolly and Carrie left Swinbrook chapel after the morning service, Christian asked them to come to the farmhouse. There was something of importance he wished to say that would affect them all.

The four gathered in the farmhouse kitchen apprehensively. They had discussed the possible reasons for such a meeting as they made their way to the farm, and all feared the worst. Perhaps Christian's ownership of the farm depended in some way upon the manor, or the Fettiplace family, and Christian had called them together to break the bad news to them.

But Christian soon made it clear that his plans had nothing to do with the fire at the manor, although he admitted that Tom being placed in charge of the manor farm did affect what he had in mind.

Quite unaware of the alarm his summons had provoked, Christian beamed at the four people assembled in the kitchen of his farmhouse. 'I have reached a momentous decision, a joyous decision, and I've brought you here to tell you about it.'

Apprehension became puzzlement. Christian was too happy to be the bearer of bad news, and yet he had told them earlier he had something to say that would affect them all. It had to involve the farm.

'I have decided to answer the Lord's call and become

a minister of the Methodist Church.'

Three of the people in the room looked at Seb. The unexpected news affected them all in some way, but it would have the greatest impact upon Seb's life.

As though unaware of the many doubts in the minds of each of his listeners, Christian went on to explain the reasons behind his momentous decision.

'Becoming a Methodist minister has been my ambition for many years. When Seb came to the village, it was as though the Lord had said, "Here you are, Christian. I've sent you a young man who loves horses as you do, and who can continue your work with them. Now you can come and work for *Me*." I applied for a place at the Methodist Institution training college in London – and have heard I have been accepted.'

As Christian beamed at his small audience, Seb asked, 'How long will you be away from Swinbrook?'

'My training will last for two years. When it's done I hope to interest the Church in a mission to the gipsies.'

'But . . . what will happen to Handley Farm?' Seb could contain the burning question no longer. 'What about me?'

'I must confess the fire at the manor has caused me some problems,' admitted Christian. 'It had been my intention to ask Tom to help manage Handley Farm, but I realise he cannot possibly take on such a task now he has been asked to perform similar duties on behalf of the manor.'

'So who'll be coming here now?' Seb asked the question that would decide his future.

'No one. I intend leaving you in charge, Seb.'

A fleeting expression of amusement crossed Christian's

face as Seb's mouth dropped open in delighted disbelief.

'I realise you lack experience, Seb, but you're not lacking in ambition and you're eager to learn. You can already manage horses better than any man I know – with the possible exception of Tom here – and you've picked up a good general knowledge of farming. I shall plan out what I propose to do on the farm for the next three years, season by season, and we'll look for a ploughman to help with your new venture. It might also be necessary to employ a good lad from the village to help. I know Tom is going to be very busy, but I'm sure he'll agree to meet up with you two or three times a week. You can tell him what you've done, what you intend doing, and seek his advice. I will, of course, pay Tom a quarterly sum in acknowledgement of his help.'

Seb's astonishment had been replaced by eagerness as Christian talked, and the farmer added, 'I've built a reputation for my horses, Seb, and I know you'll not only continue that reputation, but probably enhance it.'

Looking about him at the others, Christian said, 'There! Those are my plans for the future, now it's time for you to air your views.'

Seb was the first to speak. 'It's a wonderful opportunity, Christian, and I'm grateful for your trust in me – but you've already agreed to sell me that fifty acres of new land. Would you object if I were to buy any other land that might be on offer, and work it with the farm?'

Christian smiled. 'I've already said I admire your ambition. I can hardly say no. What are your views, Tom?'

Tom was concerned. 'Seb's good with horses, Christian. Better than me – though I might still teach him a thing or two – but the farm is a big responsibility for any young man, especially one with a London background.'

'When Seb came here he had only one way to go, Tom. That way was "up". Perhaps I see in him something of the son I would like to have had, but never did. I have every faith in him although I realise he doesn't know everything. Will you help him?'

'Of course I will, there was never any doubt of that.' Tom had seen Seb's expression of eager determination. 'You're right, Christian. Young Seb is on his way – and I'll have to work hard if I'm to keep up with him.'

'Good! I'm glad that's settled. You'll need to move to the farmhouse, Seb, and you'll be wanting help about the place.'

'I can help up here,' said Carrie, who had caught some of Seb's contagious eagerness. 'I can clean in the house, look after the chickens, and put in some time with Dolly in the dairy.'

'Thanks, Carrie.' Seb's look returned to the farmer. 'And thanks to you too, Christian. It's going to work . . . I know it is.'

When Christian left for London to begin his new life in the Methodist ministry, Seb took him to the railway station at Shipton-under-Wychwood in the farm's gig and Carrie came with him for the ride.

As the train steamed noisily into the station, Christian said his farewells, adding, 'I leave Handley Farm in your hands with every confidence, Seb. I wasn't much more than your age when I took on the farm myself. Work hard – and pray harder. It's the formula that succeeded for me, I know it will do the same for you.'

After watching the train steam away with Christian waving from an open carriage window until he was out of sight, Carrie and Seb set off on the return journey in the gig.

'You must be feeling very proud today, Seb.'

'Proud? Yes – and scared too. Very scared.'

'I don't believe that, Seb Quilter. There's not much scares you. Your mum's fairly bursting with pride for you too, you know.'

Setting the horses to a brisk trot, Seb said, 'She's very proud of you too, Carrie. When we first came here you were afraid to go outside your garden – but now look at you. You do twice as much as any other girl I know. You're teaching in the chapel most mornings, helping in the dairy and working in the house too.'

'I owe much of that to Anna – and to you.'

'Anna I can understand, she's an example to everyone – but why me?'

'You gave me lots of reasons to get out and about. To realise that a crippled leg doesn't make me some sort of oddity. I'll always be grateful to you for doing that, Seb.'

Embarrassed both by her comments and by the expression on her face, Seb squeezed the hand she was resting on the cart in front of her. 'You're a funny girl, Carrie, and no mistake.'

Carrie was uncertain whether it was what she wanted to hear him say, but she accepted his brief gesture of affection and smiled up at him. 'My knee is never going to work the way it should, Seb, but the muscles of my leg are working much better, have you noticed? I can walk for quite long distances now.'

'Yes.' Seb already had his mind on other things. 'I'm

happy for you. Hold on tight now – I'm going to whip up the horse. I want to get back to the farm. There's a whole lot of work to be done.'

That autumn was so busy for Seb he hardly had time to think his own thoughts. The clearing of Wychwood Forest had almost been completed now and the demand for ploughing increased beyond all his expectations. Taking a gamble, Seb bought a second plough and took on another ploughman. Occasionally, he would take the place of one of the men, and he also did much of the ploughing of Handley Farm's own lands.

Seb saw far less of Carrie during these weeks than he would have wished. As he walked behind the plough he had time to think of the easy relationship that had gradually built up between them. He felt a contentment when he was in her company that he missed when he did not see her for a while.

But there always seemed to be something else to be done about the farm. He was so busy for much of the time that on more than one occasion his meetings with Tom had to be conducted with Tom walking beside him as he ploughed a field.

Now Tom was managing the manor farm, Dolly was spending much time at the dairy there. Carrie had taken over many of Dolly's duties at Handley Farm, with two young girls aged ten and eleven to help her in the dairy. In exchange for their work, Carrie gave the two girls free lessons.

Harry Agg, the old man who had helped on the farm for very many years, was still employed there, but he did little more than potter, his main duties being to clean out the stables and cowshed.

Seb still contrived to spend a couple of hours with Carrie every Sunday evening to work on the farm's ledgers, carefully noting down each item of expenditure and the profit made. Sometimes they carried out the work at the Hankses' cottage and occasionally at the farm, but so tired was Seb as a result of the long days he was working that twice he fell asleep while Carrie was writing.

One evening Seb entered the farmhouse at dusk and found Carrie in the kitchen.

'What are you doing here? You should have gone home long ago.'

'You've got men coming tomorrow to do the threshing. They're renowned as a hungry lot. I stayed on to do some cooking in readiness for them. There's plenty here, so if you clean yourself up and sit down at the table I'll put something out for you too. Your mum is worried about you. She said when she saw you last you were as thin as a rake – and she's right. You need a sight more flesh on your bones.'

'I don't want that, Carrie. I want to take part in a few more races next year and you'll never hear of a plump jockey winning races.'

'There's little fear of you ever being plump, Seb Quilter, you're always far too busy. Neither will you ever make old bones if you don't take more care of yourself. Hurry up now, there's a small pie here I've made specially for you. Eat it while it's hot.'

'I don't know what I'd have done without you these last weeks, Carrie. You've been a God-send, and no mistake.'

Carrie had her back to him as she busied herself by the fire. As Seb passed by he placed his hands on her shoulders and leaned over to kiss her on the cheek. 'Thank you.'

Carrie did not turn round as Seb went out into the yard to wash. She was afraid he might see the colour he had brought to her cheeks. His gratitude – and the kiss – meant more to her than she would ever have admitted to anyone.

Carrie wished it might have been as meaningful to Seb. Unfortunately, she believed, it was no more than the gesture of a tired and grateful man.

CHAPTER FORTY-EIGHT

As autumn slipped gradually into winter so work on the farm slowed down. However, although there was less to be done, there were also fewer hours in which it could be accomplished.

Nevertheless, Seb still found time to improve his learning with Carrie. The last few months had taught him quite clearly that a good knowledge of writing, reading and arithmetic was no longer enough. Now he had a farm to run he needed to know something of farm bookkeeping.

Seb had always had an instinct for whether or not something was likely to make money, but now he was required to record farm profit and expenditure for Christian it was not enough to leave it all to Carrie.

He took to spending more time than before at the Hankses' cottage and his relationship with Carrie was an uncomplicated, comfortable one.

One cold evening, Seb returned from the cottage to Handley Farm along lanes, the banks of which were already glistening with frost. It was cold and he thrust his hands deeper inside the pockets of his coat. Shrugging the collar higher around tingling ears he thought of Carrie. He had realised some time before that he was becoming more and more attracted to her. He was also beginning to rely very heavily on her sound judgement on a number of things. Despite their closeness, Seb was not at all certain of Carrie's feelings for him. He thought he would ask his mother. She would know.

When he reached the farm, Seb carried out his usual evening routine and checked that doors of cow-sheds and stables were securely closed. The wind got up swiftly here and it was already quite strong tonight.

Having checked the main stable doors, Seb climbed the steps at the side of the stable and pushed the door to the hay-loft. It was secure. As he turned to return down the steps he was thinking of Carrie once more and not taking care where he was stepping. He trod on a patch of ice and slipped, falling down the dozen or so stone steps.

At the bottom of the steps, bruised and breathless, Seb sat up, grateful still to be in one piece. But when he tried to stand a cry of pain escaped him and he reached for the wall of the stables for support.

He had hurt his right ankle and it was too painful to put to the ground. He tried once or twice before hopping to the farmhouse, wincing in pain whenever he jolted the injured ankle.

Once inside the house Seb removed his boot and sock from the injured foot. The ankle was already swollen and painful to the touch. He thought he had probably broken it, but there was little he could do at this time of night. He made his way to bed, going backwards up the stairs, making use of his arms and one good leg.

The next morning Seb was sitting in the kitchen minus his boot and sock when Carrie came into the house. The ankle had swollen more during the night and was extremely discoloured.

'What have you done? That looks *awful*!' Carrie

dropped to her knees to examine the ankle making sympathetic noises as Seb told her how the accident had occurred.

Carrie was appalled. 'What would have happened if you'd hit your head instead of your ankle? You could have been lying out there in the farmyard all night!'

'It's no good thinking of what I *might* have done, Carrie. Can you speak to old Harry? You'll probably find him over in the cow-shed. I thought I heard him bring the cows in earlier but he's grown so deaf he didn't hear when I called him. Ask him to make some sort of crutch for me. Something I can tuck underneath my arm and use to get about with.'

'All in good time. First I'm going down to the village to fetch old Bonnie and get her to have a look at that ankle. You just sit here until I get back here with her.'

Bonnie Edgington lived in a cottage in the heart of the village. She was the midwife, nurse and layer-out of bodies. Her services were also called upon to charm away warts and cure ringworm in cattle.

The old lady was at home but she grumbled incessantly at being called upon to go out on such a chilly morning. 'That young Londoner up at the farm, you say? I can't say I'm surprised. He can't be expected to know how to stay out of trouble here in the country. From what I've heard he's come up in the world since he went to work for Christian Timms. I'd 'a thought he'd at least have the courtesy to send a pony and trap for me instead of expecting an old lady to walk all the way up to Handley Farm on such a frosty morning.'

'He'd have done it willingly had I stopped to ask him, Bonnie, but I didn't. I told him I was coming down here to fetch you, and here I am. I'm sure he'll arrange something to bring you back.'

'All right then, but you mind he does – and I hope he's got something more than milk to drink up there. That's all that Christian offered me when I went up there to lay out that poor young wife of his. All right, there's no need for that impatient look, young lady. I may not move as fast as you, but we'll be there in good time. I haven't heard of anyone dying from a broken ankle – that's if it *is* broken.'

After an examination, Bonnie declared that Seb's ankle was *not* broken. This was her diagnosis after she had pulled his foot this way and that, in a manner that brought Seb out in a sweat and had him groaning in anguish.

'It's nothing but a nasty sprain, that's all. You come back to my cottage with me, young Carrie. I'll give you a jar full of poppy seeds. Crush them to a powder and boil them, then soak the ankle when the water's cooled enough to bear. That'll bring the bruising out and the ankle will be as right as rain in a week or two.'

'I can't afford to be off work for a couple of weeks! There's too much to be done about the farm.'

'Then you'll need to go down on your knees in that chapel Christian Timms built and call on someone more highly qualified than either me or Doctor Cheatle. You'd better be quick too. We're going to have snow – and you won't be able to do much work when it arrives. Now, all that hurrying has given me a thirst. Do you have something to put the strength back in a poor old woman?'

Bonnie grumbled when Seb offered her ale, complaining that him 'being from London' she thought he'd at least have a bottle of Holland's in the house. Despite her complaint, Bonnie managed to down three pints of strong ale before being taken home in the light cart, driven by the young stable-lad.

Seb was not the best of patients. When a stick was cut for him to use as a crutch he hobbled about the yard, complaining that nothing was being done properly in his absence.

Seb also took Bonnie Edgington's snow warning seriously. When one of the men he had employed as a ploughman in the autumn came to the farm, more in hope than the expectation of finding any work, Seb was able to offer him a day's pay. After bringing the horses in from the fields and putting feed in the stables for them, his next task was to bring all the sheep in close to the farm. The cows would be dealt with by Carrie, but the bullocks too were brought in and penned securely with both shelter and fodder at hand.

True to Bonnie's prediction it began snowing that night. It was a heavy snowfall and by morning even the most prominent landmark was disguised beneath a thick covering of snow.

The cows were in the cow-shed but they needed milking. When Seb was beginning to worry about the task, Carrie arrived at the farm, carried there on the back of a horse ridden by her father. Tom was on his way to the manor farm to ensure all was well there.

'I've got a good man living in that old place of yours above the stables,' said Tom, enjoying a warm at the kitchen fire before riding on. 'But I want to satisfy myself that all's well. This is the worst snowfall we've had for years. I should complete all that needs to be done by late afternoon and I'll come back to collect Carrie on my way home.'

'All right, but don't you try to come up here if the weather's too bad.' Carrie pulled her father's coat across his chest and tucked the end of his scarf inside it. 'There's plenty of room up here for me to stay quite comfortably and there ought to be someone on hand to milk the cows, however bad the weather.'

By noon the weather had worsened and it was snowing once more.

Watching through the kitchen window as the snow fell from a leaden sky, Seb suggested that Carrie ought to try to make her way home before it deteriorated even further.

'And leave you and Christian's cows to fend for yourselves? No, Seb. You build up the fire while I go out to milk the cows. It's a bit early, but that'll be one thing less for you to worry about.'

By the time Carrie had completed her task the wind had increased in strength from the north and a fierce blizzard was setting in. It soon became so bad that Seb was concerned lest Carrie was unable to cross the farmyard from the cow-shed.

It was a great relief to him when she stumbled in through the door in a flurry of snow and he set to and made a cup of tea to warm her.

When Carrie had some feeling back in her cold limbs she began bustling around to cook them a meal while Seb sat using part of the kitchen table to work on the farm accounts in the pool of yellow light cast by the lamp.

Long before the meal was ready the kitchen was hazy with smoke, blown back down the chimney by the wind that was howling around the farmhouse.

In spite of the difficulties caused by the weather, Carrie produced a meal of baked rabbit, potatoes, swede and carrots and put it in front of Seb while the wind rattled the door and windows and an occasional gust seemed to shake the very house itself.

'I can't see your dad reaching us in this weather, even riding a horse.'

'I hope he doesn't try, there must be three- or four-foot drifts out there and it'll be worse across Handley Plain.'

They both ate, trying not to think about being in the house together, cut off from the rest of the world.

When he had finished eating, Seb hopped to the back door and opened it slightly, having great difficulty preventing the wind from blowing it open further.

'Look out here, it must be at least three feet deep outside – and this is the sheltered side! If it's drifting on the far side it will be up to the roof. I hope the stock will be all right.'

'There's nothing can be done about it now, if it's not. Close that door and keep the warmth in, Seb. Would you like more to eat?'

In the Hankses' cottage, Tom rubbed the steam from the window and peered outside, able to see nothing but heavy snowflakes melting against the windows.

'I really ought to try to get up to the farm to fetch our Carrie down.'

'Don't talk ridiculous, Tom. You couldn't make it up there even on a horse. You said so yourself when you came in – and that was some hours ago.'

'I should have gone before coming home here. At

least, I ought to have tried, but I didn't think we'd end up with a blizzard like this. I can't remember when I've ever seen the like of it.'

'You just forget about our two up at the farm and sit down here with me, by the fire.'

'But we can't just leave them up there on their own, Dolly. It ain't right.'

'Oh and what's not right about it? Tell me, Tom Hanks, what's the worst thing they could get up to between the pair of 'em?'

'You don't need me to tell you that, Dolly. You know as well as I do.'

'Perhaps I do. All right then, what hopes do you have for the future of both Seb and Carrie?'

'The same as you. I'd like to see the pair of them wed. They're made for each other. You know it, I know it and Carrie knows it, I only wish Seb did.'

'Well, can you think of a better opportunity for them to find out what's best for the both of 'em?'

'You think so? I don't know, Dolly, it still don't seem right.'

'You forget about them two, Tom Hanks. Just be thankful they're safely in away from this weather and with a roof over their heads. We should be grateful for that too, there's many in this world who haven't. Come on, let's go to bed, and if they've got any sense that's what Seb and Carrie will be doing, up at the farm.'

CHAPTER FORTY-NINE

Seb knew it was well past the time he and Carrie should have retired to their respective bedrooms, but he found the thought of mentioning bed vaguely embarrassing. Yet it was late and when the hands of the grandfather clock in the kitchen pointed to eleven-thirty he cleared his throat unnecessarily noisily and said, 'I doubt if the weather's going to clear up enough tonight for your dad to even try to get here. Anyway, he knows you're safe enough. You'll have to stay. There's a bed made up in the room across the landing from mine. But you know that already, you clean the farmhouse for me . . .'

'Yes. I think perhaps we ought to go up now and hope the weather's better in the morning.' Carrie found it as difficult to discuss bedtime as did Seb.

They both stood up, each reluctant to be the first to make a move. Eventually, Seb said, 'You'd better go upstairs first, Carrie. I'm a bit slow with this leg of mine.'

'Well, I'm not a lot faster going upstairs with mine.'

Laughter seemed to break down some of the barrier of embarrassment that had built up between them and when Carrie lit two candles she handed one to Seb and said, 'Good night, Seb. I hope your ankle doesn't keep you awake.'

'You sleep well too, Carrie.'

They stood looking at each other uncertainly, then

Carrie made her way to the door and he heard her going upstairs, with considerably more skill than he would be able to muster.

Seb made his way up the stairs in the same fashion as on the previous evening. Backwards, raising himself from step to step on his backside.

It was cold in the bedroom and the wind was extremely noisy. It howled around the house, whistled through cracks in the window-frames and rattled slates on the roof. Seb undressed and prepared for bed and had just blown out his candle when he heard a noise from the landing just outside his room.

Hopping awkwardly to the door he looked out and caught a glimpse of Carrie standing there dressed only in a linen slip, with one arm clutching a bundle of bedclothes, the other holding a candle. He was able to see no more because a draught caused by the opening of his door blew out the candle she was holding.

'I'm sorry I brought you out, Seb.' Carrie's voice came to him in the darkness. 'But it's my bedding. I don't know how long it's been on the bed, but it's far too damp to sleep in. I'll just go downstairs and air it in front of the fire for a while. You go on back to bed.'

'I'm sorry, Carrie. I should have thought of that. Here, let me help.'

'No, Seb. Your ankle . . .'

For a moment Seb had forgotten his sprained ankle but it reminded him in no uncertain fashion when he tried to put his full weight on it.

'Ouch!'

His ankle gave way and he stumbled against Carrie. Dropping the bedding in her arms she held on to him and probably prevented him falling from the narrow landing down the stairway.

'Seb, are you all right?'

'Yes, I'm fine.' Gritting his teeth against the pain, he held on to Carrie until he regained his balance. 'I just feel so damned silly and helpless. Here, let me help you pick up the bedding and we'll take it downstairs. Perhaps we can think of some way to go down together, using our two good legs.'

They both laughed and it was a pleasant feeling of togetherness.

'I dropped the candle too, Seb, and I can't seem to find it.'

'It doesn't matter. We can get downstairs all right and there'll be firelight in the kitchen.'

Seb did not want a light to show Carrie how he got down the stairs.

In the kitchen the fire was burning low but there was light enough to see the steam rising from the bedclothes as they held them out to air.

'It's a good job you didn't try to sleep in these, you'd have caught your death of cold.'

'Yes . . . but I'm sorry I disturbed you, Seb.'

It was warm in the kitchen and the fire cast a soft light on Carrie who was kneeling in front of the fire, folding the blanket she had been airing. She had taken off the ribbon that kept back her hair and it hung about her shoulders, much longer than Seb had realised.

'I'm not.'

Something in Seb's voice made Carrie look up at him sharply. What she saw brought her slowly to her feet.

In the few moments they stood looking at each other, both were acutely aware they were cut off from the rest of the world. It was just the two of them, in the warmth and near-darkness of the farmhouse kitchen.

Neither spoke, nor was there need of words, and afterwards Carrie could not recall whether Seb came to her, or she went to him. As they kissed each could feel the flimsiness of the clothing that divided their bodies, but for Carrie it did not matter. Nothing mattered now except that Seb was holding her. Kissing her.

The touch of his hand on her body made her tremble, but she did not want him to stop. Would not allow him to stop.

'Carrie . . . let's go upstairs.'

'No, Seb. Here . . . by the fire. It's warmer.'

They lay on the aired bedding in front of the fire and made love as Carrie had always hoped it might be. With a gentleness that lasted until the moment the primitive needs of their bodies demanded to be satisfied.

Afterwards, Seb lay with his head cradled against Carrie's breast for a long time. He thought she was asleep, but when he put a hand to her face he felt warm tears on her cheek.

Starting up he said, 'I'm sorry, Carrie.'

'No, Seb. I don't want you to be sorry. Not now, or ever.'

The fire had died down and Carrie said, 'Let's go upstairs now, Seb. Go to bed . . .'

Seb awoke suddenly in the morning in the belief that he could hear someone speaking. Remembering the snow, he lay back beside Carrie – and then he heard the sound again. *It was someone calling!*

Leaping from the bed, Seb put his bad foot to the

floor and cried out in agony, but he continued hopping towards the window. Rubbing away a thin film of ice, he peered through a small frame of snow – and saw Tom Hanks entering the farmyard, plodding doggedly behind a horse that was struggling to pull an improvised wooden snow-plough!

'What is it?' Carrie's voice called from the bed.

'It's your dad! He's rigged up some sort of snow-plough behind a horse.' Before he completed the sentence Carrie had tumbled from the bed and was limping rapidly from the room, in a state of total nakedness.

By the time Tom reached the house and shovelled his way to the door, Seb and Carrie were both fully dressed and Carrie was bending over the fire, coaxing life from the embers as she prepared breakfast.

'I never expected to see you – or anyone else – up here this morning,' Seb admitted honestly as he sat down at the kitchen table.

'I don't suppose you did. I said to Dolly that if I didn't do something you'd be cut off from the world for a week or more. Then I remembered this old snow-plough. I made it years and years ago, when Carrie was a small girl. I don't suppose she even remembers it.'

Carrie agreed it was an item that had completely slipped her memory, but Tom was already speaking again. 'Everything all right up here? No problems in the night?'

Seb assured the older man there had been no problems during the night, but added, 'I *am* worried about the stock, especially the sheep in the pen behind the barn.'

'Right, you save me some of that breakfast, young

Carrie, and I'll go out now and check on things about the farm.'

When Tom had gone from the house, carrying a broad-bladed, long-handled shovel, Seb asked, 'You all right, Carrie?'

'Yes.' Carrie flashed Seb a shy smile that, had he been looking at her, would have conveyed to him all the love she was feeling. But Seb was struggling up from the table. Limping awkwardly to the window, he watched Tom fight his way through the snow in the farmyard, and he thought of how close he and Carrie had come to being caught in bed together.

After Tom had returned to his cottage taking Carrie with him it snowed heavily once more, and this time the drifts in the lane to the farm defied all the efforts of Tom and his improvised horse-drawn snow-plough.

For seven days Seb was isolated at the farm, yet despite the handicap of a crutch tucked beneath one arm he managed to dig a narrow path linking the house, dairy, hen-house, stables and cow-shed. He spent a great deal of time inexpertly milking complaining cows, only to feed most of the milk to the pigs.

By the time the snow began to thaw he could walk gingerly on his injured ankle and when aid arrived at the farm in the form of Tom's snow-plough, with Tom guiding the plough and Carrie riding the horse, Seb was standing in the farmyard to greet them.

Carrie floundered excitedly through the snow to greet him and it seemed she was about to throw her arms about him. Seb stepped back quickly, embarrassed by the expression he thought he saw on Tom's face.

Carrie's arms dropped to her side and Seb immediately regretted his own bashfulness.

'You all right, Seb?'

'Fine, Carrie. Has everything been all right for you and my ma, down at the cottage?'

Carrie nodded, her eyes searching his face for something. Evidently failing to find what she sought, she turned away and entered the farmhouse.

'It's good to see you, Seb. It's been hell shut up in that cottage with two women who would both have braved the weather to come up here to see how you were if I hadn't been on hand to stop them.'

Tom spoke as he stamped snow from his boots in the doorway of the farmhouse kitchen.

'I was worried about him . . . having that bad ankle and all.' Carrie looked about her at the crackling fire and a fair semblance of tidiness in the kitchen. 'But he seems to have been doing well enough by himself. I think he must have been putting on all that business with his ankle, just to gain sympathy.'

Carrie flashed a glance in his direction and Seb blushed, believing Tom was capable of reading the same meaning into the look as he did.

Tom had noticed nothing untoward. 'How have you managed?'

'I just did what I could around the place, milking the cows and making sure everything had enough to eat. The only animals I haven't been able to check on are the sheep.'

'They looked well able to survive a week when I last looked at them, but I'll go and check again now. While I feed them Carrie can be feeding you. She and your ma have spent this last week making cakes and pies to bring up here as soon as the weather allowed.'

'Don't take any notice of him, but I have got a nice meat pie here for you. I'll build the fire up a bit more and heat it for you now. There's a couple more to be brought in from the pack on the horse. You'd best put them by in case the weather closes in again.'

Inside the kitchen, while Carrie busied herself at the range, Seb hovered behind her, wanting to touch her, but not daring to, in case she objected. Then he hesitated because he had left it too late and he was concerned that Tom would walk in through the door again at any minute.

Carrie suddenly said, 'Your mum and I *were* worried about you, Seb, but all my dad could keep saying was, "It's a good job I managed to reach you when I did, or you'd have been up at that farmhouse for another week." '

'It's something I kept thinking about, too. If I'd known what it was I would have chopped up that snow-plough before the snows arrived.'

Carrie rounded on him, her face alight with pleasure. 'Would you really, Seb?'

'Yes. Mind you, spending a week snowed-in with me would have done nothing for your reputation. When your dad eventually reached you he would have insisted that I marry you.'

Carrie lost some of her effervescence. 'No, Seb. No one's ever going to *have* to marry me, I promise you that.'

Seb realised he had inadvertently said the wrong thing, but Carrie had gone to the scullery that opened off the farmhouse kitchen. By the time he limped to the scullery door she was back again, broom in hand, and had begun attacking mud that had been tramped inside the kitchen during the past week.

'Look at this! You can see there hasn't been a woman in this house for more than a week. Never mind, we'll have it clean by the time the pie's ready.'

Carrie was still sweeping when her father returned.

'You don't have to worry about those sheep, Seb, they're as snug as bugs in a rug out there, but I've given them some more hay, just in case. This snow will have cost you a small fortune in wasted hay by the time it thaws, but it was the right thing to do, it's saved your stock.'

Tom settled himself down at the table and said, 'Now, let's have a chat about what we're going to do when this snow clears. You won't be able to do much in the fields, it'll be far too wet for a week or two. I suggest you whitewash out the pigsties and the cow-sheds. Get that ploughman to help you if he comes back up here. By the way, your ma will be able to help out at your dairy for a month or two as I'm cutting down on the number of cows at the manor. It means that Carrie won't need to work on the farm quite so often . . .'

CHAPTER FIFTY

After the floods caused by the thaw, Oxfordshire enjoyed a long dry spell of weather, with strong, drying winds. It was good news for Seb. There was still a great deal of work to be done ploughing fields reclaimed from the forests. One of his two ploughmen had left the district and Seb found himself performing a lot of the work himself. Other work was being offered too. No sooner had the late ploughing been completed than he began accepting contracts for harrowing.

During these weeks Seb rarely saw Carrie, except for a few hours each Sunday when they worked on the farm ledgers together at the Hankses' cottage, and even here they were rarely alone.

One Sunday, when Tom had gone into the garden to look at some flowers that Dolly had planted, Seb's pen paused over the sum on which he was toiling. 'We don't seem to have seen much of each other since . . . since the snows, Carrie.'

'I thought that was probably the way you wanted it to be.'

'It isn't. Look, I know you've said it doesn't matter, but I am sorry about what happened up at Handley Farm.'

'Sorry for what, that you made love to a cripple? Or sorry because it embarrasses you to be with me because of it?'

'It's neither of those things, Carrie.' Seb knew he had failed yet again to break through the barrier of embarrassment that lay between them, and he did not know what to do about it. He was having enough difficulty understanding his own feelings, without trying to fathom out Carrie's.

Seb felt happy and comfortable when he was with Carrie – at least, he had before the night they had spent snowed-in together at the farm. During that night their love-making had been something wonderful. At the time he had believed she felt the same. Since then they had been awkward in each other's company and everything seemed to have gone wrong.

When Tom and Dolly returned inside the cottage all chance of speaking privately to Carrie disappeared. Seb determined he would find time to have a long talk with her when his present hectic spell of work came to an end. He needed to speak to her – and to Tom, her father.

Four days after Seb had reached his decision about Carrie, Anna and Nahum paid a surprise visit to Handley Farm. The weather was giving promise of an early spring and they were on their way northwards, to Nahum's father.

Anna was very happy and the shape of her body broadcast the reason, even before Nahum began his explanation.

Noah Plunkett had forgiven his son and offered the marriage his blessing now that Anna was pregnant. He had asked Nahum to bring his wife home. The gipsy leader wanted his grandchild to be born in northern England, surrounded by the Plunkett family and friends.

Anna kissed and hugged Seb, but now it was in a more mature, inhibited manner than she had when they last said farewell.

There were four other caravans travelling with the young couple, but these gipsies were on their way to the old camp in the Wychwood Forest. News had reached them of the happenings at the manor and they rightly assumed that with Tom in charge of the manor farm they were not likely to be evicted from their forest camp.

The gipsies were still in the area when Christian Timms made a surprise visit to Handley Farm. He was accompanied by James Price, the Burford lawyer.

Seb was out harrowing one of his own fields when the young stable-hand came and told him of Christian's arrival. Christian wanted to see Seb at the farm – immediately.

Seb arrived at the farmhouse and feared the worst when he saw the meeting was taking place in the 'best' sitting room and not in the kitchen. His fears were fuelled when he saw the others gathered there. James Price, Tom, Dolly and Carrie were seated around the room. Surprisingly, so too were Nahum and Anna.

When it came, there was nothing at all ominous in the reason for Christian's unexpected visit . . . but it was none the less a bombshell.

Clearing his throat noisily, Price perched a pair of gold-rimmed spectacles on his nose and announced he had received a letter from India.

'I must confess, the news it contained was not at all what I had been expecting. It has caused me a great deal of work, but it has resulted in an extraordinary discovery, one that I hope may prove satisfactory to you all.'

He peered over the rim of his spectacles at each of the room's occupants in turn before continuing.

'I learned that the nearest known relative of the late Sir Nelson Fettiplace was dead. Indeed, he predeceased Sir Nelson, which made my task a little easier, inasmuch as it was not necessary for me to carry out complicated inquiries in India. However, it has been necessary for me to consult Fettiplace family records, going back very many years. To Sir Nelson's father, in fact.'

The solicitor's gaze moved around the room once more as Price warmed to his task. 'I learned, quite by chance, that when Sir Nelson's father willed this farm to Mr Timms, he also officially recognised Christian as his natural son. Something he never did with other, er . . . would-be claimants. Now, the extraordinary thing is – Mr Timms is the *only* known claimant to the Fettiplace lands.'

He smiled at the gasp produced by his revelation. 'All this will need to be verified, of course, but I can assure you my inquiries have been exhaustive. I have no hesitation whatsoever in presenting Christian Timms to you as the new lord of Swinbrook Manor, and owner of the Fettiplace lands.'

As the babble of excited talk erupted in the room, Christian stood up to speak. The news, he said, had shocked, bemused and excited him, all at the same time. He reassured everyone that it would make no difference to the course he had set for himself. Indeed, it would help to ensure the success of his plans.

He would have a farmhouse built at the manor farm and hoped that Tom would move in, as a tenant farmer. His terms were generous. For three years he would supply funds to run the farm, any profits being split equally between Tom and himself. At the end of the three years Tom would begin to pay rent – a fair rent – for the lands he farmed and would take over all farm buildings, implements and stock.

'That's wonderful news, Tom. I'm so pleased for you – and for Ma,' said Seb.

'What about you, Seb? What shall we do about you?'

Seb's spirits took a dive. He hadn't thought about himself, but with Tom taking on another farm, a farm that would one day be his own responsibility, it was hardly likely he would have time to take care of Seb too.

'I'd like you to take Handley Farm on similar terms. You can have the pick of any of the manor farm horses for breeding, to improve the standard of Handley Farm horses – providing you replace any Tom needs for general farm work.

'There's one other thing that will affect Nahum and his people – and you too, Tom. The last remaining section of Wychwood Forest belongs to the manor farm. I want your assurance that you will always allow genuine gipsies to camp there. Far too much of the forest has been cut down already, but I think there's enough to enable Nahum and his people to enjoy a traditional way of life. Is this agreed?'

'Of course.' Tom's face was scarlet with pleasure. 'I don't know how to thank you. Christian, if you were a drinking man I would say this is an occasion for a celebration.'

'I only disapprove of drinking to excess, Tom. On this occasion I think I can find a bottle of something special with which to toast the future. All our futures –

although I suggest you save the main celebration for chapel, on Sunday.'

Seb also managed to stutter his thanks to Christian before following Carrie to the kitchen where she had gone to put the kettle on the hob to make coffee for everyone.

'This is fantastic news, Carrie. Who would have expected this to happen?'

'It's wonderful.' Her manner belied her words.

'You must be overjoyed. Your dad is soon to be a tenant farmer. He's always been respected by everyone, now he'll become a man of some importance.'

'Not as important as you, Seb. You too will be a tenant farmer, as well as ploughing land for everyone; breeding your horses . . . racing.'

Carried away with his own enthusiasm, Seb said, 'It's only a beginning. I'll have some wonderful horses soon, if I get Vulcan from your dad. I can breed from him and between us, your dad and I will have the finest cart-horses and race-horses in the country, Carrie.'

'I don't doubt it, Seb, you've come a long way from the poor, sickly boy who arrived here from London only a couple of years ago.'

'We've all come a long way, Carrie, and we're going to go a lot farther . . . but come inside, I think Christian's found that bottle of brandy that I've been hoping he'd forgotten.'

CHAPTER FIFTY-ONE

The next few days were hectic ones for Seb. He needed to spend more time in Burford, discussing the terms of his future tenancy with James Price. Seb was going to be far better off than he had anticipated. In the event of Christian's death he would not only become the outright owner of Handley Farm, but Christian intended leaving him sufficient money to ensure he did not have to part with the farm in the foreseeable future.

Riding back to Swinbrook Seb became excited at the thought of discussing the future with his mother, with Tom – and with Carrie. His future was assured now, and he knew with equal certainty that he wanted Carrie to be a part of that future.

When he reached Handley Farm Seb was startled to find Anna seated outside the farmhouse door. There was no sign of Carrie and although it was milking time the cows were still in the field.

'What are you doing here, Anna? Where's Nahum – and Carrie?'

'Nahum's at the camp with the others. As for Carrie . . . that's what I've come to see you about, Seb. She's gone.'

'Gone where? She's said nothing to me.'

'No, she wouldn't. She swore me to secrecy too, but I think this is far too important – for both of you – to remain a secret.'

'What are you talking about, Anna?' Seb was thoroughly bewildered. 'Where has Carrie gone?'

'Why do you want to know, Seb? Give me an honest answer.'

'I've just been given some great news. I wanted to share it with her.'

'Only the news?'

'Yes . . . no, that *isn't* all. I have a great future here, Anna. I want her to share it with me.'

'That's what I wanted to hear. Oh, Seb, you are a fool.' Suddenly, Anna was hugging him. 'Why haven't you told Carrie? If she'd known she'd never have gone.'

'I didn't know myself until just now, as I rode home from Burford. I might have worked it out sooner had she not been so prickly lately.'

'I'm sure if you thought hard enough about it you'd know the reason for that, Seb. But we're wasting time. You must go quickly. She's on her way to Shipton.'

'Why should she be going there?'

'To catch a train. Nahum told her that a teacher's needed for one of the permanent Romany camps set up in Kent by a preacher. He said he'd mentioned her name there and promised to ask her if she would go to help them. She's on her way there now.'

'But . . . why hasn't she said anything to Tom, my ma or me about it?'

'Because she thought you'd try to stop her, and she wanted to do this on her own – that's unless you can think of some other reason. But all this talk is wasting time. Go and stop her, Seb, before she reaches Shipton.'

'How long has she been gone?'

'An hour, at least. Probably closer to an hour and a half.'

Seb recognised the disconsolate figure sitting on a milestone at the top of a hill, no more than two and a half miles from Swinbrook. Beside her was a soft bundle of clothes.

As he slowed Grye she looked up and as quickly looked down again at her feet. As Seb dismounted beside her, she spoke without looking up at him. 'What do you want? Go away.'

Seb thought she looked weary, and very unhappy.

'I've come to find you and take you home.'

'I don't want to go home, I'm going away.'

'No you're not, there's far too much for you to do at the farm.'

'Damn you, Seb! Why did you come after me? Just for once I'd like to be able to do something properly, but I never will. I'm a cripple. I can't even run away from home successfully.'

'Carrie, I shall always love that crippled leg of yours. If it hadn't been for that you'd have reached Shipton and been on a train by now.'

'Yes, and you'd have been grateful that I'd gone. When I tell you the reason I'm going you'll wish you'd let me go. If you've any sense you'll give me a ride to Shipton and put me on a train, then go back to your farm and forget all about me.'

'Why? There are any number of people they can get to teach gipsies.'

'That's not the reason I'm going away.'

'But Anna said—'

'Anna should have said nothing at all. My leaving

was supposed to be a secret between the two of us.'

Carrie looked up at him and Seb could see she had been crying. She also looked desperately tired. 'I've got to go away, Seb. I . . . I'm expecting a baby.'

Seb's expression changed from disbelief to delight in a matter of seconds. 'But . . . why didn't you tell me about this before? Why try to run away?'

'You were telling me how important you and Dad had become. I don't want to shame you both, and I don't want you to feel you have to marry me.'

'Carrie, I don't need a baby to give me a reason for marrying you. I've been hoping to find the right opportunity for weeks. I *want* to marry you.'

'Honest?'

As tears began to run down her cheeks Seb dropped the reins and allowed Grye to crop the grass on the verge as he took Carrie in his arms.

'Honest.'

'That isn't what everyone's going to say, Seb.'

'Who cares what anyone says? It won't bother me, it shouldn't bother you – and it certainly won't trouble our son.'

'I hope not.' Carrie squeezed Seb until he could hardly breathe. 'But what makes you think it's going to be a son?'

'It's bound to be a son . . . sooner or later. Come on now, we're going home. We've a wedding to arrange.'

As they returned to Swinbrook on Grye, the gipsy horse, the trees of Wychwood closed in about them and Carrie imagined the sadly diminished yet still proud forest was protecting them from the rest of the world.

She rested her head against Seb's back as, arms clasped tightly about his waist, she listened to him telling her of what the future held for them and for their family. The family that would be raised on Handley Farm, in the village of Swinbrook, with Wychwood Forest as its playground.